A Departure from the Script

a novel
by
Rochelle
Hollander
Schwab

Also by
Rochelle Hollander Schwab

In a Family Way
A Different Sin
As Far as Blood Goes

ISBN 0-7394-4409-3

Library of Congress Control Number: 2001118633

Grateful acknowledgment is made to Joseph Stein for permission to use several brief quotes from *Fiddler on the Roof*, copyright © 1964 by Joseph Stein.

Orlando Place Press
3617 Orlando Place
Alexandria, VA 22305
Phone 703-836-8964
Fax 703-836-5096
Email OrlandoPL@aol.com

Design by Communications by Design
Cover design by Communications by Design
Cover art by Jacinda Sedgley
Author photo by Kevin Kerdash

Additional Praise for *A Departure from the Script*

"With humor, warmth, pace and suspense, Rochelle Schwab weaves a tale that deftly explores the complex web of emotions set off by a series of challenges to a family's conventional notions about sexual orientation."

– Robert A. Bernstein, author of *Straight Parents, Gay Children*, and former national vice-president of Parents, Families and Friends of Lesbians and Gays (PFLAG)

"A delightful novel about family, marriage and the process of growing comfortable with all shades of the rainbow....a novel for the new millennium."

Lori L. Lake, Midwest Book Review, Sept. 2003

"Hilarious....This intimate family drama is great comedy."

Loraine Hutchins, Lambda Book Report, November-December 2002

"Unusually honest, realistically messy, and not at all easy to predict."

Sarah J., AfterEllen.com, June 2002

"In a humorous book filled with plenty of subterfuge, Sheila...learns about the meaning of love, marriage and family."

Aliza Phillips, the Forward, June 28, 2002

"Will have you laughing, teary-eyed, cheering. A must-have....Congratulations to Schwab for penning what is sure to become a classic."

Ravigo Zomana, The Virginia GayZette, May 2002

"Schwab's writing is much like her main character: warm, earthy, resolute....Her splendid ear for dialogue provides conversation that sounds overheard, not written."

— Elizabeth Millard, ForeWord Magazine, May 2002

"Delightful....tells a charming story with humor & poignancy. I found myself laughing & crying, sometimes at the same moment."

Dr. Alma Bond, Rebeccas Reads, April 26, 2003

"A delightful page turner."

—Deborah Levinson, Lesbian Worlds (lesbianworld.com

"Schwab's touch is light, but her message is earnest....as she shows how families can support and accept their children who come out to them as a gay, lesbian, or bisexual."

Nancy Pearl, Booklist, March 15, 2002

Praise for *In a Family Way*

"A vivid evocation of family life, and a real page-turner." — *San Francisco Chronicle*

"Schwab has produced a thought-provoking novel that probes the complexity of the word 'family.'" — *Small Press*

"Straight out of today's headlines, *In a Family Way* takes a dramatic look at the kinds of moral and legal issues that face lesbian and gay families, and is one of those illuminating 'social issues' novels that are an honored tradition in American literature. Highly recommended." — *Midwest Book Reviewer's Bookwatch*

"Schwab captures the joy, humor, and disorientation that comes with the territory of parenting a small child." — *The Family Next Door*

"The characters created by the author make us smile, make us weep, and give us insight into the lives of those who wish only to claim the rights inherent to any human being living in this or any other country." — *PFLAGPOLE*

"The author ... has an easy, natural way with dialogue and description, and she knits together a relatively convoluted plot without dropping a single stitch." — *the Washington Blade*

"A refreshing contribution" — *Lambda Book Report*

"*In a Family Way* is a lively and challenging investigation of the complexities of many kinds of families: the ones that are born, that are made, that are defended by love and loyalty. Rochelle Hollander Schwab has peopled her story with sympathetic characters who are never caricatures though they are, without setting out to, fighting the kinds of battles we will be seeing more and more often between 'old' and 'new' values. In Schwab's hands, these are actually as old as parenthood and the Biblical bonds between mothers, fathers, lovers. Her book does justice to the pain of the conflict." — Rosellen Brown, author of *Before and After* and *Half a Heart*

"A sweet-tempered and suspenseful tale of gay and lesbian parenting, '90s style. Rochelle Schwab is an engaging writer who should appeal to a wide audience." — Neil Miller, author of *In Search of Gay America* and *Out of the Past*

"This book is fun, sad, suspenseful, compassionate. It's filled with real conflicts, real families, and real good writing. A treat." — Mariah Burton Nelson, author of *The Stronger Women Get, the More Men Love Football*

Praise for *A Different Sin*

"Beautifully written and carefully researched...the love scenes are wonderfully sensual and moving...the queer *Gone With the Wind*!"
— Diane Raymond, co-author with Warren J. Blumenfeld,
Looking at Gay and Lesbian Life

"A well-researched, well-written, fiery historical gay novel...The sex is erotic and tasteful....All in all, an excellent novel."
— John Starr, *OUT in Virginia*

"Schwab's depiction of war's horrors has the ring of truth....Civil War enthusiasts will find much that is diverting in *A Different Sin*."
— William Lyons, *Alexandria Gazette Packet*

For Dick
and for Wendy and Jill

Acknowledgments

Several scenes in this novel are set at a support group of Parents, Families and Friends of Lesbians and Gays (PFLAG). The support group and its participants in my novel are entirely fictional, but the love, humor and courage that I found in the real-life group I've attended for many years have found their way into these pages and provided much of the inspiration for my story.

That the story evolved from inspiration to published novel is due in large part to the invaluable insights and detailed feedback I received from members of my critique group — in particular, Cathy, Kristin, Leslie and Randi, who read every word from first draft to final. Thanks, guys!

Last, but not least, I am grateful to my husband, Dick, for his patience and support.

Chapter One

A few decades of friendship are like a few decades of marriage: you get to know a person inside out — her good points and her not-so-good points. So when Lois drained her third glass of Chardonnay as she, Natalie, LaVerne and I enjoyed our monthly "ladies lunch," I knew she was ready to let loose with one of her zingers. What I didn't know was that it would be directed at me.

"Can I ask you a question, Sheila?" Lois always prefaces her queries like that. Never once does she leave a single breath's pause for an answer. "What bothers you more? Jeffrey converting to Catholicism or Jenny telling you she's a lesbian?"

I nearly choked on a mouthful of "Chocolate Decadence," which served me right. I'd promised myself to stay on my diet — had ordered tossed salad with dressing on the side — but by the time the waiter wheeled up the dessert cart I was feeling so deprived that I couldn't resist that rich, dark chocolate that caressed my taste buds like a lover's tongue. Lois forged blithely ahead, supplying her own answer since I was still sitting there, mouth opening and closing like a goldfish that's been dumped from its bowl. "It's Jeffrey converting. Am I right or am I right?"

There were maybe two seconds of silence before LaVerne shrieked, "Jenny is what? Girl, I don't believe it! I just don't believe it!" and Lois realized she'd told the secret I'd warned her was for her ears only.

"Oh, I didn't mean —" she began. "I totally forgot." She tripped over her tongue as if it was a foot.

I'd intended to tell the other two, of course. They were two of my oldest friends. And what are friends for if you can't share with them? But I'd wanted to wait till the first shock was over, till I could give them the news in a tone of voice that demanded their acceptance and their support. Now that Lois had forced my hand, I had to pull myself together. I might still be in shock, but not so much that I would stand for any negative remarks about my daughter.

"Well, it's true," I told LaVerne. "Jenny told me just last week that she thinks she's a lesbian — no, not thinks, that she's known for a while. So what? She's still the same wonderful girl that all of you have known since our kids were making mud pies together."

So they had no choice but to respond in kind, falling over themselves to reassure me that it didn't matter. "Just so long as she's happy. That's the important thing," was the way Natalie put it, with LaVerne nodding in agreement.

And before anyone could ask any more questions that might reveal my actual state of mind, the waiter arrived with the check, LaVerne started digging in her purse for her calculator and Natalie glanced at her watch and gasped, "I had no idea it was so late. I have to teach class in an hour." So I was given a reprieve until next month's get-together — or until either Natalie or LaVerne caught me on the phone.

Seeing the four of us at our monthly lunches, you would peg us as stereotypical middle-aged women with a little time on our hands, enough to keep up a friendship and indulge in the kind of exchange-of-feelings conversations women crave but so often don't get at home. You might also wonder what we all had in common: Lois and myself with our New York Jewish accents, her looking like she's just walked out of Nordstrom's on her way to the Kennedy Center, and me looking more like a refugee from Wal-Mart on my way to Weight Watchers; LaVerne, stunning in auburn corn-rows that highlight the copper tones in her mahogany skin, wearing a power suit and sneakers, her good shoes stowed at the office; and Natalie — I still think of her as Natalie, though it's years since she changed her name to Natalya — dressed in her typical uniform, black from neck to toe. Basic stagehand is how I think of it, garbed in a pretense of invisibility as if to carry props on and off stage in the darkness between scene changes. As always, Natalie's basic black was set off by something from her vast collection of colorful accessories. This afternoon she flaunted a sumptuous vest of hand-crocheted ribbon that hung halfway to her knees over her black turtleneck and tights. I try not to envy Natalie her thin body — not since she confessed to us her bouts with anorexia — but I still envy her sense of style. Whenever I outfit myself in basic black I look like what I am — a butterball of a woman who's fallen hook, line and sinker for the women's magazine line that wearing black will magically take ten pounds off your figure. This afternoon I was wearing navy slacks and a colorful, vertically striped tunic that I had liked until my husband, Dan, told me it made me look like an open beach umbrella.

Despite these stylistic differences, we'd maintained our friendship ever since we'd met, some thirty years earlier, at Parenting First — a group that taught watered-down Lamaze method to expectant mothers. Our kids had long since outgrown the weekly play group we'd started for them, but the four of us had kept up with each other at our lunchtime gabfests ever since.

Now I air-kissed Natalie and LaVerne good-bye. "Let's go," I snapped at Lois. Ever since the time she pulled into her garage without bothering to raise the garage door first, it had been tacitly understood that I would be the designated driver for future lunches.

"So I made a mistake. So sue me," she said, once we had left the District of Columbia behind and were heading down I-395 to Springfield, Virginia.

"Freud says there are no mistakes," I retorted, but weakly. I could never bring myself to hold her big mouth against her for long. I know why she drinks too much and looks for a bit of diversion from her own worries. And the troubles she's had, I wouldn't wish on my worst enemy.

"Freud was an anti-feminist sexist pig," she fired back. "And you surely weren't planning to stay in the closet about Jenny forever."

"A week," I said. "One week is not forever." Which was all the time it had been since Jenny had told me. Had *come out* to me, as she'd put it. I suddenly found myself crying, tears blurring my vision so that for a moment I was afraid I'd have to pull to the shoulder. Instead I sniffled hard once or twice and managed to blink my eyes dry.

Lois gave me a look. She appeared to be sobering up a little, frightened perhaps by the possibility of a tear-induced crash. "Well you need support to deal with this. That's what friends are for."

Some friend, I wanted to retort, who can't even keep her big mouth shut. But I had to keep my mind on my driving: I was approaching the construction zone at the "mixing bowl," where, for years, vehicles exiting

I-395 had played dodge'em with two lanes of cars and eighteen-wheelers barreling onto the highway from the Capital Beltway. It had always seemed a miracle to me that wrecked cars didn't litter the spot like broken eggshells.

"From someone who knows what I'm going through, that's who I need support from," I said instead, once I'd heaved a sigh of relief at having made it to the Springfield exit. "Not from friends who are about to *plotz* from shock. And I told you, Jenny gave me the number of a support group."

"So when are you going?" she demanded.

"I don't know. I haven't had a chance to call." I wasn't so sure I was ready for a support group, though I thought better of mentioning that to Lois.

"I wouldn't put it off if I were you," she said. After thirty years — thirty and counting, if the truth be told — she knew me.

"Who says I'm putting it off? But I want Dan and me to go together. So I've got to wait until he's ready."

"You know how long that could be?" As usual, she didn't wait for an answer. "You could be in a nursing home by that time."

"It's only been a week," I protested. "Give him time."

"Well, fine. But there's no reason for you to wait. Look, if he won't go with you, I will. Just let me know when it is, and I'll clear my calendar."

I had to admit that was a generous offer from a Realtor in the frantic tag end of the spring selling season. I told her so.

"So what are friends for?" she asked. "You'll give me a call and let me know the time?"

"I'll give you a call," I promised. "Unless Dan is willing." So one way or another, I'd boxed myself into going.

Dan had taken Jenny's revelation with such apparent unconcern that I hadn't a clue as to what he was really feeling. Still, I shouldn't have blamed Dan for covering up. I never let on to Jenny how I felt either.

Jenny had told me first, before Dan got home from work. She found me in the kitchen where I was standing at the counter making a salad, slicing tomatoes and cucumbers with movements so practiced it could have been any night in the thirty-some years of my marriage.

"Mom?" she said. Her voice was so childish and uncertain that, for an instant, I expected to see Jenny at age twelve, instead of the grown-up

Jenny, a high school English teacher going on twenty-five. And I could have traveled back in time, for all I knew. Standing at the kitchen counter, one year looks a lot like another.

Jenny's face was hesitant too, her sun-streaked blond hair still damp from the shower, her oversized white T-shirt setting off the tan she'd gotten from her summer job as a day camp swim counselor. "There's something I need to tell you," she said.

I pride myself on not being a stereotypical Jewish mother, fretting over her children as if they were hothouse flowers with the heater broken during a freeze. But something in Jenny's voice told me that whatever she was about to disclose would knock me for a loop. Even as I said, "What is it, sweetheart?" my mind was working up scenarios. What could she need to talk about? Was she about to move out? She'd been living at home, saving money, since the group house she'd lived in after college had disbanded. But moving to an apartment was to be expected at her age, nothing to require a dramatic announcement. It couldn't be job burnout — she was crazy about teaching. *Maybe she was pregnant.* No, surely she would have taken precautions, level-headed as she was. Anyhow, she hadn't mentioned a boyfriend since she'd broken up with Adam, her high school sweetheart. They'd remained friends though. In fact, he'd called her from Chicago several times this summer, chatting an hour or more each time. If they'd gotten back together again, maybe it wasn't bad news. Maybe —

"Mom," she said, breaking into my imaginings. "I've been doing a lot of thinking about myself the past few years, a lot of introspection. And I've come to realize...." She paused, shoved a strand of hair behind her ear and took a deep breath. "Maybe you've already guessed. But I've come to realize I'll never have any kind of romantic feelings for a man."

"For a man?" I echoed stupidly.

"You must have guessed?" she said again, but even as I shook my head no, the pieces were falling into place like the last pieces of a jigsaw puzzle, like the solution to the equations I'd taught my math classes before I had Jenny and her brother. No wonder she hadn't mentioned a boyfriend for years. The wonder was that I had never asked her about one.

"I've known, really, since my junior year of college," she was going on. "I should have come out to you before this. But I guess I was a little nervous about your reaction once I actually told you I was a lesbian."

"Oh, Jenny!" Instinctively, I hid my shock. "I hope nothing I've done made you feel that way. You don't ever have to hide anything about yourself from me." I threw my arms around her, holding her so close that her small high breasts pressed against my chest. We stood there, like two boxers locked in a clinch, my face and expression hidden from her, while I drew on the loving strength of Jenny's arms as she hugged me back. So when we pulled away at last, I was able to say, "It doesn't make one iota of difference. I love you, sweetheart." And congratulated myself that I hadn't met Jenny's news with rejection.

Jenny seemed to sigh with relief. "Thanks, Mom. It means a lot to hear you say that." After a second, she added, "I was going to come out to you and Dad together. But then I thought it would be easier to talk to you first."

That last took me nearly as much by surprise as her coming out had. Jenny had always been a Daddy's girl, so I was startled, maybe even a bit smug, that she'd come to me first. I didn't flatter myself for long though. I was sure Jenny had tested the waters with me because Dan's reaction was the all-important one to her.

According to Freud we were a typical family: Dan and Jenny the greatest of pals, her older brother Jeffrey and me as thick as thieves. Jenny and I had gotten past the years when her every sentence to me began with, "Oh, Mom," but it was still her father she looked to for approval. So in addition to testing the waters, Jenny needed me to give her moral support when she came out to him.

Once she'd made up her mind to tell her father, she wanted to get it over with. I persuaded her to wait till after dinner, when Dan would be agreeably full of oven-roasted chicken breast — skinless, but with my special low-cholesterol batter that seals in all the juices. So as we sat down, nothing about this night was different from any other night. We ate at the round maple table in the breakfast room, Jenny with her back to the bay window, Dan and I flanking her, the ceiling fan humming overhead. I started in on a discussion of the play my amateur theater group planned for our fall production, Jenny prompting me for details with an eagerness she'd never displayed before. After five minutes of our forced nonchalance, Dan looked first at Jenny, then at me, and said, "What's up, you two?"

So Jenny had no choice but to give her father the same news she'd confided to me two hours earlier. There was an instant of dead silence once Jenny had concluded with, "so I've realized that I'm a lesbian,

Daddy." I opened my mouth to fill it, to smooth things over. But Jenny spoke again before I could.

"I'm still the exact same person I've always been, Daddy." There was a tremulous note in her voice, the same as when she'd told me earlier.

Dan stared at her for another instant, and then he opened his mouth to speak. "So who else would you be?"

"You know what I mean." Jenny's smile was forced, and I could tell by her voice she didn't know how to take Dan's tone, which seemed to be shrugging off her news. He'd always been a kidder, but this was no time for kidding. "I haven't changed any. It's just, I have a girlfriend instead of a boyfriend."

This time her father reached out to lay a hand on hers. "Since when do you have to tell me that you're my same sweet daughter? And if you're happy with a girlfriend, well, all your mother and I want is your happiness."

Jenny's smile widened in relief and she squeezed Dan's hand back. Her eyes had filled with tears, so that she didn't see what I saw. Dan's expression had turned into a bland mask, belying his easy words. I was sure he was keeping his shock and dismay hidden, with the same skill he used for keeping his cards hidden in his Wednesday night poker group.

The next meeting of the support group Jenny had recommended turned out to be the following Sunday afternoon. True to Lois's prediction, Dan was reluctant to go. I had to nudge him, to keep reminding him that Jenny thought it would be a good idea.

"What for?" he wanted to know. "She told us. She knows we still love her. Why do we need to spend an afternoon talking about it with some group?"

I was tempted to leave it at that, but I couldn't. Not when I thought of that blank, closed expression on Dan's face. He needed the support more than I did; I was sure of that. For Jenny's sake, if not for his.

So I played my trump card. "I really don't want to go by myself. But if you're dead set against it, I'll ask Lois. I'm sure she'll go with me."

His reaction was what I'd predicted. "Whatever you do, don't tell Lois! With her big mouth...." Dan let his sentence trail off and gave a martyred sigh. "Anyway, I didn't say I *wouldn't* go, just — Oh, never mind. If it means that much to you, I'll call off my golf game and we'll both go." He waited hopefully for me to tell him not to bother rescheduling his game. I didn't. So Sunday, the two of us headed for PFLAG, Dan driv-

7

ing and me trying to decipher the directions I'd scrawled to a church down a side street off Old Keene Mill Road.

We parked in the rear of the church parking lot, stepping out of the car onto blacktop that baked under the July sun. By the time we found the entrance to the activity wing and the door with a crayoned sign taped to it that read "PFLAG here," the meeting had already started. We pushed open the door, interrupting the group's leader — facilitator she'd called herself on the phone. Some dozen other participants, the majority of them women, sat in a circle on metal folding chairs.

"Come in, come in," the facilitator said. She was a graying, grandmotherly looking woman, a bit more than plump. I'd have guessed she wore clothes a size or two bigger than mine. "I hope you're looking for PFLAG — Parents, Families and Friends of Lesbians and Gays — because you've found us," she went on. "I'm Marlene, the facilitator for this support group."

"We spoke on the phone. I'm Sheila and this is my husband, Dan."

"I'm so glad you could both make it. I was just winding up the announcements and guidelines, but the only crucial thing you need to know is that everything said here is completely confidential. Our personal stories, our names and identifying characteristics, stay in this room. So why don't you have a seat and we'll get started."

There were two empty chairs together to Marlene's right, and Dan and I took them. They were the unpadded kind of folding chairs, making me momentarily grateful for the extra padding I have in my tush. Dan, who weighs the same as he did in college, crossed and uncrossed his legs in search of a comfortable position.

Once we were seated, Marlene said, "If you've never been to a support group before, we simply go around the room, briefly introduce ourselves, and say what's brought us here today. Then we can use the remaining time to focus on whatever issues or concerns people have in more depth. You're not obligated to speak, by the way. No one is pressured here. We're all on a journey together, but everyone travels at their own speed. Well, why don't I go first. I have a son who's gay. He came out to us right after college, a little over fifteen years ago, though by then I'd guessed...."

Why hadn't I guessed about Jenny, I wondered, as Marlene went on to tell us how she and her son had danced around the topic, each afraid to actually utter the word gay, how close they were now, how she'd grieved over the fact that he would never get married. But he'd found a wonderful partner and she and her husband couldn't have been happier to include him in their family circle. "Most of you know, they split up a few months ago after twelve years together," she added. "It was hard on my husband and me as well as on our son; we'd come to love his partner as much as we would have a daughter-in-law if he'd been in a heterosexual marriage."

I'd taken the chair next to Marlene and when she was done she turned to me. "If you'd like to introduce yourself next, we'll go around counterclockwise," she said, giving me an encouraging smile.

Marlene's introduction had brought painfully to mind my daydreams of the wedding we'd give Jenny one day. Which would obviously remain nothing but daydreams. I'd have to forget my visions of making the rounds of bridal shops with her, the two of us planning and debating together over color schemes, flowers and wedding cake. Of watching the temple fill with aunts, uncles and cousins, with my mother and Dan's mother, with Lois, LaVerne, Natalie and the rest of our friends, with Dan's law partners and associates. Of how, in the Jewish tradition, we would both walk Jenny down the aisle before taking our seats in the front pew, bursting with pride, beaming through our tears, as Jenny and her dashing bridegroom stood under the canopy and took their vows. But now, put on the spot, with the expectant gazes of the other participants on me, I had a sudden attack of stage fright. Did I really want to share all that with these strangers, even if most of them smiled encouragingly when their eyes met mine? Instead, I just said, "I'm Sheila Katz. Our daughter told us she's a lesbian a week and a half ago. Maybe I should have guessed, but it was really a surprise to me. I'm here to learn." I nodded to Dan that it was his turn.

"Dan Katz," he said reluctantly, doubtless revealing his last name only because I'd automatically used it already. "I can't think of a thing to add to what my wife's told you."

"That's fine," Marlene said. "There'll be plenty of time later if you want to get more into your issues. We're glad to have you at any rate. We have more mothers than fathers in this group. Not every father is as will-ing to seek support as you are."

"I'm afraid that's my wife's doing," Dan said, but as always, when confronted by female praise he turned on his charm, sitting a little straighter and flashing Marlene a warm grin that accentuated the resem-blance to Robert Redford I'd always seen in him. I moved my hand to cover Dan's where it gripped his knee. Our fingers touched, then Dan pulled away, leaned back and crossed his arms, hands tucked into his armpits.

"We're glad you've come, whatever the cause," Marlene assured him. She nodded to the next person to introduce himself, a freckled, crew-cut boy who told the group that his parents would be visiting him from Nebraska the following month.

"I call them once a week, but it's gotten so all we talk about is the weather. I know it's gonna be like that till I come out to them, but every week I end up chickening out. But now it's like I have a deadline. I don't see how I can have them visiting me for two weeks and still keep half my life a secret. So I'm hoping to get some feedback from you parents on how to go about it."

I felt Dan give a start of surprise. Apparently he hadn't realized the support group wasn't limited to parents, but included gay people as well. Marlene had mentioned it on the phone, but I hadn't bothered passing it on. I told myself that Dan's reaction was purely surprise and not a flinch of distaste, an imperceptible one that only a wife would pick up on. It wasn't as if we didn't have gay friends, after all. I had gay friends anyway. To Dan, I supposed, they were just acquaintances.

While I was worrying about Dan's reaction, the slender, blond woman alongside the boy had taken the floor from him. "I'm Candy Sue Carter and I have a gay son," she said. She ran her fingers through her hair, an expensive shade that came from a high-priced salon rather than a drugstore counter. She looked like she'd been a high-school cheerleader and hadn't let herself go to pot after. "Most of y'all have already heard my story, so you know I never had an *idea*. Jason was a first-string quarter-back all through high school, girls calling him right and left. And then in college — Well, I won't bore y'all bragging on his accomplishments, but he was in the top 10 percent of his law school class. It just tears me up thinking how he'll never get married, never give us a grandchild. Well, y'all remember how I cried through the whole evening first time I came here."

Heads nodded around the circle. Abruptly I found my own eyes watering and had to blink back tears. When I fastened my eyes on Candy Sue once more, I had stopped envying her aerobics-trim figure long enough to empathize with her confusion and grief over the changed out-lines of her child's future.

"You've come a long way since then," Marlene interjected softly.

"It's something I've had to come to accept, much as I wish — And his... his *friend*. Well, Mark is as nice a young man...."

"Has your husband come around at all?" one of the women who hadn't yet introduced herself asked.

"Don't I wish. He's military and you know how they are. I tried telling him what I learned here, how it's not something Jason *chose* to be. But he wouldn't even go to his graduation. We nearly separated over that." She paused, fussing with her hair again. "It's been over two years since they've spoken to each other."

"I think it's harder for fathers. With sons especially," the same woman said earnestly.

"Well, I know it must be, but I wish...." And suddenly Candy Sue was turning in our direction. "How do you feel, Dan? You're a father."

Marlene leaned forward. "Candy Sue, we haven't finished going around the circle for introductions. Besides, this is all new to Dan. Give him a little time to process what he's feeling before you put him on the spot."

"I don't mind," Dan said, surprising me. He spread his hands and gave his dazzling smile again. "I really have no concerns about it."

Every female in the room seemed to beam approval at him. Dan sat back, basking in their admiration as if it was a warm bathtub.

"Well, I think that's just wonderful," Candy Sue gushed. "And you feel the same?" she asked, looking directly at me now.

I took a breath. "I should. That is, I know it shouldn't make any difference to me that Jenny is gay. I mean, some of my best friends are gay." I winced as I heard myself. "That came out wrong." I could imagine what LaVerne would say if I were to announce that some of my best friends were black.

"But I am very good friends with this gay couple who I met working in community theater. And it's never bothered me in the least that they're gay. But somehow this is different," I admitted.

"It's always different when it's your own child," Marlene said gently.

I nodded gratefully. "What I mean is, Jenny — that's our daughter — told me about this girl she teaches with who's her friend. Well, what she said was, her *girlfriend*. And then she asked if I wanted to meet her. And I said, 'Well, I guess.' And she said, 'You *guess*?' As soon as she said it, I knew how I'd disappointed her. I mean, I knew — *she* knew — that if it was a boy I'd have been really excited for her, had a million questions about him."

"But you did agree to meet her, didn't you?" Candy Sue asked.

I nodded. "I asked Jenny to invite her to our house for dinner next week. She teaches with Jenny. Physical Education. She sounds nice, from what Jenny's told me about her. But I still feel, well, kind of weird about the whole thing. And —"

"And I tell Sheila to just relax," Dan interrupted, surprising me again. "I think she's making a mountain out of a molehill."

There was a girl not much older than Jenny sitting almost directly across the circle. Petite, dark-haired, with silver dangles swinging from her ears. "Your daughter's lucky to have folks who are so supportive. My —"

"Well, isn't that what parents are for?" Dan flashed her his smile. "It's my feeling, uh —" He peered at her name tag. She was wearing denim shorts that showed off a pair of really great legs, and I saw his focus drop and linger there a moment. "It's my feeling, Alison, that we've always been a family. Had a real family dinner every night, spent time with our kids. So it's not surprising that Jenny feels free to talk to us."

Alison nodded, looking wistful, her earrings jingling like faint, far-off bells.

"Anyhow, I have a little more faith than my wife. Jenny's basic problem is, she's in a rut. Teaching school all day, stuck in a classroom, with a bunch of old-maid teachers for company, if you'll pardon the expression. It's no wonder she hasn't met a guy she can go for. It may take her a while, but she'll come around when she meets the right one. It's as simple as that."

I stared at Dan, opened my mouth to speak, closed it again.

Alison's jaw dropped as well."Oh, but," she said, then broke off, seemingly at a loss for words. "It's not like that," she said at last. "You can't just change. Your daughter might try, but it wouldn't work; she'd be living a lie. I didn't want to admit it either. It took me, God, five or six years maybe, to really face up to it, to say, yes, I'm a lesbian."

Dan jumped, so sharply that I felt his knee jerk next to mine. Though he should have guessed Alison was a lesbian — she was the only woman in the room who hadn't been ogling him. Now the rest of the group were giving nods of agreement with Alison's words. I couldn't tell if Dan was embarrassed by his faux pas. His face had closed up, the way it had after Jenny came out to him.

"Well, I appreciate your giving me your opinion," he said stiffly.

Chapter Two

*T*he evening before Jenny brought her girlfriend home for dinner, she informed Dan and me — over turbot microwaved with mustard sauce — that the two of them had found an apartment and were moving in together the first of August.

As far as I knew, nothing in the three days since we'd gone to PFLAG had shaken Dan's conviction that Jenny was going through a phase. Her new announcement didn't shake him up either. The only thing he had to say was, "I know you girls want to get settled before school starts, but if you haven't actually signed on the dotted line then let me go over the lease for you first. What's the point of having a dad in real estate law if you don't take advantage of his expertise?"

Dan was equally calm the following night, as we waited for the girls to arrive. I was the one who'd worked myself into a state, vacuuming the rugs and spending an hour deciding what to fix for dinner. Still, I had everything under control by the time Jenny parked her car at the curb. I walked into Dan's den, located across the entry foyer from the living room, and told him, "They're here." He had his blinds drawn to cut the glare on his computer screen so I peeked between them to get a first glimpse of Jenny's girlfriend. Dan was at least curious enough to join me.

"Pretty girl," he remarked, as she climbed out of the passenger side of the car. "Pretty and petite."

"She's different than I expected," I said.

"Different how?"

I was embarrassed to admit the picture I'd had in mind of a lesbian gym teacher: someone raw-boned and masculine. Now I remembered that Jenny had mentioned her friend had been a gymnast through high school and college. I could see that she had a gymnast's build: petite, as Dan had remarked, probably half a head shorter than Jenny, slender and wiry. Her face, heart-shaped and delicate, was surrounded by the kind of frizzy dark curls that we used to call a Jewish Afro back in the late sixties. Instead of the lumberjack shirt and boots I'd imagined, she was wearing a short-sleeved cotton sweater and tapered slacks.

Dan was still waiting for my response. "I don't know. Shorter maybe," I mumbled, hurrying to open the door.

"Dad, Mom, this is Tammy. My parents, Dan and Sheila Katz," Jenny said, making the introductions all in a rush. Dan seized Tammy's hand and pumped it up and down.

"We're always glad to meet one of Jenny's friends," he said, a shade too heartily.

"Tammy is my very *special* friend, Daddy," Jenny said, with a smile a novelist might have described as arch, but a mother recognized as nervous.

I opened my mouth to announce dinner before Dan could make any out-of-the-way remark, but before I got the words out, Tammy said, "You're forgetting, honey, I'd rather be called Tamara from now on." She'd said that to Jenny, and while I was struggling with an instant of shock over this girl calling Jenny "honey," she turned back to Dan and me. "My name really is Tamara, but my mother nicknamed me Tammy when I was a little kid. I've decided I'd like my name to reflect the fact that I'm a grownup now."

"It's a lovely name," I said.

"Thanks. I like that it's close to the original Hebrew name in the Old Testament. I've been trying to incorporate a little more of my Jewish heritage into my daily life."

"Well good for you!" Dan exclaimed.

I found myself warming to Tamara also, as the girls and Dan followed me down the center hall to the back of the house. The sauce was simmering on the stove for a spicy shrimp Creole that I was planning to serve with crusty French bread and hearts of palm salad. Dan and I usually ate in the breakfast room, as the builder had termed one end of our "country size" kitchen. Tonight though, I'd set the dining room table, using a pale green cloth that picked up the green figures in the cream colored Chinese carpet and made the room look like a cool oasis in the summer heat.

"Wow, we're eating in the dining room. This really is an occasion," Jenny said. Her tone was joking, but she threw me a warmly appreciative glance. I returned to the kitchen to add the shrimp while the girls and Dan nibbled cheese and crackers in the living room. When I proudly served my shrimp Creole ten minutes later though, Tamara threw Jenny a look that was distinctly unhappy. One I couldn't help picking up on.

"I hope you don't mind eating spicy food," I said to Tamara. "I should have checked with Jenny."

"It's not the spices, Mom," Jenny blurted. "I should have told you Tamara keeps kosher."

"Oh," I said. It should have dawned on me that was why she'd been taken aback. She'd just said she was trying to follow more of the Jewish traditions. And Jewish rules for keeping kosher not only preclude eating milk and meat together, but forbid pork and shellfish. So much for the shrimp that I had so laboriously peeled and deveined. "Well, let me think. I have a chicken breast left from the other night that I can pop in the microwave and —"

"Oh, no, this is fine, really. I try to keep strictly kosher in my own home, but I'm more relaxed about it outside. There's just a few foods, like bacon, I try to avoid altogether."

And shellfish, I thought.

"It's a recent development for me anyway," Tamara was going on, "just the past few months. So it's understandable that Jenny forgot to mention it to you." Tamara gave Jenny another look that made me think she'd use some other word than understandable when they were alone together. I told myself their relationship — the idea of which I'd barely begun to get used to — wasn't my concern.

"Well, if you're sure." She nodded. I sat down and started passing the salad.

Dan, who rarely picks up on looks, and to all outward appearances was blithely unconcerned about the girls' relationship, said, "It's good to see someone your age taking so much interest in her religion. Is your family religious?"

"They're Reform, but they're not observant. More what you'd call High Holy Day Jews. My mom never even bothered to clear the bread out of our house for Passover. I was pretty much the same until recently," Tamara added. "Jewish in name only."

"So what brought about the change?" Dan wanted to know.

"A workshop I went to on diversity awareness, believe it or not. It was part of training I had to take to volunteer at a rape crisis center. What the workshop leader had us do was to come up to the front of the room whenever she called out the name of a minority group we belonged to. Like, if she called out black, everyone who was black was supposed to get up and go to the front." Tamara looked from Dan to me to make sure we got it.

"The group she actually called out first was women, and I got up and went to the front. Then she called for lesbians and I got up again." I thought I saw Dan flinch at that but I was too interested to worry about him for a moment.

"So then she called other races, Asian and Native American and a bunch of ethnic and religious groups. And when I was standing at the front of the room for being Jewish, it dawned on me that I could become the victim of prejudice whether I was practicing my Judaism or not but —"

"Well said," Dan cut in. "That's what my mother used to tell us when I was a kid. Hitler didn't care whether the six million people he murdered were Orthodox or assimilated. Just their being Jewish was enough for him. I'm glad Jenny will be rooming with someone who's such a good influence. Did she tell you about her brother? He not only married a Catholic girl but converted to her religion. I thought it would give my mother a heart attack. You know what she told me at the time?"

I certainly did. If I had a dollar for every time he'd repeated what his mother told him —

"'Hitler killed six million Jews,'she told me. 'And your son just took away another one.'"

Both girls looked confused, though I didn't know whether it was on account of Dan's interrupting Tamara's story or his assumption that Jenny and Tamara were nothing but roommates. Whichever, I hoped he wasn't going to start in on Jeffrey.

However much Dan dwelt on Jeffrey's conversion, I couldn't help thinking that it was just the proverbial straw that broke the camel's back as far as their relationship was concerned. Jeffrey and Dan had (respectively) sulked and shouted their way through Jeffrey's teens. Their conflict came to the boiling point with Jeffrey's announcement, a week after his junior year in college, that no matter what his father said, he would not take the LSATs or apply to law school. Instead he was applying to the graduate school of drama at Catholic University to earn a master's degree in Performance Studies. Jeffrey made this announcement over dinner, the scene of most of the drama that takes place in our house. We were eating broiled salmon steaks, green peas and rice, and Dan had slammed his knife and fork down onto his plate with such force that grains of rice ricocheted around the table.

According to Dan, the whole thing was my fault. I was the one who had enrolled Jeffrey in a children's acting class for his eleventh birthday, who had encouraged his application to a school that would prepare him to be either a starving actor or a waiter. Unfortunately, Dan turned out to be right about Jeffrey's prospects as an actor. Despite his M.F.A. and a move to New York, he'd gotten only bit parts, all of them in off-off-Broadway productions, the longest of which ran two weeks. But he hadn't starved or waited tables. Instead, he made use of the undergraduate law-related courses Dan had insisted he take and supported himself by temping as a legal secretary. He'd met Anita, a paralegal, on one of his temp jobs.

The one saving grace for Dan was that his fear that his soft-spoken, stagestruck son might be gay was ended when Jeffrey proved his heterosexuality by getting Anita pregnant and marrying her — in that order. But remembering his anxieties about Jeffrey ("I've never yet met a male secretary who wasn't a *faygeleh*," he'd blurted on one occasion) just added to my worries about how he'd react to Jenny when it finally dawned on him that she wasn't simply going through a phase.

I told myself to stop sitting there going over past history. Tamara, who was poking food around her plate, apparently separating shrimps from Creole, still looked puzzled, but Jenny had begun to pout.

"How come we never do anything around here but talk about my brother?" she demanded. "Here I bring Tamara home to meet you and Mom, and we end up talking about Jeffrey, same as always."

"Who was talking about Jeffrey?" Dan said. "I was asking your friend about her religious views and he just happened to come into the conversation."

"But you didn't even let her finish answering your question."

Tamara looked as uncomfortable as any new boyfriend might have, stuck in the middle of a family argument. "I really didn't have any more to say. Just that I was stuck with the negatives of being Jewish, but I wasn't reaping the rewards. That is, I'd always taken it for granted, but I didn't really know that much about my own heritage."

17

"I'm beginning to feel the same way, Daddy," Jenny said, apparently forgiving her father for inserting her brother into *her* evening. She always forgave Dan a good deal faster than she forgave me. "Maybe you're right that Tammy — Tamara is a good influence on me. At least, we've joined a synagogue together, and we've decided to light candles Friday nights and keep a kosher kitchen once we move into our apartment."

"Not that we're going overboard," Tamara said. "We're not turning ultra-Orthodox or anything." When she smiled, she reminded me of the young Barbara Streisand in *The Way We Were.* "We've just decided that we enjoy setting the Sabbath aside as a special day of rest. And having separate dishes for milk and meat. But we're not going to freak out if someone uses the wrong dish towel or something."

That was something I was glad to hear her say. When we were first married, Dan's mother had bawled me out like a kid for mistakenly drying a roasting pan with the towel she'd set aside for dairy.

Dan appeared taken with Tamara as well. He gave her an approving smile and observed, "Well, it looks like you two girls are on the right path."

I got Jenny to myself for a minute, while Tamara was using the powder room. "She seems like a very nice girl," I observed cautiously.

Jenny smiled. "Isn't she wonderful, Mom? I knew you'd like her."

"I do," I assured her. "But you're sure about this move? Signing the lease and all?"

For once, Jenny didn't misunderstand me. "I've been sure since two weeks after we met. I knew the second time we went out that she was the one I wanted to spend my life with. She's — well, she's just the one, Mom."

Chapter Three

We had our next ladies' lunch three weeks after Tamara's visit. To my surprise, neither Natalie nor LaVerne had called to pump me about Jenny. I was certain they'd drill me about her now, though, and equally certain that I wasn't ready to field their questions.

It was LaVerne's turn to pick the restaurant, and she'd chosen Planet Hollywood, a noisy, kitschy place where most of the patrons looked a generation or two younger than ourselves. We trooped upstairs to nonsmoking, past Hollywood costumes in museum-style cases, and settled at a table across from a giant TV showing snippets of movie scenes.

The menu's list of merchandise for sale was longer than the list of food selections. Once we'd been served, we began catching up with each other's news. Over the years, that had consisted in large part of how our kids were doing. Before either of the others could open their mouths, Natalie leaned toward me, pitching her voice so as to be heard over the music, and asked, "So what's the latest with Jeffrey? Any luck at auditions?" As the owner of a thriving gymnastics studio, Natalie prided herself on working at least partially in the performance field; she asked about my son's auditions nearly every get-together.

I set my fork down on my plate of pasta — topped with a surprisingly good tomato sauce that I'd assured myself was low fat — and told her, "A couple of callbacks, but that's it."

"Well, it takes time. Tell him not to give up."

I shook my head ruefully. "I'm afraid he's running out of time now that Anita's expecting again. She's after him to find a full-time job so she

19

can stay home with the kids. She says that paying day care for two children will practically eat up her salary. I suppose she has a point. Of course, Stephanie is in preschool part of the day, but you wouldn't believe how tuition has gone up, even for preschool. So that's what's going on with Jeffrey."

I ate another forkful while I waited for Natalie to ask after Jenny, now that we'd started with my news. Instead, there was a pause filled only with the blare of background music. Then she said, "Well, when you consider overhead, it can't be helped. What I tell parents at the gym is —"

Simultaneously LaVerne moaned, "Don't tell me about tuition. Might as well be a rocket at Cape Kennedy, the way it keeps going up."

Had they decided to avoid the whole topic of Jenny? Instead of relief, I was startled by a surge of annoyance, of anger that took me back in time. My father had lingered two years with cancer. During that time, during the years when I grew from twelve to fourteen, not a soul had spoken the word aloud, or invited me to unburden myself. Not that Jenny's sexual orientation was akin to cancer. Yet wasn't that the way my friends were treating it with their uncharacteristic silence?

"I haven't told you Jenny's news yet," I announced, cutting into LaVerne's lament.

The two of them gave each other a look.

"How *is* Jenny?" Natalie asked finally, her voice hushed as if for a sickroom.

"She's fine." Now that I'd brought her up, there was nothing to do but continue. "She has a — a *friend,* and they just moved into an apartment together. I haven't seen it yet. Jenny says they want to finish unpacking and get a little settled in before they show it off."

"But you met this friend?" LaVerne demanded.

"Oh, yes. We had her to our house for dinner last month. A very nice girl. She teaches at the same school as Jenny. And she's Jewish too. In fact, she's Orthodox or close to it. Even keeps kosher." I made a face. "Which my darling daughter forgot to mention ahead of time. I went and served shrimp Creole for dinner."

LaVerne and Natalie laughed. Lois, who'd heard the whole thing already, looked up from her wineglass long enough to smile.

"So you're happy about it then?" Natalie wanted to know.

"I'm happy she's found someone who's right for her." I'd be happier if the someone was of the opposite sex, but I kept that to myself.

"Still," LaVerne mused, between bites of her club sandwich, "I can't get over it. Jenny turning out a lesbian. She was always such a feminine little thing. Remember how she always wanted to wear dresses?"

"She still likes dresses, actually." I tried to remember the way Jenny had explained it to me. "She just identifies more with women, so she can never get close to a man the way she can to another woman."

LaVerne looked up at the oversized TV screen, now showing a romantic montage of silver screen kisses, leading men and their ladies locked in a succession of passionate clinches. "That's what's hard to picture, her falling in love with another girl."

I could just imagine the pictures in LaVerne's mind. "She's in love with her as a *person*," I protested, trying to head off the question I was certain came next: But what do they *do* together? All three, I was sure, were wondering, but it would be Lois who would have the chutzpah to put it into words. It was Lois's kind of question, and she'd been nursing her wineglass in silence for a while.

Sure enough, Lois opened her mouth to speak. She'd reached that stage of inebriation where she pulled a ballpoint from her purse, a substitute for the cigarettes she gave up after her diagnosis of breast cancer, leaned forward and tapped imaginary ashes onto the table top. "You know, speaking of love, there's something I've been wondering. Mind if I ask you a question?"

I did mind, and was about to say so, when I realized Lois was looking not at me, but at LaVerne. "I've been wondering ever since you told us about Dennis's prostate operation. Do you and he still have a sex life since the operation? If you know what I mean," Lois added, gazing across the table at LaVerne with all the complacent expectancy of a talk show host.

"Yeah, I know what you mean," LaVerne sputtered. "Nothing wrong with our love life."

"Oh, I didn't mean there was anything wrong!" Lois assured her. "But I was reading in the paper how that kind of operation can make a man impotent and I just wondered —"

"He's not impotent. He came through the operation just fine."

"Oh, good. Then he can still get erections?"

"I just told you he could." LaVerne looked at Lois and relented a bit. "Of course, they're not like when he was twenty-five."

Natalie threw her an understanding look. "Tell me about it!" she screeched and we all howled with sympathetic laughter.

I'd put up a front at lunch, but the truth was I couldn't understand Jenny's falling in love with another girl either. It became no easier as the next few weeks went by. I accepted Jenny. How could I not accept my own daughter? And after I'd let her down by telling her I "guessed" I wanted to meet Tamara, I'd promised myself not to say or do anything else she could take as rejection. But understanding her new life was something else.

Tamara was "the one," Jenny had told me. The exact words I'd used to my own mother, when I told her that Dan and I had become engaged. I liked Tamara, found her intelligent and charming, but I still found it incomprehensible to picture Jenny falling for her the way I'd fallen for Dan. I didn't get why "identifying" with women meant Jenny couldn't relate to a man in any kind of romantic way. What was so wrong with having close women friends and *still* having a boyfriend or husband? What was it she was looking for? Why pick another girl for a *girlfriend*, a — a *spouse?*

Working on Burke Amateur Theater's fall show — for which I'd volunteered to stage manage as well as do set decorating — kept my mind off Jenny some of the time. I'd joined the group, more commonly known as BAT, when the kids were little, and in the years since had become one of the most active members.

BAT acquired its home from our founder, Philippa White, a retired drama professor who'd been eccentric even for theater circles. She'd played the role of Conjur Woman in *Dark of the Moon* — the first show I worked on — and I'd overheard more than one cast member whisper that it was a textbook example of type casting. She'd lived alone, except for a dozen or so black cats, in a ramshackle old farmhouse, set on half a dozen acres of scrubby trees that were being choked out by overgrown grape vines that twined around the trees' dying branches. It was no wonder that neighborhood children called the place the "haunted house."

By the time Philippa passed on — struck by lightning as she stood on a metal stepladder during a thunderstorm, trying to coax a stray cat down from a tree — her acreage was being eyed by real estate developers. To their chagrin, Philippa left her house and land to BAT, with the stipulation that her cats were to be cared for in their accustomed home.

If the property was ever sold, the entire proceeds would go to the local animal shelter. Which left us with no choice but to do exactly as Philippa had wished: make a theater out of the place. With the portion of liquid assets Philippa bequeathed us that weren't earmarked for lifetime care of her pets, BAT managed to convert the dilapidated barn into a theater, plus spruce up the house for rehearsal space and children's classes.

As one of the few BAT members without a "day job," I had been drafted as chief caretaker of Philippa's felines whenever we found ourselves between janitorial staff, as was presently the case. I didn't mind. As Mistress of Props I was constantly running to the theater in any case, and my friends Jack and Jim spelled me on weekends.

Jack and Jim were my gay friends. They'd met in Vietnam; Jack was an army nurse who cared for Jim after he'd been wounded. The two of them had been together ever since. Their names were as linked in everyone's minds as Jack-and-Jill: Jack-and-Jim are co-producing the next show, Jack-and-Jim are giving the cast party. I'd gone to more cast parties in their paneled rec room, with one wall full of their framed military honors, than I could remember.

As long as I'd known them, they'd never been in the closet. In fact, they'd hosted a cast party shortly after they'd remodeled their house ten years earlier. Cast and crew were given the grand tour, the highlight of which was the new master bedroom they'd created out of two smaller ones, with its king-sized water-bed and sumptuous master bath with oversized spa. The one remaining bedroom was a study where Jim, a high-paid writer of corporate video scripts, spent his spare time working on his magnum opus — a Vietnam novel he was convinced would be his generation's *War and Peace*.

I'd never given much thought to what they did in that king-size bed, or about the rest of their lifestyle either. Now, the gay lifestyle seemed to be constantly at the back of my mind.

That was the reason, I suppose, why I noticed two women wheeling their cart slowly past me as I paused to toss several boxes of Lipton's into my cart during my weekly trip to Giant Food. (BAT's upcoming fall show was one in which the actors are rarely onstage without cocktail glass in hand, requiring a stock of the tea we used for alcoholic beverages.) Like Tamara, neither woman fit the popular image of a lesbian. They were in their mid-thirties, both in the kind of tailored office clothes that indicate a quick stop on the way home from work, nothing exceptional in either woman's appearance. So I couldn't say what I was picking up on that told me the two were lesbians. Except for the way they leaned toward each other, murmuring in soft voices.

I tossed yet another box of tea into my cart and pushed it slowly after them, trying to get a better look without them noticing. They reached the end of the aisle and turned into the next. I normally went up and down every aisle too, hoping to jog my memory in case I'd forgotten to write something on my shopping list. Now I skipped the next aisle entirely, turning into the one after so I could catch a glimpse of them face-to-face. The two were just turning into the aisle from the opposite end. I gave them the once-over, though I did it without them being any the wiser, giving my best imitation of a conscientious shopper, with nothing more on her mind than finding a bargain, and looking right through them with that glazed look supermarket shoppers get.

As they passed me, I took in their hands. Each wore a matching ring on the fourth finger of her left hand, an attractive design of entwined silver and gold that looked exactly like matching wedding bands.

When I turned into the next aisle, they had stopped at the far end in front of the pet food section. They had their heads together still, and as I wheeled my cart toward them, I tried to imagine what romantic endearments they were murmuring to each other. The taller of the two women, a brunette with chin-length blunt cut hair, touched the other's hand, passing her something. A lover's note? I hurried toward them, half believing that if I only knew what lay between them, I'd understand Jenny's new lifestyle.

I needed to pick up cat food in any case. I left my cart at one end of the pet food section and began edging along it, as if indecisive about what to buy, as if I didn't know perfectly well the kitties' likes and dislikes.

I stopped two feet from the women, taking out my glasses to make a show of reading the ingredients on a can of Whiskas Mealtime. The shorter woman perused the slip of paper her lover had handed her, then murmured to her confidingly. I edged closer to catch her words.

"Well, it's up to you, sweetie," she said in a husky voice. "But with this coupon we only get sixty cents off, even after it's doubled. We'll save more just buying the Giant brand."

My questions about Jenny's new lifestyle were still unresolved when Dan and I arrived for our first visit to Jenny and Tamara's new apartment the Saturday before Labor Day. Neither of us had seen the apartment before, Jenny having declined my offers to help decorate. "That's okay, Mom. The two of us are looking forward to doing it together," she'd told me. The two of them did their own moving as well, carrying Jenny's possessions to a rented U-Haul, letting Dan help only with Jenny's desk, a golden oak roll-top I'd discovered in a second-hand shop and refinished to a mellow glow for Jenny's twelfth birthday. Some friends from their synagogue were meeting them at the apartment to help unload, they assured us.

The girls had described the apartment in glowing terms: a one-bedroom with den in a development called The Hemlocks, not far from I-95, and an easy commute to their jobs. The Hemlocks are one of the oldest garden apartment complexes in the Springfield area. Unlike most developments with woodsy names but not a tree in sight, they are situated in a stand of evergreens; the developer supposedly tagged every tree to be left standing at the time of construction. We made our way from the visitors' parking lot down a dirt path layered with pine needles that softened our footfalls. The weather was still summery, but the air smelled like a department store at the height of the Christmas shopping season.

Jenny opened the door the instant we rang the bell and gave her father a big hug, then remembered to brush my cheek with her lips. "Come sit down," she said, leading us down a short hallway that opened into the living room. "Tamara is just putting the finishing touches on dinner."

We sank down on the couch, a sleep sofa that must have been Tamara's. I'd offered Jenny the old futon that was taking up space in our rec room, but she'd turned me down. She'd taken the pine blanket chest from her room, though, and put it to use as a coffee table. A folded patchwork quilt was draped over the top and a pottery bowl was filled with tangy-smelling apples and golden ripe peaches.

On the opposite wall from the couch, the living room opened into a small alcove, just large enough for the girls' desks. I had to smile to see Jenny's roll-top with the top actually rolled down. Neatness wasn't my daughter's strong suit. In her room at home, the desktop had been heaped too high with papers to get it closed. Tamara did seem to be a good influence on her. Tamara's desk held a squared-off stack of papers, held down by a glass paperweight, and a cluster of pens in what looked to be an antique pewter mug.

"You girls have done a wonderful job of decorating in such a short time," I said, as Tamara emerged from the kitchen, a chef's apron over her slacks and her hair frizzed out from the kitchen heat.

"Hi, Mr. and Mrs. Katz," she said. "Good to see you again. I hope you're hungry — we're having veggie lasagna. It'll be ready in a half hour or so. I made it a couple of days in advance, but I just put it in the oven to reheat — sundown's still pretty late this time of year."

It *was* Saturday evening, but it hadn't occurred to me until then that Jenny and Tamara carried their observance of the Sabbath that far. I'd been brought up Reform, my mother scoffing at what she called "old-fashioned" traditions. "So who's working on the Sabbath?" she'd demand as she turned the knob on our electric oven. "When they wrote that part of the Bible, did they know that lighting an oven would be as easy as snapping your fingers?"

"It smells wonderful," Dan told Tamara, "and I'm sure it'll be worth the wait. I hope Jenny isn't making you do all the work."

"I made the salad, Daddy," Jenny assured him. "And I've got a tray of crackers and cheese ready to nibble on till the lasagna's heated. I'll just go get it."

The scents drifting from the kitchen were mouth-watering, a tantalizing blend of garlic, tomato and cheese. I was inhaling five pounds through my nose alone. I'd gain enough weight eating lasagna. If I started noshing on cheese and crackers beforehand, I'd have to ask Dan to run out and buy me a tent to wear home. So I headed Jenny off by saying, "How about giving us an apartment tour first?"

"There's really not much more to see," Jenny said, sounding so reluctant that I looked at her in surprise.

"Oh, well, if it isn't straightened up enough to show company yet," I said.

"Not that you could call your parents company," Dan put in.

Tamara gave Jenny a look that I couldn't decipher. "No, we've got most of the moving mess under control, Mrs. Katz."

"Oh please, call me Sheila," I protested.

She smiled. "Sheila, then. It's fine for you to see the rest of the place, really. Honey, why don't you show your parents around while I make the garlic bread."

Jenny gave what sounded like a subdued sigh. "Okay. Well, this is the living room of course. There's the hall you came into," she said, assuming the role of tour guide. "We've got a nice coat closet there. Big enough even for company when it's colder," she added, opening the door to show off the space.

"Then we've got a study set up for grading papers off of the living room," she said walking back into the living room and motioning for us to admire the alcove housing their desks.

"I haven't seen your desk this neat in years," I told her.

I half expected her to say, "Oh, Mom," but she just laughed. "It's good that you can't see under the roll-top, but I'm working on not being such a slob." Before I could faint with amazement, Jenny led us through the living room's sliding glass door onto the balcony.

"We really love the balcony and we're so lucky to have this view. And this is our utility shed in the corner here; every apartment has its own furnace and hot water heater. Let me get the key, and you can take a look at them, Daddy." Examining Jenny's water heater was more of an in-depth tour than I had bargained for, but I admired the wooded parkland across from their building while Dan looked in the utility shed. "We're planning to get a couple of plastic chairs and a table next spring, so we can eat outside in nice weather," Jenny went on, after the conversational possibilities of the furnace and heater had been exhausted. It wasn't like her to chatter like this about what was after all just a fairly small concrete balcony, but I listened patiently as she pointed out "our kitchen garden," a collection of potted herbs — parsley, basil, chive and others — that Tamara was doubtless responsible for. At least while I was seeing the apartment, I wasn't stuffing my face with Gouda or Brie, I reminded myself, as Jenny at last led us back inside and showed us the little dining ell off the living room, where a small square table — probably a card table — was prettily set with a blue homespun cloth and matching napkins.

Jenny showed off the compact corridor kitchen that opened onto it next, opening cabinet doors and even the refrigerator, while Tamara went on spreading sliced Italian loaves with butter and sprinkling them with fresh, minced garlic. You'd never know she'd been cooking at all, I thought, impressed by the order surrounding her. Even I wasn't that much of a neatnik.

"Okay, now follow me down the hall, and I'll show you where the bathroom is," Jenny said, after we'd stood underfoot in the kitchen while Tamara put the finishing touches on the garlic bread. "We put out guest towels." Jenny pointed them out as we reached the bathroom. The blue stripe in the towels picked up the blue of the tiles, and a white porcelain dish held an assortment of blue and white soaps, carved into the shape of shells. Very nice, I thought.

"Well, if you want to wash up or anything," Jenny murmured, backing out.

"How about finishing the tour first?" her father asked. There was only one room we hadn't seen, and I suddenly realized why Jenny had been dragging her feet in the rest of the apartment, probably hoping Tamara would announce dinner before we had a chance to reach the bedroom. The door was closed. Jenny opened it, and motioned us in.

Unlike the kitchen, the bedroom was spacious, with a wall of windows at one end. One of the interior walls was taken up by a closet, running the full length of the room. A queen-sized bed, covered with what looked like an antique patchwork quilt, stood on the other wall, flanked by two unmatched night tables.

"Isn't it great, all this closet space?" Jenny said, nervously. She pushed open one of the folding accordion doors to show it off.

"Very roomy," Dan agreed. He was looking about as if puzzled, his gaze going from the closet to the bed to the small dresser that was the only other piece of furniture in the room.

"I love the quilt," I said.

"Isn't it beautiful? Tamara's mother gave it to us. She collects them."

I'd always loved patchwork quilts myself. Our own bed, also a queen, was covered by a quilt, though it was a reproduction I'd bought in Bloomingdale's and not a genuine antique. Still, it occurred to me, the girls' bed looked remarkably like our own bed — Dan's and mine — at home.

"Well, I'd better go help Tamara put things on the table," Jenny said, after we'd all stood in silence a moment. "If you guys would like to wash up...." She gestured in the direction of the bathroom as she hurried out of the room.

Dan followed her. "But aren't you going to show us the rest — the other bedroom?" he called after her.

Jenny stopped and turned back to face him. "This is it, Daddy. Like the lease said: one bedroom with den."

"That's what I mean. I thought.... I assumed one of you would use the den for her bedroom. It's not across the hall?"

"Across the hall? There's another apartment on the other side of the hall wall. You saw the den already, Daddy. Off the living room. It's where we have our desks. I'd better go put dressing on the salad."

Jenny had turned away again as she spoke, calling the last over her shoulder as she rushed down the hall, as if she didn't want to see her father's expression.

I could have told her there was nothing to see. Dan's face had closed up as completely as a stage when the final curtain comes down on a show.

Chapter Four

As we were getting ready for bed Saturday night after our visit to the girls' apartment, I suggested Dan come with me to the next PFLAG support group. "I know you weren't crazy about it when you went with me in July, and it's not that I minded going by myself last month, but you seemed so upset that they were, well, sharing a bedroom."

"Why should I be upset?" he demanded. "Jenny is old enough to lead her own life. Anyhow, for all you know, one of them uses the sofa bed in the living room like you used to do."

Like fun, I thought. But bedtime was no time to start an argument; I slid under the covers without saying anything. As if to prove his equanimity, Dan fell asleep immediately. I was the one who lay awake trying not to picture Jenny in bed with Tamara. It was a losing battle, like trying not to think of a white elephant.

Finally I drifted off to X-rated dreams which, to my disappointment, I only partly remembered when I woke. I was consoled by the prospect of the real thing. I reached out and put my hand lightly on Dan's chest, then licked his ear as his eyes slowly opened.

Sunday morning was our usual time for making love. Unlike some of my friends, I still found sex with my husband exciting. And why not? Not only did my Dan have the body of a man twenty years younger, but he also performed like a man in his prime. No problems for us like those Natalie had once confessed over lunch. Her husband's doctor had ruled out the use of Viagra, so — on the rare occasions they still attempted it — she and Norman had to use a pump in order to raise an erection just barely firm enough for intercourse. Whenever I'd seen her and Norm since then, I couldn't help but imagine her gripping him with her strong thigh muscles, doggedly riding him to her finish with the nervous determination of a driver trying to make it to a gas station before a slow leak made her tire flat as a pancake.

For Dan and me, sex was still the bedrock of our relationship. Whatever our differences, we always made them up in bed. But now, although Dan immediately returned my caress, his own seemed half-hearted. He ran his hands perfunctorily over my breasts, gave my nipples a little squeeze, and turned his attention to the main event — which he completed in record time, leaving me still unsatisfied as he climbed out of bed mumbling something about an early tee time.

I sighed as I pulled the covers back over me, listening to the shower run, followed by his footsteps heading downstairs to the kitchen and, a few minutes later, his car engine starting. Last night's dream had been better than the real thing this morning. In the dream I'd been back in college, on the verge of doing it for the first time, back when my inexperience and imagination combined to paint sex as the ultimate mystery, a terrifying but thrilling doorway to adulthood.

Growing up in the Bronx, it was easier to fantasize about sex than to find a place or time for actually having it, especially with a mother like mine. Mama saw to it that I was never alone in our apartment with Dan. His parents' place was out of the question as well. And while suburban kids upstate might spend Saturday nights parked on lovers' lane, who had a car in the city? An out-of-town college was out of the question; I lived at home like most of the students at Hunter College. And halfway through college I was still a virgin, partly because of my mother's vigilance and partly because of my own apprehension. Nor had I intended to lose my virginity the evening it finally happened.

Dan and I had gone out for dinner at a neighborhood Chinese restaurant, with plans to see a nine o'clock movie. The feature hadn't even started when my stomach felt queasy, so much so that I made a dash to the ladies' room and threw up my shrimp chow mein. Dan was waiting in the lobby when I emerged. He put his arm around me.

"Feeling better?" he asked.

I did, a little. "But I need some fresh air." By the time Dan walked me home, I felt fine. As we stepped out of the elevator on the third floor, I apologized for making him miss the show.

"So we'll see it another time," he said as I turned my key in the lock and opened the apartment door.

"Maybe I'm allergic to shrimp."

"Maybe you've been brainwashed into an allergy. Punishment for eating *trayf*."

I laughed. "It was so yummy though."

"So are you," he told me, pulling me to him and giving me a kiss. Not his usual chaste peck for my mother's benefit, but a French kiss. His tongue, salty and sweet against mine, was as delicious as any shrimp.

"You too," I told him. "Yum, yum."

We went into the living room — which also served as my bedroom — and sat down on the sofa bed to continue our necking. Mama had switched rooms with me, moving into my old room when I started college and began staying up later than her. That didn't stop her from popping out, predictable as a cuckoo clock, the second I came home from a date. Tonight though, her mind set at ease by the expectation that we'd be out till nearly midnight, she'd gone to a Broadway show to celebrate her friend Alice's birthday.

Before you could say, "I dreamed I was sitting on the couch in my Maidenform bra," Dan and I were at second base with my blouse unbuttoned and my bra unhooked. I sighed with pleasure as Dan caressed my breasts gently with his fingertips and palms, not grabbing as if they were Silly Putty the way a couple of former boyfriends had tried. My erect nipples pressed against his chest as we fell back onto the sofa together. My skirt had ridden up around my waist and Dan's hand crept underneath.

"We shouldn't," I whispered.

"Relax. We won't do anything you don't want to." His hand, soft as his voice, was moving back and forth between my legs now, over the mound that hid my little pleasure button, stroking me with a steady silky friction that sent tingles through my nylon panties. "Sweet," he murmured, "sweet, sweet pussy." My legs parted, and I heard myself making little excited mews.

Dan's caresses sped up. I wriggled in excitement. My panties were wet, and instead of mewing like a pussycat, I was breathing as hard as if I'd sprinted up the Empire State Building. My fingers ran through Dan's hair, clasping him closer, my hips moving in instinctive rhythm. And then I was insensible to all but that warm tingling pleasure that came and came, building to one final explosion of sensation like the burst of a cork

32

from an opened bottle of champagne.

We lay still a minute afterwards, then Dan was pulling off my panties and fumbling with his zipper. "Now me," he whispered, and who could have had the heart to say no?

But today, on this Sunday morning alone in my marital bed, my own hand crept between my legs, rubbing and stroking, taking his place as I treated myself to the climax Dan had cheated me out of.

So I had something to share the following Sunday, at the September PFLAG support group, which once again I went to on my own. Not about Dan's and my sex life, of course, but about how both of us were dwelling on Jenny's. To my relief, the other parents around the circle were nodding in sympathy as I concluded.

"Oh, I know," Candy Sue said. "That was the hardest thing for me, with my son and his friend. But you've just got to put it out of your mind."

"I've been trying to," I responded. "It's just that since we visited them, well, I don't know. I keep imagining them in that bed together."

"Could I ask you a question, Sheila?" Alison put in. She was the attractive young woman who had thrown Dan for a loop when I'd dragged him to PFLAG the first time I went, just days after Jenny had come out to us at the beginning of July.

"Of course," I said.

"You said you have a married son, right?"

I nodded.

"Well, when you visit him and his wife, do you spend a lot of time wondering what they do in bed together?"

I felt my mouth drop open. When we visited Jeffrey and Anita in New York, their bed was just a handy object to throw my coat on before turning my attention to my darling granddaughter, obviously a product of at least one romp on that bed. "Well, no," I managed.

From the other side of the room, Candy Sue gave me a smile of understanding, and I forgave her her size six figure once and for all.

Now that I'd attended three support group meetings in a row, Marlene suggested I volunteer for some of the other chapter activities. "We need help getting out the monthly newsletter. And when you feel comfortable enough, we'd love to have you as one of our speakers. We're always looking for more parents to do outreach," she told me after the meeting had broken up.

Candy Sue was standing with us, and she said, "I never believed I'd be willing, but Marlene's convinced me to sign up for speakers' bureau. A lot of gay student groups ask parents to give them advice on how to come out to their families, and I thought, well that's something I could do. If you decide to do it, maybe you and I could team up."

I had no idea when I'd be ready to lecture other people's children on coming out to their parents, but my commitment to BAT's fall play gave me an excuse to put off considering it. I couldn't take on anything else at the moment, I explained to Marlene.

She gave me a warm smile. "Maybe later this winter."

It was lucky I hadn't accepted any extra responsibilities. BAT's fall show was scheduled to open Halloween weekend and, two weeks before opening night, a job crisis forced the actress playing the role of the elderly aunt to drop out of the show. Jim, who was directing, drafted me to fill her shoes.

I protested that it had been years since I'd been on stage for more than a walk-on.

"Can't be helped," Jim said. "You look the part. With make-up to age you, of course," he added before I could throw my purse at him. "More important, you've attended every rehearsal as stage manager and you know the lines. I'll get someone else to stage manage."

I'd opted for backstage work over acting once Jeffrey was born and I couldn't see my way clear to attending nightly rehearsals for weeks on end. Now, the more I thought about it, the more excited I was to have "landed" a speaking role after all those years behind the scenes. But after so many years as a techie, I was scared to death I'd make a fool of myself. It would help to have a few friendly faces in the audience opening night.

I'd already talked up the play to Jenny and Tamara, and they'd promised to come sometime during the run. Now, I gave them another call. Jenny answered, and I said, "You'll never guess what happened. The woman playing the aunt in *Postmortem* had to go on a business trip and just dropped out of the show. And the director asked me to play the part! I haven't had this big a role since before you kids were born, so I'm a nervous wreck. Anyhow, I know you and Tamara were planning to see it sometime, but I could really use the moral support opening night. It's the

Friday night after next."

"Friday night?" Jenny said, and I realized my goof. Friday night was the start of the Jewish Sabbath. I should have remembered how observant the two of them had become, how Jenny had told me weeks earlier about the gay/lesbian synagogue they'd joined.

"I forgot about it's being Friday. I mean, I remembered it was Friday but I wasn't thinking about it being the start of Sabbath. So it wouldn't work out for you girls to come opening night; you'd be going to services then. Oh well, it was just a thought."

That last sounded unconvincing even to me. A moment passed before Jenny said, "Actually, we go to services Saturday morning. But we light candles Friday nights and have Sabbath dinner; we usually have friends over for it." There was another instant of silence during which I was sure I heard her repress a sigh. "But let me check with Tamara. Can you hold on a second, Mom?" Her voice trailed off, but I heard an increasing clatter of pots and pans, as if she'd carried the phone down the hall to find Tamara in the kitchen. There was a minute or so of silence, during which the girls were apparently conferring. Then Jenny came back on the line.

"I guess we can come opening night. You don't have a leading part in a show every day, after all."

"I'm not one of the leads," I protested. "It's really an ensemble show. But that's great, if you're sure you don't mind."

"No, that's fine. Wait a second, Tamara is picking up the extension."

"Hi, Sheila. Congratulations on your part."

"Thanks," I said.

"And don't worry about the opening being Friday night. There are times when family comes ahead of following every rule. Anyway, like I told Mr. Katz — uh, Dan, we're not fanatics or anything. We mean our Judaism to be a celebration, not a prison."

The girls agreed to my suggestion that Dan and I pick them up so we could carpool opening night. BAT might not have the prestige of some of the other amateur theaters in the area, but audiences love us, especially our Halloween show. Our play-reading committee always turns up a winner, something with ghosts and ghouls, thrills and chills. By curtain time there is never an empty spot in our parking lot. And this time, the occupants of all those cars would be watching *me* play a part for the first time in years.

Postmortem is a comic mystery set during the Roaring Twenties in an isolated mansion belonging to one William Gillette, an actor whose most popular role was Sherlock Holmes. The play takes place during a weekend house party, a year to the day after Gillette's fiancee was found shot to death on the terrace. The coroner has ruled her death a suicide. Gillette suspects it was murder; he intends to discover the murderer before his guests depart. Not one of them is above suspicion.

I'd already told the girls a bit about the plot, but now I started chattering nervously as the four of us drove to BAT on opening night. "Did I mention all the characters are trapped there for the weekend? Sort of like Agatha Christie. Actually, you could call it a cross between Agatha Christie and Noel Coward. His kind of gossipy dialogue and wonderful costumes, but with a surprise ending like *Ten Little Indians*. A real fun show."

Fun was the furthest thing from my mind as Dan parked the car in the rear of BAT's lot though. I was too busy worrying that I'd forget my lines. I was playing Gillette's Aunt Lilly, his hostess since his wife's demise. As I headed for the backstage door, my mind became a total blank.

Jenny threw her arms around me for a hug and murmured, "Good luck, Mom."

"Don't wish me good luck," I said, invoking the old theatrical superstition with mock horror.

She laughed and released me. "Okay, then break a leg."

"Break a leg," Tamara echoed.

Dan squeezed my hand and pecked me on the cheek, and then I hurried backstage to get into my costume and makeup.

I wasn't onstage during the first scene — my character was nearly the last to enter — and I stood backstage trying not to bite the polish off my fingernails. Finally my cue came. I entered on automatic pilot, sure I would be unable to speak a single word.

Miraculously, my mouth opened to say my first line. I was about to breathe a sigh of relief when the realization hit me that I was in front of an audience. What if I messed up on the next cue, what if I forgot my blocking, what if — My next cue came and I remembered my line, remembered my blocking — the moves I was to make onstage. With each line, I felt more at ease. I *was* Aunt Lilly, matriarch of the family, an older but still elegant lady, graciously presiding over my nephew's stately home. For the next two hours at least, until, with the mystery solved and the murderer caught, I joined the rest of the cast in taking our bows to loud applause.

Except for a few walk-ons, my years with BAT had been spent doing set dressing, procuring props and stage-managing. In fact, I'd decorated the set for *Postmortem*, hunting down just the right chaise longue, mahogany liquor cabinet and old-fashioned Victrola. But though the backstage crew knew our work behind the scenes was essential to putting on a show, we generally got recognition only from other techies. Now, to my delight, I met with congratulations right and left. And instead of a peck on the lips and a murmured, "Nice job decorating the set," Dan was bursting with pride. "You were marvelous," he told me as he thrust a tissue-wrapped bouquet of roses into my arms. "No one would believe you just stepped into the role."

"You couldn't tell how nervous I was when I went on? I nearly missed my first cue."

Tamara, standing alongside Dan and Jenny, quickly said, "Oh, no, you were great, Sheila."

"Really, you were fine, Mom," Jenny added.

Fine was, I suppose, fine. But I couldn't help thinking that if Jeffrey could have been there, he would have laughed and said, "Stop fishing for compliments, Mom. You know you were terrific." And then enveloped me in an embrace. I stifled a sigh.

"Well, thank you," I said. "I'm glad you girls liked the show." The two of them gave each other a look that I couldn't help but notice.

"Actually —" Tamara said.

"Actually," Dan cut her off, "if we don't head over to the cast party now, we'll be half an hour getting out of the parking lot." Jenny and Tamara were going to the party with us, and whatever Tamara had been about to say, she didn't follow up during the five-minute ride to Jack and Jim's split-level.

We were met by deliciously mingling aromas of chili powder and cumin coming from the kitchen where Jack was dishing Mexican food onto pottery platters. The entry was a split foyer, half a flight leading up to the main level, the other half downstairs. Jim stood at the top of the stairs greeting guests. "Hi, come on in. Coats go in our bedroom — down the hall to your left. Good to see you, Dan. Sheila, you were fantastic!"

He enveloped me in a bear hug, his graying beard scraping against my cheek. "But tomorrow see if you can enter a couple of seconds earlier after your first cue," he added, *sotto voce.*

I laughed as we disengaged. "Save it for your director's notes. I'm sure it's not the only place I goofed. Do you remember our daughter, Jenny? And this is her —"

"Her friend, Tamara," Dan put in before I could finish my introduction.

"Of course, I remember your daughter. Long time, no see. Good to meet you, Tamara. Hope you enjoyed the show."

That last was the kind of pleasantry to which no response was expected. I could see Jim poised to turn to the next clump of people entering behind us. But Tamara took it as a serious question.

"Well, I don't mean to hurt your feelings, but I was a little upset by it."

He turned back with a look of surprise. "Upset? Really? I admit there's a lot of murder and mayhem onstage, but it's all in good fun."

"Okay, offended then. By the killer turning out to be the lesbian lover. It's such a stereotype."

"Really?" Jim is a fellow New Yorker, and like a lot of New Yorkers, views arguing as a spectator sport. Even better than watching from the sidelines is jumping into the fray himself. Without taking his eyes off Tamara, he waved at Sally Winograd and her husband, who were coming through the front door. "Coats in the bedroom, drinks downstairs," he said, and then stepped a foot or so back into the hallway, leaning one shoulder comfortably against the wall. "You thought the character was stereotypical? In what way?"

"The *situation* was stereotypical, not the character." Tamara planted herself in front of Jim. "It was just like that movie, *Basic Instinct* —"

"Wait!" Jim commanded. "Have you even *seen Basic Instinct*?"

"Well, no," Tamara admitted. "But I know that —"

"You know that it's graphic and violent and —"

"And that it implies that lesbians are all jealous murderers." Tamara was giving as good as she got. I decided she probably had some New York genes of her own. Sally and her husband, I noticed, had stopped halfway down the hall to listen, blocking the Blumenfelds, who were leaving the bedroom on their way to the bar downstairs. What with them plus Tamara, Jenny, Dan and myself, the scene in Jack and Jim's front hall was becoming the focal point of the party. Jack came out of the kitchen to see what was going on.

"Actually, I think the murderer in *Basic Instinct* was bisexual," Jim said, mildly for him.

Tamara seemed thrown off course. "Well, I guess so," she said after a moment. "But that doesn't make a difference as far as I'm concerned."

"Really? It doesn't make a difference whether you've got your facts straight or not?"

"Jim...." Jack cautioned. He walked over and rested one hand on Jim's arm with the easy familiarity of long-marrieds, about, I hoped, to suggest he could use a little help carrying the food down to the rec room. The conversation was making me uneasy. Not to mention that I'd been too nervous to eat any dinner before the show, and now was half-starved.

I knew Jim once he got wound up, though, and Tamara was obviously cut from the same cloth. "What I was *trying* to say," she went on, "is that it doesn't make a difference whether Sharon Stone was playing a lesbian character or a bi one as far as your straight audience is concerned. What they're going to remember is that a queer character was a homicidal maniac."

"So if they see *Fatal Attraction*, they see a heterosexual homicidal maniac," Jim retorted. "Is there some law that all queer characters have to be angels?"

Dan had been pressed up against me as more guests streamed into the hall, and I could feel him wince at Jim and Tamara's casual use of the "q" word — a word, I knew from my growing involvement with PFLAG, that had been reclaimed by many gays and lesbians. Still, it always gave me the same queasy feeling I'd gotten the week before when I wheeled my groceries out of Giant Food and overheard one of the two black teenagers employed to help load customers' cars say to the other, "Hey, nigger, what're you talking about!"

Dan cleared his throat with unnecessary loudness and said, "Look, we're blocking the way here, so let's —"

Our daughter cut him off. Up to now, she'd been content to let Tamara do the talking, but now she seemed to feel that her partner needed rescuing. "But Jim, don't you see," she said, "the audience knows that straight people come in both good and bad. But if the only movies or plays they see about *us* show us as villains, or unable to have a normal relationship or whatever, it just feeds into their stereotypes about lesbians and gays." Her voice was soft, but clear and carrying, and I noticed one of Jack and Jim's gay friends, who'd joined the bottleneck in the hall, nod his head in agreement.

It dawned on me that Jenny had, in effect, come out to everyone within earshot; it would be all over BAT by the time the party wound down. I certainly didn't think her being a lesbian should be some deep, dark secret, I assured myself, and yet.... I missed most of Jim's response — something about not liking any kind of censorship — as Jack finally cut in to announce that his Mexican feast was dished up and he wanted people to dig in while it was hot. "I could use a few of you to carry it downstairs," he added. "You all can continue the discussion later."

Thank God, I thought. *I* might be a little disturbed, but Dan was probably ready to *plotz* over Jenny's linking of "us" and "lesbian." Any minute he might forget himself and make some remark about lesbians or gays that could deeply wound our daughter. Not even to mention Tamara, or Jack and Jim, dear friends whom I wouldn't see hurt for a lifetime supply of Godiva. Quickly I thrust my coat at Dan, leaving him to carry it to the bedroom.

"Hand me a dish," I told Jack. "I'm starving." I dodged into the kitchen and grabbed up one of his pottery casseroles as I spoke. By the time Dan had followed me downstairs to the rec room, I had deposited the casserole on the buffet table and filled a plate with steaming hot burritos and enchiladas.

Once broken off, the discussion didn't continue, much to my relief. I spotted a free seat on the couch and headed for it. The girls had wandered over to look at Jack and Jim's wall of framed military honors, one of the few distinguishing features of their otherwise typical suburban recreation room — green-and-white checkerboard vinyl tiles, dark wood veneer paneling and a collection of mismatched furniture that had once been upstairs. Dan was planted by the wet bar, his charm turned on high as he talked with Cherry Cannon, who'd played the ingenue. His hand clenched a plastic highball glass, the only visible sign of his tension.

I sat down next to Sally Winograd and complimented her on the poster she'd designed for the show, which Jack and Jim had already added to their collection of play posters over the bar. Her compliments over my performance pushed any anxiety about Jenny's remark to the back of my mind. Sally had sat in the audience and thought the show had gone wonderfully. "Best opening night we've had in years! No really, if you missed your first cue, it must've been by a millisecond. You were great!"

By the time Dan gave me the look that's his signal he's ready to go home, I'd gone back to refill my plate twice, sampling both Jack's chili and his brownies topped with Mexican chocolate sauce (loaded with calories that I refused to calculate, it being a party, after all). And nearly every member of the cast and crew had congratulated me on my acting debut, restoring my spirits to their earlier high. I was, in fact, humming "There's No Business Like Show Business" as Dan pulled away from the curb. Which was the exact moment Jenny started in.

"Mom, I didn't want to say anything at the party. But really, you could've warned us about the play."

Jenny's voice had that accusing note I remembered from her teenage years, and my heart sank, even as I said, "It didn't occur to me there was anything to warn you *about*."

"Mom, really. Don't be dense. It's what Tamara and I were trying to get across to Jim — just the whole idea of the villain being the lesbian lover. You could've thought how we — how anyone who's lesbian — would feel about that!"

"Well, I'm sorry, but I never thought of it in connection with you girls. The whole play just seemed like a light, Noel Coward sort of thing to me. It didn't seem to bother Jim or Jack, and *they're* gay, after all, so —"

"That brings up something we need to talk about, Jenny," Dan interrupted me. "You weren't showing much common sense when you started talking about 'gays and lesbians like us' or however you put it. At Jack and Jim's place, where they're homosexual themselves and they've invited a bunch of homosexual friends, I suppose it didn't matter much. But suppose it had been tomorrow night?"

Tomorrow night, the party was at our house. I'd asked Lois, LaVerne, Natalie and the rest of our friends — including my new PFLAG buddy, Candy Sue — to wait till the second night to see the show so they could come back to our house for the party afterwards. I'd asked Jenny and Tamara to come opening night, despite its being Friday, so I'd have my family there for moral support my first time in front of an audience. *Some moral support*, I thought now.

"Mr. Katz — uh, Dan, we're not in the closet, you know." Tamara's voice was deadly earnest. I turned my head and saw that she had leaned forward as far as the taut shoulder harness would allow.

"Tamara, if you don't mind, this is just between family."

Jenny gasped at that, and mingled with my distress for her was an undercurrent of satisfaction: Let her see that her father wasn't so perfect either.

"Daddy! Tamara *is* family," she protested.

"Not so far as I'm concerned," Dan said, hitting the accelerator to beat a yellow light that was on the verge of turning red.

"Honey," I said placatingly, "I think Jenny and Tamara feel that since they're in a relationship —"

"Whatever kind of relationship they have — and I would prefer not knowing the details, thank you very much — there is such a thing as keeping your private life private. And I hope the two of you are listening to me," Dan said, his eyes suddenly glued to the rearview mirror, apparently to check their attentiveness.

"Dan, please! If you're not going to pay attention to your driving, then pull over and let me drive before you get us all killed."

"There's nothing wrong with my driving. And I would hope, Sheila, that you're going to back me up on this."

"Back you up on what? On going fifteen miles above the speed limit? Or on Jenny and Tamara staying in the closet?" The words surprised me as they flew out of my mouth, unsure as I felt about other people knowing about Jenny. "Will you please slow down!"

"Daddy, please," Jenny echoed me, and he tapped the brake a couple of times. "Don't get me wrong," she pleaded. "We're not advertising we're lesbians. I mean, we don't have gay flags on our cars or anything like that." I'd turned my head toward the girls enough to notice Tamara give Jenny a look at that, and wondered momentarily what she would have to say to her once they reached their apartment. "But when we're at a private gathering in someone's house you can't expect me to watch every word I say, worrying that I'm going to give something away."

"Well in our house that's exactly what I hope you'll do! I said before, what may be all right in that kind of theater crowd is not all right when you're around our friends."

Jenny looked like she might burst into tears, and before I knew what I was going to say, I blurted, "Our friends already know. I told Lois, and she's let it slip to Natalie and LaVerne at least."

"You went and told Lois! After I asked you not to! Why didn't you just take out a full page ad in the *Post*?"

"I just happened to mention it to her."

"And did you also just happen to remember that your daughter is a teacher? That she could lose her job over this? So you go and tell a woman who not only is an alcoholic but has a megaphone for a mouth!"

"She's not an alcoholic; she only drinks when she goes out somewhere," I mumbled, though Dan was right. I had, in fact, tried talking Lois into entering a treatment program more than once. But I wasn't in a mood to discuss my best friend's illness. Instead, I said, "And since when do you tell me what to talk to my friends about? If there's anyone whose permission I should have asked, it was Jenny's."

"That's right, Mom, you really should have asked me before you told anyone, even Aunt Lois."

I hadn't expected this response from Jenny. "I thought you weren't in the closet," I defended myself.

"I'm not. But you still should have checked with me first before you went around coming out about me. You always do that — act like I'm still a little kid that you can speak for."

Here Dan had nearly bitten Jenny's head off for an innocent remark at the cast party but Jenny was attacking *me*. "Lois is my best friend. We always talk about our families together. I didn't think you being a lesbian was something I was supposed to be ashamed of," I snapped back.

"I didn't say I was ashamed. I said it should have been my decision who I wanted to come out to."

"It's not a question of shame. It's a matter of learning some discretion," Dan put in.

"Daddy, I was *being* discreet. We were at a party where half the people were gay. And if I can't depend on my own mother not to tell everyone she knows —"

"I'd say it's fairly obvious that you can't," Dan said.

Simultaneously, Tamara demanded, "Since when is this something we have to be discreet about? If you think I'm going to pretend we're nothing but roommates —"

"I just meant —" Jenny said.

I was furious with Jenny. Before she could say another word, I snapped, "You just meant that everything that your father says is fine with you, no matter how bigoted, but when I do my best to be accepting and supportive about your orientation it gets thrown back in my face!"

"Mom, that's not fair. All I meant to say was —"

"Oh, just shut up! I don't want to hear what you meant!" I shouted, shocking everyone else into silence. I shocked myself as well — was this how a good Jewish mother talked? — but right now I didn't care. I was furious with all three of them. "I just want to thank you all very much for ruining my evening!" The three of them began speaking at once, but whether to apologize or protest I couldn't have said, because all of a sudden I was crying too loud to hear.

Chapter Five

*A*fter the blowup opening night, and a week spent dealing with Dan's recriminations and Jenny's hurt feelings, the last thing I felt ready to do was give anyone else the benefit of my wisdom on "Coming Out to Your Parents." But when Candy Sue called the following Friday, begging me to join her on a panel the next day on that very topic, her voice had the shrill edge of desperation. "It was supposed to be three of us, Marlene, Judy Peters and me. But Judy's daughter has gone into labor early; she's flying out to Oregon tonight. And the panel is at a lesbian conference, and Marlene and I have gay *sons*, so we need someone who has a lesbian daughter."

Judy Peters has not one, but *two* lesbian daughters, and a wry way of speaking that makes people hang on her every word. While I was wondering how I could fill her shoes, Candy Sue continued, "Don't get me wrong. We'd have asked you to be on the panel from the first if you hadn't been so busy with your play," and I found myself saying, "Actually, once the show is up, there really isn't much to do except show up for performances."

"Oh thank goodness!" And before I could back out, I found myself arranging to carpool to the community college where the conference was taking place.

The lobby of the college activity building was lined with tables and booths like an indoor flea market, and thronged with women noisily greeting each other, hugging, and clustering around the registration desk.

A surprising number were in their forties or fifties; most seemed never to have heard of Lady Clairol. The two dozen women waiting in the classroom where we were to give our talk looked more like girls of Jenny and Tamara's age. Their curious glances took me back to the years I'd spent teaching. The moments of stage fright with which I'd always faced a new class were coming back to me now. As if she'd guessed, Marlene turned to Candy Sue and me and murmured, "Relax. All you have to do is tell your story."

At least Marlene was speaking first. I'd heard her story before, of course. In fact, after a few months of hearing support group members tell their stories, I thought I might be able to fill in for them and give their lines in their absence. In a sense each of us parents had the same story: we each had a gay son or daughter. But each of us coped with her child's orientation in her own way. Each of us, according to Marlene's terminology and that of PFLAG brochures, was at a different stage, ranging from shock, denial, and guilt to true acceptance.

Marlene, as fit her position as support group facilitator, had progressed not only to true acceptance, but to marching in the local Gay Pride parade with our PFLAG chapter, waving a hand-lettered sign that read "Proud Mother of Gay Son." She'd passed around photos of herself and several dozen chapter members posing with their placards at the start of the parade, all of them beaming for the camera as if they were being paid for a commercial for tooth whitener. Now she was explaining to the assembled women her outrage over "Don't Ask — Don't Tell." Her son had been discharged from the Navy for admitting his sexual orientation. Marlene had spent days at the Senate committee hearings on gays in the military back in '93, her dress adorned with a button demanding "End the Ban Now." On her sweater today she wore a pin with a hot pink triangle intertwined with a fuchsia heart, the encircling lettering proclaiming "I Love My Gay Child." A second pin stated "Equal Rights Are Not Special Rights." She wore her buttons everywhere, she added, to educate anyone who happened to ask what they stood for.

Candy Sue, on the other hand, was stuck at guilt. As a Jewish mother, I recognized the signs. Candy Sue wasn't Jewish — she'd been raised Southern Baptist — but that didn't let her off the hook as far as wondering whether it was her fault her son was gay. No wonder she'd seized with such eagerness on research showing that sexual orientation could be inherited. Candy Sue can trace her family back to Jamestown. Since her son came out, she's gone over her family tree with a fine tooth comb, delighting in each bachelor uncle and old-maid aunt she finds. "And last month, I want you all to know, my sister-in-law finally broke down and let me know about her younger son, which I've suspected all along...."

As for myself, I couldn't have told you what stage I was in. I wasn't in denial like Dan. As far as I knew, I hadn't raised Jenny any differently than my friends had raised their straight daughters, so I didn't think it was anything I'd done. Or was I in denial about my own guilt, and just projecting it onto Candy Sue? She finished up her presentation to polite applause, leaving it my turn.

"I have a son and a daughter," I said, beginning my story just as I would at our monthly support group, "and my daughter came out as a lesbian this summer." The young women facing me seemed to straighten in their chairs at my mention of a lesbian daughter they could identify with, and to look at me with more than the polite interest with which they'd listened to Marlene and Candy Sue.

"So I'm really glad she told me," I finished, as I always did. "Otherwise, there would be so much about her life that she couldn't share with me — like her joining the gay/lesbian synagogue I mentioned a minute ago. It would be hard for us to be close to each other."

But how easy was it now, I asked myself, as Marlene called for questions from our audience. Why didn't anything with Jenny go the way I expected it to? Why was *I* always in the wrong and Dan perfect? Even after all he'd said in the car on the way home from the cast party, Dan had patched things up with her easily. "Daddy was just worried about our jobs," she told me. "He's just concerned about me, about me and Tamara, that we could lose our teaching jobs if it got around that we're lesbians."

And I suppose I wasn't concerned, I thought, while listening with half my mind to Marlene's response as to whether it was better to come out to parents in writing or in person. "Try combining approaches," Marlene was saying, "Write your letter, then hand it to your parents to read. Once you've given them a little time to read and digest it, you'll be available to answer their questions, and the advantage...."

My mind had gone back to Jenny again when a girl with short, dark hair and a diamond stud in her nose raised her hand. "I've come out to my parents already and they didn't throw me out or anything. But, it's like, now that I've told them, let's never mention it again. I mean, any time my sister wants to talk about her boyfriends with Mom, she's all ears. But with me, it's like, okay you told me, and I still love you and all, but now we'll never talk about it again. How do I get her to listen when I tell her about my life too?"

"Give her time," Marlene said. "It's a process. Parents often take one step forward and two steps back. How long is it since you came out to her?"

"Three months ago, right around the end of summer."

"I was just like your mother," I blurted, before Marlene could assure her that three months was hardly any time at all for a revelation like coming out. "Jenny asked if I wanted to hear about her girlfriend and I told her I guessed so."

"But then you let her tell you; that's the difference. I mean, you told us your daughter came out to you this summer too. And look how far you've come and then look where my mother is. The one time I tried to talk to her she told me she'll always love me, but she'll never be happy about my being a lesbian."

"I'm not *happy* about Jenny." The words flew out of my mouth before I could stop them. I tried to tell by the girl's expression if I'd blown her image of me without staring at the diamond blazing in her nose. I wondered if it was real, and whether this was a lesbian style that — God forbid — my daughter would adopt. Meanwhile my mouth seemed to have gotten stuck on automatic pilot. "I wouldn't have chosen for her to be a lesbian. That is, I always imagined her married and with a family, not that she doesn't have a lovely partner, but.... And that's another thing, they teach in the same school and I worry, what if someone should find out about them? And then, she's so attractive and feminine, and I hope she's not going to let herself go like —"

"It takes all of us a while," Marlene broke in, rescuing me before I could put a second foot in my mouth. "Just as it may have taken you a while to come out to yourself, you can't expect your parents to adjust immediately."

The girl nodded, her face noncommittal, and I tried to recover some vestige of stage presence. "It's like Marlene said before, most of us have a script in mind for our children's lives. So when Jenny came out to me, well, I know she's the exact same person, but all of a sudden the scenes I imagined for her have been rewritten. It's not that I think it's a phase, or that I'm trying to change her. She's a wonderful kid, and I've accepted that she's a lesbian, and all I want is for her to be happy, but sometimes....

Well, I'm still struggling. I — I guess I wasn't ready to be on a panel. I'm sorry, I'm afraid I'm not being much help to you with your parents."

To my surprise and relief the girl smiled. "Oh, but you are," she insisted. "You've given me a lot of insight into what my mom and dad are going through." Two other women nodded in agreement, and a tall blond woman in a tailored pant suit called out, "Thank you for sharing your process with us."

Marlene assured me I hadn't done that badly, once the panel had ended and we were on our way back through the booth-lined lobby. "And it'll come easier once you've taken our speaker training. By the way, if you girls wouldn't mind hanging around here a half hour or so, there are a couple of people I need to talk to."

She hurried off as soon as we assured her we wouldn't mind. Candy Sue made a beeline for the ladies' room, leaving me to look around the lobby in hopes of finding more interesting merchandise for sale than the politically correct t-shirts and pamphlets most of the organizations displayed at their tables. What I needed right now was a little retail therapy. Across the room I spotted a booth with what looked like Indian jewelry. I headed toward it like a homing pigeon.

The long table on which the jewelry had been spread out was draped with black velvet, a nice contrast to the bare, scarred tables where the organizations had laid out their tracts. The vendor behind the table was a walking advertisement for her wares. She wore a short woven jacket with a pattern reminiscent of an Indian blanket, the turquoise in the design echoed by a magnificent necklace of turquoise and silver. Perhaps to better show off the turquoise strand, her earrings were simple silver studs that echoed the silver streaks in her cropped, salt-and-pepper hair. Salt and pepper, to my mind, belongs on a kitchen table, not a woman's head. As my mother — still proudly brunette at age eighty-three — says, in this day and age there's no excuse for not washing that gray right out of your hair. On this woman, though, it didn't look bad, perhaps because her face, with its strong jawline and cheekbones, appeared almost masculine. I guessed her age at late forties to early fifties, but even without makeup, she was youthfully vibrant and unlined. If I put my mind to it, I could almost see the silver highlights as another accessory, like her necklace or the armful of silver bracelets she wore.

She caught me staring at her and, as our eyes met, she smiled. Her smile was warm and radiant like Dan's, a smile that drew you in. "Can I help you?" she asked.

"I'm just looking. I came here to be on a panel. With a couple of other mothers from PFLAG," I amplified.

"That's wonderful," she said warmly. "PFLAG is such a great organization. Well, take your time. Let me know if there's anything I can help you with."

Within minutes there was: a silver hair clip inlaid with turquoise that would be perfect for my daughter-in-law Anita's upcoming birthday. Though in other respects she's a modern woman, Anita's thick black hair falls straight to her waist like a sixties holdover. I could see the sterling clip gleaming against it now.

"I just love Indian jewelry," I told the vendor, while she rummaged around for a gift box. "I love the colors. I wish I could wear it myself, but it's just not my style."

She paused in her search. "Of course you can wear Native American designs," she assured me. "There's no one style it goes with. It's just a matter of selecting the right piece." Her gaze fell to her display of merchandise again. She reached for a choker of graduated silver beads etched with delicate, finely worked designs. She held it out for my inspection. "We call these Navajo pearls," she told me. "Here, let me show you." She walked around the table and came up behind me to fasten the choker around my neck, her fingertips brushing my skin lightly as she adjusted the necklace inside the collar of my blouse. "There!" she said, fastening the catch and moving away. "Now look at yourself in the mirror."

I did. The choker fit my neck perfectly, lending my plain, tailored blouse the elegance of pearls but with a touch of ethnic exoticism. "I love them," I told her, and she flashed me that warm smile again.

The total for the two items made me pause an instant; I could see Dan's face when he opened the Visa bill. Then I fingered my lovely new jewelry again and signed my name with a flourish.

The day after Dan and I got back from our honeymoon, Dan's mother had called me on the phone to demand, "Do you know what your mother had the nerve to tell me? At your wedding reception yet? That my Dan looks like a goy."

"Well.... I'm sure she meant it as a compliment, Rose." I knew it was the wrong thing to say as soon as the words were out of my mouth. I held my breath, hoping she wouldn't get started. I had a week's worth of dirty clothes in my laundry basket, and if I didn't get to the basement of our apartment building soon, I'd be waiting hours to use a washer.

"Since when is it a compliment to say a person doesn't look Jewish? From an anti-Semite maybe, that's who gives such a compliment."

I sighed and plopped down on the chair by the phone, knowing I was in for it now. Rose had started in on me the moment we met. She'd laid her cigarette in an ashtray and exhaled her last mouthful of smoke as she reached out a hand to take mine, her rigid handclasp holding me at arm's length rather than drawing me closer. "So this is who my Danny picked to marry," she observed. Dan has yet to convince me it was meant in a welcoming way.

All this ancient history was running through my mind because it was almost time for our annual pilgrimage to New York for Thanksgiving dinner or, as I preferred to think of it, turkey with a side helping of *tsuris* — Yiddish for the aggravation that always accompanied any occasion that brought Rose and my mother together. For the fifth year in a row, we'd be having dinner with Anita's extended family, a group so large that dinner would be served at her father's Italian restaurant, closed to the public for the occasion. Which would have been fine except for the fact that both Dan and I would be schlepping our mothers along with us to Paul's Pasta Palace.

Our mothers were both widows. After losing my father close to four decades earlier, my mother had managed both to bring me up on her own and to fashion a satisfying life for herself. Retired from thirty years of teaching, she filled her days with volunteer work for the Democratic party, an afternoon a week doing clerical work for the teachers' union, and lunches and matinees with "the girls" — those who hadn't passed away or migrated to Miami Beach. Rose, though, was still struggling to adjust to the loss of her husband four years earlier, an event that had left her largely alone in the world. Friends and relatives of her generation were falling by the wayside. And her only other child, Dan's sister, Judy — or Yehudit as she now preferred to be called — lived in Israel, having been swept off her feet by a handsome young kibbutznik during a college semester on an Israeli collective farm. The photos she sent every year showed her and her husband, bearded and handsome still, dressed in shorts and sandals. Her bare arms were tanned bronze from working in the kibbutz's orange groves, and her hair was bleached by the sun to a shade of blond that cost Candy Sue forty dollars a month.

My mother-in-law lived in a semidetached duplex less than twenty blocks from Mama's rent-controlled apartment, and you'd have thought that, alone as she was, she'd be glad to make a friend of my mother. But Rose had never forgiven her for stating the obvious — that Dan, with his classic features, sky-blue eyes and sandy hair, looked more like a goyish movie star than a nice Jewish boy from the Bronx. Not that Rose herself didn't burst with pride over Dan and Judy's blond, all-American looks. Nor did she hesitate to accept compliments on their behalf — just so long as you in no way implied her children might look Christian.

I was sure it was because Jenny was a feminine version of her father — a near twin to the snapshots of her Aunt Yehudit at Jenny's age — that she was her grandmother Rose's favorite. Jeffrey, who'd inherited my olive skin and tendency to plumpness, had always come off second best.

Since his marriage to Anita, Jeffrey had put on a good twenty pounds of what his mother-in-law, Linda, termed "happy fat." Happy it might be, but I was convinced that if it weren't for his weight, Jeffrey would long since have been cast in a Broadway show. And with the holiday season just starting, he'd probably be a good five pounds heavier by the time he made his New Year's resolutions.

So, unfortunately, would I. The yearly hurdle of Thanksgiving dinner alone could put five pounds on my hips. Paul and Linda spared no effort in preparing a spread to die for. In addition to all the traditional dishes — turkey with chestnut dressing, sweet potatoes, cranberry-orange relish, and pumpkin pie — we'd be gorging on side dishes like gnocchi and three-cheese lasagna, with a finale of decadently rich, creamy tiramisu.

With Thanksgiving looming, I was trying on the three dressy outfits I'd bought last year, to see whether there was a chance I could wear one of them on turkey day, or whether I'd have to head out to the mall to shop for the next larger size. Unfortunately, this was an all-too-familiar scenario. I had just wriggled into my black sheath dress when Dan appeared in the bedroom.

"Are we supposed to go out tonight?" he wanted to know.

"I was thinking of wearing it Thanksgiving. What do you think? Does it look too bad on me?"

Dan looked me up and down, pausing long enough to pretend there was a possibility I could wear a dress that would split at the seams if I sat down, let alone let Linda heap my plate with one of her too-generous helpings. "Maybe with a better girdle," he said finally. "I wouldn't say it's the most flattering thing you own. What about that blue pants outfit, the one with the big blouse?"

The blue silk pants and tunic had been one of my favorites until it became so tight that the elastic of the waistband threatened to cut off my circulation. Now it was in the closet of the sitting room adjoining our bedroom, where I kept my "out of size" clothes. I'd once seen LaVerne's overflow closet, where she kept out-of-season clothes, neatly arranged from down jacket through swimsuits. My closet was similarly neat, but where LaVerne's clothes just awaited a change of season until she could wear them again, my closet was sectioned into the number of pounds I needed to lose to get into each garment. The blue silk trousers and tunic were — rather optimistically — placed in the five-pound-or-less section, though it looked like before long I'd have to move them into the five-to-ten-pound category. I pulled off the black sheath, walked into the sitting room, and hung it next to the pants.

Dan followed along after me. "Why don't you get yourself something new," he offered. I nodded glumly. No woman loves shopping more than I do, but it's a lot less fun to shop for larger sizes than smaller ones.

"Speaking of Thanksgiving," Dan added, "Will Jenny be ready to leave for New York as soon as she gets off teaching Wednesday?"

It had been over a week since I'd talked with Jenny, and Thanksgiving hadn't come up, maybe because I'd been too busy telling her about the panel I'd been on (carefully omitting my faux pas) and the vendor I'd stumbled on with the enticing Indian jewelry. "Actually I don't know what plans she and Tamara have for the holiday," I told Dan.

"Well, I'm sure Jenny plans to be with her family. Suppose you give her a call and see if she wants to be picked up or if she's planning on leaving her car here for that weekend."

"To tell the truth, Mom, Tamara and I aren't sure if we're ready to face that mob in New York," Jenny told me when I phoned her. "We're debating starting our own tradition, and inviting a few of our friends. But we're not going to be apart on Thanksgiving. I hope that's understood."

"Of course it is," I assured her, deciding to be generous on Dan's behalf. "I'm sure Dad meant the two of you when he asked me about your plans." I privately doubted that. What I didn't doubt was that Rose would be peevish for days if her favorite grandchild skipped a family occasion.

I reminded Jenny of how much her grandmother looked forward to seeing her.

She sighed. "I'll check with Tamara again. We'll probably go."

Despite the day-before-Thanksgiving traffic, Dan was mellow on the drive to New York, including Tamara in the conversation, though I knew he'd have been happier if she wasn't along.

While we were talking, though, I could sense — from the way he kept going "uh huh, uh huh"in that way people have when they're really going over their grocery list or planning their next vacation — that he was just waiting for a pause in the conversation to bring up what was actually on his mind. Sure enough, in the midst of a story Jenny was telling about one of her classes, he said, "That reminds me. You had a phone call from Adam this afternoon." He paused expectantly and I noticed he'd tensed up waiting for her reaction.

"Adam? You should have told me before we left, Daddy, so I could have called him back."

"You'll have plenty of chance," Dan told her, relieved and hearty. "He found a new job. He's moving back to our area."

"Oh, he got the job. That's wonderful!" Jenny replied to her father, and even I noticed her voice was filled with pleasure.

Dan glanced back over his shoulder — a move that always makes me grab the door handle for dear life — but in Tamara's direction, not Jenny's. "Jenny's old boyfriend," he informed her. Tamara nodded. Her hair hid her face from me, so I couldn't see her expression. Presumably Jenny had told her about Adam, but who knew? Dan, though, sounded so self-satisfied that I wondered if he was harboring fantasies of Adam and Jenny taking up where they'd left off. I wasn't about to ask.

"Will you watch where you're driving," I told him. He faced front again, and I released my grip on the door.

"I knew he'd applied for a job with the *Journal* papers, but he wasn't at all sure he'd get it," Jenny was continuing. "I'll call him when we get back then, and arrange to get together," she said happily.

Traffic was heavy enough that it was nearly midnight before we reached the Bronx and dropped Jenny and Tamara at Rose's place. The girls were sleeping in Judy's old room, still furnished with the twin bed set Judy had received for her twelfth birthday, while Dan and I were staying in my mother's apartment. By the time we found a parking spot on her street it was too late to do more than give her a hug and fall onto the sleep sofa. But I braced myself for her questions in the morning. Mama's no dummy. I wondered how long it would take her to guess that Jenny and Tamara were more than just friends. I hadn't told either of our mothers about Jenny, other than to say she'd invited a friend to join us for Thanksgiving. The day after Jenny had jumped down my throat for telling Lois about her sexual orientation, I'd promised her that, in the future, I'd leave it up to her to decide who she wanted to come out to.

To my relief, on Thanksgiving morning Mama's conversation centered entirely on arrangements, a phenomenon I'd noticed among older people. "I'm slowest, so I'll be first in the shower, then Sheila, and Dan last while we're dressing, because we girls always take longer. And when we go in the car, remember I need to sit up front on account of my arthritis...."

When we pulled into her driveway, Rose glared at my mother sitting in the van's front passenger seat, then flounced into the seat behind her. "Here, darling, you sit next to me," she commanded Jenny, before Jenny had even finished greeting Mama and introducing "my friend, Tamara," to her. Rose had completely ignored the fact that I was already sitting in the seat next to her, but unless I wanted a fight on my hands, I had no alternative but to move from my seat behind Dan to the rear. Tamara climbed in next to me and we set out for Long Island.

You'd think Rose would be mollified by sharing the middle seat with her darling granddaughter, but we'd barely turned off Sedgwick onto Kingsbridge before she started in. "I wouldn't eat a bite of the turkey today. Not one bite."

"So who's holding a gun to your head?" my mother asked her. Mama doesn't normally pick fights, but Rose always brings out the worst in her.

"You won't have to," Jenny assured Rose before she could make a dig back. "I talked to Jeffrey and Anita the other day, and she told me her mother is making a veggie lasagna especially for you."

"But the dishes, darling, you know they don't keep the dairy dishes separate from the meat dishes," Rose explained, the way she did every year. "Not to mention the soap they use..." I lost interest in her concerns over keeping kosher, wondering what Jenny had told her brother and his wife.

By the time we were inching our way down the Bronx River Parkway I'd stopped wondering and begun to worry. I'd have to take Jeffrey aside and warn him not to say anything that might give Jenny and Tamara away, I decided, just as Rose got around to telling Dan, "It's bad enough your son had to go and marry a goy but to convert out of his own religion...." as she did every time we were thrown together.

Dan was turning defensive, as he did every year. "Don't blame me. I saw to it he was Bar Mitzvahed —" at which my mother naturally put in, "So I suppose you're blaming my daughter?" At this point, I'd generally add my own two cents. Instead, I sighed deeply and tried not to imagine how Rose would take the news that her darling Jenny was a lesbian.

Jenny, as *she* always did, was changing the subject, telling her two grandmothers a funny story about her class. I turned to Tamara with a wry smile and upturned palm, as if to say, "Families. What can you do?" She gave me a strained smile and turned toward the window as if to enjoy the scenery, though it was obvious that her view of the Long Island Sound was all but hidden by the bumper-to-bumper traffic in the right-hand lane. I permitted myself another sigh. Then I let my eyes close and my head rest against the seat back.

I'd intended just to rest my eyes, but when they opened we were pulling into the shopping center parking lot in front of Paul's Pasta Palace. Jeffrey and Anita had arrived just ahead of us and Stephanie pulled loose from her mother's hand to give her Aunt Jenny a hug and a kiss. Next she flung herself at Dan and me. While Dan was asking, "How's my favorite granddaughter?" Jenny, enveloped in a bear hug by Jeffrey, gave her brother a hug and kiss in return.

"Jenny kissed me!" he crowed.

"Don't you dare start!" Jenny told him. "My mom named me for this romantic poem she fell in love with," she added to Tamara. "That's the title if you'd believe it; it's the sappiest thing you ever heard."

"It's a beautiful poem," I protested. "And I needed a name that started with J because you're also named in honor of your grandfather Joseph."

The two grandmas were hovering, waiting to hug their great-grand-child, and my mother explained to Tamara, "It's a Jewish tradition, naming a baby after a dead family member."

At which Rose had to put in her two cents. "Don't you think she knows? You can't tell by looking, she's a Jewish girl? You don't think at least one of your grandchildren keeps company with other Jews?"

"Grandma," Jenny murmured. "But it didn't have to be Jenny," she went on to Tamara. "It's not even Jennifer, just Jenny because she was so crazy about that poem. When I was a kid, she used to recite it every single time she tucked me in, until I told her if I heard it once more I'd open my mouth and scream and I wouldn't stop till the alarm went off the next morning."

Tamara laughed.

"Anyway," Jenny continued, "This guy with the big mouth and the long memory is my brother, Jeffrey, and this is my sister-in-law, Anita."

"We've heard so much about you," Anita said.

Jeffrey took Tamara's extended hand in both of his. I could see my plan for getting him aside for a few words was down the drain.

"It's great to finally meet you," Jeffrey said. "Welcome to the family."

We pulled open the door, which displayed a large CLOSED sign to ward off the general public, and were greeted by an aroma of sage, garlic and other mouth-watering spices. Anita's mother, Linda, bustled over to welcome us with smiles and hugs. "Come in, come in, wonderful to see you," she said over the hubbub of talk and laughter from family members there ahead of us. "I hope you didn't run into too much traffic. Jenny! You've gotten prettier than ever. And this must be?"

"Jenny's friend, Tamara," Dan said before Jenny could open her mouth.

"So glad to meet you, Tamara. Good to see you, Myrna," she said to Mama. "Rose, I've made you my special spinach lasagna," she added, giving my mother-in-law a quick embrace. "No meat. Nothing but assorted cheeses and a touch of cream, so you don't have to be afraid to eat."

"Sounds wonderful, Mom," Anita said, as Rose gave a halfhearted murmur of thanks. "I hope you made plenty!"

"What do you think? Of course I did. Enough for the whole crowd."

I groaned, and Linda turned on me with mock severity, "This is no day to diet, Sheila. Right, Steffi?" she said, scooping up our granddaughter for a hug. "Sit down, make yourselves at home," she added, setting Steffi down and turning to greet the next batch of arrivals.

To Linda, the restaurant was home, or close to it. She'd been head chef since she and Paul opened the place ten years after they married. Their kids had grown up as much there as in their apartment, which I marveled at every time I observed Anita's size-six figure. For this occasion, Linda and Paul had replaced the red-and-white-checked tablecloths with cloths of ivory damask and pushed the separate tables together into a U-shaped arrangement. Dinner — golden brown turkey, baked ham, creamy spinach lasagna and an assortment of traditional and nontraditional side dishes from savory stuffing and candied sweet potatoes to gnocchi and antipasto salad — was set out buffet style on an overloaded table by the kitchen door.

Anita settled Stephanie at the "children's table" — one of the long legs of the U. The rest of us filled our plates, Tamara, Jenny and Rose making selections that would do the least damage to their kosher standards, and found seats near the end of the table where Paul and Linda presided.

Paul tapped his glass with his spoon to signal for quiet for the grace. "Bless us O Lord, and these Thy gifts, which we are about to receive from Thy bounty, through Christ our Lord. Amen." The assembled family members crossed themselves — all but Dan, myself, our mothers, Jenny and Tamara. I kept my head bowed so as not to glimpse the looks on Rose's and Dan's faces as our son made the sign of the cross along with the others; truthfully, I hoped Jeffrey didn't pick up on my own instinctive wince of dismay.

Rose, thank God, kept her mouth shut as grace ended and we began to eat — perhaps because she was so busy shoveling food into it. Despite her kvetching in the car on the way over, she was wolfing down the lasagna with enormous relish. She was sitting by Mama, and I couldn't help but notice that my mother was making a production of cutting up the slice of baked ham she'd taken, to get Rose's goat, I was sure.

I winked at Mama and took a bite of ham myself. I can't resist Linda's baked ham, but I couldn't bring myself to flaunt it the way Mama did. The piece I'd taken was hidden by a generous helping of moist, dark turkey, not to mention the side dishes, relish, and a small — okay, medium — square of lasagna. It was, after all, Thanksgiving, I told myself. And I felt relatively slim in my new dress, an ethnic print that swung loose from the shoulders with no waistline. I'd found the dress in a boutique in Alexandria, and accessorized it with the Navajo pearls I'd bought from the vendor at the lesbian conference. I took a forkful of lasagna, relishing its creamy richness.

Between bites I agreed with Mama that we'd have to ask Linda for the recipe — though naturally we'd substitute low-fat cheese. With half an ear, I could hear Rose chatting with Jenny, and Dan giving Paul a mile-by-mile rundown of our drive from Washington. They were still on the subject of traffic and routes when we had filled dessert plates with pump-kin pie and cannoli, now comparing the wisdom of taking old U.S. 40 rather than I-95.

"Are you guys still at it?" Linda asked. "Have you ever noticed," she added, her voice pitched to reach all the females around her, "how when men get together they never talk about anything but maps and mileage? You'd think the only reason they take a trip is so they can discuss which way they should have gone and which way they'll go home."

It was true, and we all laughed. Paul snorted. "Well then, not to change the subject," he said, "it's good your whole family could be here for the holiday, what with your lovely daughter braving the traffic to drive up with you. And her friend —" He gestured toward Tamara.

"Tamara." She smiled at him.

"Yes, yes, I remember. Well, you're a brave girl to subject yourself to this mob scene. Dan mentioned that you came to do some sightseeing, thought you'd take advantage of a ride to New York. But I bet you didn't bargain for this zoo."

Tamara looked startled. "We are hoping to go to the Metropolitan Museum of Art tomorrow. But my main reason for coming was to meet more of Jenny's family. And to be with her for the holiday, of course."

"Really?" Paul said in a bewildered voice, and I knew the other shoe was about to drop even before Dan opened his mouth.

"What Tamara means is she couldn't make the trip to see her own family this year, so rather than be alone on a big holiday, why not spend it with a friend? She and Jenny teach together you know, and —"

I tuned out the rest as Tamara gave Dan a look. She turned to Jenny, apparently waiting for Jenny to set the record straight, it being Jenny's family, after all. Jenny, though, seemed to have nothing to say, staring at her plate and biting her lower lip. It was Jeffrey who leaned across the table and demanded, "Dad, will you cut the crap! Why are you afraid to say that Jenny and Tamara are a couple, so they're here together like any other couple?"

In the dead silence that enveloped us for the next few seconds, I thought I could hear Paul's mouth drop open. Dan's knuckles whitened on his fork. I set my own fork down on my plate; there'd be no way to get any more pie down past the lump in my throat. The far ends of the table hadn't heard anything yet. I could hear snatches of ordinary conversations — ("Reviewers said.... Half price tickets..." "So Anita's expecting again? Does she know yet what she'll have?") — and found myself calculating how many minutes it would take before Jeffrey's announcement reached the rest of them.

Then Anita was speaking angrily into Jeffrey's ear, while Linda stared at Jenny in her flowered Laura Ashley dress and murmured, "Oh no, it couldn't be, no one could be more feminine..." Jenny, still apparently struck dumb, sat twisting her good linen napkin into a rope. Dan had leaned across me to shoot Jeffrey a look that could have killed, hissing, "Will you keep your big mouth shut!" Rose was demanding "What? What did he say? Will someone tell me what's going on?" and Mama, looking stricken, was staring at me with reproach in her eyes.

Only one person was looking at Jeffrey with anything approaching gratitude, and that person was Tamara.

The dinner was beginning to break up into after-dinner visiting. The kids were up from their chairs and chasing each other around the outskirts of the room. Grown siblings and cousins were hitching their chairs together for a second cup of coffee, while Linda's sisters and sisters-in-law brushed off her protestations and began clearing the dessert dishes and organizing the cleanup. Normally I would have felt compelled to help, but Dan — apparently too overcome with embarrassment to stay even another half hour — hustled us out, shutting Rose up temporarily with a whispered promise to explain things later. "Not in front of other people, Ma. This isn't anyone else's business."

We said goodbye to Paul and Linda, both of whom were tactfully pretending that nothing had happened, and headed for the car. Dan turned the ignition key before the girls, lagging behind and apparently in the midst of an argument, had even reached it. The second Dan started the engine, Mama turned on me. "How could you keep something like this from your own mother?" She was sitting next to me in the middle seat, Rose having sat herself down in the front this time, and Rose swiveled her head to demand, "Something like what? Do you mind finally telling me what you're talking about!"

Mama gave a heartfelt sigh. "Only that our granddaughter and her friend — according to what her own brother says and I didn't hear her denying it — are lesbians."

"They're what? *What* did you say?"

"Lesbians, Rose. I can't believe you've never heard the word. Have you heard of girls being *that way*, being — let me think back — bed partners?"

Rose drew her breath in so sharply it seemed to whistle into her lungs. "My Jenny? She and — No, I don't believe it!" The girls had finally caught up to us. As Jenny, followed by Tamara, climbed into the back, Rose demanded, "Tell me this isn't true, Jenny! What your grandma Myrna says, that you two are, are.... You're friends, right? That's what you told me last night, no? The two of you are friends."

"We are friends, Grandma," Jenny said miserably. "Tamara is my very best friend in the whole world. But she's also my, my —" Jenny paused, obviously casting about for a term that Rose could relate to. "She's my everything, Grandma," she finished at last.

Tamara gave her a look. "Your everything who you won't even acknowledge." She was speaking for Jenny's ears only, but I pride myself on my hearing.

"I can't believe it," Rose said. "You knew this?" she demanded of Dan. "You gave your stamp of approval to this?"

"It's not a question of approving. Look, you know from your own experience that there are times when the worst thing you can do is put your foot down. When it comes to a child outgrowing a phase —"

I looked over my shoulder again to see Jenny's reaction to that little remark, but she and Tamara were so engrossed in angry whispers that it had gone right over her head. I couldn't make out any of their words, especially with Mama going on at me for not having let her know.

"You didn't tell your own mother. I can't get over it. And it's not that you didn't have every opportunity. I asked you on the phone, just last week, had Jenny met anyone yet and what did you say —"

I began telling Mama that it wasn't something I felt I could communicate over the phone and of course I'd planned, or rather I was sure Jenny had planned, once we all had time to sit down and visit together —

Rose's shrill tones cut right through my murmurs to Mama. "It's not going to go on under my roof; that's one thing I'll tell you right now!"

There was an instant of silence and then Tamara, her voice as furious as I'd ever heard it, informed her, "You don't need to worry, Mrs. Katz. Jenny can do whatever she wants, stay or leave, but I'm catching the train back home tonight."

Chapter Six

"So Tamara packed up and left," I told our lunch bunch the following week. "Jenny drove her to Penn Station; then she went back to Rose's house for the rest of the weekend." I paused for a bite of quiche. Lois had heard the story on the way to the restaurant, but LaVerne and Natalie watched me eat as if they were waiting for a commercial to end on their favorite soap opera. "Jenny didn't tell me what Rose had to say to her, but would you believe that Rose is furious at *me*? If there's something wrong with Jenny — according to Rose's way of thinking, that is — then it's got to be her mother's fault."

Natalie raised her hand to head me off. She'd heard my complaints about my mother-in-law too many times. "What about the girls?" she demanded. "Have they made up yet?"

I shrugged. "Jenny says they've realized they can't just go on the way they have, that they've got to rethink their relationship. That's what she said when I called her the day after we drove home. She wouldn't go into any more details."

"You're lucky to get that much from one of your kids," LaVerne told me. "It sounds to me like they're on the verge of breaking up."

I ate another creamy, delicious bite. I shouldn't have ordered quiche, but after the nightmare of Thanksgiving weekend I needed *something* good. "I couldn't tell from her voice at all. Usually, I can pick up on what she really means, but.... They're both back in their apartment though, so —"

"Well, suppose they did call it quits?" Natalie demanded, before I could finish my thought. "Would that be so terrible? If she realizes this whole gay thing is just a phase?"

"Cause you can't tell me the Jenny I know is *really* a lesbian," LaVerne put in.

"And if she's not with this girl any more, then she still might meet someone. A boy she could go for," Natalie added, as if she thought I didn't know what she was getting at.

I shook my head. "That's not the way it works —" I started, and then I remembered Jenny's excitement over seeing Adam again after two years. "Actually, she's getting together with her old boyfriend next weekend," I blurted. "But I'm sure it's just for old times' sake."

"Don't be so sure," Natalie said.

Lois put down her glass of wine to join in. "Whether she meets a boy or not, if this Tamara person is a louse, it's good Jenny's finding it out now rather than later. Not like me and the rat."

The rat was Lois's ex-husband, Bernie, who walked out on her two months after her mastectomy. The four of us — Lois, LaVerne, Natalie and I — never mentioned his name again, though we discussed him plenty. "The rat," we've called him ever since, as in "The rat is late with his child support for a change," to which the rest of us invariably chimed in, "Some change."

"I wouldn't call Tamara a louse," I protested.

"Girl, I don't see how you can take up for her like that! Didn't you just tell us she picked a fight at Thanksgiving dinner in front of the whole family?" LaVerne demanded.

"That's the way it turned out," I admitted, "but I don't think that's what she had in mind."

"Well, shoving all that gay stuff in their faces," LaVerne went on.

"But from her point of view, it was like...like asking Jeffrey not to mention that Anita's his wife. Anyway, it was Jeffrey who actually outed them at Thanksgiving. And Jenny was defending Tamara to the rest of us all weekend. I just wish that Tamara had stayed and helped Jenny out instead of leaving her in the lurch." I sighed and, while my mouth was open, ate the last bite of quiche. "I hate to see Jenny so unhappy," I said as I set my fork down on my empty plate.

"One way or another, she'll work things out. You can't live her life for her," Lois told me, as she had in the car on the way over.

LaVerne nodded vigorously. "Tell me about kids! Here's Dennis Jr. still shacking with Shawna, and now she's expecting another this spring.

The both of them still in school, and you know who's paying for it. I've given up even *trying* to talk to him. But last time I got Shawna alone, I said to her, 'You're smart enough to be working on a master's degree; how come you're not smart enough to make that son of mine do the right thing by you and make it legal?'"

LaVerne's complaints about her son were a staple of our lunches, as were her proud reports on the progress of her grandson, little Denzel. Natalie stopped her before she could pull out her latest photos. "Listen, don't give up hope for Jenny so easy. For all you know, she might still get back with the boyfriend — I forget his name."

"Adam," I mumbled. I should have been educating Natalie on the fact that if Jenny was a lesbian, her orientation would still be toward other women, whether she broke up with Tamara or not. But I was thrown by a surge of hope completely inappropriate for a PFLAG mom who had progressed to being a permanent member of the speakers' bureau. So I only added, weakly, "I'm sure they're just friends."

Our conversation turned to holiday shopping, and it dawned on me that what with everything going on in my life, I was weeks behind. Normally I had presents in the mail by this time of year. I hated facing the malls in December. Natalie noticed my Navaho pearls just then — I'd taken to wearing them everywhere — and as she leaned forward to admire them, I made up my mind to do as much of my shopping as I could in the quaint boutiques in Alexandria's Old Town, starting the next morning with the shop owned by the vendor who had sold me the necklace.

Old Town is long on charm and short on parking space, so I got going as soon as I'd cleared away our breakfast dishes the next day. I lucked into a spot a block away from the address on the business card the vendor had given me. Her shop, The Soaring Eagle, was in a building that had been converted for commercial use from an eighteenth century townhouse, and boasted a plaque designating it as a historic structure. The storefront was set back from the street in a tiny courtyard. I walked down a short path of uneven red bricks to the door and turned the knob. To my disappointment, it was locked.

The display window was covered by a wrought-iron grillwork. Frustrated, I peered through the grill at necklaces fashioned of delicately intertwined silver strands, bracelets and watchbands inlaid with turquoise and coral, and perfectly formed pottery bowls in deep reds and black. In the middle of the window, a hand-lettered sign advised me the shop was CLOSED. As I looked in, a light went on toward the back of the store. I could make out someone moving about. It was a few minutes before ten; doubtless the shop was about to open. I was getting chilly standing outside; I rang the doorbell, hoping to be let in a few minutes early.

The person inside — who I could see now was my vendor — fiddled with the lock a moment and then pulled open the door a few inches. She was wearing a long bathrobe that looked like it was fashioned from an Indian blanket. "I'm sorry," she began, "we don't open till eleven —" Her face suddenly lit up with recognition. "Well, hi! If it isn't my PFLAG mom. I'm getting a late start this morning; I was just finishing breakfast. Look, I can't leave you standing out in the cold. Would you like to join me for a cup of coffee?"

As she opened the door, I noticed for the first time the small card with hours, also neatly hand-lettered. "I'm sorry to barge in," I said, embarrassed. "I didn't notice the sign with your hours. But I'd love some coffee, if it's not too much trouble."

"No trouble. I live over the shop and I just made a fresh pot. Come this way," she added, leading me through a curtained door at the rear of the store. "We probably should open earlier, but we don't get much business till lunch-time. I just came down to get the mail. Things were so hectic in the shop yesterday that I forgot to bring it upstairs."

"I'm sorry I didn't notice your hours," I apologized again, following her through a crowded storeroom and up a narrow staircase. "They were on the card you gave me too, now that I think of it. Anyway, I'm amazed you remember me. You must've had so many customers that day."

"You were the only one from PFLAG," she told me as we entered her kitchen. "I'm Naomi Pearlman, by the way. I remember your last name is Katz. I've forgotten your first name though. Here, have a seat and I'll pour us some coffee."

"It smells wonderful," I said as I breathed in the aroma of fresh coffee. Columbian, I thought. "My name's Sheila. I love the colors in your robe," I added as she set a pottery mug in front of me and poured coffee from an old-fashioned stove-top percolator. "It looks like one of those Indian blankets."

Naomi smiled. "It is. I found it on one of my buying trips out West. A friend who sews turned it into a robe for my birthday." She warmed her cup with a little more coffee and sat across from me. "Sugar, milk?" She gestured toward a carton of milk and a sugar bowl already on the table.

"Do you have any NutraSweet? I'm trying to lose weight."

She shook her head. "Sorry. I don't use anything with chemical additives. Anyway, why let the patriarchy define how you should look? I like to see a woman with a little healthy flesh on her."

"Let the what do what?" I mumbled, spooning sugar into my coffee cup and wondering if I should be offended by Naomi's description of "a little healthy flesh." She leaned forward to slide the sugar back in her direction when I'd finished, and I caught a glimpse of her own firm flesh and modest cleavage. She seemed to be nude under her robe, and I caught myself wondering what the heavy wool must feel like on her naked skin. It was an oddly unsettling thought. I decided to change the subject. "Naomi Pearlman," I repeated her name. "So you're Jewish, then?"

"Afraid not. Pearlman is my ex-husband's name. He's Jewish. I decided to keep my married name when we divorced, so my kids and I wouldn't have different last names."

"I thought you were a lesbian," I blurted. "Oh, I'm sorry. It's just, meeting you at a lesbian conference —"

"Don't apologize. Lesbian is a noun, not an insult. As a matter of fact, I am a lesbian, though it took me twelve years of marriage before I realized it."

"Oh," I managed, feeling like a fool. "I didn't mean anything by it. That is —"

Naomi took pity on me. "My fault. I confused you."

"But if you were married for twelve years? You didn't *hate* having sex with your husband that whole time, did you?" It dawned on me that it was the kind of intrusive question Lois would ask. "Sorry," I apologized. "That's an awfully nosy question."

She laughed. "Yes, it is. But the answer is no, it wasn't awful all the time. And my ex and I are still good friends. But it gradually dawned on me that I'm more attuned to women. Emotionally attuned, not just physically. Coming out of marriage isn't as unusual as you might think. It can take years to find out who you really are."

I nodded, although I still couldn't comprehend why being attuned to women meant having to give up men. "Still, it must have been such a change for you."

"It was. In fact, I made a total life change, starting with my first name. My parents named me Jane. As in *Sally, Dick and Jane.* I always hated it."

That I could empathize with. I'd never cared for my first name either. "But why Naomi? It's such a Jewish name, and if you're not Jewish yourself...."

"I've always thought it had a beautiful sound to it. But mainly because the Biblical story of Ruth and Naomi is a celebration of love between two women."

Whatever Biblical scribe had set down the story of Ruth leaving everything behind to follow her mother-in-law had never had a mother-in-law like mine, but I nodded again anyway.

"Of course, I could have taken a name like Sappho or Dykewomin, the way some dykes I know did, but my kids were still in school at the time and I needed to sign report cards and meet their teachers."

"I can just imagine," I said, nearly choking on the last of my coffee. "This is my mother, Dykewomin Pearlman."

Naomi grinned. "Naomi does blend a lot better into mainstream culture." She glanced at her watch, then drained the rest of her cup in one swallow. "I'd better get into clothes if I'm going to open the shop on time." She gestured toward my empty cup. "More coffee?"

I shook my head. "I'm fine, thanks."

She stood up from the table. "I'll just be a few minutes." The apartment was laid out like a railroad flat. I was sitting with my back to the living room. Naomi pushed open the door facing me, revealing an unmade queen-sized bed. Curled up in the middle was a large orange-colored Persian cat twice the size of any of the kitties at BAT. As the door opened he stood up and stretched. Then he jumped from the bed, raced through the kitchen and made a flying leap onto my lap. Startled, I jumped up myself, spilling him to the floor. He gave me a reproachful meow and sprang up onto the chair again.

"Sorry about that," Naomi called. "You were sitting on his chair. Why don't you come in here, and we can continue our conversation while I dress."

There was nowhere to sit in the bedroom but the bed, so I pulled up the quilt a bit and plopped down on it. "He's a beautiful cat."

"Isn't he? His name's Ginger. I adopted him from the animal shelter right after I bought this place. He likes to lord it over me, but what kind of self-respecting dyke would I be if I didn't keep a cat?"

"Is it a prerequisite?" I asked her. "I hadn't realized."

Naomi laughed. "You have a sense of humor. I like that." She opened a dresser drawer and pulled out panties and a turtleneck, then threw off her robe and perched on the edge of the bed a few feet from me to pull on her underwear. As I'd suspected, she was nude under the robe, a fact that didn't seem to faze her. I turned my eyes away from Naomi to discover I was then staring at her image in a full length mirror fastened to the closet door: small, high breasts, broad shoulders and slender, firm arms, only a hint of paunch above a triangle of pubic hair that was still a rich, chestnut brown. Her legs and underarms were unshaven, and her naked body gave off a faint odor of sweat mingled with that of a spicy scented soap.

I redirected my gaze to a painting of a sunset hanging next to the door, studying the vivid swirls of red and purple as she slipped on her panties and shirt. "I like that painting," I told her. "Is it from a gallery out West?"

Naomi gave me a warm, wide smile. "Thanks for the compliment. I did it myself, actually. I wanted to capture those incredible colors in a more personal way than just taking a photo."

"Well, I love it! I didn't know you were an artist too. Did you take art in school?"

"Only a couple of courses. I wanted to major in art in college, but I got a lot of family pressure to pick something practical. And you know how back then, if you were a woman —"

"You ended up in one of the 'helping professions,'" I interrupted, and we both laughed.

"Exactly. I got a Master's in social work and worked in the field most of my marriage," she said as she walked to the closet for a pair of slacks and embroidered denim vest. "By the time my marriage was ending, I was also suffering total job burnout."

"I know just what you mean!" I told her, amazed at the parallels between Naomi's life and my own. An hour ago I'd have sworn we had nothing in common. "What I wanted to major in was theater. But my mother pushed me into an ed major instead, because teaching would give me something to 'fall back on' in case my husband couldn't support me. I couldn't bring myself to go back to it once my kids were old enough. So then you opened this place?"

"Not quite that easily. I always loved Native American crafts, so I found a job in a gallery selling them and spent a few years learning all I could. My partner and I finally opened The Soaring Eagle a little over six years ago."

So she had a partner, I mused. I'd had the impression she lived alone. I must have been mistaken.

"She had to go out of town for a family emergency — one reason I'm so swamped this week. Running a business can be draining in its own way, but I wouldn't give it up for anything." She walked over to the dresser, opened the lid on a large jewelry box, and selected a strand of turquoise and another of tiny carved birds. She fastened both around her neck and studied the effect in the mirror. "Just being around these beautiful creations all day nourishes my spirit. So what do you do now? Besides being a PFLAG mom?"

"PFLAG's a recent development. My daughter just came out a few months ago. Aside from that, I'm nothing special, just a housewife."

"Uh huh." I had the sinking feeling I was losing Naomi's interest. She stuck her foot into an ankle-high leather boot and asked, "No hobbies? Did you give up your interest in theater after high school?"

"Well, actually," I said, wondering how I'd come to leave it out, "I've been involved for years with one of the amateur groups in the area. Burke Amateur Theater. BAT for short. You've probably never heard of it. We're a pretty laid-back bunch, not like Little Theatre of Alexandria or some of the other community theater groups. We're not into heavy drama; we do plays that have more general appeal. But we've got a large following, especially for our fall show. Our theater was converted from a barn behind a creepy old house that everyone got to calling 'the haunted house,' so we open our season every Halloween with either a thriller or a ghost story."

"Sounds fun."

"Oh, it keeps me busy," I murmured, the way I would to one of Dan's associates that I was meeting for the first time, the way Dan might describe it himself. Then I looked up and met Naomi's expectant gaze.

"Actually, it's more than that," I confessed. "I usually work as a techie. I've done a little of everything — props, stage managing, you name it. I guess you could call set decoration my specialty. And when you start with that bare space, and then the set designer creates the stage set — well, the set decorator works with the designer to furnish his design. To take the basic outlines of a living room, say, and transform it into a living room in a Beverly Hills mansion, or into a peasant's hut in a nineteenth-century Russian village. Your set is the first thing the audience sees when the curtain goes up. I like to think it sets the tone of the play. I can become totally engrossed in finding just the right accessories. It's like creating a whole little world."

"Sounds a lot like painting," Naomi said, and gave me that smile of hers.

I smiled back. "Well, it fulfills most of my creative urges, the way I guess painting does for you. But I was going to say, in our last play I had a speaking role. More than a walk-on, that is. I acted when I was in school, but the rehearsals took up too much time once I had kids. I'd forgotten how much I loved it. Playing this part, it's like I was transformed into a new person, into the character I was playing. Now I can't wait until there's another role that's right for me to try out for. I don't know why I'm going on and on about it," I murmured, suddenly shy.

"Because I asked you. And because I love hearing you talk about it." She gave me another smile. A moment went by. "Matter of fact, I've always thought I'd like to work on a show — someday when I've got the time. Speaking of which, I ought to be getting downstairs."

I followed her from the room. "It doesn't have to take that much time. Not working backstage, anyway. A lot of people just help out a few hours with set construction. If you're interested," I said, as she reached the staircase, "BAT could use your help painting flats for scenery. We'll start work on our next show in January, and we're short on real artistic talent."

She paused a moment to look over her shoulder at me. "When you put it like that, January and February are our slow period. So I just might. Why not?"

The next PFLAG meeting was packed, a common occurrence around major holidays, Candy Sue explained as we strolled in together, both of us — as usual — without our spouses. The imminence of family gatherings brought out panicky gay men and lesbians searching for tips on dealing with parents. So I found myself looking into two dozen attentive pairs of eyes as I described the debacle of our Thanksgiving dinner, hoping that no one was expecting any helpful hints for family harmony from me.

I stumbled through my story of how Jeffrey had outed Jenny and

Tamara. Unfortunately, I had no happy ending. "I'm afraid the whole family is still upset. Dan's furious at Jeffrey, and Jenny let on to me that she and Tamara are still having problems over Jenny not introducing Tamara as her partner in the first place." The gay men and lesbians looked back at me with dismay. This wasn't the encouraging scenario they'd hoped to hear. "But there is one bright note," I told them, and the lesbian couple sitting opposite me sat up straighter and gave each other's hands a little squeeze. "My husband's mother is beginning to come around. Jenny had a big talk with her while we were still in New York, and apparently they've talked on the phone several times since then. Last night Jenny told me that Rose has come to understand that she can't help being a lesbian, that it isn't a choice on her part."

I didn't add what Rose had said when *I'd* talked on the phone with her: "A choice is deserting your own religion like your son did." Nor did I bother adding my own mother's comments. Instead, I murmured, "So that's how things stand right now," and nodded to Marlene, who was sitting next to me, that I was through.

Normally Marlene broke the ice by telling her story first. This afternoon, she'd waited until last. She looked around the circle and said, "I hear a lot of issues around coming out tonight, and we'll have time to get back to everyone's concerns before we break up for the evening. But I have a different twist to my story today. The old-timers here know that my son came out over fifteen years ago. And that a year ago he broke up with his partner of twelve years, so he's been having a rough time lately. Well, last week he called to tell me there's someone new in his life. But you can't imagine who!"

Marlene paused so dramatically that Billy, the boy from Nebraska who'd been at the first support group I'd attended, and who was preparing to go home for the first time since coming out to his parents, called out, "Greg Louganis?"

"No, not a gay celebrity. Nothing like that." Marlene hesitated again, then her words came all in a rush. "He's got a girl. That is, a woman friend. But she's more than a friend — they're actually considering marriage. Only now — well, what do I do?" she asked plaintively, with none of the self-assured leadership her voice usually displayed. "I've told every single person I know that Matthew is gay. What am I supposed to tell them now?"

We all stared at her. Then Candy Sue said, "You suppose he was mistaken about being gay in the first place?" She was sitting on the edge of her seat, both hands gripping her purse.

It wasn't like Marlene to ignore Candy Sue's question, but she went on as if she hadn't heard her. "Of course, all I want is Matthew's happiness, and I'll support him in whatever he decides. But where does it leave *me*? I've been facilitating this support group ten years, I was just elected president of the chapter. PFLAG is a big part of my life. And if my son is in a straight relationship, if he isn't gay anymore...." She shrugged plump shoulders and turned her hands up helplessly. "Well, that's my issue for today."

We observed another moment of silence. Then a gay man new to the group, a bearded redhead whose name had slipped my mind, spoke up. "Hey look, if your son was with another man for twelve years, he's not *straight*. He's bisexual. And just didn't know it till he found the right person." He grinned. "So don't sweat it. He's still part of the community. You can still tell everyone your son is queer."

"Can you believe it?" Candy Sue demanded of me, as we walked to our cars together after the meeting. "Can you just believe it? Marlene's upset that her son might get *married*?" She came to a dead stop and grabbed my arm. "I know I'm not supposed to say it, but I would fall down on my knees and give thanks if Jason were ever to tell me he'd fallen in love with a girl. Not that I don't accept him the way he is, you understand, and I'm glad he's found someone as sweet as Mark. But when Marlene told us how her son is thinking of getting married, how he could still give her grandchildren — well, you can't imagine how that made me feel."

I was afraid I could. "It's funny," I confessed to her, while we both fished in our purses for our keys. "I don't know why I didn't mention it in the support group, but Jenny has started seeing her old boyfriend again. She had brunch with him last Sunday, and apparently they're planning to go out again next week. She told me she'd forgotten what a great guy he is. Of course they're just friends, but —"

"But look at Marlene's son. You never can tell — miracles can happen. Honey, I'll be praying for them."

Chapter Seven

"You're late," Dan observed as I walked into the front hall to hang my coat in the closet.

"I had coffee with Candy Sue after the meeting." I grabbed Dan's jacket from the Victorian hall tree where he'd tossed it, and hung it in the closet next to mine. He stood in the doorway of his den watching me. I've told him a thousand times that an antique hall tree is meant as an ornament, not a coat rack, but every time he's replied that he'll stop hanging his things on it as soon as I explain to his satisfaction the point of spending $479 on a piece of furniture that can't be used. So I didn't waste my breath again. Anyhow, my mind was still on Candy Sue. "She's worked herself into a state. Marlene's son told her he's dating a woman — you can imagine what a surprise that was — and now Candy Sue has taken a step backwards and is sure that Jason can turn straight if she just prays hard enough."

Abruptly I realized what I'd done. "Oh, no! I shouldn't have told you about Marlene — everything that goes on at the meeting is supposed to be confidential. Don't repeat it to anyone."

"Who do you expect me to tell? What do you think, I go around advertising that I have a lesbian daughter? Anyhow," Dan added in a tone of satisfaction, "that may be changing very soon."

"What may be changing?" I asked him as I headed toward the kitchen. I needed to relax before starting dinner. I poured us each a glass of red wine — good for lowering blood pressure and raising good cholesterol — and planted myself on the couch in the family room. Dan lowered himself into his recliner across from me.

"That really says something," he said. "Your friend Marlene is willing to tell the whole world her son is a *faygeleh*, but let him get into a normal relationship and you have to clam up like it was some kind of dirty secret." He took a swallow of wine and picked up the TV clicker.

"His relationship with Kevin was normal, too," I protested, before he could turn on the CNN news. "What did you start to tell me about? What's going to change?"

"Our daughter and her friend Tamara. She called while you were out. She's planning to spend her Christmas vacation at home with us — without Tamara. If you ask me, that's a relationship that's run its course."

I thought about that a moment. "It's a shame in a way. I like Tamara. But honey, don't you see that even if they do break up that it's not going to change Jenny's orientation?"

"Ah," he said, with the same *ta da* in his voice that his computer makes when he boots it up. "I didn't finish. We had a nice, long chat. I asked her what she and Adam talked about on their date last weekend, after not seeing each other for two years. And what do you suppose?"

There was no need to suppose, since Dan was obviously about to tell me. Nevertheless I demanded, "Well what?" Jenny and Adam had been friends, after all, since the year they'd both been ten and she had dressed as Esther and he as King Ahasuerus at the temple Purim party. They'd started dating in tenth grade. "What did they talk about?" I repeated.

"About two people getting back together again after they've broken up."

When I was growing up, Mama always trimmed a tree at Christmastime. If anyone had the nerve to tell her it was out of place in a Jewish household, she'd answer back, "Since when is it a crime to decorate a Hanukkah bush? There's not one thing Christian about it. When you show me where it talks about evergreens in the New Testament, then I'll stop bringing one into my house."

Rose, on the other hand, never thought things through. Anything smacking of Christianity was like a red flag to a bull as far as she was concerned. Never mind how little it actually had to do with the Christian religion. Despite that — or, according to Dan, because of that — I'd followed Mama's lead and put up a tree of my own every year since Jeffrey and Jenny were little. Why deprive children of what had become a secular winter holiday that all their friends got to celebrate? Especially when I tied my decorating scheme into our own holiday by hanging the tree with tiny dreydels so it really was a Hanukkah bush.

I was just putting on the last string of Hanukkah lights when Jenny drove up. The dreydels were hung, along with the blue and white glass balls and the handmade ornaments left over from elementary-school art projects that I couldn't bring myself to dispose of. The tree was set up in its customary place in front of the living room windows and I switched on the string of lights — also in my blue-and-white color scheme — to welcome Jenny as she came up the front walk.

"Your timing is perfect," I told her, after a kiss hello. "I just put the finishing touches on the tree."

"You didn't need to bother on my account. I'll go take my stuff upstairs before Daddy gets home."

I overlooked her tone of impatience. She was probably just tired after a term of teaching. "What bother? You know how I love decorating for holidays. I found a gorgeous blue spruce. Remember how you and Jeffrey always went along to help pick out the tree? The two of you used to get so excited when we put it up."

Jenny had started toward the stairs with her suitcase, but now she set it down on the bottom step and turned to face me. "Mom, I'm not a kid anymore."

This time her voice held the unmistakable teenage whine I thought she'd outgrown years ago. "Who said you were? I was just reminiscing."

"But you expect me to be the same person I was then. When you know that I'm trying to live my Judaism a little more than we ever did in this house. So I don't know why you expect me to get all excited that you've put up a Christmas tree again."

"It's a Hanukkah bush," I said automatically. "I happen to think it's nice to have that fresh pine scent in the middle of winter. And it's not just on your account. You know that Jeffrey and Anita are driving down the day after Christmas; I'm keeping their presents here for them, and I want Steffi to find them under the tree."

"It figures," Jenny said, half under her breath, grabbing up her bag and starting upstairs again. I trailed after her, determined to get to the bottom of this.

"What figures?" I demanded. "What's going on that you can't walk in the house and give me one pleasant word?"

Jenny pushed open the door to her old bedroom and dropped her suitcase onto the bed. "Mom, from the moment I walked in the house you've been pretending that you put all these Christmas decorations up like some kind of welcome home for me. When it's perfectly obvious that Jeffrey's the one you were really thinking about."

"I was thinking about both of you," I informed her. "Besides, I told you — I want Steffi to see the tree. She's only four, remember?"

Jenny opened her case, pulled out a half dozen bras and panties and put them away in the top drawer of her old dresser. "Steffi is going to have a tree in her own house and in her New York grandparents' house. She's old enough to understand that other religions celebrate differently from hers. But you're leaning over backwards to have everything perfect for Jeffrey's family without even thinking about my feelings. Looking at our house from the street, you'd never guess we're Jewish."

It was bad enough that Jenny had to walk into the house and start recycling old sibling squabbles. Now I was getting Rose redux. "Jenny, it seems to me lately I've been doing nothing *but* think of you. Educating myself, spending half my time at PFLAG. And you never objected to a tree before. Just because Tamara has swayed you —"

"Mom, that's exactly what I mean. Here, you don't have the slightest difficulty accepting that Jeffrey has converted out of his religion. But when I'm doing my best to observe my *own* religion, you act like I've been brainwashed. The only reason you're blaming Tamara is because you can't accept that I'm a lesbian."

This was so patently unfair it took my breath away. "*I'm* the one who can't accept that you're a lesbian?" I said, once I could talk again. "When I'm the one who's tried to educate myself? When I'm the one who's on the PFLAG speakers' bureau?" Though I hadn't mentioned her father by name — hadn't even been thinking of him when I opened my mouth — the implication was clear. Jenny picked up on it immediately. And hastened to defend him, even though just one month earlier Dan had done everything in his power to keep her orientation a secret from Anita's family.

"That's not very fair, Mom," she told me. "You weren't any more ready to come out of the closet about me than Daddy was. You didn't even tell Grandma Myrna. And Daddy was right about what happened at Thanksgiving. Jeffrey had no right to come out about me at dinner. I'm the one who should have introduced Tamara as my partner from the beginning."

I could imagine Dan's reaction if Jenny had come out at the beginning of dinner. I bit my tongue before I could run him down any further.

"But you go on and on about PFLAG," Jenny went on. "I mean I think it's great you're going, don't get me wrong. But —"

"Wait a minute," I said, suddenly remembering the fight in the car after *Postmortem*. "You practically jumped down my throat a couple of months ago when I told you I'd come out to Aunt Lois. And now you're mad because I *didn't* tell your grandma. I don't think that's very fair to me."

"But then you go and have a tree, when you know how observant Tamara is," Jenny continued, as if I'd been talking to the wall.

"Don't give me that, Jenny," I said, in a tone of voice I hadn't used with her for some time. "You know perfectly well we've always had a tree. I mean a Hanukkah bush. Just like your grandma Myrna. It has nothing to do with Tamara. And besides, you told us she wasn't coming here over the holidays. Didn't you?"

"Well.... I guess I did tell Daddy that. But —"

"And," I interrupted, pressing my advantage before Jenny could start in again, "as a matter of fact, I got Tamara a Hanukkah gift. A very nice menorah." This was a little white lie. To be honest, I'd forgotten all about Tamara while doing my holiday shopping. I wasn't about to let that on to Jenny, who would take it as further proof I didn't accept her lesbianism — I'd never forgotten to buy a gift for Anita, after all. Whoever said honesty is the best policy knew nothing about families.

"I didn't want to take a chance with clothes, not knowing her size," I embroidered, "and I knew she — well, both of you — must light Hanukkah candles. So I thought, even if she has a traditional candelabrum, you see artists making menorahs in such beautiful designs now...."

"I'm sure she'll love a new menorah, Mom," Jenny said, sounding like my sweet daughter again.

"I haven't wrapped it yet," I said hastily. "I ran out of Hanukkah paper, thought I'd pick up some more when I get groceries tomorrow. You can take it to her after the holidays," I added. "Unless she's planning to stop by here before then."

"She's not. It's like I told Daddy. We agreed not to see each others' families till we get our issues worked out."

"Your father thought the two of you seemed on the verge of breaking up," I ventured.

"Mom," Jenny said, the whine creeping back into her voice, "I told you, we've got to work on our issues. It's too soon to know whether we'll stay together or not."

I left Jenny to finish unpacking. Before going downstairs again, I jotted a reminder in my date book. I'd noticed a shop in Old Town that had a nice selection of menorahs not far from The Soaring Eagle. And as long as I was down there, I'd stop by and say hi to Naomi. Why not, I thought, with a surge of unexpected pleasure.

Mama called the day after Jenny's arrival to let me know she'd be coming for a visit along with Jeffrey's family, "hitching a ride" with them, as she put it. Right away, I knew I was in for it. As I confided to Lois in a forty-five-minute phone call, "Remember how you told me I needed to start an exercise program? Well, I'm about to start one: walking on eggs."

Not that this was new for me. I'd been walking on eggs with Rose since day one. But Mama and I usually got along famously, like two sisters, she liked to tell her friends. Since neither Mama nor I actually had a sister, she had an idealized view of sisterhood, according to *my* friends. But you get the picture.

Ever since Thanksgiving, though, my mother had been blaming me for not telling her — or warning her, as she put it — about Jenny.

"Because I didn't think it was my place to tell you if Jenny wasn't ready to," I'd explained to her at least half a dozen times.

"So instead you have to tell a whole restaurant full of people?"

"Mama, that wasn't my doing." I didn't remind her whose doing it was. No point getting her angry at her grandson. It was enough that she was so upset over Jenny, which frankly left me dumbfounded. It was what I'd expected from Rose, who blindly adhered to every Orthodox Jewish precept no matter how little sense it made. But not from my mother, a liberal Democrat, freethinker, and veteran of more civil-rights marches than she could count.

Yet it was my mother-in-law who seemed to be accepting Jenny's lesbianism while my mother — as if never to take the same side as Rose — was lining up with Dan to tacitly condemn it.

"I've been talking with Jenny over the phone," Rose had announced, also by long-distance phone. At least, thank goodness, she wouldn't be gracing our home with her presence, as long as the Hanukkah bush stayed up. "I was wrong to be angry with her. She hasn't changed a bit — she's still my same *shana maidel*. She can't help who she has feelings for. It's not as if she had married out of her religion, after all, or God forbid, converted like your son did."

So could Jeffrey help who *he* had feelings for? I kept the thought to myself. I wasn't up to starting in with Rose.

"And from what Jenny tells me, her friend is a very good influence on her," Rose went on, while I was biting my tongue about Jeffrey. "The two of them have joined a synagogue and keep a kosher kitchen. So at least one of your children is trying to be a good Jew."

But from the moment Mama arrived, with Jeffrey's family, the day after Christmas, she lost no opportunity to tell me that Jenny was just going through a phase. Normally, the way I get along with Rose is the way Dan gets along with Mama. Now, rather than running interference between my mother and my husband, I found myself on the defensive against the two of them.

"Jenny's just calling herself a lesbian to be fashionable," Mama said Saturday night after supper. Anita had taken Steffi up for her bath. The rest of us, with the exception of Jenny, who'd gone out to dinner with Adam, were having decaf in the family room. "All the college girls think they have to give up men to prove what big feminists they are. But it won't last."

Our daughter hadn't been a "college girl" for several years. Nevertheless, Dan lost no time in seconding her views. "Myrna, you've hit the nail on the head. And to prove it, she's started seeing her old high-school sweetheart again."

"She's seen a lot of him, but she's not *seeing* him," I protested, though weakly. Jenny *had* been seeing an awful lot of Adam.

Mama looked a bit confused at the distinction between seen and seeing. Sometimes I have to remind myself she is eighty-three. Jeffrey leaned forward to explain. "What Mom meant, Grandma —"

"What Sheila means," Dan interrupted, "is that she's made up her mind our daughter is a lesbian, and is doing all she can to encourage her in that lifestyle."

"To support her," I retorted. "And it's not a lifestyle. She's not living any differently than she would be if Tamara were a boy."

Mama, Dan and Jeffrey had all opened their mouths to speak when we heard the front door opening, and Jenny's footsteps heading toward the family room. "Hi everyone," she said. "Sorry to leave you guys while you're visiting, but since Adam landed a job as a reporter, he only has a few evenings free."

"So how was your date?" Mama demanded.

Jenny sat down next to her. "It wasn't a date, Grandma, just dinner with an old friend."

"But you enjoyed seeing him, didn't you?" Mama prodded.

"Oh, yeah, it's great that he's back in this area. We were good friends in high school, but then he went off to Chicago for college, so we're really picking up from where we left off six, seven years ago."

"Do you still find that much to talk about?" Anita asked as she came into the room. "I always find when I see friends I haven't seen for a while, there isn't that much between us. Once we're done with all the do-you-remembers, I mean."

"Oh, not Adam and me. We've been talking over everything. Our jobs, where we're going in life, what goes into maintaining a relationship with another person, you name it. He was talking tonight about how he finally feels ready to make a commitment, maybe even think about marriage. Say, is Steffi asleep yet? Let me go up and say good night to her."

The instant Jenny had gone upstairs, Dan turned to Jeffrey. "Well, Mr. Big Mouth, it looks like you'll have to let your in-laws' family know you were not only speaking out of turn last month, but dead wrong about your sister."

I'd been holding my breath, waiting for another blow-up between Dan and Jeffrey ever since he'd arrived the day before. Now, sure enough, Jeffrey yelled, "Dad, you are so full of —" at which point Anita broke in to head him off.

"I promised Steffi you'd be up to read her a story. She's waiting for you. Right now!" she ordered. I breathed a sigh of relief as Jeffrey stood up to obey her. I needed another family fight like I needed an extra twenty pounds.

Jeffrey clumped up the stairs, grumbling under his breath. "To get back to what I was saying," Dan told the rest of us, "Jenny hasn't mentioned Tamara once during this visit, and she's done nothing but rave about Adam. If you ask me, it's just a matter of time until this whole lesbian thing blows over."

My mother nodded. "It's what I was just saying. Dan, I always said I'd tell you if you were ever right. And you're right now."

Dan grinned at Mama and settled himself more comfortably in his chair. "You know," he said, "Adam always struck me as a mensch, even back in high school. Jenny could do a lot worse for herself. She definitely could do a lot worse."

"Then Jenny *has* gone back to her old boyfriend. I told you she would," LaVerne crowed at our next lunch bunch get-together. We were meeting at Jaleo, a popular tapas place near Pennsylvania Avenue. It was mid-January, the holidays finally behind us, the city bustling with excited preparations for the following week's inauguration of George W. Bush as president. I was more excited about the start of work on BAT's spring production just a few days away, even more so than usual since I'd talked Naomi into a commitment to work on the show. The only thing my friends wanted to hear, though, was news from the boyfriend front.

"All I said was that Jenny and Adam have had dinner together a few times," I said, trying not to notice the man at the next table lifting his fork in pleased anticipation as the waiter set down a slice of dark chocolate cake bordered by fresh raspberries in sauce. It was too soon after New Year's to break my annual resolution to lose weight. "You sound just like Dan. He's convinced himself it's just a matter of time till they announce their engagement."

"I'm going by what you didn't say. You haven't mentioned word one about that girlfriend of hers. Is she even still in the picture?" LaVerne demanded on a note of triumph.

It was true that Jenny hadn't brought up Tamara since telling me they had to "work on their issues." But I wasn't about to draw conclusions from that. Jenny had never confided in me the way I'd hoped.

"Actually, the main reason Dan's gotten all worked up is because of the sheets," I blurted without meaning to. Having opened my mouth, I had to go on and explain. "When Jenny left to go back to her apartment, she asked if I could lend her a set of sheets to use on their sofa bed. She said it was because they're having a houseguest stay a couple of weeks."

"So?" Natalie asked. She seemed distracted, and I wondered what was going on with her.

"So Dan says he doesn't buy her explanation of a houseguest. He thinks Jenny is planning to use the couch herself, that she just wants to save face by not moving back home. He says he wouldn't be surprised if the next thing she tells us is that Adam and she are setting up housekeeping." I took a last bite of spinach sauteed in olive oil with raisins, pine nuts and apples and put down my fork, carefully averting my gaze from our chocolate-devouring neighbor.

"Girl, that is one open-minded man. Shawna's father nearly blew a gasket when she and Dennis Jr. started shacking together. But I bet you anything he's right. Didn't Jenny go with Adam in high school? Maybe she had a bad experience with some guy she met in college, and overreacted by thinking she could give up men. But now that she's started seeing Adam again, she's come to her senses."

I started to shake my head when Marlene popped into my mind. "It's funny you should say that," I admitted. "There's a woman I met in PFLAG whose son broke up with his partner recently, and now he's living with a woman."

"Well, what did I tell you?" LaVerne said. "It'll be the same with Jenny."

"But on the other hand," I added, "her son was with his partner for years. So a couple of other people said he must be bisexual."

"Labels don't matter," LaVerne responded. "What's important is that Jenny find someone she can make a life with. And maybe I'm old-fashioned, but to me that includes a family and kids."

"And a good sex life," Natalie put in.

"Whose sex life are we talking about?" Lois asked, returning from the ladies' room, where she'd spent the last ten minutes.

"Not mine," Natalie said. "How can you talk about something that doesn't exist?"

I breathed a sigh of relief. My daughter's sex life wasn't something I was prepared to discuss. But now that Natalie had gotten started on the sad state of her sex life with Norman, I didn't need to worry. Sure enough, the next thing out of Natalie's mouth was, "It's nonexistent with Norman, at any rate. It's gotten so I've been thinking of having an affair."

"So what's new? For the last five years you've been thinking," Lois told her, with the exaggerated New York accent she always adopts after a few drinks. She was drinking sangria instead of wine this afternoon. She picked up her glass and drained it, and then started looking around for the waiter.

For Natalie to be thinking of an affair was nothing new. What came next out of her mouth was. "Well, actually — No, maybe I shouldn't say.

You girls promise you won't tell?"

Once we'd all sworn that wild horses couldn't make us tell, Natalie said, "I told you girls that I hired a new assistant coach at the gymnastics studio a few months ago? Roberto. Mexican, in his late twenties, and a sweet, sweet guy. And, drop dead gorgeous. Dark hair, dark eyes, moves like a dream. So last week," Natalie lowered her voice till we all had to lean together to hear her over the clatter of utensils and conversation surrounding us. The waiter approached, and she broke off.

"So last week," I prompted, once he'd taken Lois's order for another sangria and mine for black coffee.

"Well, just the two of us were left putting things away. We'd finished stacking the exercise mats when we looked at each other and, well, it happened." Natalie stopped and gave the same blissful sigh that our neighbor was giving over the last of his cake.

LaVerne shook her head. "I don't believe it! Right there on the exercise mats? I just don't believe it!"

"So don't," Natalie retorted. She took a sip from her water glass and laid her fork across her barely touched paella, from which the tantalizing scents of saffron and garlic still rose.

Lois picked up her spoon and started fishing the liquor-soaked fruits from the bottom of her glass. "Well, tell us the rest of the story. What was it *like*?"

"Like? Unbelievable, simply unbelievable. I'd forgotten what it was like to make love with someone young and — what's the word I'm looking for? And *virile*. An erection you could hang a towel on. Take all the time you want for foreplay instead of rushing to get it over with before it deflates."

LaVerne gave an involuntary sigh and I guessed that Dennis's prostate operation hadn't left him in as virile a condition as she'd made out a few months back. "But now what happens? Every day when you go into work and have to look him in the face?"

Natalie smiled. "That's the best part. All the anticipation. All through class and team practice when I watch him spotting the girls on the uneven bars, watch that *body* of his, and then think how in a few hours.... Let me tell you, it's like being a teenager and starting dating all over again. Plus, we speak the same language. Norman has two topics of conversation: his dental practice and the Redskins. And he's such a couch potato I keep expecting him to grow more eyes."

"And if he finds out?" LaVerne asked her.

She nodded to the bus boy to remove her plate. "I don't see how."

We woke to rain the following Sunday: cold, steady, drumming-on-the-roof rain, my favorite kind of weather for Sunday morning. Dan and I were cocooned together under our down quilt, and he turned to me as I stretched luxuriously. "It's so cozy lying here," I said sleepily, the way I do nearly every Sunday morning in winter. "I feel like a cat curled up in front of the fireplace."

"My favorite pussy," he murmured in return, as he always does. He reached down and stroked me between my legs until I purred with pleasure. I turned toward him, throwing one leg over his a moment, then pulling away so I could catch his nipples between my fingertips and give them the little squeeze that always turned him on.

Again in return, exactly as I was expecting, Dan cupped my breasts in his hands and began fondling them, burying his face between them and sucking on my nipples. My big bazooms — as Dan calls them when we're alone — have always been my best feature, as far as he's concerned. I worry that my waistline may be getting too big for his taste, but never my boobs.

I ran my hands through his hair as he nuzzled me, thinking back to when we were first married. I'd be sitting at the dinette table once I'd done the supper dishes, doing lesson plans and correcting homework. As I'd pick up one of my two colored pencils — blue to praise a perfect paper, red to circle mistakes and order "study your multiplication tables" — Dan would embrace me from behind, red leatherette chair and all. "How about doing that in the morning," he'd whisper into my neck, his hands slipping under my blouse to feel me up until I was as ready for bed as he was.

Now I found myself wondering just how many times we'd made love in the thirty plus years of our marriage. Once a day most weekdays, twice daily on weekends for the first year. Five times fifty-two plus four times fifty-two for Saturdays and Sundays. Seven days a week the next year so there would be one step less: simply multiply fifty-two by seven.

It would have to be an algebraic equation, I thought, opening my legs on cue as Dan finally slid his hands toward my crotch again. If X stands for one X-rated event and Y for number of times a year. Only Y would diminish annually for the next couple of decades, until stabilizing at our present Sunday morning routine. Too many variables to do in my head. Dan slipped the tip of his finger inside the way I like, and I gave a little squeal of enjoyment and left off my computations.

My hands slid down Dan's body, caressing him in the well-rehearsed routine that would excite him most efficiently. My senses were fixed on what was going on in our bed this morning now as we escalated toward that inevitable moment when I inserted a discreet dab of lubricating KY jelly — hormone replacement therapy helps, but not quite enough — and locked my legs around his thrusting hips.

It wasn't until that final burst of pleasure had died down that my mind wandered again, this time to Natalie's confession. What would it be like to go to bed with someone new, someone whose touch was not as familiar on my body as that of my own hands in the shower? To tentatively stroke a stranger, to feel unfamiliar skin under my own palms and fingertips? It must be like the excitement of a play's first read-through, where everything is still unsettled — blocking, pace, understanding of your character's motivation — compared to the comfort of settling into a role well into the production's run.

Chapter Eight

*B*AT's spring show was *Fiddler on the Roof*. I'd agreed to do set decoration and had talked Naomi into doing the scenery. New techies were harder to come by than new would-be actors, so when I introduced her to the rest of the production crew at our first meeting, I practically sang, "This is Naomi, everyone. I've roped her into doing scene painting — she's a terrific artist, wait'll you see. Naomi, these are our hosts, Jack, and his partner, Jim. Jack's producing and Jim is directing. Bill here is doing the set design; you'll probably be working pretty closely with him," I continued as I went around the room, ending up with, "I'm doing set dressing. So I'll be working closely with you too."

"And you said working on the show wouldn't take much of my time," Naomi said ruefully, a couple of hours later. I'd offered to treat her to a cup of coffee after the production meeting was over and we'd gone to a nearby Starbucks. I'd ordered a cup of black decaf; Naomi had a double mocha latte that steamed aromatically in front of her.

I laughed. "You'll love every minute of it, so stop kvetching." I took a sip of my bitter, calorie-free brew, then inhaled the delicious scent of chocolate rising from Naomi's glass. "That smells wonderful. I don't see how you keep so slim. I can gain five pounds just from looking at it."

"Excuse me a second," Naomi said. She got up, but instead of heading to the restroom as I expected, strode to the counter. Doubtless to get a cookie to eat with her drink, I was musing enviously, when she returned to the table and set a mocha latte squarely in front of me.

"What are you doing?" I sputtered. "I told you I'm on a diet."

"Diet some other time. I can't stand seeing you deprive yourself because you think every woman has to look like some anorexic Barbie doll."

"But —"

Naomi leaned forward. "But nothing. Drink up, or I'll go back and buy the fudge brownie too."

With a threat like that I had no choice. I sipped the latte, letting the rich, melted chocolate swirl over my tongue. "I should be mad at you," I told her when I could bring myself to set down the heavenly confection. "You don't know what it's like to have to count every calorie, not with your figure."

She shrugged. "I guess I burn them off waiting on customers. But frankly, I think most women look better with a little padding. Sexier. My first lover was twice your size and I loved every inch of her."

It was hard to picture Naomi, with her love of beautiful objects, falling for someone twice my size.

"It must have been her personality that attracted you," I said, reaching for my latte again. "Where did you meet her?"

"It's funny, but I don't actually remember the first time we met."

"Sorry, I didn't mean to pry. You don't need to tell me."

Naomi smiled. "No, I meant that I already knew her, years before I knew I was a lesbian. Before either of us knew. We were neighbors — and best friends."

"You're kidding!"

"Nope."

"It's hard for me to imagine." I paused to take another sip. "I mean, I've had a best friend for years too. We met in a course we took when we were expecting our first babies, Parenting First, it was called. In fact, she and I are friendly with two other girls from the same course. We still get together for lunch once a month, if we can manage it."

"But you can't imagine getting into a relationship with her?"

"We *have* a relationship. We're close friends, like I told you. We do things together, we confide in one another, tell each other our troubles. But a relationship like you're talking about, no. That I can't imagine. I mean it's not just that I can't imagine going to bed with Lois, which in my wildest dreams I couldn't. But when we get together, especially with LaVerne and Natalie, and we're all talking together, a lot of our conversation revolves around husbands. Or ex-husband, in Lois's case. It's like —" I paused to think. "Like one of those God's-Eyes they have kids make in day camp. You know, with four sticks wrapped with yarn to form a pattern. It's as if our relationship with men is providing the pattern, the structure for the way the four of us relate to one another."

Naomi nodded. "I like that. Your analysis, that is, not what it describes. I have no desire to have my relationships with other women circumscribed by the patriarchy." She smiled. "So if you can't imagine a romantic relationship with your friend Lois, what woman could you imagine one with?"

I stared at Naomi. "Why in the world would you ask me that? You know I'm straight!"

"That's what I used to tell myself too." She smiled again, wider this time. "I'm just teasing you. I was curious as to who you would pick."

I looked at her strong, expectant face. A little smile still hovered on her lips. Someone like you, I thought for a split second. I shook my head quickly, before she could read my mind. "No one, I'm afraid. Now offer me Robert Redford...."

She laughed, and I hastened to change the subject. "So what happened with you and your friend? You did say you split up, didn't you?"

Naomi shrugged. "It didn't work out for us to live together. But we're still best friends."

"That's more than I can say for any of the divorced couples I know," I said, Lois and the rat being a case in point. "But your present, um, lover doesn't mind?"

"I don't have a present lover. I was in long-term relationships with two other women after Melanie, and no, neither of them minded. But I'm single right now."

I could have sworn that queen-sized bed of hers had been rumpled on both sides, but maybe the cat had been responsible for that. "But you've mentioned your partner several times," I blurted.

"I have a *business* partner. She and I own The Soaring Eagle together."

"Oh. Then I must've misunderstood you. I thought when you said partner — my daughter told me the word lover is outdated now, that partner is the preferred term. So...."

Naomi laughed again. "You're right, partner is P.C. now. It's also a little confusing when you own a business with someone. Ginny and I used to work together, and both got disenchanted with social work around the same time. We pooled our resources to open the shop. We're good friends, but definitely not lovers. She and her husband just celebrated their twenty-fifth anniversary."

"So she's not a lesbian?"

"Is there some reason she has to be?"

"I just thought, since you're a lesbian...." I said, lowering my voice as the couple at the next table walked past us on their way out, giving us what I was sure was a curious glance.

"You don't need to whisper. I'm not embarrassed by the word lesbian."

"I just didn't see any point in broadcasting...." I stopped myself before I could offend Naomi any further. "Sorry. I remember you made a point of telling me that lesbian is a noun, not an insult," I added, enunciating clearly and unnecessarily loudly.

"My exact words. You've got a good memory," Naomi said, apparently mollified. "Anyway," she added, gathering up her used cup and napkin for the trash, "to answer your question, I have straight friends as well as lesbian. I don't know why that should surprise you. After all, you're my friend, aren't you?"

One double mocha latte shouldn't have made a difference in the fit of my good pants, I told myself the following morning as I struggled to simultaneously hold in my tummy and yank up the zipper. But even with my best panty girdle, it was clear they were headed for the out-of-size closet. That closet was already jam-packed with clothes, while the walk-in in our bedroom held fewer and fewer things I could actually wear. Besides the elastic-waisted warm-up suits I wore around the house, the only garment that still fit comfortably was the ethnic print dress I'd bought for Thanksgiving dinner.

The boutique where I'd bought the dress had sent me an advertisement a few days earlier for its winter clearance. The shop had been filled, I remembered, with clothes that were not only attractive but cut to be comfortable. I pulled on my navy warm-up suit — dark colors are the most slimming — and headed for Old Town. Two hours later, I left the store with a shopping bag full of bargains: two pairs of "daytime" slacks, presentable enough to wear to our ladies' lunches, three coordinated tunics that could be mixed and matched with the pants, and a dressy outfit of midnight-blue raw-silk trousers that fell into soft folds from a drawstring waist and a hip-length jacket in the same deep color but threaded with subtle vertical stripes of metallic silver thread.

On impulse, I had the clerk pack my warm-ups with my other purchases, and wore one of my new pairs of slacks with a top of hand-woven Guatemalan cotton. I might as well drop in at The Soaring Eagle while I was in Alexandria. It was Naomi who'd told me about the boutique in the first place; why not wear one of my finds to stop by and thank her?

A customer strolled past me out the door when I entered; Naomi was otherwise alone in the shop. "Well, hi! What are you doing in my neck of the woods?" she greeted me.

"Clothes shopping. At the place you told me about, Wardrobe for a Small World. I bought this outfit there," I said, slipping off my car coat to show her.

"Hey, that's a gorgeous tunic! It looks great on you."

"Well, thanks. Though I don't know that anything looks *great* on me at this weight. But at least it's comfortable, which is more than I can say for most of the stuff in my closet. You know, it's really your fault I had to buy new clothes. Encouraging me to stuff myself so I can't get into anything I own!"

Naomi laughed. "I still say you look fine."

"No really," I said, "I bought these for a stopgap. I'm going to lose weight and get back into the rest of my things. It's one of my resolutions."

"Why not just resolve to be happy with yourself the way you are?"

I gave her a look. "When I have a figure like yours, I'll be happy with myself the way I am." I began to pull on my coat again, then confessed, "But lately I keep cheating on my diet, not just last night. I don't know what's come over me. I think maybe it's because of *Fiddler*. Tryouts are next week and I've got my heart set on getting a part. I've been spending all my spare time practicing for auditions, and I've worked myself into such a state that I've been eating everything in sight."

Now I felt embarrassed. I'd mentioned to a number of people — Dan, Lois, a few friends at BAT — that I meant to try out "just for fun," but not how much I really wanted a part. Naomi just nodded calmly.

"Which part is it you want?" she asked me.

I was dying to play Tevye's wife, Golde, but I couldn't bring myself to say I was after one of the major roles. "Oh, I'd be thrilled just to be in the chorus. It's stupid for me even to try out for anything else. I've only had one part in my life since college that wasn't a walk-on, and even that wasn't in a musical."

"So? That's no reason not to try out. It's never stupid to go for what you really want."

"I'm planning to audition. I just don't want to get my hopes too high. Anyway, I've got to be going."

"Wait a minute." Naomi slid open the glass door to one of the under-counter display shelves, reached in to take something out, and came out from behind the counter. "Here, I want you to have this," she said, handing me what looked like a small carved charm on a black, silken cord.

"It's a bear fetish," she explained solemnly. "To bring you good luck in the tryouts."

I cupped the tiny, stylized bear in the palm of my hand. It was carved of sky-blue turquoise and wrapped in sterling silver wire that ended in a loop attaching it to the cord. "I can't just take this," I protested. "Let me pay you for it."

"I'm *giving* it to you. So to use a terrible stereotype, don't make me an Indian-giver." She reached out and took the fetish from me. Then she slipped it over my head. "Just be sure to wear it to the auditions, because a bear fetish not only brings luck, it brings confidence to its wearer."

She spoke with such conviction that she had me half convinced of its magical powers. I fingered the little bear, now dangling between my breasts, and smiled. "All right, I will. And thank you."

"You're welcome. And knock them dead at the auditions."

"I'll do my best." Impulsively, I reached out to give Naomi a hug. She threw her arms around me in return, the bear fetish caught snugly between our breasts as we bear hugged.

Mama brought me up to laugh at superstitions. So when I called to tell her that I'd landed the part of Golde, I didn't mention the turquoise bear pendant nestled between my breasts. But I stroked it gratefully as I said, "I still can't believe it! I'm pinching myself to see if I'm dreaming."

"So if you're dreaming, then who am I talking to on the phone? Seriously, why shouldn't you have gotten the part? You've always had a nice voice."

I had to admit, my voice wasn't bad. But it wasn't that spectacular either. I'd beaten out a couple of other women with better ranges, sweeter tones. Fortunately, Golde couldn't be summed up by the word *sweet.* Tevye's wife, Golde, has a sharp tongue that she uses as frequently as she does her kitchen knives.

What gave me the edge, according to Jim, who was directing, was an authentic "Jewish accent." Jim isn't Jewish. He's Catholic, though fallen away with a vengeance, and comes from an Irish-American family. Nevertheless he speaks with the same "accent" as me: neither Jewish nor a brogue, but Bronx, New York. I told that to Mama. "But I didn't go out of my way to point it out to Jim," I added. "I don't want him to change his mind and find someone else from New York with tons more acting experience than I have."

"Who says you have no experience? You're a mother, Golde is a mother. You have the — what's the word I'm looking for? The *life* experience to understand how to play her," Mama assured me.

"I suppose." I wasn't so sure I liked Mama's implication that I was typecast as Golde, whose only interest, outside of her constant tasks of cleaning and cooking for her family, was to marry off her daughters.

As if reading my mind, Mama asked, "So what else is new? What's going on with Jenny? Is she still living with that girlfriend of hers?"

"Her name's Tamara. And yes, she and Jenny are still living together. That's all I can tell you; I haven't exchanged more than two words with Jenny since the end of Christmas vacation. She says she's snowed under."

"So, maybe I shouldn't say it, but Jenny's not like you were. She doesn't tell you everything she's doing, the way you did me."

It still amazes me that my mother thinks I never kept any secrets from her. To this day, she believes I was a virgin on my wedding day. Before I could pursue the thought, Mama wanted to know, "What about that boy she's seeing? The one she used to go out with?"

"Mama, she told you he's just a friend."

"You're sure?" I could hear the letdown in her voice.

I was sure, except for one thing. But I didn't want to mention it, and revive my mother's hopes of Jenny leading a "normal" life. Or of getting up my own hopes, which I knew I shouldn't have, of Jenny coming around to heterosexual love and marriage.

I'd waited too long to answer, because now Mama, once again demonstrating her talent for reading my mind, demanded, "What, what is it? There's something you're not telling me."

"It's nothing, really, so don't make a big thing of it. But I stopped by the other night. Jenny had asked if they could borrow an extra blanket for the Hide-A-Bed. They have a houseguest and she said it gets cold in their living room with the sliding glass door. She doesn't think it's insulated glass."

"When you're not paying long distance, you can tell me about the glass. But if Jenny is sleeping in the living room —"

"You're not listening. I just told you, she says they have a house-guest. But what I was about to say, there was a big stack of magazines on their coffee table. And I couldn't help noticing that most of them were bridal magazines."

"*Bridal* magazines?"

"You know what I mean, all full of articles on how to get ready for your big day." The kind I'd dreamed of thumbing through with my daughter, the two of us jotting down ideas on wedding gowns, caterers and the most romantic setting to hold a reception. I didn't say that to Mama. Instead, I added, "And catalogs from places like Williams-Sonoma, with porcelain place settings and Calphalon cookware circled in red ink."

"Well, didn't you ask —"

"I was going to ask, you know, casually, if they were for some kind of class project. But then the phone rang and Jenny answered it. It was Adam calling her," I added, before I could stop myself.

"Adam! The boyfriend, right? Well, what did I tell you?"

"Mama, I already told you, they're just friends."

"Have you told Dan about the bridal magazines?" Mama asked, ignoring that last.

The last thing I needed was to put any more ideas in Dan's head. "There's nothing to tell him. For all I know, the magazines belong to their houseguest."

"If they even have a houseguest," she retorted.

"Mama, let's just drop it," I said.

I knew my mother, though. She'd manage to let it out, "accidently on purpose." So now I'd have to tell Dan, or Mama would do it for me.

The state of Jenny's love life could wait till I gave Dan *my* news. I'd phoned Mama as soon as Jim, who was directing *Fiddler on the Roof*, called to let me know that I'd gotten the part — right after I called Lois and Naomi. I hadn't tried to reach Dan, knowing he would be out of the office at a settlement.

So now, instead of just saying, "Hi, honey," from the kitchen as he walked in from the garage, I met him with, "You won't believe it! Jim cast me as Golde."

"Well, *mazel tov*! What did I tell you?" Dan planted a kiss on my lips, shrugged off his coat and tossed it onto the Victorian hall tree. I reached for it and hung it in the coat closet.

"We start rehearsals tomorrow evening," I told him.

"Then I take it this is the last decent meal we'll have for the next couple of months," he said, appreciatively sniffing the coq a vin simmering on the stove. "Just kidding," he added, before I could belt him. "You owe it to yourself to do something besides backstage work. In fact, I'd say this calls for champagne," he added. "Don't we have a bottle left over from New Year's Eve?"

He located the bottle in the refrigerator, popped the cork and poured two flutes. We took our champagne into the family room and sat on the sofa, Dan next to me instead of in his recliner. "*L'chaim*," Dan said, raising his glass as he gave the traditional Jewish toast — to life. Then he clinked his glass gently against mine — champagne flutes don't come cheap — and added, "and to your new life as an actress."

I sipped my bubbly and sighed happily as Dan's arm encircled my shoulders. I'd put a selection of dreamy big band tunes on the CD player earlier. The only light in the family room came from the fire I'd started in the fireplace. From where we sat, you'd never guess the stacked logs were made of ceramic and the roaring yellow flames had been started with a flick of a switch. Gas or not, there's nothing more romantic than a blazing fire, especially with the two of us alone in the house and the insulated drapes drawn across the sliding glass door. No one to see us, no one to walk in on us, a big, soft couch to stretch out on....

I set my glass down on the coffee table, rubbed my cheek against Dan's silver-blond stubble, and turned to give him a kiss. He returned it, his tongue sliding into my mouth and teasing mine. After a long moment, we drew back, I undid his necktie and slipped it from under his collar. Dan was still holding his flute; he took a last sip and set it down next to mine. Then he reached for me, took the necktie from my hand and folded it neatly.

"Well, I'd better get washed up for supper. It is ready, isn't it? I've got a ton of paperwork to get through tonight." He leaned forward, lips puckered, to give me a peck that just missed the corner of my mouth, and followed it up with his leer. "I'll be looking forward to Sunday morning," he breathed sexily, as he stood to head upstairs.

As Tevye might have said, would it have been such a crime to make love on a Wednesday evening? But my Dan was a creature of schedule. Sunday morning had become our time for "making whoopie" ever since he'd read — in a newsletter on *Keeping Your Love Life Alive for Life,* which we'd once subscribed to — that middle-aged men have their strongest erections first thing in the morning.

In any event, Dan *was* overworked this time of year; he gave tax advice as a sideline to real-estate law. And I had plenty to do with my evening as well. I wanted to make a good start on learning my lines, so as not to be totally dependent on the script at the first read-through the following night. And that meant I'd better start this evening. Tomorrow was our monthly ladies' lunch, and by the time I picked up Lois and brought her back, half the day would be gone.

By bedtime, I'd read through the script twice, marking my cues and further familiarizing myself with my lines. I slipped under the covers, looking forward to the beginning of rehearsals and to additional congratulations from Natalie and LaVerne.

I couldn't help looking forward to hearing about the progress of Natalie's affair as well. Having a friend confide in you that she's taken a lover is like watching a daytime soap — the totally safe titillation of surrogate sex. LaVerne, whom I'd spoken with a couple of weeks earlier, found Natalie's adventure genuinely shocking. But Lois and I agreed that if we were in Natalie's place we might well do the same. I drifted off to sleep, smug in the knowledge that Dan might wait till Sunday to make love, but, unlike Norman, when the time came he'd be able to do it.

Suddenly it seemed it was morning, wintry sun peeking through the center of the window where the drapes closed. Dan's side of the bed was already empty, the quilt shoved back on rumpled flannel sheets. Why not go thank Naomi for that good-luck charm in person, I asked myself. It was a bit out of the way to stop in Old Town before picking up Lois, but so what. One moment, I was lying in bed, the thought half formed in my mind; next thing I found myself standing in Naomi's shop, saying, "I just stopped by to thank you again."

She gave me her dazzling smile. "You're very welcome again. But we can't talk out here." She came from behind the counter, took me by the hand and led me through the curtained back doorway into the storeroom. We stood together in the shadowy darkness, next to cardboard boxes and a carved totem pole, and Naomi gave me a hug, as she had when she'd given me the bear fetish. Only this time her lips pressed against mine, the way no one but Dan's had for years. I found myself kissing her back. Why not? I thought. What harm could one kiss do?

The bear was between our breasts again, and Naomi reached a hand between us to finger it. "Told you he'd bring you luck at tryouts," she whispered, and went back to kissing me, while her hand now caressed my breasts until my nipples stood erect against her.

"Oh, is it a he?" I whispered back.

"No, you're right, it's a she-bear. A wonderful, warm, sexy she-bear. Like you."

I loved it when she said that. But I didn't want to stop kissing her, so I said, "Never mind the bear," and pressed my lips against hers yet again, my tongue darting in and out, playing with hers. My body was pressed against hers too, ripples of excitement radiating downwards till I moved my pelvis rhythmically against Naomi's, alive down there with electric tingles that sparked stronger every moment like an explosion about to go off.

My breath was coming as fast as if I'd been running for a bus. Naomi's breath came as fast as mine, and then a phone rang in her shop. I was so excited my legs were weak, so I clung to her and said, "Don't answer it."

"No, I've got to get it. But don't move. Wait right here."

I could see the totem leering at me, so I said, "No, I'll go upstairs and wait in your bedroom."

"Even better." She let go of me and ran for the phone, but it kept on ringing, so I reached out a hand for it.

"Were you in the shower, Sheila?" Lois's voice wanted to know. "I've been ringing and ringing."

I opened my eyes to rumpled covers. Not Naomi's. Mine and Dan's. My right hand gripped the receiver of the bedside phone, my left hand was still stroking between my legs.

"No, I must have overslept," I managed.

"Well, you'd better check your machine. It didn't pick up. I was just calling to let you know I'll be at the real-estate office, not my home office today. Pick me up there, okay?"

"Okay."

"You're still asleep. What did I say?"

"Pick you up at the real-estate office," I repeated. "Lois, I had the craziest dream," I told her drowsily.

"Tell it to me later. I've got to go."

But as I came fully awake, I knew I had no intention of ever telling her about it.

Chapter Nine

I'd been looking forward to excited congratulations from Natalie and LaVerne, but both of them had news that trumped mine. LaVerne's news was good. Her son, Dennis Jr., was finally marrying Shawna. The wedding was scheduled for the eighth of July. "Shawna figures she's waited this long, she might as well wait till she's out of maternity clothes. Why walk down the aisle in a maternity wedding gown? And you better believe her folks are tickled. They're going to go all out — half a dozen bridesmaids, so many flowers you'll think the church is a florist's shop. Our grandson, Denzel, is going to be ringbearer. The invitations aren't out yet; I'm still working on my list to give Shawna's mom, but you girls are on it so keep the date open."

Natalie's news was not so good. She'd been discovered by Norman, caught with her tights down and her legs wrapped around the waist of her young stud — to use Norman's phraseology.

"Thought you said there was no way he'd ever find out. What happened?" LaVerne demanded.

Natalie shrugged. "He walked in on us at the gymnastics studio. I forgot to lock the outside door. I turned off the light in the lobby like always, but somehow I forgot the door was unlocked. And you know that window with one-way glass for the parents to watch their little darlings from the lobby? Well...."

Lois set down her wineglass, and I laid my fork on top of my salmon fettuccine. (What harm could one splurge do, I'd reasoned.) All three of us stared at Natalie. In the fifteen years she'd owned Natalya's School of

Gymnastics, Norman had never deigned to drop by before. As far as he was concerned, the gym was her "little hobby" and hardly worthy of his high-paid time.

"Out of the blue, he just happened to walk in?" Lois asked, for all of us.

"He claims when I was late getting home, he got concerned I was having car trouble. I had a hard time starting it a couple of mornings last week. But I'm sure I told him I had the battery replaced since then."

"Then you must have given him some clue you were playing around," LaVerne told her.

Natalie gave LaVerne a look. "After thirty years of putting up with Norm's stuff without once being unfaithful, it seems to me that a few hours spent with someone who actually cares about me and my needs isn't exactly *playing around*."

"So what happens now?" Lois asked hastily, before LaVerne could respond. "You are staying together, am I right? After thirty years."

Natalie shrugged again, with what I was sure was forced nonchalance. I couldn't help noticing that her all-black outfit today made her look haggard instead of stylish. "We haven't gotten that far. Right now we're in a holding pattern, just circling around the subject."

"Why not ask yourself that question Ann Landers always asks, 'Would you be better off with him or without him?'" I offered. I didn't doubt the answer would be with him. Norman might not be the easiest person in the world to live with, but to give up on your marriage after all those years....

"Except that by letting him catch her, she's put the ball in his court," LaVerne said, with a touch of self-righteousness. "At whatever you want to call it — playing around or getting her needs met."

Before Natalie could take offense, Lois leaned toward her and took my feelings a step further. "Look, it wouldn't hurt to see a marriage counselor before you do anything rash. If you ask me, the two of you should've gone years ago. But if you do end up divorcing, make sure you get a damn good lawyer. You don't want to be left out in the cold, money-wise, the way the rat left me." She sat back, picked up her glass, put it down again. "By the way, don't let LaVerne upset you. Remember, she's an accountant, not a lawyer. It doesn't make any difference to a settlement who was stepping out on the other. And believe me, from a few of the things you've told us over the years, if I was married to a cold fish like Norman, I'd be playing around too."

The only playing around *I'd* done had been in my dream, but that dream kept haunting me. Which was unusual for me. Normally I forget my dreams by the time I sit down to breakfast, unless I tell them to Dan when I wake up. But this was one dream I hadn't told him about. I didn't know what he would make of it, but I preferred not to find out. I didn't know what to make of it myself, for that matter. I liked Naomi a lot, but not in that way. How could I? I was a married woman.

Still, I'd now met enough people, including Naomi, who'd married before realizing they were attracted to their own sex to know that being married was no proof of heterosexuality. It was one thing to accept that my daughter was a lesbian, but even to entertain such a notion about myself at this time in my life.... Which probably explained why I was lying in bed Sunday morning, whiling away the time waiting for Dan to wake up, making a list of as many sexual fantasies as I could remember that revolved around the male sex. A mental list. I wasn't about to write them down for him to come across. I doubted that sharing sexual fantasies about other men with your husband would be exactly what Ann Landers would suggest for improving your marriage.

I'd gotten to the one where I get cast as an extra in the film *The Way We Were*, starring my all-time movie idol, Robert Redford. It's back in the seventies, before I put on all this weight, and I'm wearing a red angora sweater with a deep V-neck that shows off my cleavage. I want to stand out. I want him to notice me.

But there are hordes of extras, and the only glimpse I catch of Redford is when I stroll down the sidewalk swinging a shopping bag from Bloomies in the scene where he and Barbara Streisand meet years after their divorce. Then as I'm starting for home after the day's shooting is done, he appears in front of me and smiles in a way that sends shivers right down to my panties.

"Don't go," he begs me. "The way you fill that sweater, I couldn't keep my eyes off you." He leads me to his trailer, shuts the door behind us and takes me in his arms. From outside I can hear the footsteps of people hurrying by, none of them knowing that a few feet away, *Robert Redford* is rubbing the palm of one hand in slow circles over the furry angora stretched taut over my breasts, then sliding it into the V-neck to tease my erect nipples, while the other deftly creeps up my back to unhook my bra.

Or that I'm so weak in the knees, I have to press up close against him, my pelvis throbbing against his hard thigh in a rehearsal of the pleasures awaiting me. Or that he whispers, "Beautiful, God, you're so beautiful. If only you were my leading lady," as he lays me down on a soft couch.

When he smiles I see an echo of Dan's, only sexier, so much, much sexier. And who wants to remember a husband at a time like this? So I shut everything else from my mind but the thrill of running my fingers through that tousled blond hair, caressing his muscular shoulders and tight butt. My pelvis is rocking against him, my legs parting, and I feel — Dan's hand on my shoulder.

"You awake?" he whispered. "Ready for some action?"

I opened my eyes and smiled at him. "Uh huh."

"You're grinning like a Cheshire cat. What were you thinking about?"

I grinned wider. "You," I said.

That afternoon at PFLAG, after Marlene had updated us on her son's continuing heterosexual romance, I volunteered my own confusion over the meaning of Jenny's renewed involvement with Adam. "And then I went and told my husband about his calling her, and about the bridal magazines in her apartment. So he's sure that she's gotten through her 'lesbian phase' — that's the way he put it — and is just trying to ease out of her relationship with Tamara without a lot of hurt feelings. And to tell the truth, I was beginning to think the same way."

I paused a second after that confession, all eyes on me. "But then the very next day, Jenny called to say she hadn't meant to be rude taking Adam's phone call while I was there, it's just they had so much to talk about, she wasn't thinking."

"Did you ask her what was going on between them?" Candy Sue cut in, too eager to wait for me to tell my story my own way.

I shook my head. "I didn't want her to think I was prying. Or, assuming Dan is wrong, that I suddenly didn't accept her lesbianism. But I did say, you know, kind of casually, that I hoped she and Tamara wouldn't be too busy to drop by. That maybe they could come for dinner on a night I didn't have rehearsal. I thought that would give her an opening if she wanted to tell me anything. So then she said that it wasn't just a case of being busy. That she and Tamara are seeing someone she called a couples counselor. And this counselor advised them to limit their contact with the rest of the family until they've worked through their issues together. So that's why she hasn't brought Tamara over since what happened at Thanksgiving. And I suppose why she hasn't talked much with Dan and me lately either — so we won't start in asking her a lot of questions she isn't ready to answer. In fact, she didn't stay on the phone with me more than a couple of minutes altogether."

I looked around the circle. With the exception of Candy Sue, everyone looked happy for Jenny and Tamara, had started nodding in relief when I'd told them about the counselor. "But since then, I've been wondering whether I ought to tell Dan about them seeing the counselor, or just wait and see if they get things worked out between them," I went on. "I mean, now that I've got him thinking they're about to break up, I suppose I ought to set him straight. But on the other hand, he's in such a good mood over what I told him already that maybe I should just leave well enough alone until something happens one way or the other."

"Well if you want my top-of-the-head feelings —"

I nodded affirmatively at Chuck, a newish member of the support group, who'd admitted last month to being a therapist himself.

"As I hear what you're saying, you don't want to exclude Dan from the loop. You want to do your best to keep the relationship between your husband and your daughter on an even keel. Would that be an accurate summary so far?"

I wasn't sure that's the way I would have phrased it, but it sounded close enough, so I nodded again.

Chuck stroked his beard, a graying Vandyke. "I empathize with your feelings. You remember how I had to get over my own hurt when I learned that my son had come out to his mother six months before he approached me with the news. And that I was angry with my wife for not sharing it with me at the time. But once I had a chance to process, I realized she did the right thing. In the long run, whenever you allow yourself to become a go-between for two other people, you're actually impeding the growth of their own unique relationship. Your daughter and your husband need to work out their communication problems on their own. Their relationship will be stronger in the end — the way it became for my son and myself."

It had never occurred to me that Jenny and Dan needed to work at developing a relationship. *I* was the one who had always felt odd man out from their easy camaraderie. But who was I not to take the good advice of a psychologist?

Especially when it gave me the smug feeling of knowing that, for a change, my daughter was closer to me than she was to her father.

For the next few weeks, my life revolved around the upcoming production of *Fiddler*. Jim had increased our rehearsal schedule to four evenings a week, which meant I was usually leaving the house just as Dan got home from work, our conversation consisting of my reassurances that his dinner was keeping warm in the oven.

Not that I minded a heavy rehearsal schedule. Golde was a major role and I'd be onstage in front of my closest and most critical friends, not to mention my entire family. Mama, Rose, Jeffrey and Anita would be driving down from New York together.

Mama had told me she'd be there opening night as soon as I told her I'd landed the part, and Jeffrey and Anita had assured me they "wouldn't miss it for the world," despite the fact that Anita would be in her seventh month by then. Rose would be there as well. I doubted she'd have made a special trip to see me in a play. But the first night of Passover was just two days after opening night, so it fell to me to make the Seder. Though she'd have preferred to prepare it herself in her own kosher kitchen, there was no way Rose would skip a family Seder. And she did let slip that *Fiddler on the Roof* was her all-time favorite musical.

"How many musicals have such feeling, such a Jewish heart?" she told me over the phone. "In fact, if you ask my opinion, it's funny you should be playing Golde, who keeps every tradition, who teaches her children to make marriages in their own religion."

I didn't point out that one of Golde's daughters winds up marrying a Christian anyhow. Or tell her how sick I was of her constant digs about Jeffrey. Why prolong a conversation with Rose any longer than absolutely necessary? I managed a civil goodbye and hung up before I should start bleeding all over myself from biting my tongue.

I was more worried over my lack of acting experience than whether Rose thought it was incongruous to cast me as Golde. The last thing I wanted was for Jim to regret choosing me for the role, or to damage BAT's reputation as a theater.

For one reason or another, perhaps our start as a "haunted" house, or the play-reading committee's consistent choice of family fare over cutting-edge drama, or the cats that had free run of the place and wandered onstage unexpectedly or curled up in the lap of some audience member,

BAT had never been ranked with the most prestigious amateur theaters in Northern Virginia. Not to mention that Phillipa was land-poor, and a good chunk of the liquid assets she did leave was earmarked for the lifetime care of her kitties. Technically, we were in the bargain basement. Our sound equipment needed replacing; our computerized light board was obsolete.

Still, we had one advantage over most community theaters: Owning our facilities meant we didn't need to share our space with any other group. We didn't need to tear down our set after Saturday night performances to accommodate church services Sunday morning. Nor did the construction crew have to build sets on a cold parking lot outside some self-storage unit and schlep them to the theater in a rented truck. Our crew could work comfortably in the workshop we converted from Philippa's garage. Or, with a set like the one we needed for *Fiddler*, build the whole thing right onstage.

Which meant, now that construction was done and set painting about to begin, I couldn't help but run into Naomi.

Not that I'd been avoiding her. I'd just been too busy to drop in at The Soaring Eagle for a schmooze. But when I walked into the theater for rehearsal four weeks before the show opened, I found that the set crew had finished construction and Naomi was already putting the finishing touches on one of the two shutters of Tevye's ramshackle home. Our youngest cat, Nudnik, sat alongside her, apparently watching with critical interest.

Nudnik is a long-haired black cat who showed up at BAT on Friday the thirteenth a couple of years back, rubbing against my legs and meowing for a handout, doubtless guided to us by some feline grapevine. Philippa's will didn't require us to take in additional stray cats, but, as I explained to the rest of the board, it was undeniably what she would have wanted. We could scarcely turn away a black cat who appeared in a haunted house at the stroke of midnight during the teardown of *Bell, Book and Candle*. I wanted to call her Midnight, but Sam Blumenfeld overruled me. Her name means pest in Yiddish, and it fits her to a tee.

Nudnik ran to me, meowing, as I walked onstage, breaking Naomi's concentration. She turned to look at me, and then smiled. "Hi stranger."

"Hi yourself," I said. Nudnik continued meowing, and I bent down and scooped her up. "You don't belong in here," I scolded. She purred in response, perhaps because I was simultaneously rubbing her behind the ears the way she liked. "Sorry," I told Naomi. "The kitties are always sneaking in."

Her smile widened. "I don't mind. As long as she doesn't lend an actual paw to the painting. So you're a cat person, too. You didn't tell me."

For an instant I could barely breathe. Was there some hidden meaning in her remark? Hadn't we discussed the bond between lesbians and their cats? So now, after what had happened between us, did she assume that I — I gave myself a mental shake. What had gone on between us had been in my dream, of which Naomi was naturally oblivious. No wonder she was staring at me so quizzically now.

"This one's a sweetie," I answered. "She's charmed everyone, even the non-cat people. But I'm not supposed to be here. I forgot you were starting on the painting tonight. Jim told everyone we'd rehearse in the house so we won't get in your way. I'd better get over there before I hold things up."

Naomi nodded. "But how about coffee later?"

I hesitated only an instant. I'd missed talking with Naomi the past couple of weeks. And whatever I'd dreamed about her, it was hardly likely she'd had the same dream. "Okay, great. I'll come get you when rehearsal is over."

We were rehearsing the scene where Tevye awakens from a terrible dream: Golde's grandmother has returned from the dead to warn them against going through with an arranged marriage between their oldest daughter, Tzeitel, and a wealthy but much older butcher she doesn't love. The dream is a fabrication on Tevye's part to keep Golde from finding out that he has already given in to Tzeitel's pleas to marry her childhood sweetheart. Tevye and the rest of the company enact his nightmare, which culminates in the return of the butcher's dead wife, Fruma-Sarah, full of rage and threats of vengeance at the thought of her husband remarrying. While the others — particularly Fruma-Sarah — had a frenzied dance number, I merely had to sit up in bed listening with exclamations of increasing horror until I concluded that if my dead grandmother had taken the trouble to appear to us, we should take her advice and let Tzeitel marry her sweetheart.

I thought the scene went well. But Jim had nothing but criticism. "Grandma Tzeitel needs to make her entrance earlier, Phyllis. You should appear on the scene as soon as Tevye starts across the stage to greet you. Pat, you're coming on too low-key. Fruma-Sarah has to inspire fear. The chorus should be quaking in their boots when they call you the 'butcher's dear, darling, departed wife.' Keep in mind you want Tevye pissing in his pants when you grab him by the throat. His daughter is about to steal your husband and you're giving him a taste of what *she'll* get if he doesn't call off their wedding."

He glanced down at his notes again. "That brings me to you, Sheila. You need to work on your motivation. You're letter-perfect, but it's not enough to mouth the lines. Golde has her heart set on seeing her daughter married well, and now she's decided they have to go back on their agreement with one of the richest men in town and let Tzeitel marry a poverty-stricken nobody. You've got to show me the emotions that brought about that change of heart."

"I'll try," I said, struggling up from the cushions we'd laid down on the practice-room floor in lieu of a bed.

"Don't just try. Try harder. Seriously, talk to me before you leave tonight. I'll give you some pointers. Okay, everyone. I want to run through this whole scene again Sunday afternoon, starting 2 p.m."

I gave a mock groan. "I'll have to miss the PFLAG support group. That's exactly when we meet."

Jim gave me a look. "Tough. You know what a rehearsal schedule is like."

As producer of the show, Jack had been sitting in on the rehearsal. He came over to Jim and me as the rest of the cast started filing out and asked, "Is everything all right, Sheila? I know it can be rough when children first come out to their parents and —"

"I'm fine about Jenny," I said, interrupting him before he could offer to find someone to stand in for me Sunday and precipitate a fight with Jim. Anyway, how could I tell my closest gay friends that I was too upset about my daughter coming out to me to miss a support group meeting eight months after that fact? "I was kidding. I know we need the rehearsal time. It's just that our support group has gotten to be like a soap opera that's only on once a month. For instance, one of the women has a son who told her he was gay years ago, and he was in a relationship with another man most of that time. But now he's fallen in love with a woman. And half the group says he was really bisexual all along, and the other half says —"

"He's not," Jim cut in. "Maybe he's gone back in the closet for one reason or another. But if he was with another man all those years he's gay. Period. You don't suddenly change sexual orientation the way you'd change your clothes."

Jack grinned in the mischievous way he has when he thinks Jim is getting a touch too strident. "Oh, I don't know about that, sweetheart. I've been thinking lately I could go for some attractive lady. Particularly if she was a rich widow."

Jim burst out laughing. "Right. And be sure and tell her how much BAT needs a new light board while you're at it." Still laughing, he grabbed Jack by the shoulders and kissed him. With no one but me left hanging around — and presumably the mother of a lesbian daughter could be counted on to understand — Jack put his arms around his partner and kissed him back. When they finally let go of each other, Jim stood grinning at Jack. "And if she can make you feel like this, I'll eat my words."

I found Naomi cleaning paintbrushes; we headed for Starbucks again. This time I ordered a Chocolate Brownie Frappuccino without her twisting my arm, and sat sipping the rich chocolate with pleasure.

"How did your rehearsal go?" she asked me, after I'd complimented the work she'd done so far on the scenery.

"So-so. The dancing had a lot of energy, but Jim really tore into everyone's performances. Particularly mine."

"Oh?" Naomi folded her hands under her chin, waiting for me to continue. She'd dressed to paint flats in an old gray sweatshirt that complemented her short, silvery hair. She'd left her jewelry off, making her appearance more than usually androgynous but nevertheless awfully attractive.

"He told me I need to work on my motivation. So I asked him afterwards what he meant, and he said that I hadn't convinced him that I believed in Tevye's dream and was willing to change my daughter's whole future on account of it. He says I've got to remember that I'm — that is, my character, Golde, is — a superstitious woman. And that I would have no trouble believing my grandmother would come back from the afterlife and warn me off the butcher."

Naomi had been listening with what appeared genuine interest, not like the perfunctory attention I might have gotten from Dan or the lunch bunch. "So why do you think you have a problem with it?"

"I was just asking myself that. Actually, till I talked to Jim a few minutes ago, I hadn't realized how much I was conscious of playing a part in that scene. It's a little hard to explain."

"Take your time," Naomi said, in that warm, attentive way of hers.

"Well, I think — it's not that I'm having a problem remembering the lines or anything. I don't even *have* a lot of lines in the dream scene. I've just got to listen and be horrified by the danger that my grandma has warned us of. But the thing is, I was brought up not to be superstitious. Everything else in Golde's character comes easily to me. I can understand the kind of hard life she has, from remembering my grandparents' stories. And the way that affects her marriage. And I can believe how much she wants for her daughters to have an easier life than she has. But I don't believe in people coming back from the dead. And I've never believed that dreams have any meaning."

So what about the dream I'd been struggling to forget the past few weeks? I'd been concentrating on my problems playing Golde, but the images of that dream now came back in an embarrassing rush. I forced them to the back of my mind. "So I guess all that is coming through in the way I play the scene," I concluded.

"Uh huh," Naomi said. We both sipped in silence a moment. "Maybe you need to look at it from a different perspective," she said finally. "You're saying you can't get into your character because you don't believe this dream is some kind of visit from the supernatural. But suppose you look at it the way a modern woman who's not ignorant of psychology would, as a message from your subconscious?"

"But it's Tevye's dream, not Golde's," I protested.

"That's okay," Naomi said calmly. "Golde can still find a message for herself, a message *from* herself. For instance, how about this? Golde's own marriage was arranged, wasn't it?"

I nodded. "That was the tradition then. That's what the play says, anyway."

"So Golde had no choice but to accept it," Naomi continued. "She's been married to Tevye twenty-five years, and, as one of her lines says, she just 'supposes' she loves him. Now she and Tevye are arranging for *their* daughter to marry someone she doesn't love. But say Tevye's dream takes Golde back to the time when she was a young girl and still had romantic fantasies. When she might have been secretly in love with someone other than Tevye. Do you see what I'm saying?"

"Well...."

Naomi reached across the table and put her hand on mine. I tried not to jump. No electric sparks, I assured myself. Just a hand, warm and a little dry. "Put yourself in Golde's place. That's what you have to do, right?" she said, retrieving her hand and reaching now for a spoon to scoop out the foam remaining at the bottom of her cup.

"Right." I wasn't sure if that was how Jim — or his god, Stanislavsky — would have phrased it, but it seemed to me to get at the essence of motivation.

"Then instead of worrying about whether you believe in ghosts, think about how this dream is reminding you of how you felt when you were Tzeitel's age. How it's brought back all kinds of memories and emotions that you haven't let yourself dwell on in quite a while, but are still there in your unconscious mind. And whether you want to put your daughter through the same unhappiness, even if she will be better off financially. Does that make sense to you?"

I nodded again, vigorously this time. "That's it! Of course! And you know, Tzeitel's sweetheart, Motel, was always coming over to their house. Golde brushes it off because he was her friend since they were toddlers. But I bet, underneath, she realized that the two of them were in love. So then, if hearing Tevye's dream brings back all those memories and makes her empathize with her daughter like you said, she can justify breaking the agreement they had with the butcher and letting Tzeitel and Motel get married. Which was the advice her grandma was giving, according to Tevye."

I'd been babbling so excitedly that Naomi laughed. "Glad I could be of help."

"I don't know why I didn't figure it out for myself. Just because the play has Golde taking the dream literally doesn't mean I have to."

She smiled. "Maybe you would have come up with another interpretation that would work just as well for you."

"Maybe. But I've never been good at interpreting dreams. I think they're fascinating, but...."

"But you no doubt took a psychology course in college that taught that the images in dreams had only one interpretation. Probably Freudian. I take dreams very seriously, myself. I think they're an important route to self-knowledge. But the two of us could dream about the same thing, and it wouldn't have the same meaning for you as it would for me."

I nearly *plotzed*. Surely Naomi didn't also dream that she and I —

"For instance," she went on. "Say we both dream that we're on a crowded dance floor with our partner," she smiled, "or your husband, for you. Suddenly you realize that everyone else has gotten off the floor and is just watching the two of you dance. Wouldn't that have a different meaning to you if you were an expert dancer who participated regularly in dance contests than if you were the kind of dancer who described herself as having 'two left feet'?"

No, of course she hadn't! It was a purely hypothetical situation. "That makes sense," I said. "But what if —"

"What if what?" Naomi asked, when several moments had gone by without my finishing my question.

I shook my head, appalled at myself. Had I actually been on the verge of blurting out, *what if you suddenly found yourself dancing with a partner of a different sex than you expected*? "I can't remember what I was going to say," I mumbled. "Chalk it up to menopause. Does terrible things to your memory."

She laughed again. "Don't I know! Well, let me know if it ever comes back to you."

Chapter Ten

N ow that I'd broken the ice with Naomi again, we got together for coffee a few more times on the nights she and her helpers were painting scenery. The insights I got from her seemed to do the trick. At least, after Sunday's rehearsal Jim grudgingly admitted that my performance had improved. (Jim's praise is always grudging until the show is actually up.) "He says I've gotten the feeling he was after, and that's a lot coming from him at this point in the show," I reported to Naomi on the phone the first Sunday evening in April. "He was really pleased with the whole scene. In fact, he admitted that the show is coming together."

That was a good thing as opening night was the following Friday. Only four more rehearsals and we'd be performing in front of an audience. And eight of the seats in that audience would be occupied by members of my family.

"I've reserved a block of eight tickets," I told my mother on the phone Tuesday night.

There was a moment's silence during which I knew my mother was whipping out her pocket calculator to check my arrangements. My mother deals with the memory lapses that come with age by a strict reliance on electronic gadgets. "Eight," she said after another second or two. "Rose is still coming?"

"Far as I know."

"I'll look forward to seeing her," she fibbed.

"That makes two of us," I said, and we laughed together.

"And Anita told me she's letting Steffi stay up for the show," Mama went on. "So eight tickets means you've gotten one for Jenny and one for whoever she's coming with. Any chance she's coming with her old boyfriend, or will it still be that roommate of hers?"

I hadn't talked with Jenny in the past week or two. Now I gave her a call.

"Just wanted to double check arrangements for opening night. It's this Friday, remember. Do you and Tamara need a ride to the theater?" I asked, not prying, but leaving an opening for Jenny to volunteer any change in her love life.

Which she didn't. "No, that's fine. Tell Daddy not to worry about picking us up. He'll have enough people to arrange for as is."

Jeffrey and the rest arrived at our house so late that I barely had time to get supper on the table before leaving for the theater, and no time to eat myself. Not that I could have eaten anything, in any case. The butterflies in my stomach left no room for food.

I parked in the rear of the lot, surprised to see Naomi's van already there, over an hour before the start of the play. Naomi herself was backstage in the crowded women's dressing room, with a paint-spattered rag of a man's shirt thrown over what looked like a dressy sweater and slacks.

"What are you doing here so early?" I asked her. "I thought you were going to watch the show from out front."

"I am. But there was a last minute emergency with the scenery."

Just what we needed opening night. "What kind of emergency?" I said. Emergency or not, I was running late and I had to get into my costume, so I stowed my purse and began unbuttoning my blouse.

"There were several lines of scratches on one of the flats — on the outside wall of Tevye's house."

"Who would have done something like that?" I demanded, before realizing the answer to my question. Naomi had already reached the same conclusion.

"It looked like cat scratches," she told me.

I hung my blouse on the rack alongside the street clothes of the other women changing, slipped off my shoes and undid the zipper on my slacks. "And I bet I know just which one it was." I tugged the pants down and stepped out of them. "Nudnik, my sweetie of a stray. This is the thanks I get for taking her in. You know I'll catch the blame, even though I always check for cats when I go in or out of the theater."

112

Naomi laughed. "Whichever one it was didn't sign its work. Anyway it was easily fixed. I don't think the audience will notice. But I'm the one who knew what colors were blended for each flat, so I had to come repaint it," she added. "And as long as I was here early, I thought I'd pop into the dressing room and tell you to break a leg."

I turned back to Naomi from hanging up my slacks, suddenly acutely aware that I was standing in front of her in nothing but my bra and panties.

"Thanks," I said, and slid the dress I was to wear over my head so fast that I got it back to front. My first scene was during the preparations for Sabbath, when Golde would still be wearing a faded old housedress. The dress, a thrift shop find, had had a long zipper running up the back from waistline to neck, which the costume designer had replaced with Velcro. So now I stood in front of Naomi with that Velcro undone from throat to navel.

When Naomi stopped laughing, she asked, "Need some help?"

"I can manage," I said quickly, yanking the dress over my head and turning it around. I put it on properly and then remembered that I did need help after all. I could hardly walk past Naomi to ask anyone else. "Actually, if you could just zip me up. Velcro me up, that is."

"No problem," Naomi smiled. "Here, turn around. And relax," she added as her fingers slid up my spine, causing me to shiver involuntarily. "Everyone gets stage fright before opening. You're going to be terrific."

At least Naomi had put down my reaction to stage fright and not to her presence in the dressing room. Why shouldn't she? The room held over a dozen women, everybody in the middle of changing from street clothes into costumes. I'd undressed in front of them without a qualm the night before. So it made no sense for Naomi's being there to bother me. I had no reason to think she was interested in me or that she'd come to ogle me.

"Thanks," I told her again. "It's hard not to get stage fright. But I'd better hurry and get my hair covered now." A Jewish woman in the Orthodox culture portrayed in *Fiddler on the Roof* would never appear in public with her head uncovered, so I'd be wearing a scarf or hat of some kind throughout the show. I reached for a tube of gel to slick down my hair, hoping Naomi would take the hint and go. Instead, she stood and watched while I shoved my gelled hair back from my face and covered it with an old fashioned hairnet of the sort my grandma used to wear. My hairdresser would have died if she could have seen what I'd done to her hard work.

For the Sabbath meal, I was to wear a figured silk square, but in this scene — where I was still cooking — I wore a faded cotton scarf that could have passed for a dustrag. It was tricky to tie on myself, so I looked around for Sally, who was working wardrobe. I spotted her across the room, helping one of the two little girls who were the youngest of my five stage daughters.

"Want me to fix it on you? I'm good with scarves," Naomi offered. She folded it into a triangle, then positioned the flat edge across my forehead. "Hold your finger here," she directed, moving behind me. I could feel her hands on me again as she pulled the ends into a secure knot. Her breath was warm on the back of my neck. She reached around to make sure the scarf was still centered in the middle of my forehead, her breasts pressing into my back, and I found myself holding my breath.

"There," she said, and the pressure was gone. "Let me check to make sure your hair isn't sticking out anywhere, and then we'll put some bobby pins in to hold it." Hearing Naomi's nonchalant voice, so completely unaware of my awareness of *her*, I flushed with embarrassment all over again. After all, I thought, as I sat down to put on a pair of low-heeled black oxfords, I was the one who'd dreamed about her, not the other way around.

This wasn't the time to worry about dreams. I could feel a trickle of nervous perspiration between my breasts as the hubbub of arriving audience members filtered backstage from the lobby. Chatter backstage died down, so that we wouldn't be heard out front, and in the relative quiet I could hear the musicians tuning their instruments, a sign that there were only minutes left before the start of the play. The crowded dressing room smelled of make-up and sweat. My stage-fright had increased tenfold, and I was certain that not another person in the cast could be as scared as I was.

I should have worn my bear pendant. The notion flashed through my mind as I moved into position to be ready for my first entrance. Then the poignant melody of the fiddler on the roof sounded, Tevye spoke his first line, and I was oblivious to everything but my concentration on the show. As if in a dream, I entered on cue along with the rest of the chorus, the mamas and papas of the village.

Then I was opening my mouth and singing "Tradition," not quite believing I was actually onstage, singing in front of an audience.

At the conclusion of the song the scene changes from the village street to the interior of Tevye and Golde's house. Golde is preparing the Sabbath meal when Yente the matchmaker arrives with news. Wanting to talk with Yente privately, Golde tells the children they can go and play. "You have feet? Go," I said to the two youngest and was surprised by the sound of laughter from the audience. It wasn't *that* funny a line. Just then I heard — and felt — the reason: a plaintive meow followed by Nudnik rubbing up against my leg.

For an instant, as the audience's giggles doubled, I was about to *plotz*. Tzeitel, who had the next line, was dumbstruck, and the two little girls, who should have exited already, were standing there staring. *Think*, I commanded myself. What would Golde do? Then it came to me. I bent down and scooped up Nudnik, turned to the less excitable of the two children and thrust Nudnik into her arms. "And take your cat with you," I ad libbed. "If the good Lord intended us to keep cats in the house, then why would He have created barn mice?"

The appreciative burst of laughter that followed made me feel suddenly at home in Golde's kitchen.

Despite crossing paths with a black cat, the rest of the show went off without a hitch. I was mobbed by family and friends in the lobby after we'd taken our bows. Dan presented me with a huge bouquet of red roses, then said, practically singing out the words, "Will you look who's here with Jenny!"

I turned to Jenny, half hidden behind Anita and Jeffrey. At her side was not Tamara, but her old boyfriend, Adam. "It's good to have you back with us again," Dan boomed out, while Jenny was congratulating me.

"I'm glad to be back here as well." Adam turned to me. "Congratulations, you were great!"

"It was so sweet of you to come," I said.

"I wouldn't have missed it. Not once Jenny told me you had one of the lead parts. I had no idea you were such a good actress, Mrs. Katz," Adam said.

"She's been hiding her light under a bushel basket," Dan told him. "But I think you'll see her onstage a lot more from now on. By the way, Adam, no need to be so formal. Dan and Sheila are fine."

Adam smiled and said, "Well, it was good seeing you all again."

"Adam has to get up early, so we're going to leave now, Mom," Jenny told me, while Dan was telling Adam yet again how glad he was to see him. The noise level in the lobby had increased so that Jenny had to speak right into my ear as she added, "Tamara wanted me to give you her regrets. She's having a lot of cramps with her period, and the only thing she's up to is curling up with a heating pad. So she told Adam to use her ticket. But she is planning to see the show — probably next Saturday evening."

She and Adam left. I was hugged in turn by the rest of my family: Jeffrey, Anita, a sleepy Stephanie, Mama, and even Rose. "A wonderful show," she told me. "Such a beautiful celebration of Jewish life, I think God will forgive me for riding in a car Friday night to see it. And you weren't half bad as Golde, either," she added.

"Not bad!" Mama said. "Well that's damning with faint praise!" Seeing Rose's puzzlement, she translated for her benefit. "You don't have to be so stingy with your compliments, Rose. Sheila was terrific in the part!"

"So did I say she was awful? In fact —"

Whatever Rose was about to add was interrupted by the lunch bunch, maneuvering their way to me through the lobby, which was jam-packed with the rest of the cast members and *their* friends and family. Naomi was on their heels. While I was introducing her to the others, Jim and Jack came up to us.

"Quick thinking with that ad lib," Jim complimented me, then couldn't resist adding, "though if we ran this place like a theater instead of an animal shelter, we wouldn't have so many feline walk-ons."

I had to admit he had a point: it was a joke among local theater groups that BAT was staging the area's longest running production of *Cats*. Before I could come up with a reply, Jack asked, "Are you all joining us at the cast party?"

Steffi was half asleep in Jeffrey's arms, and the rest of the family looked equally ready for bed. I was wondering how rude it would be not to accompany everyone home when Jeffrey said, in his sweet, understanding way, "I think we're all tired, Mom. Why don't you go on to the party and celebrate? We have all day tomorrow and Sunday to visit."

I woke up late on Saturday — the consequence of staying at the cast party till one in the morning — to find the others already done with breakfast. Cold cereal. Loss of one Brownie point with Rose for me. My mother-in-law may not turn on her own stove on the Sabbath, but that wouldn't have stopped her from eating heartily of the cheese omelettes I had meant to prepare. I'd have to make up for it tomorrow.

My son and his family, plus Mama, were in the family room, still in their robes. I gave Steffi a kiss, barely disturbing her concentration on her Saturday morning cartoons, and sat down with them.

"Dan took Rose to services," Mama informed me. "So while they're out, tell me. What was Jenny whispering in your ear last night?"

It took me a minute to figure out what Mama meant. "No big secret; she was just explaining why Tamara couldn't make it last night."

The phone shrilled. I murmured "Excuse me," to Mama and hurried into the kitchen to answer it. It was Jenny, asking if I needed help getting ready for the Seder the next day.

"It's sweet of you to offer," I told her. "Actually, I'm finished with everything that can be done in advance."

"Well, in that case, I think I'll stay for the Shabbat luncheon after services at Bet Chaverim." Bet Chaverim was the gay/lesbian synagogue she and Tamara had joined. "We discuss a weekly Torah section afterwards and this week's topic is pretty interesting. Oh, but then —"

"But what?" I asked.

"Well, I was planning to come to the house to visit after. But I have to be at Bet Chaverim tonight too. There's a community Seder tomorrow, and I promised to help with food preparation. Actually, Tamara's the one on the food committee, but I'm taking her place because she still has bad cramps. So if I stay for the Shabbat lunch and discussion, there won't be any point in my coming to the house. I'd have just a half hour or so before I had to turn around and head back. But I hate to disappoint Grandma by not spending any time before the Seder with her."

Jenny had two grandmas visiting this weekend, but I knew which one she meant. She'd been Rose's favorite and vice-versa from infancy. "Your Grandma Rose won't be here herself. She went to services with your father, and they're eating lunch at the deli afterwards."

"Well, in that case...." Jenny said.

"But I'll tell you what your Grandma Rose *would* enjoy," I said, suddenly inspired. "If you take her out to a kosher restaurant for brunch tomorrow. Somewhere the two of you can have a nice long schmooze. To be perfectly honest, that would be more help to me than anything you can do in the kitchen. I have plenty of people here already, and you know Rose is older than Mama — I don't want her to overdo." What I really didn't want was to have Rose looking over my shoulder all day, having a fit if she found a stray crumb of bread left in my cabinets.

Jenny knew that, of course, but it was better left unspoken. She said, "That's a great idea, Mom. Oh, I almost forgot! Adam was going to go out of town but his plans fell through and he didn't have a Seder to go to. I knew you wouldn't mind if I invited him to join us."

Jeffrey and Anita decided to drag Steffi away from the TV and take her to the Museum of Natural History to see the dinosaurs. With no one else home, I told Mama I was taking her out to lunch.

"Jenny's boyfriend is a looker," she said to me, once we were sitting in a booth at Applebee's, waiting for our order of Caesar salad and iced tea. "Tall, dark and handsome. They make a very striking couple."

"They always did look good together. Remember how they were crowned king and queen at their senior prom in high school?" I still had the picture in one of my albums. Who would have known, looking at Jenny glowing in Adam's arms, how things would turn out? "But Mama, remember not to slip up and call him her boyfriend anymore. They're just friends now."

The waiter set down our plates. Mama took her silverware from the napkin it had been wrapped in and placed the fork and knife across her plate so they wouldn't pick up germs from the table, then spread the napkin on her lap. "They're just friends, and yet the two of them came to the play together last night?"

"Because Tamara couldn't make it, so he used her ticket."

Mama picked up her fork and put it down again. "I forgot to ask if they use pasteurized eggs in the dressing."

"I'm sure they do, Mama."

"I just hope you're right. Food-borne illnesses are increasing, you know. You can't be too careful." I sighed loudly and she finally ate a forkful of salad. "But to get back to Jenny," she went on between bites, "when I was here at Christmastime she was going out with him. And now it's over three months later, and they're still going out. How many times have you seen the girlfriend in all that time?"

Only when I'd stopped by their apartment. "Tamara hasn't been to our house lately. But —"

"Don't give me buts. Let me finish what I was saying," Mama commanded. "Jenny hasn't brought her by for months. And last night she was out on a date with what's-his-name, Adam, in a place where she knew she'd be seen by dozens of people she knows. If you ask me —"

"It wasn't a date, Mama. I told you. Tamara had bad menstrual cramps. Otherwise she would have come to the play with Jenny. The two of them are still together."

I could see that took the wind out of Mama's sails, but after a sip or two of iced tea, she came back with, "Still together in the same apartment, you mean. But you told me that Jenny's sleeping on the sofa bed in the living room."

"When did I ever —"

"You expect me to remember the date of every conversation at my age? Back when you told me about dropping in on them to lend Jenny a blanket for the Hide-A-Bed and finding all those bridal magazines."

"Well, since you remember every word I say so well, then you know I told you they had a friend staying there then."

"Tell me, how did I come to raise such a naive daughter? You never heard *friend* used as a euphemism before? Remember Marjorie, who got pregnant in high school, and who came to ask me if I knew where her *friend* could get an abortion? And —"

"Okay, okay, you've made your point. But if they're on the verge of breaking up, then why would Jenny have invited Tamara to our house for the Seder tomorrow?"

Mama only paused a second. "Well, didn't you tell me that Tamara is from the Midwest? Maybe she wasn't able to get home for Passover. You know, even a secular Jew wants to take part in a Seder at Passover, and if this girl is as religious as you've told me, it could be that Jenny invited her simply because she didn't have another Seder to go to. You know how thoughtful Jenny is."

"I know, Mama. In fact she's asked Adam to join us tomorrow because his plans fell through, but —"

"She's invited Adam for tomorrow!" Mama set down her fork and gave me her full attention. "Can I say something, Sheila?" It was the kind of rhetorical question that didn't require an answer, so she didn't wait for one. "It was a shock for you, a big adjustment, when Jenny told you she thought she was a lesbian." Mama lowered her voice as she uttered that word, even though we were in a high-backed booth, with noisy conversations going on all around us. "But she's your daughter, you love her, so naturally you tried to accept it. I'm sure it wasn't easy for you," Mama added, and I nodded.

"But you worked hard at it, you went to that support group, and you finally got used to the idea. And now you've succeeded so well at seeing Jenny in a new light, that you can't accept the possibility that she might have only been flirting with a sexual preference that wasn't right for her."

"But, Mama —"

She shushed me. "Let me finish. You don't have any trouble accepting that Jenny went for years with a boy, and that now they can just be friends instead of boyfriend and girlfriend. Is it so impossible that she may have ended her fling with that girl, but still be friendly with her? Friendly enough to room with her still, and to ask her to your house for Passover?"

For a moment, my mother almost had me convinced. Naomi was still best friends with her ex-lover, wasn't she? And look at Marlene's son. Hadn't he fallen in love with a member of the opposite sex after breaking up with his partner? Jenny *had* been seeing a lot of Adam, now that I thought about it. It could just be that they would end up as a couple after all! I might yet be a mother-of-the-bride. My mind filled with visions of mother-daughter shopping trips to bridal salons, florist shops, caterers, of every seat in the temple filled as Jenny and Adam stood together under the wedding canopy....

"Is it so impossible, Sheila?" Mama repeated gently.

Abruptly, my little fantasy bubble popped. How could I have forgotten that Jenny had told me, just weeks earlier, of the work she and Tamara had been doing with the couples counselor? And that Tamara hadn't been to our house the past few months only because the counselor thought it would strengthen their relationship in the long run to limit contact with our family?

So, most likely, Jenny planned on bringing Tamara home with her again because they'd finally mended their relationship, rather than — as Mama suggested — simply so that Tamara could sit down to a family Seder. "Mama," I started, about to set her straight, when the bus boy came over to ask if he could take our plates. In the moment or two that he spent clattering them onto his tray, I remembered the advice that Chuck — the therapist with the gay son — had given me at PFLAG. It wasn't my place to repeat everything Jenny had told me to the family at large. When Jenny was ready to update the others on the state of her relationship with Tamara, she would do so on her own.

So now, as I signaled the waiter to bring me the check, I said only, "I don't suppose it's impossible, but I'm not the person to ask. If you want to know more about what's going on in Jenny's life, you'll have to ask her."

Mama and Rose spent the afternoon resting, while Dan entertained Steffi, and Jeffrey and Anita helped me run last-minute errands. I had no intention of cooking supper, so that evening, after the usual argument over what restaurant Rose could bring herself to eat at, we headed out for Chinese as we always did. We went in two cars so I could leave for the theater right from the restaurant. Jeffrey and my mother came along to see the play again, while the rest headed home. The three of us dropped by the cast party afterwards; Mama said she didn't mind, and Jeffrey was eager to shmooze with the old-timers who remembered him from back when he'd started taking children's classes at BAT. Everyone, including Dan, was asleep by the time we got home.

Sunday morning, Jenny took Rose to brunch, while Dan and Jeffrey took Steffi to the National Zoo. Mama, Anita and I set the table and cooked the meal. By the time everything was done, there was barely time to shower and change. Which explains how I never got around to mentioning to Dan that Adam was coming to Seder, until he was actually standing at our front door that evening.

When we sat down fifteen minutes later, Dan was beaming so broadly over Adam's presence that he could have been posing for a toothpaste commercial. His good humor was only increased by the fact that Tamara wasn't there — still under the weather, in fact she thought she might have a touch of stomach flu, Jenny had told me hurriedly as I checked the roast chicken.

From his vantage point at the head of the table, Dan surveyed Adam, Jenny and the rest of us with the fond regard of a biblical patriarch. I lit the holiday candles and said the blessing over them, hoping Rose noticed that I was as capable of being observant in real life, when the occasion demanded, as onstage. Then it was up to Dan to lead us through the rest of the service. As part of the Seder, wineglasses are filled four times. I'd set out grape juice for Steffi. For the rest of us, I'd bought several bottles of a good, kosher Israeli wine, instead of the syrupy sweet Mogen David that had been the only wine on our parents' Seder table. Though, just as I'd expected, while the wine was being passed around to fill the glasses for the first time, my mother-in-law demanded, "You don't have any Mogen David? Nothing but that sour-tasting stuff?"

"Right here, Rose," I told her, passing it down. "I remembered it's your favorite." I winked discreetly at Mama, who likes to think of herself as something of a wine connoisseur.

Dan continued the service with the blessing over the wine and we all raised our glasses for the first cup of wine. Jeffrey, Anita, Jenny and Adam took only a few sips of their "first glass." But after knocking myself out with preparations all day, I *needed* a drink. Mama's glass too was nearly empty when she set it down, with Dan and even Rose not far behind.

In the Orthodox tradition, the entire company would then have washed our hands at the table. My good damask cloth was crowded enough with nine place settings, our sterling candlesticks, and the varied Passover symbols without finding room for finger bowls for everyone. In addition to the wine there was Elijah's cup, to welcome the prophet and offer hospitality to strangers; the Seder plate with three matzos, symbolizing the unleavened bread the Jews ate on the flight from Egypt; a roasted shank bone of lamb, representing the sacrificial lamb of Passover; a roasted egg, representing the burnt offerings brought to the Temple in olden days; the parsley, symbol of springtime; horseradish or bitter herbs, as a reminder of the bitterness of slavery; and haroset, the mixture of apples, nuts, cinnamon and wine that resembles the mortar the Hebrew slaves used as they built Egypt's monuments. But to placate Rose, I'd set a bowl by Dan's plate for him to rinse his hands in. After he'd dribbled water over his hands, the blessing was said, and the parsley was passed around, dipped into the salt water that symbolized the tears of suffering, and eaten. Dan broke the middle matzo in half and, with a little sleight-of-hand, hid half for Steffi — as the only child present — to find later.

Holding the Seder plate, Dan began reading, "See the bread of suffering which our forefathers ate in Egypt. All you who are hungry, come eat with us! All you who are in need, come, celebrate the Passover with us. This year we are here. May next year find us celebrating the Passover in Israel. This year men are enslaved; may next year see them free." The wineglasses were filled again and though it wasn't yet time to drink another ceremonial cup, I noticed Mama take a few sips.

"Well," Dan said. "Your turn, Jenny." By tradition, the youngest child asks the Four Questions, which are then answered by continuing the retelling of the story of Passover. As the youngest, Jenny had continued asking the questions long past childhood. But now, she shook her head.

"Not me, Daddy. Steffi's old enough. She's getting to be a big girl."

Steffi, of course, was delighted. "I'm gonna be five soon. And Aunt Jenny's gonna help me."

"We went over them together a little while ago." Jenny turned to Steffi. "Remember the first one, Steffi?"

She nodded. "Why we can't eat bread with supper, and we have to eat...."

"Matzos," Jenny prompted, after a moment. The rest of us sat beaming as Steffi — with help from Jenny — got through the rest of the Four Questions asking why this night is different from all other nights.

"Good job," Jenny and her parents told her, nearly in unison.

"Not just good. *Beautiful*," Rose said. "Such a smart girl you are to remember all that in one afternoon. Such a pleasure to see her learn a little bit of her heritage," Rose went on, speaking now to the rest of the table rather than Stephanie. "Even if her father has given up being a Jew."

I've always thought Jeffrey must be a saint to put up with Rose without blowing up. But my sweet son just said to her, mildly, "You know I still consider myself Jewish, Grandma."

"So what kind of person says he's a Jew, but then he gives up his own faith and goes to church every Sunday?" she came back at him.

"But I haven't given up my faith. Christianity is a house that's built on a Jewish foundation. I still believe the Old Testament. I've just *extended* my beliefs. Once you start to study —"

"Study nothing! Your daughter, here, should be learning the Jewish religion, but —"

"Rose, enough already!" my mother cut in, just as Anita was about to open her mouth to explain how they were planning to teach their kids about Judaism when they were old enough to understand, the way she had the last time Rose started. "Jenny has a guest here, remember."

Jenny was sitting by Rose, and now she touched her shoulder and reminded her, "We need to get on with the rest of the Seder, Grandma, or we won't answer the Four Questions for Steffi."

"You're right, darling. So what are we waiting for? Are we having a Seder or not?"

Everyone but Steffi then read along with Dan, "We were Pharaoh's slaves in Egypt, but the Lord our God rescued us with a mighty hand and an outstretched arm. If He had not brought our forefathers out of

Egypt, then we and our children and our children's children might still be enslaved to Pharaoh in Egypt. Therefore, even if all of us were men of learning and understanding, ripe in age and wisdom, and well versed in Torah, it would still be our duty each year to repeat the story of the exodus from Egypt."

The Haggadah continues with pages of commentary and elaboration. I could see Steffi's eyes glaze over with boredom by the time we reached the ten plagues and sang a rousing chorus of "Dayenu," saying that each of God's miracles by itself would have been sufficient to satisfy us. Then we ate the matzo with the horseradish and haroset, Dan read the passage commanding each generation to look on themselves as having been personally brought forth from Egypt, and after another blessing for the wine, we drank the second cup. Finally, it was time to eat — despite Rose's grumbles over the few pages Dan had skipped.

I filled everyone's bowls with homemade chicken soup and matzo balls, and for a few minutes heard nothing but the sounds of satisfied slurping. Then Adam said, "This is delicious, Mrs. Katz. I really appreciate you folks letting me join you on such short notice."

Dan waved away his thanks. "No need to stand on ceremony with us. I hope you consider this your second home."

"How are your parents?" I asked. Adam's parents had moved to Vero Beach, Florida, two years earlier, after his father took early retirement.

"Fine, thanks. They love Florida, play golf three times a week."

"But they must miss you at their Seder table," Rose said. "I'm surprised you didn't make a trip down there."

That was just like Rose, to criticize a boy she hadn't seen since he was in high school. Adam didn't take offense. "I planned to. But I got a last-minute assignment, and if you want to get anywhere in the news business.... And Jennifer originally planned to go down with me, but —"

"Really!" Dan cut in. "Well, we're absolutely delighted that you and Jenny could join us here," he said, just as Jeffrey asked, "Are you with the *Washington Post*?"

"With the *Journal* — they have a chain of suburban papers," Adam said, as I started to clear the soup bowls. Jenny jumped up to help me carry them into the kitchen and bring out the gefilte fish.

"From a jar you got this?" Rose demanded, after her first bite.

Sometimes my mother-in-law leaves me speechless. From the corner of my eye I saw Mama about to start, but before she opened her mouth,

Jenny said, "It's my favorite kind, Grandma. But really, the point of the Seder isn't what we eat, is it? It's getting together as a family, to celebrate our deliverance from slavery. And then to turn our joy at our own freedom into a commitment to work for freedom wherever it's denied people in today's world."

Jenny was the only one in the family who could get away with telling Rose off like that. Rose patted her hand, beaming, and said, "You're right, darling. It's to celebrate our Jewish religion that's important, not what we eat. I can eat gourmet some other time. And you," she added, turning to Adam. "You're also religious?"

"I try to be. I guess a lot of people in our generation have gone back to being more observant than our parents."

"Good for you!"

Before Rose could add any more about which member of Adam's generation was *not* an observant Jew, Mama — who'd been rolling her eyes at me since Rose's remark about the fish — said, "Sheila, I'd ask for seconds on the gefilte fish, only I don't want to spoil my appetite for your roast chicken. But would you mind passing the wine? I'd like a glass with dinner. The good stuff, not the Mogen David."

I passed her the Israeli wine. She'd been drinking more than usual, but then who wouldn't if she was sharing a room with Rose? The wine was making Mama a bit more combative, not rising above Rose's little jabs the way I tried to. While I was trying to come up with a change of subject, Dan did it for me, turning to Adam to ask, "Now that you've landed a newspaper job, do you see much of a future for print journalism?"

"Oh, I think so. Newspapers have a readership base among older readers, and that's the fastest growing segment of the population. But in terms of my own career, I'm trying to position myself to be able to move into Web technology when the opportunity arises."

Dan was nodding approvingly when Mama said, "And what about the rest of your future plans?"

I gave Mama a look, which she chose to ignore. Adam looked at her inquisitively.

"A little bird told me there are wedding bells in your future."

Adam smiled. "Jenny told you about the engagement? Everything's still up in the air, as far as actual plans go. I mean, I haven't even told my folks yet, because we've had a lot of issues to work out. But we have gotten to the point of beginning to discuss living arrangements. And I guess

Jennifer is already trying to pull together some ideas for the ceremony itself. I know she's collected a stack of bridal magazines at any rate."

"What did I tell you!" Mama said triumphantly. Everyone looked at her, with the exception of Jenny, who had started whispering a simplified explanation of the Passover service to Stephanie. "So when are you planning to let your parents know the good news?"

"Mama, don't be so nosey," I said, but Adam gave a good-natured laugh.

"That's okay, Mrs. Katz. It's not like it's a state secret. Actually, we had hoped to break the news to my folks over Passover, but the way it's worked out I'm not sure just when we can get down there. I'd like to tell them in person, not just in a phone call."

"But was I right or was I right?" Mama demanded. "Didn't I tell you yesterday, Sheila, when we had lunch together?"

It was obvious my mother was building up to embarrass Jenny, who I was certain would have confided in me if she and Adam were planning to marry. Not to mention Adam, who was already looking discomfited over Mama's inordinate interest in his wedding plans. I should have told her to watch it with the wine, I thought, as I gave her another look. "Mama, please, let's drop it."

She ignored that too. "And you, Jenny. You don't want to make an announcement either?"

Jenny broke off telling Steffi that her grandfather had hidden a piece of the matzo for her to find later, and looked at Mama, startled. "What did you say, Grandma? I wasn't listening. I was trying to explain a little more about the Seder to Steffi."

"I said Adam just said he doesn't want to tell his family about getting married over the phone. But here you are with your whole family gathered. What better time to share your news?"

"Well, I do have an announcement. But I really wanted to tell Daddy and Mom privately first."

I nearly jumped out of my skin. Was Mama right, after all?

From the opposite end of the table, Rose called down, "You have news for us, darling?"

"She's getting married!" Mama answered for her.

Jenny turned to Adam. "You went and told them?"

"No, all I told them about —"

"That you're making wedding plans," Mama broke in. "Go on,

Jenny. It's too late to keep us in the dark."

"You're gonna get married, Aunt Jenny?"

Jenny smiled down at Steffi. "Well, yes, honey, I am. I mean, we are, going to have a wedding ceremony, but —"

But Dan cut her off. "*Mazel Tov*! This is the most wonderful news you could have given us! Right Sheila?"

I was sitting with my mouth open wide enough to catch flies, my heart suddenly pounding in my chest with excitement. "Well, it's quite a surprise, but —"

"I knew it would be, Mom," Jenny said. "That's why I wanted to tell you and Dad before everyone else. And of course to wait till Tamara could be here with me. But she'll be thrilled that you and Dad are so —"

"Tamara?" Dan broke in. "What in the world does she have to do with it?"

Jenny stared at him a moment. A long moment. "Tamara and I are planning to get married. We can't marry legally, of course, but we are going to have a wedding ceremony. And make our vows to each other." Another moment of dead silence went by. "What did you think I meant, Daddy?"

Chapter Eleven

For a few instants, everyone was dumbstruck. Then Rose asked, "This is some joke you're making, darling?"

At the same time, Mama said, "But we all thought you and Adam — He just told us —"

Jenny had kept her eyes fixed on her father's face, but now she and Adam gave each other a look of surprise. "Me and Adam!" she said. "Why would you think that? You know I'm a lesbian."

"But he *said*. Not five minutes ago. I asked him about his plans and he said, 'Jenny was going to go to Florida with me, Jenny is getting ideas from bridal magazines.' Your mother told me, you and that girl broke up, it's why you've been sleeping on the couch and —"

"I never said —" I protested.

Adam broke in. "Wait. There's a misunderstanding here. I thought Jenny had already told you all that I got engaged a few weeks ago."

"I don't think I ever got around to it," she said. "I don't know where you got all that other stuff, Grandma, about me and Tamara. I told Mom she and I were seeing a counselor to get our relationship back on track."

"Well thank you for mentioning it, Sheila," Dan snapped. "And letting us all make fools of ourselves."

"Who's eating his words now, Dad?" Jeffrey put in.

Adam, obviously trying to smooth things over, said, "It's a natural mistake, Mr. Katz. My fiancee's name is Jennifer. So Jenny's grandmother just misunderstood when I was talking about her."

"Who would expect such a coincidence? Two Jennys?" Mama said.

"Grandma, Adam said *Jennifer*, not Jenny," Jenny informed her. "And it happens to be a very common name."

Anita, in the soothing tone she used when Steffi was upset, said, "Well, anyway. So you and your friend are planning some kind of commitment ceremony?"

"Right," Jenny said, sounding mollified. "Actually we're planning a regular Jewish wedding under a canopy. We've been talking with our rabbi about adapting the traditional liturgy. We haven't set a date yet, but it'll be late this summer sometime." Jenny took a breath. "So that's my announcement."

"Plan it for a three-day weekend, if you can," Anita suggested. "It's a long drive with kids. You are having it in Washington?"

"Yeah, all our friends are in this area. It'll be at our synagogue. Bet Chaverim."

"We'll be looking forward to it," Anita said. "Won't we, Jeffrey?" she added, and Jeffrey got out of his seat and came around the table to give Jenny a hug. "Congratulations! I mean, *Mazel tov*! Give Tamara our congratulations too. I'm glad you guys worked things out."

Jenny hugged her brother back and gave Anita a radiant smile. Then she took another breath. "Well, like I said before, I know this is a surprise, and if there's anything you want to ask me. Mom?" I felt like a poor student too much at sea even to frame a question. I managed to shake my head, though Jenny, her eyes again focused on Dan, didn't notice. "Daddy? Do you have any questions?"

"Just one," he said slowly. "Have you completely lost your mind?"

"I still don't see why you had to tell Daddy all that stuff about me and Tamara breaking up," Jenny said accusingly. It was the following evening, and I'd driven to her apartment after she'd hung up on me twice. I'd figured, rightly, that she might bring herself to slam down the receiver on her mother, but not to leave me standing out in the hall.

Adam had explained the whole mix-up during the rest of the Seder dinner: he and *Jennifer* had met in college, but broke up when career plans took them to opposite coasts. *Jenny* was a platonic friend; she'd acted as a sounding board while he and Jennifer tried to rekindle their relationship. They'd worked things out and Jennifer had been Jenny and Tamara's houseguest while interviewing for jobs in the area; she couldn't stay with Adam because he was staying with friends himself at the time.

Jennifer, now Adam's fiancee, would be moving to D.C. to start her new job in June.

Now, with Tamara out for the evening, and just the two of us sitting on opposite ends of the sofa, I retorted to Jenny, "I told you last night, I never said anything like that to your father. I told him you wanted to borrow some bedding for your sleep sofa. Period. The rest came from my mother. You know how older people can embroider things. I might've mentioned to her that you had a bunch of bridal magazines lying around. But just to make conversation," I fibbed.

My explanation met with angry silence on Jenny's part, so I counterattacked. "Besides, don't you think *you* should have told Daddy about you and Tamara getting counseling? The reason I didn't, as a matter of fact, is that I got some advice from a therapist." I carefully didn't mention that it was "top of his head" at a support group meeting. Instead I went on, "And he told me that I shouldn't be interfering in your relationship with your father by doing your communicating for you."

Jenny shrugged.

I held my tongue.

"I suppose you're right," she said grudgingly, after a moment. "But how was I to know he had all those ideas about me getting back with Adam? And that he would freak out over Tamara and me having a wedding ceremony?"

"I had no idea he was so much in denial myself," I fibbed again. "You know he doesn't like to open up about his feelings."

"But he said he accepted me. When I first came out to him, he said all he wanted was my happiness."

"He does, sweetheart. I know he does," I assured her, all nurturing mother at the unhappiness in her voice. "He's just...well, parents go through stages, and sometimes it's two steps forward and one step back. We talk about it a lot at PFLAG. Having a commitment ceremony was a step he just wasn't ready to hear about. You know, maybe you — and Tamara too, the two of you — should come to a support group with me. A lot of times you get better insights from people facing the same issues who aren't members of your family."

"Mom," Jenny said, with that old exasperation in her voice, as if I was the one who'd blown up at her the night before. "Okay, I'll talk to Tamara. I suppose we could go to a session of the support group with you and Daddy if you think it'll help. But having a wedding isn't an issue that we're going to negotiate about. We love each other and we're committed to each other just the same as — as Jeffrey and Anita. And we're going to get married just the same as them. I mean, not according to the state of Virginia, but *we'll* know we're married."

To tell the truth, I felt in danger of taking a step backwards myself. I'd accepted Jenny's relationship with Tamara — or thought I had. But the image of the two of them *marrying* — standing under a wedding canopy together — had thrown me for a loop. While I was struggling for words, I remembered what she'd said about coming to PFLAG. "Sweetheart, I'm afraid it would just be the three of us going to the support group. You know Daddy isn't into that kind of thing."

"Mom, I really don't care whether Daddy goes to the support group. But I want him to be at my wedding!"

Jenny sounded so close to tears that I moved over to sit beside her and put an arm around her shoulders. "Well, it's not like you have it scheduled for tomorrow," I said. "I'm sure that given some time to adjust to the idea —"

"Mom," Jenny broke in. "What about you?"

"What about me?"

"*You* understand why we want to have a wedding, don't you? I mean, I can count on *your* support, can't I?"

If the truth be told, I wasn't sure I did understand. But I wasn't about to tell the truth. Not the truth, the whole truth and nothing but the truth. Instead, I said, "Of course you have my support, sweetheart."

"Thanks, Mom," Jenny said, with what sounded like a giant sigh of relief. She suddenly threw her arms around me and we hugged one another fiercely.

As far as I was concerned, Chuck's advice had backfired, the only desirable consequence being that Jenny was now showering me with confidences in a way I'd wished she would for years. But at home, I went back to my old role of smoothing things over, giving Dan the same explanation that I had given Jenny about not wanting to interfere with their relationship.

"The two of you have always been so close, I just assumed you and she were talking. But honey, you really hurt her feelings by jumping down her throat the way you did. She had no idea that you would react like that. After all, you did tell her that you accepted her when she came out to you."

Dan gave me a look. "Of course I accept her. What did you think, I was going to disown my own daughter because she says she's gay? But this idea of some mock wedding ceremony —"

"I know, it's pretty unexpected. It was a big surprise to me, too. I didn't realize she was thinking of anything like that. But honey, if she and Tamara are certain they want to stay together, then it's only natural for them to want a commitment ceremony." I carefully avoided the word wedding. "You weren't upset when Jack and Jim invited us to their commitment ceremony a few years ago," I suddenly remembered.

"Jack and Jim aren't my daughter," Dan snapped.

I thought back to what Marlene had said the first time I'd gone to PFLAG. "It's always harder when it's your own child," I told him. "But we've got to make the effort. Maybe you should go to the next support group with me."

Dan gave me another look. "I've already told you I'm not interested in sitting in a room with a bunch of strangers exchanging confidences." He walked into his den and shut the door behind him.

With a house full of company, Dan and I had skipped our usual lovemaking Sunday morning. That might have explained why I felt a bit horny by Wednesday. But not why I'd awakened from another X-rated dream about Naomi. Once again, I'd stopped by The Soaring Eagle. This time, the phone didn't intrude on our kisses. She led me up the stairs to her bedroom with its unmade bed and pulled me down next to her.

"Aren't you wearing your fetish anymore?" she inquired, when we stopped kissing for a moment to take a breath. I murmured, "That's for me to know and you to find out." So her hand slid inside my blouse looking for the tiny bear, but instead found my breasts, the nipples already standing erect even before she unbuttoned my blouse and took it off me. "Mmnn, nice," I purred, as she unhooked my bra and flung it aside. I closed my eyes as her hands caressed my breasts. Then I opened them again. "But it's not fair," I told her. "I have my clothes off, and you don't."

"Well, that's easily remedied," she said, laughing, and as if by magic her turtleneck was off, revealing her breasts, small and high on her chest, just as I remembered from that time I'd watched her dress. But this time, her smile invited me to reach out and stroke them, her nipples firming under my touch. I let my hand wander down toward that triangle of chestnut brown pubic hair I'd glimpsed. My eyes were still closed as my hand moved and then, with a suddenness that took my breath away, my fingers were entangled in the fur of Naomi's Persian cat, who had landed with an abrupt plop between us.

I woke with a frustrated start, to discover my fingers entwined in Dan's lush pubic hair, and hear his voice in my ear telling me, "Not this morning, honey. I have an early meeting."

I'd intended to run down to Old Town to buy a baby present for LaVerne's new granddaughter. LaVerne had called with the news that her son's fiancee had given birth the day before, and I decided to bring the present to our monthly get-together that afternoon. But the dream unsettled me enough that I went to Springfield Mall instead, where I'd have no opportunity — or temptation — to drop in on Naomi.

We were meeting that afternoon at an upscale pizza place that LaVerne had suggested, mainly for its convenience to her son's apartment, where she was staying a few days to help out. "Thank   God Shawna waited till after the income-tax deadline to deliver, so I could take the time off," LaVerne said, once she'd passed around a copy of the newborn's hour-old picture, and the rest of us had told her — disregarding the fact that, like all newborn babies, she resembled nothing so much as a wrinkled prune — how absolutely adorable she was, and how perfectly the name Jasmine suited her.

I had promised to stay a week with Jeffrey and Anita once she'd given birth. Fortunately, Anita wasn't due until after BAT's production of *Fiddler on the Roof* had closed. I chimed in with that information. As soon as I'd finished with the topic of Jeffrey's family, Natalie asked, "And Jenny? I assume that was her boyfriend with her at the opening of your play? You didn't tell us how cute he was. Seriously cute."

"Didn't I tell you she'd get over that lesbian stage?" LaVerne said.

"Well, you were wrong," I said. "Tamara was sick the night of the play. That's the only reason Jenny came with Adam. Like I told you, they're just friends. In fact, he just got engaged to someone else." I didn't add anything about Jenny's plans for a commitment ceremony with Tamara. I'd defended it to Dan — I couldn't do anything else if I was to give Jenny the support she expected — but I couldn't bring myself to mention it to my friends right now. Instead, I changed the subject. "So now you've heard all the news I have to tell. Natalie, what's happening with you and Norm?"

Natalie gave me a look. "If you can remember all those lines for the play, you can remember that it's nearly twenty years since I changed my name to Natalya. But since you ask, we're still living in the same house." Natalie picked at her green salad without dressing, which was just what *I* should have ordered. But Naomi's lectures had had a bad influence on me; I'd gotten what I felt like — the shrimp and pesto pizza. I took a bite, savoring the oily mix of garlic and basil, while waiting for Natalie to continue. We both sipped our Diet Cokes, and then she added, "But that's as far as it goes. Whole days can go by without our exchanging a single word. Not that I care."

"Listen to yourself, girl," LaVerne put in. "You expect Norman to feel like talking to you, the way you've been running around on him? You'd better see a marriage counselor before he decides to move out on you altogether."

Natalie gave LaVerne a look now. "If I had the time or money to see a counselor, I'd spend it on Roberto instead. And what makes you think Norman would be so willing to go to a marriage counselor? It's been years since he gave a flying fuck about my needs."

"Look, don't bite my head off. I'm only thinking of your welfare. And as far as needs go, I can tell you from personal experience there's help for Norm's problem now. I wasn't going to tell you girls something this personal," LaVerne went on, after a pause punctuated only by the clink of Lois's wineglass as she set it down to give LaVerne her full attention. "But Dennis's doctor gave him a prescription for Viagra a couple of months ago, and just between us it's done wonders for our sex life. He's like a new man."

Natalie smirked. "It happens I *have* a new man."

"If you're going to put playing around in the same class with being married for as many years as you have," LaVerne came back at her.

"Let me tell you, I get more true love from Roberto in a day than Norm ever gave me in a year. And don't give me that goody-two-shoes attitude. You're telling me that none of you have ever considered having an affair?"

Natalie was glaring at LaVerne, but Lois was the one who answered, having apparently given up on learning any more particulars of LaVerne and Dennis's sex life. "Not me. I left the affairs to the rat," Lois said.

There was an awkward silence, broken only by LaVerne finally saying, "I believe in sticking to my wedding vows."

You'd have thought that Natalie would be fazed by Lois's implied criticism, not to mention LaVerne's. She turned to me with no change in expression. "I suppose you never gave a second's thought to having an affair either?"

I opened my mouth to tell her that Dan's lovemaking still satisfied me, when I remembered waking up that morning breathless from Naomi's kisses, my nipples still tingling from her caresses. "Only in my dreams," I said.

Chapter Twelve

"*That's* my little brother?" Steffi asked, in a voice so disappointed that we all laughed. Immediately a chorus of half a dozen voices drowned one another out reassuring her that her baby brother would grow big enough to play with her. Whether or not it takes a village to raise a child, we apparently believed it took one to birth a child, judging by the number of family members crowded into the birthing room to welcome Anita and Jeffrey's new son.

Back when I was pregnant with Jeffrey, I had to beg the obstetrician to let Dan into the delivery room. Anita, by contrast, had not only Jeffrey but her mother, Linda, acting as labor coaches, and two sisters with her into the bargain — to play the role of cheerleaders, I supposed. The rest of us had stayed in the waiting room with Steffi until the nurse called us in, a few minutes after the baby was born.

Jeffrey picked Steffi up to give her a better look at the baby. "Remember, we told you your brother would be tiny when he was born, so he could fit inside Mommy," he reminded her.

"And you said maybe I could see him get borned. I wanted to see him."

Anita's younger sister, Cathy, who'd videotaped the birth, piped up, "When you're a little older you can watch the tape I made."

Linda gave her a look. "In twenty years maybe. Meanwhile, Cathy, you'd better be careful sitting down so you don't squash your brains."

"But I *wanted* —" Steffi began.

Quickly Anita said, "Look, Steffi, see this funny cord on his middle.

That's like a big straw that he got his food through when he was inside Mommy. And when it falls off it'll leave a little stump to be a belly button just like you have." She gave Steffi a gentle poke in her belly button and Steffi giggled. "And now look," Anita went on. "He's going to learn how to drink milk from Mommy's nipples just like you used to."

Whining forgotten, Steffi's face screwed up in concentration as the baby rooted around for his mother's breast. "*I'm* too big to drink like that anymore," she announced.

"You absolutely are," Anita agreed. "That's why you get to spend the night with your grandma and grandpa. So you give Mommy a big hug and kiss now, and I'll be home tomorrow."

I thought back to the five blissful days that I'd rested in the hospital after Jeffrey's birth, and the three our insurance plan had allowed when Jenny was born. Anita didn't seem at all fazed by the prospect of going home twenty-four hours after giving birth. My admiration for my daughter-in-law went up another notch as I assured her I'd stay on a week to help out after she went home.

"Time for Anita to get some rest," Linda said in a no-nonsense tone of voice, as she began shooing everyone from the room. "Steffi is coming home with Paul and me, and we'll keep her overnight. Jeffrey, I know you want to stay with Anita, but she needs to nap now. And your parents and sister want to run up to the Bronx and see your grandmas. This is a good chance for you to visit with your family. Go on all of you and have a nice lunch."

Obediently, the four of us trooped to our car. Anita's doctor had told her early in the week that if she didn't go into labor by Friday, she would induce it. Given this news, Dan and I had made up our minds to drive to New York Thursday afternoon, with Jenny deciding to take a day of personal leave and join us.

Jenny hadn't been by our house in the three weeks following Passover. As far as I knew she hadn't talked with her father either. Dan hadn't mentioned Jenny and Tamara's commitment ceremony since his outburst at the Seder, as if he could prevent it from taking place by ignoring it. But I didn't expect his forbearance to last during the drive to New York. The last thing I'd wanted was a family fight while Dan was at the wheel of the car. So I'd immediately started reminiscing on how different childbirth was back when our own two were born. Who would have believed that a couple could now learn the sex of the baby in advance? As

I knew he would, Dan chimed in with the story of Jenny's birth, how our doctor had triumphantly proclaimed, "It's a boy!" and then sheepishly corrected himself, explaining it had been a long day and he'd mistaken the emerging umbilical cord for a penis. When I glanced back, I saw that Jenny had been lulled by the familiar story. Head pillowed on her arm, she was fast asleep, reminding me of the way she used to sleep through our trips to New York at Steffi's age.

Now that Anita had given birth, the only thing on Dan's mind — as the four of us headed over the Triborough Bridge to the Bronx — was the new arrival. By the time we'd picked up Rose and Mama and driven to a kosher deli near the Jerome Street el, it was closer to supper than lunch. I couldn't help giving in to the tantalizing smells of vinegary pickles, corned beef and pastrami and ordering the combination platter.

Jeffrey, of course, had to retell the entire story of Anita's labor and delivery for Mama and Rose. Not that he minded — he was bubbling over with excitement. "He's so alert, you can tell he's going to be just as smart as Steffi. Weight? Eight pounds even. And wait till you see his hair. A full head of hair, black like Anita's."

"And you named him what?" Rose asked. "Your father told me on the phone but I told myself I must have heard wrong." From her tone of voice it was obvious she'd heard perfectly well. Only my mother-in-law could have chosen such a moment to go on the attack.

Jeffrey's voice was midway between apologetic and defensive. "It's Jeffrey Paul, Grandma. Anita thinks a boy should carry on his father's name. The middle name is after *her* father."

"And this is a name for a Jewish baby?" This was a rhetorical question on Rose's part. Jewish custom says that a child should never be named after a living relative. While here was Jeffrey's son named after not one, but *two* living relatives. "In case you've forgotten, you made a big point of telling everyone at the Seder last month that you still consider yourself a good Jew." Rose popped half a knish in her big mouth, which didn't shut her up for a minute. "But what am I saying? An old woman who can't remember for ten minutes that your son has a Catholic mother, that you've seen to it that your children weren't even born Jews."

As all of us knew, Jewish law doesn't consider the child of a non-Jewish mother to be Jewish. And Rose simply couldn't miss an occasion to badger poor Jeffrey about his religion.

Jeffrey set down his fork, his face screwed up in an earnest search for words to mollify his grandmother. It crossed my mind that Dan had tried to force our son into the wrong profession entirely. The kind of thinking on your feet that lawyers have to do had never been his strong suit. I was about to open my mouth and put Rose in her place when Mama came to Jeffrey's defense. "Rose, the only reason Jews don't name a baby after someone living is superstition: an old wives' tale that says the Angel of Death might take the wrong soul by mistake."

I looked at Mama in surprise. She'd gone along with the custom's opposite side of the coin, insisting with both my children that I honor my father, Joseph, their deceased grandfather, by giving them names starting with the letter J. But I certainly wasn't going to take issue with my mother over her defense of Jeffrey. I opened my mouth, but instead of telling Rose off, took a bite of a sandwich worth meeting the Angel of Death for, a spicy combination of meats on real Jewish rye spread thickly with mustard.

Jeffrey was still struggling for words when Jenny came to his rescue. "That's right, there's actually no Jewish law against naming a baby after a living person. In fact, a lot of Jewish families have begun naming children after living relatives. Like in Tamara's family, her grandfather is Stanley, and her father is Stanley Jr."

Nobody else in the family, not even Dan, commands Rose's respect the way Jenny does. So Rose just nodded. "I never knew that about the names. But more important, your brother's children are lost to the Jewish people."

"Actually," Jenny said again, "Reform Judaism considers them Jewish if either of their parents are. It's just the more Orthodox that says a child can only be called Jewish if he has a Jewish mother." That was news even to me, but I could see Rose light up as Jenny went on to say, "We were just discussing it in a Torah study group Tamara and I are in."

"It's such a pleasure to listen to you," Rose told her. "Even an old woman like myself can learn something about her religion from you. But to get back —"

Jeffrey had been nodding gratefully as Jenny spoke. Now he hastened to change the subject before Rose could start in on his children again. "How's Tamara doing, Jen? Have you guys got any further with your plans?"

She nodded. "We had a preliminary talk with our rabbi. We'll get together with her again and discuss everything in more detail when we get closer to the date. That's still a little iffy. We put in a request for a Sunday afternoon the end of August. But the church secretary said she couldn't promise anything so far in advance because they hadn't set the date for church dinners and stuff. So —"

"What's this about a church?" Rose interrupted. "Since when do *you* go to church?"

"I don't go to church. Our congregation can't afford its own building for a synagogue yet, so we rent space from a church. It works out because we don't have services the same day of the week, but we have to work around their schedule for special events."

Dan had been eating a platter of New York bagel and lox in exhausted silence. He'd been too excited over his grandson's impending arrival to sleep the night before. But now he shoved back his plate and said, "If this special event you're talking about is that mock wedding ceremony —"

"It's not mock," Jenny said in a hurt voice. "It's real to Tamara and me. I told you that, Daddy."

My mother beat Dan in responding. "Jenny, listen to me. There was too much confusion at the Seder for me to speak my piece. So I want to say to you now, I know you're very fond of your friend and she of you. But putting on a public spectacle to celebrate your friendship isn't a smart thing to do. At the least, wait a year or two." Dan seemed about to interrupt, but Mama waved him to silence. "After all the two of you weren't even speaking to each other last fall," she continued. "Now you're friends again, but you may very well find that a few years down the road, given a little added maturity, you'll have outgrown this whole phase."

"Grandma!"

But Jenny was cut off by Rose, saying, "That's exactly what I hope for with this whole Catholic business. That you'll get over this phase, Jeffrey, and let your wife know you want to give your little ones a Jewish upbringing. Your sister just said: to the Reform, they're still Jews. Well, better they should be Reform than nothing. At the very least — I'm sure, for health reasons if nothing else, you're planning to have your son circumcised. I beg of you, at the very least, wait the eight days and have a proper *bris*," she said, her voice rising loud enough that the couple at the next table turned to look at her. "For my sake."

Jeffrey sighed. "He's already been circumcised, Grandma. We arranged in advance to have it done right after his birth. I'm sure it's been done by now. Anyway —"

"Anyway," Rose interrupted. "Why would I think you'd do anything for *my* sake? Did you even think of honoring your *other* grandfather, my Morris, may he rest in peace? Did you even think to yourself, let me give my Grandma Rose a little *naches*?"

All the *naches* — the joy — that Jeffrey had shown at the beginning of the meal had leaked out of him like air from a birthday balloon as a result of Rose's jabs. "Anita wanted, that is, we both thought, I mean Jeffy is carrying on *my* name, and his middle name is after one of *his* grandfathers." He sighed again in the face of Rose's stony silence and looked at his watch. "Visiting hours end in a couple of hours, so if we're going to drive you guys down to see him we ought to get going. That is, if you're interested in seeing him at all, Grandma," he said, looking directly at Rose.

Rose looked at him in astonishment. "You think I wouldn't want to see my great-grandson? Just because I have some criticisms for his father?" She reached across the Formica-topped table and patted Jeffrey's hand. "When you love somebody, you tell them their faults."

The first thing Dan said to me when I returned home after the week with Jeffrey and Anita was, "I had a long talk with Jenny on the ride home, and I told her that she could go ahead with whatever plans for that commitment ceremony she and Tamara wanted to make, but the two of us weren't going to have any part in it. I think I got that through her head this time."

I gave Dan a look, too astounded to know whether to bawl him out for putting words in my mouth or to demand to know what Jenny's reply had been. Before I could do either, he added, "You got a long distance call the other day from Tamara's mother. She asked for you by name, so I left it on the machine for you to return, but I'm sure she's calling to talk over how we can put an end to this foolishness."

I went into Dan's den where we kept the answering machine, and plopped into his leather chair to listen to the message and return the call. At a woman's, "Hello," I said, "Hi, this is Sheila Katz. I'm returning a call from Debby Goldberg."

"How wonderful to hear your voice," hers cut in. "This is Tamara's mother, Debby. Isn't it exciting about our daughters! I can't wait to meet you and your husband, and Jenny, of course. Tamara's been telling me so much about her."

141

Was Dan in for a surprise, I thought, with a surge of satisfaction. "Uh, your daughter, what we've seen of her. She seems like a lovely person. Um —"

She gave a tinkling laugh. "I know the whole idea of their having a wedding came as a surprise to you. My husband and I were bowled over at first too. But why shouldn't they, after all? So why I'm calling is, I know the girls want to pay for things themselves, but with them both being teachers, they aren't exactly flush. And usually the parents of the bride shoulder most of the expenses. But this isn't exactly usual, is it? With two brides?"

I shook my head, forgetting that she could hardly see me.

"So what Stan and I thought," she went on, "was that we two couples could decide how much we'd help them out and simply split it down the middle. If that's agreeable to you." Without a pause she added, "We married off one daughter not too long ago, so I can tell you that when it comes to planning a wedding it's none too soon to start. And it's always the mothers who end up doing it, isn't it? Now before we even get as far as calling caterers and all that, we have to get a firm figure from the girls on the number of friends they want to invite. And that will give you and me some idea of what kind of limits we want to set in drawing up our own guest lists."

I didn't need to consult with Dan to know the number he'd include in his guest list: a big, round zero. And if the truth were told, my own list wouldn't be much longer. I still hadn't brought myself to share Jenny's plans with anyone outside those family members who'd heard them directly from her. Not even with my best friend Lois. I wasn't about to let on to Debby Goldberg though. I didn't know if Tamara's mother had ever gone to a PFLAG support group, but she'd obviously traveled a lot further down the road toward true acceptance than I had. I mumbled something about having to talk things over with my husband and that I'd get back to her.

Dan was planted in his recliner in the family room. "So what did she suggest?" he asked.

"She asked for our guest list," I told him.

He put his feet down with a thump. "This isn't a joking matter, Sheila."

"I'm not joking," I snapped. "You said a few minutes ago you talked to Jenny. What did *she* say?"

"She mostly listened to me for a change. I told her that she'd been doing a lot of talking about what she wanted and I felt it was important for her to hear our position."

I gave him a look. "So you put words in my mouth."

"I didn't say a word to Jenny that wasn't simple common sense. And I would hope you'll tell her that when you talk to her. Your own mother after all —"

I left him talking to himself and went to the bedroom phone to call Jenny. Tamara was the one who answered. "I just got back from New York, and I need to talk to Jenny," I said, trying not to sound flustered at getting her rather than my daughter.

"Jenny just ran out to buy milk. But she definitely wants to talk with you, Mrs. Katz. She's been pretty upset about what her father said. I told her she ought to call you at her brother's, but she said it would be a madhouse there and anyway, she wanted to talk to you face-to-face."

I took a deep breath. "I'm coming over right now." I hung up without even a goodbye. On my way down to the garage, I paused to tell Dan I was going over to the girls' apartment. "I need to talk to Jenny in person."

He glanced meaningfully at his watch. "It's almost dinnertime, you know."

"I'm sure you can find yourself something in the refrigerator." I closed the door behind me.

Jenny was not only back from the grocery store when I arrived, but she and Tamara were about to eat. The air was pleasantly scented with nutmeg from a quiche Tamara was just setting on the table. "I've set a place for you, Mrs. Katz," she said, in a carefully neutral voice.

"Sheila, please," I murmured, hoping that neither of the girls picked up on the fact that I hadn't exactly counted on Tamara's presence during my talk with Jenny. I was sure they'd take that as a sign of homophobia on my part. After all, would I expect to drop in on Jeffrey and find that Anita had conveniently absented herself? "Oh, I won't eat anything. I didn't mean to barge in at dinnertime," I said, sitting at the place Tamara indicated, but turning to Jenny. "It's just that Daddy told you I said some things, I'm not sure —"

"He said you were as much against our having a wedding as he was. That it was as big a shock to you as to him."

"I never said anything like that!"

143

"I *knew* you hadn't," Jenny said with a mixture of such triumph and relief that it was obvious she'd known no such thing.

I made up my mind to give Dan a piece of it when I got home. "I might have told him it came as a surprise when you first mentioned it," I said, pausing to give myself time to think. I needed to walk on eggs here. At least that was something I had plenty of practice at. I did it routinely with Jenny, and even with Jeffrey when the subject of religion came up. It occurred to me that Mama's generation expected their children to watch every word with them as a matter of course. But *my* children expected the same from *me*. When would it be my turn for anyone to walk on eggs with me?

Before I could go on, Tamara chimed in. "It's natural that you might have been surprised, Mrs. — uh, Sheila. Here have some quiche," she went on, cutting a large slice and sliding it onto my plate. "You can't just sit there and watch us eat."

With the tantalizing scent of the quiche right under my nose, I picked up my fork obediently.

"I hope it's okay. I might've added a little too much nutmeg," Tamara said, as I took my first bite.

"Oh no, it's delicious." And so rich, she must have used real cream.

"It wouldn't have been such a surprise if Grandma Myrna hadn't gotten all those ideas about me and Adam and forced me into telling everyone at Passover. We were planning to sit down with just you and Daddy first. But she had to bring it up at the Seder. And then she and Daddy ganged up against me in New York."

The salad bowl was sitting in front of Jenny, but she was too wound up in what she was saying to pass it. I reached for it and took a healthy helping. "Your grandma is just worried about what might happen with your job if people found out about your plans," I said carefully. "I mean with you being a teacher...."

"Mom, I don't *care* if people find out. In fact, that's the main issue Tamara and I had to work out between us, that we're going to be honest about ourselves and not afraid to let people know who we are."

"But if you were to lose your jobs on account of it —" I blurted around a mouthful of lettuce.

Jenny sighed. "We're not going to lose our jobs."

"There are places that might happen," Tamara put in. "But luckily, discrimination on account of sexual orientation is illegal in Alexandria."

"But even if it wasn't," Jenny said, "I've made up my mind. I'm not going to hide in the closet. I mean, I'm crazy about teaching, but I'd go into some other field altogether rather than tell lies about myself every day."

I'd heard variations of Jenny's declaration at every support group I attended. I certainly couldn't argue with it, not if I wanted to stay on her good side, so I nodded in what I hoped was a supportive fashion and let another forkful of quiche slide down my throat.

Tamara gave me a sudden, radiant smile. "I told Jenny you'd understand. Didn't I, honey?" she said. She reached for Jenny's unoccupied hand and held it a moment; the two of them gave each other one of those just-between-us smiles you see couples share. "Like I said a few minutes ago, Sheila, we realize this came as a surprise to you. My mom and dad were kind of taken aback at first too. But I had a long talk with them. I pointed out that when parents say something along the lines of, 'Well, we accept you, but let's not advertise the fact that you're gay,' then they aren't *really* accepting you. And that for them to say Jenny and I weren't entitled to a wedding meant that they thought I wasn't as good as Stacy. That's my sister. Anyway, it completely changed their outlook. They're really behind us now."

It had certainly sounded like it from Debby Goldberg's call. "That reminds me," I said. "Your mother called me this evening. She wants the two of us to get together and plan your — your ceremony."

After what Tamara had just said, you would have thought that would make her happy. Instead, she rolled her eyes, something that until that moment I'd thought was an invention of cliche-wielding novelists. "That's all we need. No offense, Sheila. But Jenny and I don't want some kind of circus like Stacy and Michael's wedding."

"A circus?" I said.

Tamara shrugged. "Well just for starters, instead of having the ceremony in our temple, my mother talked Stacy into this upscale catering hall that has what they call their Chapel of Wedded Bliss. The highlight is this raised platform at the back of the chapel. Not a platform, a small stage, a — What do you call it, honey? You're the English teacher."

"A dais," Jenny said.

"Oh, right. Thanks. So anyway, instead of having the bride enter from the rear of the chapel in a normal way, this place turns off all the lights and the bride goes through a door from an antechamber that leads onto this dais. *Then*, when the lights go back on, they shine a spotlight on her — like she's Miss America or something — and it follows her down the steps to where her parents are waiting to march down the aisle with her. And they keep the spotlight trained on her till she's actually standing under the canopy."

I couldn't think of anything to say but, "Oh." I polished off the last of my quiche, looked longingly at the remaining pie, then gave myself a mental shake and took a bite of salad — a red leaf lettuce with tangy balsamic vinegar dressing.

"Not to mention that the whole affair didn't start until after sundown on Saturday. Which meant Stacy and Michael didn't get away until way after midnight. Because we had to have drinks and hors d'oeuvres first, *before* the ceremony, just like it was a cocktail party, and that went on for an hour, hour and a half," Tamara said. She was clearly on a roll. "Then, of course, there was the seated dinner after the ceremony, with a six-piece band for dancing. And to top it all off, out of the three hundred people there, maybe twenty or thirty were friends of Stacy's or Michael's and another few dozen were relatives of our family or his. The rest were all business associates of Dad's that he and my mother owed invitations to."

I said the first thing that came to mind. "Well, at least they must have gotten a lot of nice wedding presents."

Tamara laughed. "Yeah, they did. A dozen Mr. Coffees alone." She pushed the pie tin of quiche toward me. "Please, have another piece."

While I was succumbing to temptation, she said, "So you can see what I mean about my mother."

It was one thing for Tamara to criticize her mother, another for me. Luckily, Jenny jumped into the conversation. "What Tamara is getting at, is that all we want is a simple religious ceremony in front of our own congregation."

"Exactly," Tamara said. "Not a big extravaganza. Something that has meaning to the two of us. And the people close to us."

Just a small, private affair, I thought with relief. The girls' gay and lesbian friends from their synagogue. The two sets of parents. I'd work on Dan to bring him around. Rose and Mama, if they were willing to attend. Jeffrey and Anita. Tamara's sister and her husband, naturally. *Her* grandparents, if they were still around and willing to attend. "So basically you want to keep it to close family," I summed up.

146

"That's it," Jenny said, beaming at me. "Well, of course you'll want to invite Aunt Lois and them. And their kids who are my age — those are the ones I'm friendliest with. Or do you think we'd have to invite all of them, so as not to hurt anyone's feelings? My mother met her three best friends when she was pregnant with my brother," she explained in an aside to Tamara, without waiting for me to reply to her question about "Lois and them's" children. "For years they got together with us kids and had a play group. We'd play and they'd gab."

"And I'm sure there's some of your good friends from BAT," she went on to me. "And there's a couple of people I teach with I'd want to include, and same goes for Tamara."

Tamara nodded. "Jenny and I have to put our heads together and make up a list of who we want to invite. And, like she was saying, you and my mother will have people you'll want to add." She looked at me with that earnest expression of hers. "It's not that we don't want any input from you at all, Sheila. Or from my mother. But we're celebrating *our* marriage. And we want to be the ones to plan it." The two of them turned to smile at each other; then they leaned together for a kiss. I felt myself flinch. Luckily they were too engrossed to notice.

After a moment Jenny turned to me. "It's really wonderful that you're behind us, Mom."

"Of course I am, sweetheart," I told her. I ignored a dozen butterflies suddenly competing for space in my stomach and reached over to hug her.

"And there are lots of ways you can help us if you want," she added, hugging me back.

"Just let me know what I can do," I said.

"Well," she said, sitting back again. "There are just so many details. My wedding gown for one. We're both going to wear dresses, I mean one of us isn't going to be in a tuxedo or anything like that. Stacy has offered to let Tamara wear her gown, so she's already set. But I need to go shopping for the right one. That's something you might like to do, Mom. Go shopping with me for a wedding gown."

It was a moment before I could speak. "I've dreamed about it for years," I told her.

Chapter Thirteen

S o now Jenny had cast me as Mother of the Bride while Dan was demanding that I have nothing to do with her plans. Once he had left for work the following morning, I headed for the kitchen phone. I desperately needed to talk to someone. The question was, who? Normally I'd turn to Lois, but I still couldn't bring myself to tell her about the girls' ceremony, though I'd have to sooner or later if I was to send her an invitation.

But right now I needed to talk with someone I could count on not to *plotz* in shock at the very thought of a traditional Jewish wedding between Jenny and another woman. That's what our PFLAG support group was for, but I didn't feel like waiting until the next meeting. I could, of course, call one of the other members. I'd become friendly with both Candy Sue and Marlene. Candy Sue, though, had taken several steps backward since the meeting where Marlene had told us her gay son was planning to marry a woman. And Marlene would greet my news with such sincere congratulations that I knew I'd never confess my true feelings to her.

I was sipping my second cup of coffee, still undecided over who — if anyone — to call, when Naomi called me.

"Hi, stranger," she said. "Any chance you're free for lunch today? You got me hooked on theater again. I told Jack and Jim I'd do set design for the next show. I've got some ideas I'm raring to get going on, but I thought it would be a good idea for the two of us to touch base first. They said you're doing set dressing."

"The next show?" I repeated, so blankly that Naomi said, "*Plaza*

Suite, by Neil Simon, remember? Are you all right, Sheila? You sound out of it. I didn't wake you up, did I?"

"No, I've been up for hours. I was just distracted. There's a problem that's come up about Jenny. My daughter. That is, it *shouldn't* be a problem, but...."

Naomi's warm voice interrupted. "When it comes to emotions there aren't any shoulds or shouldn'ts. If you're upset, you're upset, and until you deal with whatever it is, you won't be able to focus on anything else. So before we even mention the play, why don't you tell me all about it over lunch?"

Naomi was waiting for me in front of Santa Fe East, the Old Town restaurant she had suggested. "I was afraid you might miss the entrance," she said, as she led me down a narrow path between two buildings. Once inside, we followed the hostess past a dimly lit bar area decorated with wooden carvings. From the surprisingly bright and airy dining area, French doors opened onto a courtyard filled with wrought iron tables and chairs. She seated us at a table for two; almost immediately a waiter appeared, greeted Naomi by name and asked if we'd care to order drinks while looking over the menu.

"They have wonderful margaritas here," Naomi said. "I'll have one on the rocks," she told the waiter.

He turned expectantly to me. "I shouldn't," I said. But suddenly I didn't feel like drinking iced tea while Naomi sipped her tangy-sweet margarita. "Oh, I guess I'll have one too."

Once we'd ordered — the chicken special for Naomi, rainbow trout for me — and our drinks had been set in front of us, Naomi said, "What is it that has you so upset about your daughter?"

"I hardly know where to start." I lifted my glass, sipping my margarita over the salty rim. "It's just — well, she and Tamara want to get married. That's what they're calling it, not even a commitment ceremony, they say they want a wedding." With that, I was launched into the whole *megillah*, not leaving out a thing, as if I were filling Naomi in on six months of a soap opera she'd missed. "So I told Jenny and Tamara I supported them, I promised Jenny I'd shop for a *wedding gown* with her. But with Dan a hundred percent opposed to the whole idea...."

"What you're saying is that you're between the proverbial rock and the hard place."

I took another swallow of my drink. "I guess. No, I don't know. That is, the whole idea of a lesbian wedding —" I said, suddenly glad that it was still early for lunch and we had the place virtually to ourselves. "Jenny thinks I'm totally all right with it. And I know I *should* be. But I just have this feeling of unreality about the whole thing, as if I'm in a play acting out a part." I broke off as the waiter approached and set our plates in front of us, cheerily bidding us to enjoy.

"Like I told you on the phone, there's no use saying you should or shouldn't feel a certain way. You feel what you feel. This looks delicious," Naomi added, picking up her fork.

My own dish looked equally yummy, but instead of digging in I said, "I shouldn't even be saying all this to you. I mean, I hope you're not taking it as an insult."

"Not at all."

I gave a sigh of relief and started in on my lunch. It *was* delicious: succulent fork-tender trout, topped with marvelous little roasted shrimps and accompanied by rice seasoned with cilantro.

"You've only known about your daughter a few months," Naomi continued. "It's not surprising that you aren't ready to send up lavender balloons to celebrate her union with her partner."

She'd hit the nail on the head. "That sounds just like what Jenny is expecting from me. And you're right, I'm not ready to send up balloons. Even after going to PFLAG for months. But I was afraid you wouldn't understand."

Naomi smiled. "I may have given you the wrong impression. I'm completely comfortable with my sexuality now, but you should have seen me ten, twelve years ago. I was a wreck when I first realized I loved Jody. Even though I thought it was fine for other people to be lesbian or gay."

I sipped my drink again. "I'm so glad I talked to you. I've been feeling like there was no one I could talk to about it — that I'd have to wait for the next PFLAG support group. I haven't mentioned it to any of my friends yet."

"Except me," Naomi said and flashed me another smile.

I smiled back at her. "Except you," I said.

I picked up my glass again, surprised to find it nearly drained. Our waiter materialized, asking if I cared for another. I did. I had to drive home, though; I normally left the lunchtime drinking to Lois. Still, with a big lunch.... And I wouldn't go right home, I decided. I needed some new clothes for spring anyway; I'd spend the afternoon shopping in Old Town.

Naomi ordered a refill too. She raised her glass when it arrived. "To friendship."

"To friendship," I toasted her back.

I felt better, even though I was no closer to resolving the issue between Jenny and Dan. I relaxed and looked at the decor I'd been too busy talking to notice before. The restaurant was decorated in a Southwestern scheme, with Indian — or as Naomi would say, Native American — artifacts and carvings. The wall across the room from me was painted with three mock windows that looked out on a Southwestern desert "landscape." No wonder this was one of Naomi's favorite places to eat. With her carved silver bracelets and strands of turquoise she looked as if she could have stepped out of that landscape.

This afternoon she was also wearing turquoise and sterling earrings, the silver of the earrings setting off the silvery highlights in her hair. None of my other friends would have dreamed of letting her hair go gray. I'd bought my first bottle of Miss Clairol the day I found my first gray hair; my hair was now a soft honey brown that my hairdresser felt would give a more natural look than trying to match my original dark brown. Yet Naomi's salt-and-pepper hair made her handsome face even more attractive. She looked up from her plate, caught me staring, and gave me a quizzical smile. I could feel myself blushing and hoped she mistook the heat coloring my face for a hot flash.

I reached for my margarita, took a long swallow and said, "I was just admiring your jewelry. And thinking how it fits right in with the Southwestern setting."

Naomi laughed. "It's my favorite part of the country. Taking buying trips out there is one of the things I like best about the business I'm in."

"I've never been," I said. "We've flown to California on vacation a couple of times, but I've never seen anything else of the Southwest."

"Oh, you have to!" she said. "The beauty is so...so intense." She picked up her glass, turned it to where the rim was still encrusted with salt, and drank. "You know, Jody had never seen it either. For our first anniversary we took a trip out to Arizona and New Mexico. One night we borrowed a tent and camped out in the desert. We made love under a blanket of stars. It was the most glorious experience I'd had in my life." She smiled and then looked back at me. "I hope I'm not embarrassing you."

I shook my head. "Not at all." Which, surprisingly, was the truth. I'd been upset by a little kiss between Jenny and Tamara, but the thought of Naomi and her lover making love under the stars left me unfazed. Was it because — as Dan had said about Jack and Jim — Naomi wasn't my daughter? Or because I was only hearing about it, rather than seeing it with my own eyes? But looking at Naomi, I could imagine her lying naked on a sleeping bag. She and Jody would have zipped their bags together and spread them out on a bed of soft sand. Jody's body would be soft and yielding as the sandy ground. Naomi had told me once that Jody was twice my size. I couldn't quite picture her jumbo-sized lover, but I could easily see Naomi's nude body in my mind's eye. I'd been able to close my eyes and see her since the first time I'd barged into her shop and she invited me upstairs for coffee while she dressed. And despite all the spicy aromas rising from my plate and from the lime in the drink I raised to my lips again, I could still smell Naomi's personal scent.

"I still dream of going back one day," Naomi said, and I started, wondering how much of what she'd been saying I missed. "Of course it's over with Jody, but someday with the right woman....whoever she turns out to be."

"So you're daydreaming about meeting someone new," I said playfully.

"Sometimes. But actually I was talking about real dreams. Nighttime ones. A lot of the time I dream about places. Landscapes that I remember, the first faint tinges of pink in the sky as the sun rises over the desert, the way the shapes of rocks and cactus emerge from the darkness as if they were being created all over again. I fell in love with that landscape. And I do think my sleeping mind is sending me a message: that's a place I need to be one day, not just for a visit but for good."

She turned the glass and sipped again. "So how about you? Where are you dreaming of?"

"Me?" I said. "I hardly ever dream about other places. Well, sometimes the apartment I grew up in, or something like that, but nothing exotic. In fact, I hardly even notice my surroundings in dreams. Which is funny, because when I'm awake I'm always noticing how people's homes are decorated, all that kind of thing. But when I dream, it's mostly about people."

"I think that's what most people dream about. But which people? Your family? The kids you went to school with? Or famous movie stars?"

I laughed. "All of them. A lot of dreams about my own kids when they were children. So if your mind is sending messages like you say, maybe I wish they were little again. But I've had my share of fantasies with leading men too. And I dream about my friends. Like...well, I've dreamed about you a lot, for instance."

"About me? Well, what was I doing in your dream?"

"Oh we weren't really doing anything. Your cat jumped up on the bed before anything could happen between us," I blurted, before I could think what I was saying.

Naomi stared at me a second, then broke into delighted laughter. "We were *making love* in your dream?"

It was too late to call my words back. The heat in my face was twice as intense as before. I picked up my glass, filled with nothing but dregs of ice now, and held it to my cheek. "No, I just told you. The cat got in the way before anything could happen."

She laughed again. "Next time we'll have to make sure to close him out of the room."

This was what came from drinking at lunch. I set my empty glass down on the table. "There isn't going to be a next time. We're just talking about a crazy dream I had."

"But I'm flattered that you invited me into your dream world," Naomi said, still smiling.

I gave her a look. "Naomi, maybe your dreams are messages from your subconscious or whatever, but mine are just dreams. They don't mean anything." But when I'd dreamed about her a half-dozen times — and always in compromising situations? That was a question I couldn't answer, or deal with right now either. "I mean, it's not that I think you're unattractive, I think you are, I mean you're very pretty —" Or did you say pretty to a lesbian? "Uh, very handsome I mean, you're a very attractive person. It's just that I'm not —" Not what? Not attracted to her, when my cunt had been throbbing against hers in those dreams? My head was swimming. "I never should have had those margaritas," I said.

"Me either," she said lightly. "And as a matter of fact, I find you attractive too. But don't worry," she added in a more serious vein. "I'm not going to try to seduce you." She looked at me searchingly. "It's obvious that you're upset about your sexuality. Did you know that's fairly common among mothers of lesbians?"

Naomi had seen through me so clearly there was no point in deny-

153

ing it. "Really? I don't think any of the mothers I know —"

"I learned it from the therapist I saw when I was struggling with my own coming out issues," she cut in. "If the mother identifies closely with her daughter, sees her as an extension of herself, then when her daughter comes out she might start wondering about her own sexual orientation."

If either of my kids seemed like an extension of myself, it was Jeffrey, but I didn't bother to argue the point. I nodded.

"Besides," Naomi went on, "suppose you *do* discover that you're capable of being attracted to another woman? You'll still be the same person you've always been; you'll just have a little more self-knowledge." The waiter returned to suggest dessert. We shook our heads, and asked for the check.

I fumbled for my wallet. "You're the one who should be a speaker for PFLAG, not me. That's exactly the advice we give people coming out to their parents, that they should remind them they're still the same person."

"As a matter of fact, I went to a few PFLAG support group sessions when I was coming out. And did my best to remember what I learned there. Now put that money away. I asked you to lunch. This is my treat."

"I can't let you —"

She waved away the twenty I was holding out to her. "You can take me to lunch next time. We need to get together again, you know. We haven't said a word about the set design for *Plaza Suite*."

I'd almost forgotten the reason Naomi had suggested lunch. Right now the play was the last thing on my mind, but I said, "Well, in that case...."

"I've got to get back to the shop now," she said as we walked out. "But give me a call this evening, and we'll pick a day."

I nodded.

"And relax," she added. "You've loaded yourself down with worries. Your daughter, your husband, your sexual orientation."

"I'm not worried about my —" I started automatically, but she cut off my protest.

"It won't be the end of the world if you discover that you're not strictly heterosexual. I can testify to that. In fact, for me it opened up a whole new world." She stopped suddenly, halfway down the secluded pathway leading to the sidewalk, and enveloped me in a bear hug. "Take care now," she added, giving me a quick kiss on the cheek. I had turned toward her to hug her back, and for a fraction of a second our lips met. Then we pulled back and went on down the path, going our separate ways as we reached the street.

It was good I'd decided to spend a couple of hours shopping, I told myself, as I headed toward Wardrobe for a Small World. The drinks were still affecting me. Why else would the thought be running through my mind that Naomi's lips were more enticing than even the fudge brownie I'd nearly succumbed to for dessert?

This seemed to be my week for lunching out, what with the lunch bunch getting together at Kramerbooks & Afterwords Café three days after my lunch with Naomi. Parking was tight near Dupont Circle. LaVerne and Natalie had already been seated by the time I walked in with Lois. We ordered — I stuck to the salad special and a glass of iced tea today — and the second the waiter headed off, Natalie said, "Well, girls, I've got some news. I finally found time to go apartment hunting."

Thank goodness, I thought. If Natalie had made up her mind to separate from Norm, we'd be talking about it for the rest of lunch. There would be no chance for anyone to ask about — or for me to dwell on — what was going on in my own life. I settled back comfortably and asked, "Have you actually moved out on Norm then, Natal — Natalya?"

"This coming weekend. I've put a deposit on a studio apartment over in River Towers. A bit small, but it'll do for the time being. Roberto is going to help me move my things over there Saturday morning, while Norm's at the golf course."

"You shouldn't be the one to move out," Lois advised. She sipped her wine and added, "You're giving Norman too much advantage if you leave him in possession of the house."

Natalie shrugged. "You sound like my lawyer. But Norm can keep the house, as far as I'm concerned. I've taken care of that mausoleum long enough. I just want a nice, efficient apartment. All I really need is a microwave and a comfortable couch. That, and the queen-sized waterbed I'm buying."

Natalie and Norman owned a six-bedroom stone Tudor, furnished with antiques and original works of art that Norm's prosperous orthodontic practice had paid for. Whenever we'd gotten together with our families, I could sense Norm totaling up the potential profit of each child's smile. I knew exactly which watercolor Jeffrey's mouth had purchased.

Their house was a showplace and I didn't see how Natalie could give it up with so little regret. *My* home was my castle, my nest that I had feathered with patchwork quilts, golden oak collectibles and cozy country touches, and I couldn't imagine just walking away from it the way Natalie was doing from hers.

"So," LaVerne said, "you're going to be shacking up with Roberto now?"

Luckily, Natalie was in too good a mood to take offense. She merely said, "I'm renting the apartment on my own. Maybe later on, once the divorce is final, we'll talk about finding a bigger place and moving in together."

The waiter placed our salads in front of us as Lois said, "You don't mean you're thinking of a permanent arrangement? Do you mind if I ask you a question?" she went on, spearing a shrimp from her salad. "Aren't you close to twenty-five years older than him?" Not that she needed to ask. Lois never forgot a detail like someone's age.

"Age isn't important," Natalie retorted. "Not when two people have as much in common as Roberto and I do, when they have the same interests and the same worldview and —"

"And when they can't keep their hands off each other," LaVerne put in.

"That too," Natalie agreed smugly, sounding like the proverbial cat who ate the cream, though she'd hardly allowed anything with more calories than diet soda to pass her lips as long as I'd known her.

"Uh huh," LaVerne said. "But like Lois was saying, how long is that going to last when he's young enough to be your son?"

Natalie gave LaVerne a look that lingered on her well-padded frame. Like me, LaVerne could pose for the "Before" picture of a diet pill ad; unlike me, she claims to relish being a "full-figured, feminine woman." She wears her extra pounds as if they were the robes of an African queen.

"If you keep yourself in shape the way I have," Natalie told LaVerne, after she'd finished running her eyes over LaVerne's ample bosom and double chin, "there's no reason not to have an active sex life your entire life." Natalie flicked her bleached blond hair back behind her ears and shoved away her salad before she could add an ounce to her hundred-pound frame.

"It so happens that I have a very satisfactory sex life," LaVerne snapped back. "And for your information —"

I opened my mouth before the two of them could really get into it. "Speaking of information, doesn't research show that women don't reach their sexual peak until their later years?" I'd said it simply to forestall a squabble, but when I thought of it, *I* certainly felt as sexual as I had at any time in my life. I might not look sexy by society's standards, but that had nothing to do with what I was capable of in bed. Nor, I was sure, with what Natalie could do with Roberto, or LaVerne with Dennis. And who said a mature woman wasn't attractive anyway? Look at Naomi, with her silver hair and musky, ripe body. I'd bet she was plenty capable of using that body, of arousing a partner with her hands and mouth....

"Everyone knows that women's sexual appetites increase with age," Lois said. I jerked back to our conversation with a guilty start. Lois set down her wineglass and addressed Natalie. "That's why, speaking as your friend," she told her, "I want to warn you to be on your guard. You don't want to waste your divorce settlement on a gigolo."

Natalie dropped her napkin onto her plate, scattering several leaves of baby lettuce. "I can't believe you said that! Just because Roberto's a few years younger than me you think there's nothing about me that could attract him outside of the few dollars I have in my bank account. I don't know if it's just jealousy on your part or —"

"I don't know why you think I should be jealous," Lois interrupted, leaning toward Natalie. "Believe me, after spending eighteen years with the rat, I'm more than happy to live the rest of my life without another man. And we both know that LaVerne and Sheila are too happily married to be jealous for a moment. I just had your welfare in mind."

"If you say so," Natalie said. She turned to LaVerne. "Getting back to the subject of shacking up, what's happening with your son's wedding? Is it still on, or did he and Shawna decide to just keep living together?"

"Of course it's still on!"

"Well I haven't gotten an invitation yet. Have you decided not to invite me, since I'd be coming with Roberto instead of Norm?"

"Girl, I don't know what's come over you today. I'm not about to drop one of my best friends just because your marriage is breaking up. Of course you're invited — Shawna's mother just hasn't gotten the invitations out yet."

It occurred to me that the topic of Dennis, Jr. and Shawna's wedding had given me a natural opening to mention the girls' ceremony, which I was going to have to bring up sooner or later if I intended to invite the lunch bunch to it.

After letting the margaritas I'd had with Naomi go to my head, I'd sworn never to drink at lunch again. But right now I was tempted to reach for Lois' wineglass before opening my mouth. Stupid, I told myself. These were my closest friends, and if I couldn't talk to them.... "Speaking of wedding invitations," I said brightly, after gulping down a mouthful of iced tea instead. "You girls will be getting one from Jenny in a little bit." As the three of them turned to stare at me, I quickly added, "No, she hasn't gotten back together with Adam. Jenny and Tamara have decided to have a commitment ceremony. But they're taking it as seriously as if they were planning their wedding, so that's what they're calling it." I went on into a startled silence: "A wedding. With the two of them standing under the canopy and all."

"A wedding?" LaVerne echoed.

"When did all this come up? You never said a word to me about it," Lois accused.

"Because I figured I'd tell everyone at lunch today," I fibbed. "I didn't want to repeat myself." At least, I thought, the other two wouldn't have their noses out of joint at Lois always getting my news before them.

"You aren't serious, are you?" Natalie said.

"Why shouldn't I be?" I demanded, with a lot more conviction than I felt. "I've already told you about Jenny coming out as a lesbian. So why shouldn't she have the same right to — to celebrate having found the person she wants to spend her life with?"

I'd gotten so carried away on my daughter's behalf that the two women eating at the table closest to ours turned to stare at me. Lois laid her fork on her salad plate and drank half her wineglass in one swallow. "Well, of course it's good that she's with someone she likes, but a wedding? A traditional Jewish wedding, under the *chuppah*? Let me ask you a question. Do you really think they'll find a rabbi to —"

"They already have a rabbi," I cut in. "A lesbian rabbi from their synagogue. And yes, I mean a regular Jewish wedding, breaking the glass, the whole bit. With a kosher caterer for the reception. Why shouldn't they?" I demanded, so stoutly that the three of them seemed dumbstruck and our eavesdropping neighbors turned their eyes, if not their ears, to their own table.

I waited for someone to ask what Dan thought, but instead LaVerne asked, "And you're doing the planning for this — this event? It's supposed to be the mother of the bride who makes all the arrangements, you know. That's how come Shawna's mother is in charge of their wedding. If it was up to me to do it, they'd be on their honeymoon by now."

"You're living in the past," I told her. "Most couples plan their own weddings these days. The girls are doing most of their planning. But I said I'd help," I admitted. "And Tamara's mother said she would too. We've got two brides after all, so we have two mothers of the bride," I pointed out, taking perverse pleasure in pitching my voice in the direction of the next table.

Another few moments of silence went by. "Well," LaVerne finally said, "I'll give you a call before I go shopping for something to wear to Dennis Jr. and Shawna's wedding. We can look for mother-of-the-bride dresses together."

Within one week, Jenny had asked me to help her pick out a wedding gown and LaVerne had suggested we shop for mother-of-the-bride dresses. I needed some retail therapy, all right, but nothing that involved setting foot in a bridal shop. Not with the whole subject of weddings still a sore subject between Dan and me. It was lucky I had BAT's upcoming show, Neil Simon's *Plaza Suite*, to take my mind off the situation.

I not only had landed a part, but had signed up for set decoration as well. Naomi was designing the set, and a week after our drunken lunch at Santa Fe East we were getting together again. This time I was determined to stick to the subject of the play. At my suggestion, we met for coffee, a beverage much less likely to get me in trouble than margaritas, though I did let Naomi talk me into one of Starbucks' rich fudge brownies with it.

Much to my relief, Naomi was all business, pulling out a preliminary sketch of the set — a suite in the Plaza Hotel — and setting it on the counter between us. "I've put the bedroom area stage left, with the door to the bathroom all the way upstage for the bride to make her entrance." The location of the bathroom mattered. *Plaza Suite* consists of three separate one-acts; each of the acts is a complete, short play, all taking place in the same luxury hotel suite. The action of the third one-act revolves around a bride who gets cold feet, and locks herself inside the bathroom minutes before her wedding. I nodded.

"The two windows will be here, and I imagine you'll want to position the dresser between them," Naomi went on. "Then the couch will have to go stage right."

"I hope I can find someone willing to lend a nice-looking one. Not something that looks like it came from a garage sale." I took a sip of coffee and scraped the last bit of icing from my cake plate. "And drapes. Oh, and paintings for the walls. You know. Something bland but tasteful." I thought a moment. "No one I know has anything that would look right. Any chance you could do a few hotel-style pictures?"

She nodded solemnly. "Something bland but tasteful. My specialty."

"I didn't mean that you aren't capable of something better than that! I love that sunset you have hanging in your bedroom." The one I'd noticed while trying not to notice her nude body, as she'd casually tossed off her robe to dress in front of me. "I mean those colors, the way that reddish glow reflects off the clouds, it's just marvelous," I babbled on, willing my memory to stay focused on the painting. "I just thought for the show —"

Naomi laughed. "Relax, I was teasing you. I know what you meant. And I'm really flattered you remember that painting. I didn't know you'd even seen it."

"You don't remember? I thought you opened your shop at ten, and you invited me up for coffee? And then I had to come sit in the bedroom because your cat wanted the kitchen chair."

"Oh, that's right. He's a real tyrant, isn't he? Always getting in the way at the wrong moment." She was looking at me with a little smile, and I was sure she was remembering the dream I'd blurted to her the week before.

"Well anyway, about the paintings for the show," I said hurriedly.

"I can probably do something that will work." She glanced at her watch, back to her businesslike attitude. "Well, now that we've touched base, I'd better get back to the shop."

"So when do you get out West on another buying trip?" I asked, as we walked out.

"Toward the middle of summer. I'm planning it to tie in with the national PFLAG convention; I've signed up for a sales table. It's in Scottsdale, Arizona, this year."

"I know. Our facilitator keeps talking it up at support group. But she's the only one from our chapter who's going. Arizona in summer isn't that tempting."

Naomi laughed. "You'd probably spend 90 percent of your time inside. But it's a dry heat out there, not like the humidity we have around here. And it does cool off a bit at night."

Once the sun was down it would be pleasant enough outside, I thought, pleasant enough to make love under the stars the way Naomi had described. "I'll think of you out there in that hundred-degree *dry* heat," I said, willing myself to think of her with her clothes on.

She laughed again. "Well, I'll say goodbye. Unless you're planning to come in and shop."

Startled, I realized that I'd walked Naomi all the way to her shop — only two blocks from Starbucks, but two blocks in the opposite direction from my car. "Well, now that I'm here," I started to say, when I caught a glimpse of my watch. "Oh, no, my meter just expired. I'd better run."

It was just my luck that the meter maid was sticking a ticket under my windshield wipers as I panted up to my car. She gave me a triumphant smirk as she hopped back on her scooter and rounded the corner.

When I got home, I dropped my purse with the twenty-dollar ticket on the staircase, and checked the answering machine. Two callers had left messages: Jenny, and Debby Goldberg. My daughter, I felt up to talking to. Debby Goldberg I wasn't so sure about.

"Hi, Mom. I called about our wedding," Jenny said when she heard my voice.

I covered the mouthpiece with my hand so she wouldn't hear my sigh.

"We have a problem," she continued. "We can't get the church for our date."

"Oh." Oh seemed an inadequate response to the disappointment in Jenny's voice, so I added, "That's a shame."

"In fact we can't get it for any Sunday in August. We want a summer wedding, before we have to start teaching, and you know there's a mourning period during most of July — that's when it falls this year anyway — when observant Jews can't get married."

I hadn't known. "Oh," I said again.

"Only it seems the church has this summer program.... Anyway, we're having a terrible time finding somewhere else to have the wedding."

"Have you thought of our temple?" I blurted before I could bite my tongue. Dan would *plotz*. He would die. He'd kill me first, and Jenny would have to arrange a double funeral on top of her wedding.

"Mom, I really don't think they'd agree to a lesbian wedding."

"I could talk to the rabbi," I said weakly, just in case she'd heard the sigh of relief I had just heaved. If she took me up on it, I'd kill myself and save Dan the trouble. "Of course, I don't really know him that well. I haven't been active in the temple; I'm more of a High Holiday Jew, but —"

"Don't talk to anyone," she cut in. "This is our wedding we're talking about. We want to get married somewhere that we'll feel welcome, not where we're some kind of civil-rights test case. There are a couple of welcoming congregations in the area, but I've already checked with them and the date is taken."

"Oh," I said again. "Well.... It doesn't actually have to be in a synagogue, does it?"

There was a moment's silence. Then Jenny said, "No, really it can be almost anywhere as long as it's under a canopy. I just thought since we have so many people to invite from our congregation...."

It was plain that any hope of a private family affair was out the window. I stifled another sigh.

Jenny went on, oblivious. "Tamara's mother has been pushing us to have it in a hotel, but...."

"That reminds me," I said. "She left a message on our machine today. I'd better return her call." Before your father gets home, I'd been about to add, but thought better of it. "I'll talk to you in a day or two, sweetheart. Maybe we'll come up with another location by then."

When I reached Debby Goldberg, she was as up as Jenny was down. "I've made up a checklist. We're on an incredibly tight schedule here, so the sooner we reserve a place the better. Just between us, it's just as well that church is booked up. We can put on a much nicer affair in a hotel ballroom."

I was beginning to see what Tamara had meant about her mother. "Uh, Mrs. Goldberg —"

"Please, let's not be so formal. After all, we're going to be family, right?"

It seemed that way. "Debby, then. What I was going to say, the girls want to stay within a budget. And a hotel —"

"You're right, absolutely. We can't expect the two of them to foot the bill for the whole affair. Let them pick up the incidentals, their rabbi and whatnot. We two couples can divvy up the major expenses, like we agreed last time we talked."

I looked down at myself. My stomach still stuck out as much as ever. You'd think being run over by a steamroller would have flattened it a bit.

"Debby," I said loudly. "My husband isn't — That is, he still has a lot of questions about the whole thing and —"

"So did Stan to begin with. But I put it to him, why shouldn't Tamara have as much of a celebration as Stacy did? Are she and your daughter any less deserving because they happen to love each other?"

"No, of course not," I said. Marlene would just love her. She'd have her signed up for every committee in our PFLAG chapter. "Still, I have no idea how much a hotel ballroom costs but —"

"Oh, I know. Tamara told me your other child is a son. So you didn't have to do any of the planning for his wedding; the bride's mother did it all."

Linda had not only helped her daughter plan that wedding, she'd laughed and danced till the heel broke off her lavender dyed-to-match-her-mother-of-the-bride-dress-pumps. That had been five years back, with Anita stunning in a princess-cut wedding gown that hid her pregnancy from all but the nosiest and shrewdest of eyes. (Namely Lois's, who had tipsily accosted the newlyweds at the reception with, "Do you mind if I ask you a question?") Dan had been so enchanted by his granddaughter from the moment he laid eyes on her, that I'd all but forgotten how he'd threatened not to attend right up until two days before their wedding.

"So," Debby said, and I jumped, wondering how long I'd been reminiscing while she was rattling on at long-distance rates. "Since I'm the one with experience in putting on a wedding, it's unfair to put the whole burden of calling up hotels and dealing with caterers on you. And we really should meet each other, don't you think? I've been looking for an excuse to visit your area anyway. We used to live there, you know, when my husband was with the first Bush administration. I'll give you another call soon as I've made travel arrangements. I can't wait to meet you and your daughter. And your husband, too, of course."

I laid the phone gingerly back on its base, as if it were a letter bomb I'd found at my front door, and hurried to the kitchen. My plans for supper had involved a chicken recipe Natalie once passed along to me called "Hurried Honied Baked Chicken," which required nothing more elaborate than pouring several tablespoons of honey over the chicken parts and sticking them in the oven for an hour. Now, as I stuck the package of chicken in the microwave to defrost, I thumbed through the more elaborate recipes in my cookbook, settling instead on my specialty, coq au vin.

I pulled a kitchen stool up to the counter to begin mincing parsley and garlic and planning what else to serve. I wanted Dan agreeably full of my best culinary efforts when I broached the subject of Jenny's wedding.

Honey, we can't let her down, I rehearsed in my head as I put a bottle of Riesling in the refrigerator to chill and then grated lemon peel for home-made lemon meringue pie.

We can't let her feel that we don't accept who she is, I practiced, as I showered and changed into my most flattering casual top and pants.

She's our daughter and we love her. We have to give her our support, I concluded as Dan's car pulled into the driveway and the garage door opened, with a rumbling like the lowering of a drawbridge, to grant access to the lord and master of the manor.

"What's all this? We're having a dinner party and you forgot to tell me?" he said, coming into the kitchen where I was just opening the wine.

I gave him a kiss. "Nope. Just had a little extra time today, so I thought I'd make a nice dinner for the two of us."

"So what have you been doing all day besides putting Julia Child to shame?" Dan asked, once we were seated at the table savoring the rich mushroom and wine sauce.

"Getting a start on the set decorating for *Plaza Suite.* I had coffee with Naomi Pearlman, who's designing the set, to talk over our ideas. You remember her, don't you? She did set painting for *Fiddler?*"

"Uh, huh. Good-looking woman." He gave me a wink and grin reminiscent of Bill Clinton before he'd heard of Kenneth Starr and added, "I wouldn't kick her out of my bed."

Neither would I, it occurred to me. I quickly shoved that thought back into my subconscious, laughed as Dan had intended, and started in on a nervous monologue about how Naomi's set design would work around the limitations of our stage.

"Anything else new? Any calls?" Dan asked, once I'd told him how lucky it was that Naomi could paint the pictures I needed for the walls of the hotel suite. He meant calls for him, of course, but it was my opportunity to bring up Topic A. I took a deep breath.

"Honey, we have to talk."

"Oh, and what have we been doing up to now? At least you've been talking and I've been listening. Not that I don't want to hear more about your activities, but I just wondered if anyone had called —"

"Tamara's mother called about the girls'...the girls' commitment ceremony. It seems they can't get their synagogue, or, you know, the church they rent from, the night they want it. So Debby was thinking that if they had it someplace else, like a hotel, then she and her husband and you and me could split —"

"I hope you told her that we have no intention —"

"I told her you're not sold on the idea."

"Now that is the understatement of the year. Debby. Debby the Ditz, I'd call her."

"She is a bit much," I said with feeling. I wet my whistle with a sip of wine and went on. "But honey, about the girls' ceremony, shouldn't you think twice before you just condemn it out of hand? Remember how you felt when Jeffrey and Anita got married? You were saying at one point that you wouldn't even go to their wedding. And now, well now, can you imagine not having Stephanie or the baby?"

Dan put down his fork to give full attention toward delivering his opinion. "You're comparing apples and oranges. Of course I wasn't jumping for joy that your son gave up his religion to marry a shiksa. Though as it turns out, he did pick a sweet girl with a good level head on her shoulders. But at least it was a bona fide marriage, between a man and a woman. And, as you pointed out, Anita *was* carrying our grandchild."

I supposed that Jenny and Tamara could give us a grandchild too, if they went the turkey baster route, but this didn't seem the time to bring it up.

"But if this ceremony means so much to Jenny —"

"Sheila, I love my daughter as much as you do. But I've told you, and I'll tell her to her face, this whole idea is totally meshuga. More than crazy. It's a travesty. If Jenny insists on going ahead with it, that's her business. But the two of us are not going to be involved. Now, as far as I'm concerned the subject is closed."

I, on the other hand, had promised *my* daughter I would be involved in her wedding, a fact I hadn't yet mentioned to Dan. There was of course no time like the present.

"So what did you want to talk about?" Dan asked.

"Talk about?"

"You said you wanted to talk before we got off track with that phone call from that ditzy mother of Tamara's."

"I just wanted to tell you...."

"Yes?" Dan prompted. He lifted the lid off the serving dish of coq

165

au vin, and ladled another generous spoonful onto his plate. "Great meal, by the way."

On the other hand, some other time might be better. "Oh, I don't know. I've gotten a little nervous over everything I've taken on. Doing set decoration on top of getting a part in the show. I'm only in one act, but it's still a big time commitment."

"So that's why you've gone to all this trouble with dinner," Dan said. "Because we'll be having catch-as-catch-can for the next couple of months while you're in rehearsal."

I laughed. "I'll have to teach you how to cook. But seriously, I'm worried about spreading myself too thin. You're right, it's going to take a lot of rehearsing — I'm onstage for the whole act. I don't want to mess up, you know."

"Honey, you're worrying for nothing. You're a natural actress. You were inspired as Golde."

When you cook and clean for someone for thirty years sometimes it's hard to remember why you took on the job, but when Dan talks to me like that, I remember why it was I married him. I reached across the table and squeezed his hand, nearly causing him to spill his wine. "You're sweet."

"And don't worry about being gone evenings. You don't have to cater to me like this every night."

I squeezed his fingers again. "I'll play Julia Child again once the show is over."

He gave me his Robert Redford smile. "I'll hold you to that. And is that what you were so worried about telling me? That's what we had to talk about?"

With an opening like this how could I not tell him that I'd promised Jenny and Tamara to help with their wedding? "Well actually, there is something else," I began.

"I knew it. Well, what? I'm sure whatever it is isn't the end of the world." Dan was looking at me with loving interest, his eyes as close to bedroom eyes as they ever got on a weekday.

I opened my mouth to tell him, closed it, and then opened it again. "I'm afraid I got a twenty-dollar parking ticket today."

Chapter Fourteen

*T*he Broadway production of *Plaza Suite* cast the same actress, Maureen Stapleton, as the female half of each of the three unhappy couples portrayed in the three one-act plays that make up the show. BAT, not being Broadway, likes to broaden opportunities for amateur actors. I would appear only in act three. I'd been cast as a frantic mother-of-the-bride who tries to cajole a daughter with cold feet out of the suite's bathroom and downstairs to get married, while my stage husband attempts to blast her out with tirades and tricks.

It crossed my mind as I started home from rehearsal the night after our gourmet dinner, that it was ironic that I should be playing a woman so eager to be mother-of-the-bride when in real life it was a role I'd taken on with reluctance.

Which reminded me of Debby. I'd left Dan with the impression I was having nothing to do with Jenny's plans, while at that very moment Debby the Ditz could be calling our house and asking Dan to relay the message that she'd be arriving the next day to visit wedding caterers with me. It was past ten in the evening, late to call; luckily it *was* an hour earlier in Chicago. At the next red light, I pulled my phone out of my purse and punched in her number.

"Debby?" I said when she answered. "It's Sheila. Jenny's mother. I hope I'm not calling too late." There really was no way for her to respond but to assure me the hour was fine.

"I was out for the evening — a rehearsal for a play I'm in — and thought you might have been trying to reach me. In fact, I'm still out, calling from my car, but I just thought I'd better call you back before it got even later." I sounded as scatterbrained as *her*, but if she'd talked to Dan I wanted to know it now.

"What a coincidence. I just now got my plane reservations, and I was wondering if it was too late to call *you*." I breathed a sigh of relief. She was still going on about how she didn't mean it was too late for her, but it was an hour later in Washington, wasn't it, though she supposed all us theater people were such night owls.

I cut in on her. "Well, we do have a lot of late rehearsals." I hadn't worked out how to phrase what came next, so I just babbled on as if the two of us were two Chatty Cathy dolls. "Debby, before I forget — no, really the reason I called you was.... Well, to be honest, I've got to work on Dan to bring him around. You know how men can be." I waited for her lilting laugh to assure me that she did indeed know how men could be. "So as far as helping the girls plan their wedding, let's leave our hubbies out of it a while. In fact, it might be just as well" — I gave a falsely lilting laugh of my own here — "if you don't call me at my house. Let me give you my cell phone number and you can use that. Okay?"

There was a moment of silence on her part and I held my breath till she said, "Something like this really is easier without involving the guys right now, isn't it? Now let me give you my flight number. Any chance you might be able to pick me up at Dulles Airport?"

I picked Debby out immediately from the arriving passengers when I met her plane three days later — an older version of Tamara, infuriatingly trim in black stirrup pants and a belted aqua tunic. Her hair though, I couldn't help noticing with a little burst of satisfaction, was dyed a jet black that contrasted tellingly with the lines around her brightly lipsticked mouth. I waved at her and she rushed toward me, threw her arms around me and transferred a carbon copy of her lips to my cheek. "It's so wonderful to meet you! I can't wait to get started," she bubbled as I led her to the car with as much good humor as I could muster.

By rights, I should have invited Tamara's mother to stay at my house. We had plenty of room — I'd redecorated Jenny and Jeffrey's old rooms into guest rooms as inviting as any I'd seen in *House Beautiful*. But with Dan in the dark as to my involvement with the girls' wedding, having Debby the Ditz as a houseguest was out of the question. Instead we checked Debby in at a nearby Sheraton, after a lunch of salad with no dressing during which she complained with every other bite about how much weight she'd been putting on. Charitably, I didn't grab the sash from her twenty-four inch waist and strangle her with it.

Jenny had given me the key to their apartment in case we arrived there before she and Tamara returned from teaching. But by the time Debby had unpacked and checked out the hotel's fitness room, the girls were unlocking their front door. Tamara and her mother hugged and kissed with a fervor that gave me a twinge of envy. They stepped back from one another and Debby threw her arms around Jenny, even before Tamara had finished introducing them. I had to hand it to Debby. She might be a bit much, but she greeted my daughter with a good deal more warmth than I had Tamara when Jenny first introduced her.

Tamara showed her mother around the apartment, with Debby keeping up a continuous cooing about how cute the place was. Once they'd finished the tour, the four of us sat in the living room with glasses of diet soda, Debby in the overstuffed chair and the girls side by side on the sofa, with me squeezed in alongside Jenny. Debby whipped a spiral notebook out of her handbag.

"I've made a list of everything we need to do between now and your wedding date," she said, without a sign of flinching at the "W" word. "Decide on a color scheme, finish the guest list, have invitations printed, select a band and photographer, order the wedding cake and so on. But the absolute first priority is to find and reserve a site. Make that two sites, one for the ceremony itself and one for the reception. Unless, of course, we find a facility that can handle both events." Debby focused her gaze on me. "I found a simply marvelous place when Tammy's sister got married. A catering hall with a wonderful ballroom for receptions and a simply inspired chef — I wish you could've tasted the meal he and his staff produced. California cuisine that would rival the finest restaurants in San Francisco. And their chapel, they call it the Chapel of Wedded Bliss —"

"Was the most garish, tacky setting you could have come up with," Tamara cut in, rolling her eyes the way she had a few weeks earlier when she'd gone on about what a "circus" her sister's wedding had been.

"Stacy adored it," Debby shot back. "All her friends were getting married at the club, and it was just the same old, same old. Not that there's anything wrong with a country club setting. In fact, it just occurred to me, Sheila, if you and your husband belong to a club —"

We did but, "My husband would have a fit." When the kids had been younger, Dan had taken Jenny there for swim-team practice and taught her to play golf, while Jeffrey tagged along with me to BAT. I wondered if she was remembering that now. "I'm afraid he's still dead set against the girls having a wedding."

Jenny knew that. What she didn't know was that I was here behind Dan's back. So before she let it slip to him that we'd been planning her wedding, I had to tell her, hopefully without hurting her more. "In fact," I added, "I haven't mentioned anything to Daddy yet about Debby being here or about us getting together to plan things, so if you talk to him...."

"I'm not going to talk to him about the wedding, Mom. I haven't said a thing to him about it since Anita had the baby. I talked to him in the car all the way back from New York, and he didn't hear a thing I said. It's like he's totally stopped caring about me," Jenny said. She sounded close to tears.

Tamara put her arm around Jenny's shoulder. She and Debby both appeared to be about to speak, but I beat them to it. "Sweetheart, Daddy loves you very much. He told me so just the other day. He's just having more trouble than I expected adjusting to all this. It's like we talk about at PFLAG," I said, trying to think how Marlene would have put it to the support group. "Parents have a script written out in their heads for their children. And Daddy is having a hard time accepting that your life isn't going according to that script. But it doesn't mean he doesn't care about —"

"Mom," Jenny interrupted, "if he doesn't accept me, then —"

"He will." Jenny's misery put words in my mouth. "I give you my word," I promised my daughter. "On your wedding day, Daddy will walk you down the aisle."

I had a rehearsal that night, and the delicious smells of tomatoes and garlic coming from a Crock-Pot Tamara had going reminded me I barely had time to get Dan's supper on the table — as he'd predicted, something "catch-as-catch-can." Before I left, Debby and I agreed we'd each spend the following day phoning possible wedding sites, and then get together with the girls in the evening.

Needless to say, I had no idea how I was going to make good on my promise. Jenny had tacitly agreed to let me do the communicating with Dan, but I was still nowhere near telling him about my participation in the wedding — let alone demanding his. I had no rehearsal the following evening, but I left for the girls' apartment after supper, with the excuse that some details about the play needed to be ironed out. It wasn't exactly a fib. When weren't there details to iron out?

After a day spent on the phone, I hadn't come up with a single site that would fit within the girls' budget. "We want to keep the whole thing under a thousand dollars, tops," Tamara had said airily, the week before, though even I, who hadn't planned a wedding since my own, knew what wishful thinking that was.

Debby, on the other hand, had come up with a list of half a dozen places she felt would be "delightful." She'd been at Jenny and Tamara's apartment the better part of the afternoon, and when I arrived that evening it was clear that the honeymoon stage of her visit with Tamara was over.

I'd already eaten supper with Dan, but gave in to Tamara's urging to join the three of them for dessert. She slid me a slice of mouth-watering strawberry shortcake and went on with the argument they'd obviously been having before I arrived. "Mother, how many times do I have to tell you, Jenny and I want a simple, religious ceremony, not —"

"Tammy —"

"And I wish you'd call me Tamara. I'm not a little kid anymore."

Tamara's mother turned to me. "Thank goodness you're finally here. I've just been trying to make the point that there's no reason on earth that the girls can't have their religious ceremony in a beautiful setting. I'm sure you agree."

Put like that, it sounded perfectly reasonable. But the calls I'd made to the types of places I imagined Debby would consider "beautiful" had left me reeling with sticker shock. "But we do have to take the girls' budget into account," I reminded her.

She gave her trill of a laugh "That's what we parents are for. To pick up the slack and give them a nice send-off."

Which would be fine if Jenny were having a "normal" wedding. I knew Dan would be willing to go all out if it had been Adam that Jenny was marrying. But he'd put his foot down. I didn't know Debby well enough to know if she had financial resources in her own name. I didn't. Dan and I had quite a nice bank account, but a joint one. I'd be hard-pressed to explain taking anything more than incidentals out of it.

While I was searching for words to explain this to Debby, she went blithely on. "I was just reminding the girls how incredibly tight our time frame is. I've come up with several possibilities, but we'll have to move fast to reserve one. Now, the hotels I've talked to all require that you use their in-house caterer, but with a package deal like that you do have the advantage —"

"Mother! How many times do I have to tell you that the food has to be kosher!"

I had to empathize with Debby. That last had sounded like a blast from Tamara's teenage past. "Certainly, we'd tell them not to mix milk and meat," Debby said, with a hurt look.

Tamara gave an exaggerated sigh. "If you ever listened to me, you'd know there's a lot more to keeping kosher than just not having milk and meat at the same meal. Like, do you expect a hotel to keep a separate set of dishes and pots for milk and for meat?"

"I don't know what you're trying to prove by suddenly turning so Orthodox," Debby said. I could see Tamara was about to blow up again, but before she could, Jenny put a hand on her arm and said, in an amazingly mature voice, "Tamara and I aren't really Orthodox, Debby, and we don't necessarily keep kosher outside of our house. But our wedding is very special to us, and we want to celebrate it in an observant Jewish fashion. Besides, even if we didn't care about keeping kosher, there are people in our congregation who do. We don't want to be in the position of keeping anyone from celebrating with us, especially our rabbi."

"Oh." Debby thought a moment. "Well, there must be some good kosher caterers around."

"I'm sure there are," Jenny said. "But actually, our congregation has just formed a committee to provide food for weddings."

This was news to me as well as Debby. "Really?" she said, after a moment.

Jenny nodded. "For our Seder and Sabbath luncheons too. If we want to eat in the building, people have to prepare the food at home and bring it in. I mean, it's a church building so of course the kitchen isn't kosher. It's worked out great so far. People rotate on and off the committee, so the whole thing operates like an ongoing potluck."

Debby seemed stunned by the thought. "You mean you're planning to have a *potluck* for your reception?"

"Why not?" I found myself saying. "Potlucks are an old lesbian tradition."

The girls burst out laughing.

"That's great, Mom," Jenny told me, and I couldn't help beaming.

"Well, the idea of a potluck is very nice," Debby said weakly. "But when you're trying to put on an elegant wedding...."

"*You're* the one trying to put on an elegant wedding, not Jenny and me," Tamara said. "We've told you, we want a nice, simple ceremony. But you keep trying to turn our wedding into a spectacle like Stacy's, into some kind of — of theatrical production."

I nearly jumped out of my chair as inspiration struck. "That's it!" I said. "Why not hold your wedding at BAT?" All three of them turned to stare at me.

"Our amateur theater group has its own building," I explained to Debby. "An old estate, actually," I embroidered. "A gentleman's farm, with a barn that's been remodeled for use as a theater. We won't be doing a show then," I said, mentally checking dates, "so it'll be available.

"The theater would be ideal for the wedding," I went on. "It's about the size of a country church. And the house has kitchen facilities. For heating things up," I added hastily before Jenny or Tamara could remind me it wasn't kosher. "You can use our kitchen if you bring your own pots and pans, can't you?"

Tamara nodded.

"Mom, that's a marvelous idea," Jenny said. "But do you think they'll rent it out?"

I nodded happily at her praise. "I don't see why not. We never have before, but there's a first time for everything." And I wasn't on the board of directors for nothing. "I'll bring it up at the board meeting Saturday."

"You want to hold it *here*?" Sam Blumenfeld asked.

"Why not?" I said. The eight board members, myself included, were sitting in the back parlor of BAT's house, around a coffee table strewn with scripts and emptied Diet Coke cans. "The place needs to be cleaned up some, but I'll certainly pay a cleaning company — in addition to whatever rent we decide on. We've been looking for ways to raise a little extra money. Though not too much extra, I hope," I added, smiling. "Jenny and Tamara are trying to do this on a shoestring." Sam was our treasurer, and his voice carried a lot of weight in any financial decisions we made.

He was frowning now, but when he spoke again, after a pause even longer than usual for him, his objection wasn't financial. "It's not the amount I'm worrying about, Sheila. We draw a family-type audience. We have to consider what the community reaction will be to our hosting a lesbian wedding."

Whatever reservations I had about the girls' ceremony were momentarily blown away. "Sam, all *I'm* considering is how my daughter is going to feel if I have to tell her the board thinks she's not good enough to hold her wedding here." Not even to mention how Jack and Jim — who three years ago had celebrated the thirtieth year of their relationship with a gala commitment ceremony at the Ramada — were feeling at Sam's words.

"I'm not saying anything against Jenny," Sam stammered. "Just that the take at our box office could be affected."

Before I could come back at him, Jim, who I'd noticed from the corner of my eye had been quietly working up to the boiling point, snapped, "Sam, if keeping our bottom line in the black means that BAT is going to knuckle under to bigotry, then I'm resigning as a member right now. And that goes for Jack too." Jim spoke for them both, as always.

Without Jack and Jim — current president and artistic director, respectively — BAT would probably fold. The two of them had been pillars of the group for years. Sam knew this, of course, leaving him little recourse but to mumble, "I never said we should be prejudiced; I was just pointing it out as an item of information."

"Well, of course we'll rent to Jenny and her friend," Sally Winograd said, before any more ugliness could break out. "I so move." Once Sally's motion had carried unanimously, we still had to settle on the amount of rent.

A few moments before Sam had said he wasn't worried about the amount, but now he gave his opinion that, "If we're going to rent the place out, we should ask market rates. At least $500."

"I don't think we need to make such a big profit off Sheila," Sally said quickly. "In fact, considering how much she does for this group, I don't think we should charge her anything."

To tell the truth, that's what I'd been hoping for. But I *had* presented it to the board as a money-making proposition. And though $500 was more than I'd hoped to pay, it was peanuts compared to the sites Debby had suggested. I thought a moment. "I insist on paying something. But how about if we split the difference and make it $250?" I pulled out my checkbook as soon as the rest of the board had agreed. "Let me give it to you right now so I won't forget," I said, thrusting the check at Sam.

I'd written the check months before I would have needed to, and now I was faced with the problem of how to explain it to Dan. He was in his recliner in the family room when I got home. He put down his *Sports Illustrated* to ask, "Have a good meeting?"

"Pretty good." I came up behind him and started rubbing his neck.

"Ah, that's nice. So did you get your problems worked out?"

"Problems?"

"You said when you went out the other night that some kind of snag had come up in the play that needed to be worked out," he reminded me.

Inspiration struck. "It was basically money problems," I said as I began kneading his shoulder muscles. "We're running a little over budget on this production. We've had to spend more on props than I'd planned." Which happened to be perfectly true. "I hope you don't mind," I went on, as my massage elicited a rumble of pleasure from Dan, "but I offered to give BAT a donation to make up some of the shortfall. And I went ahead and gave the treasurer a check on the spot."

Sally Winograd, who was doing costumes for *Plaza Suite*, called me the next day. "I meant to ask yesterday, at the board meeting, if you have anything in your closet that would work for the show. Otherwise, give me your dress size. I'm on my way out to hit a few thrift shops for costumes."

My role of mother-of-the-bride called for a cocktail dress, a fancy one in which I would look my best. That, needless to say, was how I hoped to look for the girls' ceremony as well. Jenny and Tamara's wedding was months off, but Debby had just reminded me that we needed to "coordinate" our dresses for it.

Debby would look good in anything she wore, while I most decidedly would not. Traditionally, the mother of the bride chooses her dress before the groom's mother. With two brides and two mothers-of, tradition obviously fell by the wayside. My best chance at looking halfway decent was to make my selection first, and let Debby coordinate with *me*. I'd already planned a shopping trip, taking LaVerne up on her offer to go together. The only thing I hadn't figured out was how I'd explain buying a dressy dress to Dan when, as far as he knew, we had no occasion calling for one on our calendar. A solution came to me now.

"Not at the moment, but you know, I've been planning to look for something dressy. So what I'm thinking is, why not kill two birds with one stone? Let me go shopping for something I can get some use out of once

175

the show is over, and you won't have to play guessing games about what might fit me."

"Now this one is a few dollars more than you had in mind," the saleslady admitted, holding the dress, on its padded hanger, in front of me. "But it's so special, I just wanted you to see it."

"How much more?" LaVerne murmured, as I took it from the woman's hands.

I winced as I glanced at the discreetly hand-lettered price tag. "Four-hundred-fifty." But I had to admit that the dress was special. Even if this hadn't been the seventh shop LaVerne and I had visited over as many lunch hours. Even if LaVerne, who'd found a striking, African-inspired gown three boutiques ago, wasn't growing tired of schlepping from store to store with me. Even if Sally hadn't been pressing me about whether I'd found a suitable dress for a costume.

This dress was more than suitable for making me look my best. I could see that even before I took it into the fitting room, a room that, despite its full-length mirror and brocaded chair, doubled as the boutique's bathroom. I slipped the dress over my head. Pale blue silk, gleaming subtly with metallic gold threads, it skimmed gracefully over my body. I emerged from the room and preened in front of the three-way mirror outside. "So what do you think?" I asked — of LaVerne, not of the saleswoman. She was on commission; LaVerne wasn't.

"It looks great," LaVerne said. "It's definitely the best one you've tried."

I nodded happily. The price was steep, but for a dress this gorgeous.... I'd get my money's worth. This wasn't some frumpy frock that would go straight to the back of my closet after the wedding. It was something I could wear time and time again, the kind of thing that LaVerne and I had hoped to find by bypassing traditional bridal shops.

"But let me get this straight," she added now. "You're going to pay $450 for a dress to wear onstage, night after night, crawl around in it on your hands and knees, and then expect to wear it to this affair Jenny and her friend are having?"

I'd been imagining myself dancing with Dan to the strains of big band music, but at that my bubble burst. "I don't really crawl around the floor," I said weakly. "Just kneel down in front of the keyhole to see what my daughter is doing in the bathroom."

The saleslady's eyebrows rose so high, I was afraid they'd hit the ceiling. "I'm in a play; I'm playing the mother-of-the bride," I hurried to explain. "I was hoping to find something I could wear in the play that I could use afterward as well." I decided not to add it was for my daughter's lesbian wedding. I looked at the price tag again and sighed. "This is beautiful, but...."

"Oh, you're an actress," she said brightly. "How exciting! Have I seen you in anything?" Before I could confess to how very unlikely that was, she said, "Now let me think. I didn't realize you were looking for a *costume.*"

"Not a costume exactly —" I said, but she was heading toward the back of the store, calling over her shoulder, "Let me take a look in the stockroom."

I looked mournfully at my reflection in the blue silk. I was sure it took at least ten pounds off me. But LaVerne had a point. "I suppose you're right. This is too good a dress to do double duty," I told her.

"So is anything else you're liable to find in an upscale place like this. Speaking of double duty, let me use this dressing room before she comes back." LaVerne brushed past me. I returned to gazing in the three-way mirror. I looked closer to fifteen pounds lighter than ten, I decided, and the gold threads brought out the highlights in my hair. From behind the closed door of the fitting room, the toilet flushed, then LaVerne emerged, carrying the brocade chair with her. She set it down and lowered herself onto it just as the saleslady returned.

"There isn't too much back there in your size, but I think this one just might work for you." This one was a yellowish chartreuse, in satin so shiny it could have doubled as a traffic signal.

"I don't know," I said doubtfully. "The color...."

"Pistachio green," the saleslady broke in. "It's very flattering on, really."

On a twenty-year-old blond bombshell maybe. LaVerne looked at her watch and heaved a sigh. "You might as well try it on," she told me.

Reluctantly, I took off the blue and emerged from the fitting room in the chartreuse. "Well?" I said, again to LaVerne. She gave me a good look, one that took in the sallow cast the chartreuse gave my complexion and the way the fitted bodice emphasized my hips.

"The play you're in is by Neil Simon, right? It looks like something you could wear for one of his comedies."

"Sally would love it," I agreed. "And it's more in my price range. But can you see me wearing this to the wedding?"

"You said you were looking for a costume," the saleslady reminded me. "Though with a little more makeup — and maybe a tad more control in your undergarments — there's no reason you couldn't get some more use out of it."

I stared at my backside in the mirror, trying to imagine it with a tad more control.

"It *is* a designer original. But I'll be honest with you. This number hasn't done that well. I can let you have it at half off. It's a steal, really, at that price. Under a hundred dollars."

Ninety-nine, to be precise. I looked at LaVerne. "What do you think?" I asked her.

"If you want to spend that much for something to wear in a play then go ahead and get it." She looked down at her watch, and then pushed herself to her feet. "I've got to get going, Sheila. I'm in the middle of an audit."

I sighed. "I did promise Sally I'd buy my own costume. I hate to back out now. Or to start schlepping around thrift stores.... And, you're right, this would work perfectly for *Plaza Suite*." In fact I was sure that Norma — the character I portrayed — would love the chartreuse. "But I love the blue dress," I wailed.

LaVerne stopped in the middle of slipping into her London Fog. "Girl, ask yourself this. Even if you weren't afraid of messing up a $450 dress, do you really want whoever you invite to Jenny's affair to see you wearing the exact same thing they saw on you in the play?"

She had a point there. One I'd completely overlooked in my focus on keeping my involvement in the girls' wedding from Dan.

"Solution's right in front of your nose," LaVerne added, as she picked up her handbag. "Go ahead and get them both."

I didn't get any further with Dan in the next couple of weeks, and arrived at PFLAG hoping for feedback from other members of the support group. I was last when we went around the circle telling our stories. When I'd finished, Chuck, the therapist whose advice had boomeranged at the Seder, said, "Let me see if I understand. Are you saying you're actively involved with your daughter's wedding, but you're effectively in the closet as far as your husband goes?"

His therapeutic tone of voice irked me after the bad advice he'd given me before. "Well, my dress is in the closet at any rate," I retorted. "At the very back. I haven't shown it to Dan yet."

Candy Sue and a few of the others laughed, but Chuck focused on me even more earnestly. "Sheila, as a rule, PFLAG doesn't try to push people into a timetable for coming out. Isn't that right?" he asked Marlene, who nodded. "We know everyone is on their own journey," Chuck continued. "But I'm afraid your daughter's wedding plans have imposed a timetable on you. And the longer you wait.... How do you think your husband will feel when he finally opens that closet door?"

I had not one, but two, dresses at the back of my closet. The back of my "out-of-size" closet, where Dan would never in a million years look. And no matter what Chuck had said at PFLAG, I wasn't ready to tell Dan that I was helping the girls with their wedding plans. Still, I had to tell him something about my purchase; the Visa bill would be coming any day now.

The solution came to me while I was fixing dinner, one of Dan's favorites, grilled lamb chops with mint jelly. "I forgot to tell you," I said casually, as we were getting ready for bed that night. "I found a dress. I told you, didn't I, that I was looking for something to wear during the run of *Plaza Suite* that I could get some more use out of afterwards? Well, I found the perfect thing a couple of weeks ago. It was more expensive than I had in mind, but —"

"You told me you were going to buy your own costume, yes. What you didn't tell me is why you're suddenly carrying the whole organization on your shoulders. If BAT is so financially troubled —"

"It's not that," I said hastily. "That is, it did help Sally stretch our costume budget a little further for me to buy something on my own. But the real reason is, I just thought how I might as well kill two birds with one stone. I've been needing something a little dressier than what I have, you know, something I can wear to the law association banquet or — well, there are so many dressy occasions at the temple...."

"So do I get to see this dress?" Dan asked. "Aren't you going to model it for me?"

I pulled it from the bedroom closet, where I'd moved it after dinner, and slipped it over my head. With just the light from our bedside lamps, the color wasn't quite as ghastly on me, I hoped. "I'll have a girdle under it when I wear it, of course," I said nervously.

"Well," Dan said, obviously going by the maxim that if you can't find anything good to say about something, then say nothing.

"It's a designer original," I added. "It was on half-price sale."

"So how much did it set us back?"

I took a deep breath. "The bill came to a little over $500."

Dan's eyebrows rose like those of the saleslady. "Five —"

"Oh, I know," I said quickly. "I never meant to spend near that much. But LaVerne took me to this wonderful boutique in Georgetown and, well, when I spotted this it was love at first sight. It's one-of-a-kind. Something I'll never see myself coming and going in."

And with good cause. There was a reason this little chartreuse number had been languishing in the back of the shop. I could see in Dan's face that he knew that as well as I did. But he was treading on thin ice. He couldn't very well say, "Honey, you look like a fat frog in that." Not if he knew what was good for him.

He sighed, a heartfelt, defeated sigh. "If it makes you happy. But I hope you're done shopping for a while, honey."

Chapter Fifteen

*D*ebby had called almost daily, in the month since her visit, to discuss details that absolutely couldn't be overlooked in planning the wedding. "I'd hate to see her phone bill," I told the lunch bunch two days after I showed Dan my chartreuse horror.

"Huh," LaVerne said. "That from a woman who pays a hundred dollars for a costume to wear in a play."

I hadn't told LaVerne the whole story, not the part about pulling the wool over Dan's eyes — or the silk and satin, so to speak. I shrugged. "It's still a designer original. I'll take it to one of those resale shops after the show."

"If they'll have it," LaVerne snorted. "Wait till you girls see it. You'll die laughing."

"I hope so," I told them. "It *is* a comedy. Thank God we open this Friday. Between rehearsals and set decoration, I've run myself ragged. And Tamara's mother, Debby the Ditz, has been bugging me nonstop. What color scheme have the girls decided on? Don't I think they should at least consider a kosher caterer? Don't I like the idea of throw-away cameras on the tables? Have I finished my guest list yet?"

"Speaking of guest lists," LaVerne said, before anyone could raise her eyebrows over the girls' plans, "Shawna's mother finally put the invitations in the mail yesterday."

"Where did she mail mine?" asked Natalie.

"To your house, I assume. I gave her everyone's home address."

"You know I'm not living there any more."

"I gave her that address months ago. How was I supposed to know you'd be moving out? Anyway, Norm is still there, isn't he?"

"You didn't invite Norman! Tell me you didn't invite Norman."

LaVerne had just speared a fat shrimp from her salad. She put her fork back on her plate again. "You were both on the list I gave her. I just told you, that was months ago — you know how long it's taken her to organize this wedding."

Natalie groaned theatrically. "You expect me to come to their wedding with my ex-husband?"

"So come separately." LaVerne popped the shrimp in her mouth and ate it. "I'm not going to un-invite him. I'll see to it you're not sitting at the same table, but I'm not going to hurt Norm's feelings by telling him he's not welcome."

"The point is, I'm with Roberto now. And if I'm going to your son's wedding, that's who I expect to go with."

"Girl, if you knew how stingy Shawna's mother is with the number of invitations she's allotted us!"

Nearly simultaneously, Lois exclaimed, "So we get to meet Roberto after hearing so much about him!"

LaVerne sighed. Then, making a show of reluctance so as not to admit she was as curious to meet this Roberto as Lois and I, she said, "I can't promise anything, but I'll see if I can talk her into an extra invitation."

Natalie nodded, apparently mollified. Lois sipped her wine meditatively, then suddenly looked at Natalie. "What do you mean ex-husband? You haven't even filed for divorce yet, right?"

Natalie shrugged. "You know, I realized twenty years ago that Norman and I have nothing in common. Not one single thing."

"So?"

"So as far as I'm concerned, I've been divorced for years."

Natalie's statement got me wondering: What did Dan and I have in common? An odd thing to question after thirty years of marriage, like Tevye plaintively begging Golde to tell him if she loved him. Or maybe question wasn't really the right word. It had been obvious for years that Dan and I had no more interests in common than Natalie and Norman did. In fact, as I told Naomi the following afternoon, "My husband and I never do anything together. I go to rehearsals every night, but he never sets foot in the theater till opening night when he goes to see the show.

And he gave up, years ago, trying to teach me golf or drag me to the pool in summer."

"It isn't necessary for a couple to do everything together. People need some space of their own. Here, I just made these yesterday," Naomi said, slicing two home-baked brownies from an aluminum foil pan and passing me the larger. I'd gone to The Soaring Eagle to pick up the paintings Naomi had done for the set of *Plaza Suite*, and she'd left the shop in her business partner's hands and invited me upstairs for an afternoon coffee break.

"At least give me the smaller one," I said, switching the two plates. "I'm fat enough already. Even if I wanted to swim, I wouldn't let anyone see me in a bathing suit."

Naomi put down her coffee cup. "There you go again making yourself miserable because you've bought into some Madison Avenue image of what a woman is supposed to look like. Why don't you just learn to accept yourself like you are?"

"Easy for you to say. If I looked as good in my clothes as you do, I'd accept myself the way I am too."

"Probably not," she retorted, though she was smiling at my compliment. "You'd find something —"

"The only thing I complain about is my weight," I interrupted, "And if I do say so, staying out of the sun has been good for my complexion." Which had yet to develop the lines and beginning wrinkles that Debby's foundation didn't quite conceal. "A lot of people tell me I look younger than I am."

Naomi smiled again. "You do. You look like you could still be in your forties. You have beautiful skin," she added. She was looking at me in a way that made me blush, and I quickly changed the subject.

"What were we talking about anyway, before we got sidetracked?"

She thought. "Couples, I think. Whether or not they have to do everything together."

"I didn't say a couple has to do everything together," I said. "But I've been thinking ever since my friend Natalie brought it up at lunch, that Dan and I don't even talk about anything but our house and the family. I find more to talk about with my women friends. Like you, for instance. I mean, really, I have a lot more in common with you than I do with him."

Luckily Naomi had to get back to the shop before I could blurt out anything further. I didn't know what was going on with me. Maybe, I mused, as I lugged Naomi's two framed landscapes back to my car, it was simply what she had suggested when I'd let on to her that she was playing a starring role in my erotic dreams: I saw Jenny as such an extension of myself, identified with her so strongly, that if Jenny announced she was a lesbian, then I promptly developed lesbian longings as well. But whatever the reason, when Naomi looked at me in the way she just had, I was half hoping that she would lean across the table to stroke my face with her fingertips, run her hands through my hair and press her lips to mine.

When I'd met Dan, he couldn't keep his hands off me, and vice versa. But after thirty years of marriage, our sex life had become a routinized romp in the hay. I suspected Dan checked it off mentally on his Sunday to-do list: have sex with wife; read *Washington Post* sports and business sections; play eighteen holes of golf. I hadn't known I wanted more till I met Naomi.

No one expects the honeymoon stage to last forever. It's a truism that once you have children, passionate mating gives way to PTA meetings. As I'd told Naomi, the strongest bond between Dan and me was our home and family. In retrospect, it seemed as if we'd seen eye to eye on everything when the kids were little. We had simultaneously fallen in love with our house the moment we crossed the threshold of the builder's model; agreed that one boy and one girl was the perfect family; agreed that he would provide the financial support for our family while I stayed at home to provide our children a proper upbringing.

It was only when a teenaged Jeffrey started spending all his spare time at acting classes and auditions that Dan started raising his eyebrows and then his voice. And when Jeffrey first informed us of Anita's pregnancy and their plans to marry, Dan's dismay was mitigated only by his relief at this proof that his son was no *faygeleh*. "With all the Jewish girls in New York you have to give up your own religion for a shiksa?" he thundered at him, though at least not in front of Anita.

I was quickly won over by my sweet-tempered future daughter-in-law. It took Dan longer. It wasn't until Stephanie was born, and gripped her grandfather's finger in her little fist for the first time, that his anger melted like a Hershey bar left sitting in a parked car on a hot day.

But if the strongest bond between Dan and me was our family, how badly would it be strained when I told him of my role in Jenny and

Tamara's upcoming nuptials? This time there was no adorable grandchild on the way. As I pulled into our garage, I wondered how in the world I would keep my promise to Jenny that her father would walk her down the aisle. Because so far at least, far from melting like chocolate, his resistance had the consistency of rock candy.

The phone was ringing as I walked into the house. I caught it on the fourth ring, before the machine could pick up. "Mom, listen," Jenny said in a rush. "There's a new klezmer band everyone says is great. The Capitol Klezmers. Tamara and I are thinking of getting them for the wedding, but we've never heard them play. They're going to be at the Birchmere for one night, but the problem is we've got a teacher's meeting. So I thought, you've got a good ear for music, if you'd go listen to them and tell us how they sound —"

"Oh sweetheart," I cut in, "I'd like to help you, but I've got rehearsal every night this week. This Friday is opening night, you know."

"I know, Mom. But this group is playing the Birchmere a week from Tuesday. You don't rehearse once the show is open, do you?"

"We might have a pickup rehearsal Thursday, but Tuesday I'm free. Though I hate to leave your father when I've been out so many nights with the show."

"I thought Dad loved Jewish music."

"You're right, he does." Though he wouldn't love the reason we were going. But I didn't need to tell him, did I? "I wasn't thinking. I've gotten used to running out to BAT every night without him."

"Tamara and I are looking forward to seeing the show Saturday night," Jenny said. "I know you'll be great, Mom. Oh, by the way. Tamara's mother sent us her list of people she wants to invite and Tamara and I are just about done with ours. And we really have to look at the total figure before we can go over our budget and plan the food and all. So do you think you could let us have your guest list Saturday night?"

I hung up and sat down at the planning desk in the kitchen, where I could keep an eye on supper. Staring at a blank sheet of paper, I told myself that at least I wouldn't have to worry about paring down my guest list to fit into the girls' budget. Who could I invite to my daughter's lesbian wedding, after all? Not Dan's law partners, whom he would surely have invited if Jenny were marrying, say, Adam. None of our neighbors or friends from temple. None of.... I sighed. Put down my pencil and picked it up again.

Jeffrey would come to support his sister. And Anita. She'd have to bring the baby — she was nursing — and Steffi could hardly be left out if her baby brother was there. Rose had been surprisingly amenable to Jenny's plans. Jenny was her favorite grandchild, after all. And I would simply insist that Mama attend. Five people — not counting little Jeffrey, who needn't be taken into account as far as planning the food went.

Though of course I was overlooking the lunch bunch, all of whom already knew about Jenny's plans and expected to be invited. Lois, I scribbled. LaVerne and Dennis, Natalie and — Natalie had made it clear that she and Norman were no longer a couple, but like LaVerne I could hardly slight Norm. Carefully I printed Norman's name, then on the line below, Natalie and Roberto. I looked at what I'd written a moment, then remembered to cross out Natalie and substitute Natalya.

Jenny had reminded me about my three best friends' children. She'd attended their birthday parties through childhood, from the time when there had been just one candle on their cakes. The kids saw each other less than their mothers did now, but I dutifully added them to the list. Which then meant penciling in Shawna's name by Dennis Jr.'s, plus the rest of the kids' spouses or significant others.

My own closest friends besides the lunch bunch were the people I worked with in BAT, but I'd made a few friends since joining PFLAG. Marlene and her husband. Candy Sue, no matter how many steps backwards she'd taken. I added them as well. The seven other members of BAT's current board of directors. I hesitated a moment before putting down Sam Blumenfeld's name, but it would be awkward to invite everyone but him and his wife, Zelda. He was famous for his blunt manner; he hadn't meant to be insulting about leasing the theater for Jenny's wedding.

Seven board members, five spouses or partners. I counted up, surprised to find that I'd come up with forty-two people, not including little Jeffrey. Had I left anyone out? I scanned my list. Not a person on it from Anita's family. I wouldn't leave out her parents, Paul and Linda, if Jenny were marrying Adam, I told myself as I wrote down their names. Or my sister-in-law, Yehudit. It was unlikely she and her family would make the trip from Israel, but why hurt her feelings by excluding her?

I double-checked my list again. Then I added one last name: Naomi's.

"What are you working on so intently?" Dan's voice boomed out behind me.

I jumped. "You scared me; I didn't hear the garage door. A list of people who want reservations to *Plaza Suite*," I added, folding it quickly before he could get more than a glimpse.

"Looks like a hit, by the length of it."

"I hope so." I got up to check on the pot roast I had simmering in the Crock-Pot. "By the way, I was thinking it would be fun for us to go out together for a change, once the show is open. Someone told me there's a new Klezmer band that's supposed to be really good playing the Birchmere next week. I thought I'd get us tickets. My treat."

Plaza Suite's opening night went better than I could have hoped. I was playing the mother of a bride whose cold feet have led her to lock herself in the bathroom of our hotel suite, minutes before her wedding is scheduled to begin. When the curtain rose, revealing me onstage in my chartreuse ensemble — Sally Winograd not only loved the dress but had found me a hat to match — the lunch bunch led the audience in laughter before I got the first line out of my mouth. Roars of laughter continued as her father and I tried to beg, bribe and bully her to come out and get married.

The opening night party was at my house. Potluck, but since most of the cast and crew could be counted on to arrive with nothing more than chips or dip and a ravenous appetite, I'd cooked a turkey the day before to slice up for the buffet table, and prepared a pasta salad and relish tray. I looked forward to eating someone else's cooking the following Tuesday, even if the Birchmere had built a reputation for music rather than food.

Jenny had warned me to arrive early if we wanted to get seats close to the stage, but the music hall was three-quarters full by the time Dan and I arrived. We settled down at a table in the rear and ordered. The food wasn't bad, the beer — from the Birchmere's own microbrewery — better.

The type of Jewish music termed klezmer has been variously described as a mishmash of traditional Yiddish folk songs, dances, Jewish jazz and ethnic music with an attitude. The six band members constituting the Capitol Klezmers could have been described as having attitude as well. All had shoulder-length brown hair, covered with colorful kerchiefs. The four women had their scarves tied back in traditional fashion, while the men, both wearing ponytails at the napes of their necks, might have been sporting the head wraps of pirates on the high seas. Their first number, greeted with enthusiastic applause, was a spirited medley of dances.

I was applauding their second number when it dawned on me that most, if not all, of the six musicians were lesbian or gay. I couldn't have said why. Not their costumes — leather vests over open-necked shirts, with baggy pants for the guys and long peasant skirts for the women. Perhaps I was developing the "gaydar" Jim and Jack had once laughingly described to me. Or maybe it was the audience: most of the tables were filled with same-sex groups of wildly clapping young people. Too bad Jenny couldn't have been here, I thought. It was a shame she had to miss this performance.

I wondered suddenly if Dan was picking up on the orientation of the band members or on how many gay and lesbian folk were in the audience. As far as I could tell, he seemed happily oblivious. The Capitol Klezmers started the next song, the voice of the vocalist forming a lilting counterpart to the strains of fiddles, piano, bass and clarinet, and Dan whispered to me, "Terrific group. I'm glad you thought of this." He gave my hand a squeeze and I sighed happily as I settled back to listen.

"We're going to take a break after our next number," the woman who was bandleader announced an hour into the concert. "We call this our wedding medley. For those of you not fortunate enough to have attended a Jewish wedding, to dance at a wedding is like the eleventh commandment for Jews. And during the break, by the way, if your feet should dance you right into Birchmere's store outside the double doors, you'll find our new CD on sale there." She grinned, and then raised her violin to a plump chin as the Capitol Klezmers burst into a hora. Dan drummed his fingers on the table and my feet tapped to the rhythm of the circle dance. Since I'd put on so much weight, I'd been too self-conscious to enjoy dancing, but this music was making me wish I was on a dance floor.

"They're wonderful. I've got to get that CD!" I said to Dan when the medley ended. "Didn't that make you just want to get up and dance the hora?" I added as he followed me out of the concert hall.

"I could hardly keep my feet still. It's a pity though."

His expression had sobered, and I glanced at him, startled. "What is?"

"It just crossed my mind how perfect a group like this would be for a wedding. If our daughter were having a real wedding, that is."

Well, if I had anything to say about it, he'd be dancing the hora at our daughter's wedding. If only —

"Say, isn't that Jenny?" Dan broke into my thoughts.

I looked where he was pointing. Sure enough, Jenny *was* there, toward the front of the ladies' room line, a line that extended into the hall outside the rest room. After she'd made a point of telling me she'd be stuck at a teachers' meeting this evening. She wouldn't have any reason to lie — unless she was planning some kind of confrontation over the wedding with Dan that I wasn't at all ready for.

"You'd think she could have come over to say hello," Dan said. "It's not like her to be holding a grudge about this wedding business."

"It's so crowded in here she probably didn't see us. We didn't see *her* till just now," I pointed out.

"Well, let's say hello now."

I grabbed Dan before he could start down the hall. "Not when she's walking into the ladies' room. You go buy that CD," I commanded, giving him a nudge in the direction of the store. "I'll tell Jenny we're here. I've got to go anyway," I fibbed, breathing a sigh of relief as I saw Jenny actually enter the ladies' room. I hurried up to the front of the line, murmuring, "Just going to wash my hands," to the first woman outside the door as I went in. The line for the toilets continued inside the rest room; some four or five women were still ahead of Jenny. "I thought you had a teachers' meeting tonight," I said to her.

"Oh, hi, Mom. I was going to look for you on the way back to our table. No, we lucked out. There was a power outage at school so the meeting's been postponed till next week. I guess I should have called, but I figured you'd already bought tickets. Anyway, I thought you'd enjoy them. Aren't they great?"

I nodded. "Your father and I both love the music. Of course I didn't tell him why I wanted to come."

"But Mom, don't you think we ought to talk to him about it?" Jenny asked. "I don't feel right with you doing all this planning behind his back."

"Well, of course I'm going to tell him," I assured her. "But this isn't the right time for it, to spring it on him in the middle of the Birchmere."

"I suppose." A toilet flushed, a stall door opened, and Jenny inched ahead in line. "Oh, did I tell you that Tamara's sister is going to let her wear her wedding gown?" she said. "It's really beautiful. Don't tell Tamara

I said it, but I bet Stacy's wedding wasn't half as tacky as she makes out."

I laughed.

"Stacy is going to be Tamara's maid of honor too," she went on. "The Jewish tradition really calls for each of us to have two attendants, to be like right and left hands. But it's not a rule or anything. We're only having one each. And Tamara's mother insists on calling Stacy her maid of honor."

"Uh huh," I said. I thought a moment. "So you're supposed to pick someone too?" I asked, wondering if any of the women in line were picking up on the fact that this was a wedding with two brides but no groom.

"I already have," she said happily. A girl emerged from the toilet in front of her, leaving her first in line. "You go on in, Mom," she offered.

I hadn't thought I needed to use the facilities when I followed Jenny into the rest room, but I did now. Badly. I looked guiltily at the woman behind me, whom I'd told I was just going to freshen up. "I don't mean to cut in," I mumbled.

She gave a resigned sigh. "Be my guest."

I entered quickly. Jenny's feet moved into the adjacent stall as I unzipped my slacks. "So who's your maid of honor, I mean right hand?" I asked as I let loose my waterfall with a great gush of relief. "One of your friends from the synagogue?"

"No, I don't know anyone there well enough yet. I asked Anita, but she was afraid the baby would want to nurse in the middle of the ceremony. So I picked someone who was a really close friend instead," she said, over an echoing stream.

I reached for the toilet tissue, trying to remember which girls she'd been friendly with in school. "So who is it, then?"

Over the flush of a toilet she said, "Can't you guess? He's my best friend, really. It's Adam."

After working for months to get a show up, it's always amazing how quickly closing night comes. The last performance of *Plaza Suite* was Saturday night, three weeks and a day since we'd opened, and it seemed the weeks had just flown. That's how it is when a show is going well, and this one had. No missed cues, no flubbed lines. The set looked good, the scenery never seemed on the verge of falling down and, with the approach of summer, the kitties stayed off the stage and outdoors where they belonged.

The first two acts of the last performance went smoothly as ice cream. Then came act three. My act. As my character, Norma, I had to do a frantic balancing act: simultaneously try to talk my daughter, the reluctant bride, out of the bathroom; stave off her impatient about-to-be in-laws; and stop Roy, my irate husband, from blaming me for the whole thing. Shortly into the act, Roy demands that I look through the keyhole to see exactly what Mimsey is doing in the bolted bathroom of our hotel room. Reluctantly, I obey.

On cue, I got down on one knee. From that perspective I caught the gleam of a pair of glowing green eyes just about to emerge from under the bed. One of the kitties, of course, and doubtless the one *I'd* been responsible for BAT adopting. The audience didn't realize yet that there was a cat onstage, and wouldn't if I could help it. Subtly I shifted my weight in the direction of the bed, at the same time trying to shoo Nudnik back under the bed, gesturing with my free hand in a way that was imperceptible to all but feline eyes.

At that point, the script called for me to give a cry of frustration because I had torn my pantyhose. Instead, as I balanced on one knee and one hand, my dress somehow caught under my slipping knee and hand. The fabric tore, with a noise that sent Nudnik scampering back under the bed. I struggled to my feet, again as called for in the script. I was now supposed to bemoan the fact that I had ripped my pantyhose. Except that it seemed pointless for me to go on about my ruined hose, when I was standing there holding together the shreds of a designer cocktail dress.

"Oh, my God!" I ad libbed instead. "I tore my dress!"

Unfortunately, the script calls for Norma to keep on kvetching about her torn hose. But *I* now had to substitute lines about restoring a satin gown.

"Bergdoff's is across the street. They're sure to have a seamstress," I improvised, praying it wasn't as obvious to the audience as it was to me that this dress was beyond repair.

The only thing that prevented total chaos is that Roy and Norma rarely listen to one another, so that Jack, who was playing Roy, simply came in on cue with his own lines, at the end of each of my ad libs. ("Give me a credit card. I'll call their personal shopper and have her meet me with something in my size.")

Our last performance, and I'd ruined it. I didn't even feel like going to the party. Dan had come to the show for closing night, and I told him I didn't want to go when he met me after I'd changed out of my costume.

"But Sam will take it personally if I don't show up," I added. Sam Blumenfeld had produced *Plaza Suite*, and he was expecting the entire cast and crew at his house for a gala producer's party.

"Honey, you'll feel better once you listen to what people who saw the show said," he reassured me, as he started the car. "You carried it off so well everybody thought that's the way Neil Simon wrote the play. Didn't you hear the audience roaring?"

"Sam won't roar," I said gloomily. "He'll blame me for taking that cat in to begin with."

"Forget Sam. The play's over. You can relax now. But it's a shame you ruined that dress when you were so crazy about it."

I could hear Dan thinking $500 down the drain, but he was kind enough not to say it out loud. I felt a rush of love and appreciation for him. "It's just a seam," I lied. "I'll have to have it cleaned before I can wear it again, in any case. There's a tailor who works for the cleaner; I'll ask him to sew it up."

"Well it didn't spoil the show at all," he repeated. "Funniest show I've seen in years. Funny and yet not-so-funny too."

"Maybe I was trying too hard to cover up."

"Not your performance. The play itself. You know, everyone thinks Neil Simon is only interested in writing one-liners. But I read his autobiography, and he takes himself much more seriously than that. For instance, he wrote the first act to take a look at how the husband's fear of growing older leads him to have an affair and probably to the breakup of his marriage."

"Uh huh," I said.

Dan slowed for a turn. "He said he hopes the audience will see themselves in his characters. It makes me wonder."

"What makes you wonder?" I asked. "You sound so serious all of a sudden."

"I am. I was thinking about how the act you were in concludes. Before the groom finally talks his fiancee into coming out of the bathroom and getting married, she confesses to her father that the reason she's suddenly got cold feet is she's afraid her marriage will end up like her parents' marriage."

"And so what about it?"

"So it got me to wondering if that's Jenny's problem. That she's decided to become a lesbian because we somehow haven't set her a good example of married life."

Before I could remind Dan that Jenny's orientation wasn't a choice, we were pulling onto Sam's street. It obviously wasn't time for a serious discussion, but maybe on the way home or the next morning. Dan's question gave me the opening I'd been looking for to broach the subject of how much the wedding meant to our daughter, and my considerable role in helping her carry it off.

Sam's wife, Zelda, had prepared a feast. And to my surprise, Sam hastened to congratulate me for ad-libbing my way out of the dress disaster. "You're a trouper, Sheila, a real trouper. That's all I can say."

Which was seconded by nearly everyone there. "I could never have found you a better costume," Sally said, throwing her arms around me. "Really, it worked so well, it's too bad you couldn't have ripped it in every performance! I wish we could extend the play another three weeks, patch that garment up with Velcro, and incorporate it into the show. But anyway, you'll never have to wear that monstrosity again."

Naomi embraced me next, pulling me into a bear hug that for a moment reminded me of all those X-rated dreams. Before I could pursue the thought, Jack was telling me that he and I made a great couple — theatrically speaking — and our guest director was telling me I was a pleasure to work with. By the time I made my way to the buffet table, my spirits had lifted dramatically. I heaped my plate — this was a celebration, after all — and looked around for Dan. I finally spotted him sitting on the love seat in the corner with Naomi. Dan was turning on the charm, the way he did whenever he spoke to an attractive woman, nodding appreciatively as she talked, his face lighting up with his irresistible Robert Redford grin. If I hadn't known she was a lesbian, it might have given me pause.

"It looked like you were having quite a conversation with Naomi," I couldn't help saying to him, as we were getting ready to leave an hour and a half later.

"She has some very interesting views on what it would take to make welfare reform work. Did you know she used to be a social worker? It's a pleasure to find someone who can carry on a conversation about something besides missed cues and when the next audition is. Do you have your purse?"

"I left it in the bedroom," I told him. "I'll just be a minute; I've got to run into the powder room before we leave."

He nodded. "See you in a minute then. Let me go find Zelda to thank her."

When I emerged, Dan had found Sam rather than Zelda, and was talking earnestly with him.

"Thanks for a great party," I said to Sam as I joined them. "And thank Zelda for me. Everything was marvelous; she ought to write a cookbook."

"I'll tell her," Sam said. He turned back to Dan. "And I do admire what you're doing; it takes a lot of courage. Good luck."

"So what are you doing that Sam admires?" I asked, after Dan and I had walked to the car without a word between us.

Dan opened my car door, waited for me to seat myself, closed it, walked to the driver's side, got in and started the engine. Still in perfect silence. It was a warm night, but the atmosphere in the car would have been ideal for a performance of the Ice Capades. And the air conditioner wasn't even running.

"Is something the matter?" I asked, though after thirty years of marriage it was a rhetorical question. I didn't need to be told when Dan's mood had swung one hundred eighty degrees.

Dan gave me a look. "Why should anything be the matter, Sheila? Just because Sam felt he needed to congratulate me on how broad-minded I was being, to rent the theater for my daughter's lesbian wedding."

"Oh," I said.

He swung away from the curb, racing the engine unnecessarily. "You gave BAT $250 to rent the place, behind my back, and all you have to say for yourself is 'oh'?"

Unfortunately, it was.

"I assume that was the money you told me you'd given as a donation. Do you realize that I wrote it down in our tax records, that I would have taken an illegal deduction?"

"I was planning to tell you about it, honey," I said, finding my voice at last. "Way before you had to do our taxes."

"But not before you made me feel like a fool, with your theater buddies knowing more about what's going on in my house than I do. And I suppose this isn't the only lie you've told me."

A moment went by.

"Well? What else have you lied to me about?"

Too much to remember, taken off guard as I was. "The dress I bought for my costume," I said at last. "That I told you I paid five hundred for, so I'd have a dress I could wear to —"

"To this *event* of Jenny's," he said with disbelief. "You went and spent $550 for a dress that, if you want to know the truth, is the most unflattering thing I've ever seen you in, then you wear it in a play where you treat it like a rag —"

"I didn't spend the money on that dress," I said quickly. "That's what I told you a little fib about."

He took his eyes from the road to give me another look. "A little fib is when you tell a phone solicitor you're on the way out the door. A $550 purchase is not a little fib. And don't compound it by telling me you didn't spend the money. It was on last month's Visa statement."

"I didn't say that I didn't spend the money. I meant, I didn't spend that kind of money on something to wear for a costume. The dress I wore for the play is something I spotted on the markdown rack that I thought would work well for a comedy. But I bought another, really beautiful dress at the same time, that I haven't showed you yet. One that really is worth the money," I babbled on. "Not like the chartreuse. That one is history. You've seen the last of it."

Dan exhaled. "Well," he said drily, "thank heaven for small favors."

I woke late the next morning, but though it was Sunday, I wasn't greeted by Dan's amorous advances. Instead, I found him in the kitchen, reading the Sunday *New York Times* over a cup of coffee. The sink held the cereal bowl he'd used for his solitary breakfast.

"You're not still mad?" I asked. I poured myself a cup of coffee and sat down opposite him.

Dan put down the paper to give me a look. "You think I don't have good reason to be angry? After the way you snuck around behind my back? When I expressly told you we were having nothing to do with this scheme of Jenny's!"

Until that moment I'd been feeling apologetic. Now I felt like fighting back. "You mean when you told me to behave like we don't accept our daughter, like we don't care about her at all! Do you realize how it makes Jenny feel when you talk about her...her ceremony like that?"

"Don't put words in my mouth, Sheila! This has nothing to do with accepting her."

"Speaking of putting words in someone's mouth," I said, "what about the way *you* spent the whole drive home after Anita had the baby, telling Jenny that I was going to go back on my word to her? That I wasn't going to keep the promise I made to support her?" I took a sip of coffee. I'd forgotten to add NutraSweet; the black coffee was bitter in my mouth.

"If by support, you mean spending hundreds of dollars of my hard-earned money —"

"Since when is our joint checking account *your* money?" I ripped open the packet of sugar substitute so quickly it spilled over the table.

Dan gave me another look. "Aren't you going to clean that up?" he said, after a moment.

I'd been about to. Instead, I sat unmoving while I told Dan, "If you're about to remind me that you're the one who brings home the bacon —"

"That does happen to be the case."

I got up and went to the sink for the sponge. "I should have said brings home the brisket. I know you'd die if I ever brought a pound of bacon home. Though I've never understood why, when you've eaten shellfish for years."

"This isn't a joking matter," he snapped.

"You're right, it's not. So let me remind *you*, that you wouldn't be earning the money you do if I hadn't put you through law school." I wiped up the spilled NutraSweet, put back the sponge and sat down again. My coffee still tasted bitter, but I left well enough alone. Hadn't I read somewhere that eating too many artificial sweeteners somehow led to weight gain? "Did I ever tell you that Mama wanted me to stay in school and get my Master's, and I told her I was already getting a graduate degree? My P.H.T. Putting Hubby Through."

"If you didn't tell me, she did. Now will you cut the comedy! You're not playing Neil Simon any more. I'm trying to have a serious discussion here. I think I have a right to be a little upset."

I took another swallow of bitter coffee. "You do," I admitted. "I shouldn't have lied to you. I'm sorry."

Dan nodded magnanimously. "Well, at least —"

"Let me finish," I said. "I shouldn't have done things behind your back. I should have had the nerve to stand up to you and tell you I was going to do what was right by Jenny. So I'm going to stop sneaking around from now on. I want you to know I'm through taking orders from you! I promised Jenny and Tamara I'd support them every step of the way and that's just what I intend to do. And that includes financial support. Like Debby Goldberg says, we can't expect the girls to pay for the whole thing. And by the way, I'm not talking about hundreds of *our* hard-earned money. It's more likely to be thousands. Don't you have any idea what weddings cost nowadays?"

Chapter Sixteen

*I*f my life were a one-act, Dan and I would have resolved our fight, one way or another, by the end of the scene. Either he'd have stormed off to call a divorce lawyer or, won over by my heartfelt arguments, taken me apologetically in his arms as he promised to walk Jenny down the aisle to the tune of "Here Come the Brides." Instead, Dan stormed off to keep his golf date, while I, fight or no fight, had to be at the strike of *Plaza Suite* in a little over an hour.

Normally, I find striking a set — dismantling the scenery that has taken weeks to build — depressing. But I wasn't sorry to tear down this set, where the conflict onstage was resolved far more quickly and easily than was likely in my real-life role of mother-of-the-bride. On top of everything else, the theater was a mess. If Debby Goldberg saw this place right now, she'd *plotz*. The sunlight streaming through the opened doors illuminated not just the stacked-up flats, waiting to be carried to storage, but the scuffed-up floorboards, the banged-up folding chairs, the dust swirling off the faded black curtain and the cobwebs in the rafters that created an atmosphere appropriate to our Halloween thriller all year round.

I'd once read a lighthearted guide to keeping house that suggested that rather than clean before a party, the hostess arrange an eye-catching vase of fresh flowers. Jenny and Tamara would have flowers, but it was going to take a lot more than flowers before the remodeled barn and adjoining house that were the heart of BAT resembled anything like the gentleman's farm I had so foolishly described to Debby. It could be done, of course. I'd get a recommendation for a good cleaning company, have the floors waxed. There must be a rental company that could supply attractive cushions for the two hundred folding chairs. I'd have to make a list, I thought, as suddenly energized as if I were in the beginning stages of decorating for a new play. All it would take was a little money.

My bubble burst. "Not a cent!" I could hear Dan thundering. I gave a despairing sigh, loud enough that Jack paused in prying nails from the floor to tell me, "Hang in there. Almost done." He gave me a good look then, and added, "Is everything all right, Sheila?"

Everything but the fact that Dan and I had reached an impasse, an impending crisis in our marriage. This didn't seem the time or place to discuss it, not with Sam Blumenfeld and three or four others working within earshot. "Oh, it's always a letdown when a show's over. And I was just realizing how shabby this place looks in daylight. How much work it's going to take to get it ready for Jenny and Tamara to have their ceremony here. I don't know what I was thinking of when I suggested it to them."

Sam, making no pretense of not overhearing, called out, "You get what you pay for," as he maneuvered one end of a flat out the stage door.

Jack stared after him a moment. To my surprise then, he set down his hammer to take my hands in his. "I just wanted to tell you what a wonderful thing you and Dan are doing to put on this wedding for your daughter. I can't tell you how much seeing that kind of support from parents means to me as a gay man. And if there's anything that Jim and I can do — anything at all — to help make it a success, don't hesitate to call on us."

My main responsibility at strike was getting the items I'd borrowed for the set back to their owners. Luckily, the two couples who owned the bedroom and sitting-room furniture had brought vans to transport them home. All I had to worry about were a few odds and ends: the bedspread from my spare room, a couple of lamps and Naomi's paintings. I bundled them into my van, half-tempted to drive directly to The Soaring Eagle and pour out the mess I'd made of things into Naomi's sympathetic ears. But she'd be busy with customers on a Sunday afternoon, the reason she'd begged off helping with strike. And I was too exhausted to head anywhere but a hot bath.

Dan was still out, probably at the club, having a bite with his golfing buddies after their game. Which was fine with me. When we bought the house, we'd opted for the master bath upgrade with a luxuriously oversized whirlpool, and now I sank gratefully into warm water and turned the jets to high. I closed my eyes and let the noisily bubbling water soothe me. A good half-hour went by before I was startled by the phone. I've never been able to let a phone ring, so I emerged dripping from the tub, wrapped myself in a towel and padded into the bedroom, leaving damp footprints on the Oriental carpet. I grabbed up the phone from my nightstand and perched on the edge of the bed.

The call was from Jenny. "I'm glad I caught you, Mom," she said. "Tamara and I talked to the Capitol Klezmers bandleader the other week, and they're a lot more expensive than we thought they'd be. To get them for four hours is going to be $1,200. They have the date free, and she said they'd give us right-of-first-refusal for it, but now there's someone else interested for the same day so we have to make up our minds by tomorrow evening."

Jenny paused for breath and I said, "I don't know how that compares to other groups, but they really have a wonderful sound."

"Oh I know! We went to a bar mitzvah at Bet Chaverim yesterday, and the group that played doesn't charge near as much, but they didn't compare. Tamara says the Capitol Klezmers are nearly as good as the Klezmatics."

The Klezmatics had recorded with Itzhak Perlman and had a widespread reputation. I wasn't sure if this local group was on quite that level, but I knew longing when I heard it. "If it's a matter of money —"

"I really didn't call to ask you for money, Mom."

But, I thought.

"But we really underestimated what everything would cost," Jenny continued. "I mean, the food won't be all that much with the potluck committee doing it, and it was brilliant of you to think of the theater and to rent it at such a low cost."

If you don't count the cost to my marriage. I didn't say that to Jenny, of course. Instead, I kept up a stream of *mm hmmns* and *uh huhs*, as Jenny said earnestly, "Still, there are so many incidentals. Table rentals, flowers, the *chuppah*. Of course the *chuppah* isn't incidental. If you don't have a canopy to stand under, then you simply don't have a Jewish wedding." She paused for breath.

I said, "You're right, that's the only thing essential for a Jewish wedding."

"But music is almost as important, Mom. Like the bandleader said, it's practically the eleventh commandment for Jews to dance at a wedding. It's one of the oldest Jewish traditions."

I didn't ask my daughter whether there was such a thing as a traditional Jewish lesbian wedding. I got back to the point of her call instead. "Well, then, if you're sure this band is the one you want —"

"Tamara's mother said if they're a top band, the price isn't out of line at all," Jenny interrupted. "She said if we wanted to, just to send the bill to her and her husband. But we hate to ask them to pay the whole thing." She paused again, briefly. "From what Tamara says, they'd have no trouble affording it. But she feels that the more her parents pay for, then the more Debby will try to take over all the wedding arrangements."

An expression I'd heard Mama use came to mind: the one who pays is the one who says. It wouldn't surprise me if Debby subscribed to that philosophy. "Actually, Debby suggested to me that she and her husband split some of the wedding costs with Daddy and me."

"That would be much better, if you were willing. But I thought Daddy didn't even know you were helping us plan the wedding."

"No, he knows about it now. I told him last night." There was no need, I decided, to mention the circumstances under which Dan had found me out. "I was going to tell you that before we hung up. And I had another long talk with Daddy this morning, but I'm afraid he still feels —"

Dan's voice suddenly demanded, "Is that Jenny on the phone? What are you telling her I feel?" I hadn't heard him come in; my back was to the door, and our carpeted stairs muffled footsteps. I jumped as he grabbed the phone from me.

"This is Daddy, Jenny," he told her. "I don't know what your mother has been telling you about me, but I hope you know that I'm as concerned about your happiness as she is."

"I wasn't saying anything about you," I protested. Dan ignored me.

"That's why I think this...this demonstration you and Tamara have planned is such a mistake. I know you think it's what you want now, but it's liable to come back to haunt you in the future when you want to change jobs or —"

Dan broke off as Jenny apparently cut in with a response. I couldn't hear what she was saying, though not for lack of trying. When Jeffrey and Anita called, Dan and I routinely got on extensions, but I didn't think I could pick up another phone under the circumstances, especially since it meant I'd have to go running through the house wearing nothing but a towel to reach one. Instead, I walked to my dressing table, a few feet from where Dan was now sitting on the foot of the bed. I pretended to be engrossed in moisturizing my face, while keeping my ears cocked.

"Times haven't changed that much," Dan said now, responding to whatever our daughter had told him. "And a teacher is expected to exhibit a certain amount of propriety in her private life." Another, briefer pause. "I didn't say there was anything *wrong* with being gay, if that's what you think you are, simply that there's no need to advertise —"

This time I could hear Jenny's voice through the receiver, though not her words.

"I'm sorry, sweetheart," Dan said back to her, "but no matter what you call it, it's not a wedding. A wedding is between a man and a woman. Period. You can be best friends with Tamara, but you can't marry her."

Another stream of protest from Jenny's end.

"Jenny, for someone who claims to be as religious as you have lately, you don't seem very interested in following one of the basic tenets of Judaism. There is simply no way you can reconcile this affair with the Jewish religion. No, hear me out. Maybe your mother can square it with her conscience, but there's no way I can condone what you're doing." Dan drummed his fingers on his knee, listening to Jenny, and then said sharply, "No, it is not the same as Jeffrey and Anita. Of course I didn't want your brother to marry outside his religion but like I told your mother, that was an entirely different matter — Jenny, will you let me finish!" After the briefest of pauses, Dan said, "All right, let me put it this way. When Tamara makes you pregnant, then I'll agree that the best course is for you two to marry."

I couldn't believe he'd said that, but before I could yell at him or grab the phone myself to try to smooth things over, he was apologizing to Jenny. "Look, sweetheart, don't cry. I wasn't trying to hurt your feelings. I was just trying to point out that there's a basic difference in a relationship between a man and a woman and one between two women, no matter how fond you are of each other." He sighed. "Of course I still love you even if you're a lesbian. Don't you know I could never stop loving my baby girl? That's why I only want what's best for you." Another pause. Dan sighed. "Do me a favor, at least, and give my objections some thought, will you? All right, call me if you want to talk some more."

He hung up the phone and I said, "Why did you hang up? I wasn't done talking with her."

Dan gave me a look. "Don't you think you've done enough to encourage her? Do you *want* her to ruin her life?"

"She's not going to ruin her life. If anyone's ruining things for her, it's you. You just told her how much you love her, but how do you expect her to believe you, if you don't even accept her for who she is?"

"For who she is? I suppose that's some kind of catchword you picked up in that support group of yours. Well, I happen to think a little more of my daughter than to reduce her to her — her love life."

"You think so much of her that you had to insult her and make her cry! If you really cared about her, you'd put a little effort into understanding her. The way I've tried to," I said. The bath towel slipped from my shoulders and I clutched it around me.

Dan's shoulders slumped. "I happen to care about Jenny every bit as much as you do. I'm not going to get into some ridiculous fight over which one of us loves her more." He looked suddenly exhausted, his bowed head showing all the gray that usually blended unobtrusively into the blond. All the *tsuris* over Jenny was aging him, I thought with a pang. I sat on the bed next to him.

"I'm not trying to pick a fight, honey," I told him. "I know you're trying to do what you think is right." I reached out to touch his shoulder and the towel I had draped around me fell off, leaving me nude, still glowing from my hot bath. I'd intended to make another effort at explaining to Dan why he was wrong. Instead, I let my hand creep up to his neck and rub it in the way that he liked. "Let's stop fighting about this," I purred.

According to our personal script, Dan should have responded to my cue with, "So you want to make love, not war." We hadn't lived through the sixties for nothing; the motto of the flower children had averted dozens of fights. I waited expectantly, still massaging his neck. I was suddenly ready and willing to kiss and make up. And eager as well; we hadn't "done it" that morning, after all.

But Dan's next line wasn't according to script. "Lay off, will you," he said irritably. "I'm not in the mood."

Dan didn't discover the $600 check I'd given Jenny to cover half of the Capitol Klezmers' fee until he got home from work Friday and checked our online bank statement. I hadn't mentioned it to him; it seemed wiser to wait until the check had cleared. So Friday evening, as soon as AOL had bid him *"Good*bye," Dan emerged from his den demanding to know exactly what I'd given Jenny the money for.

"It's for the band for the girls' reception," I said blandly. I was toss-ing the salad, and I kept right on as I added, "They're getting the group we heard at the Birchmere. They're a little on the steep side, but —"

"I thought it was something along those lines!" Dan snapped. "So, after all your apologies, you've gone behind my back again."

I set the tossed salad on the table. "I didn't go behind your back. I told you I was going to help the girls. Do you want red or white wine with dinner? We're having salmon so I think either would work."

Dan smacked his hand on the table hard enough to give the lettuce leaves an extra toss. "Forget dinner. And forget whatever game you're playing. You've done precisely what I asked you not to do. What do I have to do? Confiscate the checkbook to get you to stop ignoring me?"

"There's always Visa," I chirped.

"Dammit, Sheila!"

"I'm just trying to stop you from making a federal case out of this. We can afford to help Jenny out and you know it."

"And *you* know that this has nothing to do with what we can afford! I'd be glad to help her if she needed the money for anything else, but not for this scheme of hers."

The microwave beeped that the salmon was done. I took it out, removed the plastic wrap and set it on the table along with a serving dish of rice. "Getting married isn't a scheme; it's a celebration." I felt pleased with myself for thinking up the phrase; I'd have to remember to repeat it to the PFLAG support group. I took the bottle of white wine from the refrigerator. "I've made up my mind. White is better with fish."

"I'm warning you Sheila —"

"Warn me later. Dinner is ready." I got out the corkscrew and thrust it and the wine bottle at Dan. "Here, open this, will you?"

My attempt at jollying Dan out of his anger was a flop. He stayed furious the rest of Friday night and Saturday, and on Sunday morning was even less in the mood than he'd been the week before. I really need-ed to go to the support group that afternoon, but it was also the afternoon of Dennis Jr. and Shawna's wedding. Fight or no fight, Dan and I had to show up. Together. And if we didn't want to start people talking, we had to at least look as if we were getting along.

Which I could tell wasn't going to be easy from the moment I pulled my outfit from the closet. "You're wearing *that*?" he wanted to know.

That was the raw-silk pants suit that had been one of my first purchases at Wardrobe for a Small Planet, a seasonless fabric in a cut that flattered my figure as much as anything could. "What's wrong with it?" I wanted to know.

"It's slacks. You should wear a dress to a wedding. Like that $450 number that you haven't even shown me yet."

It was clear from the tone of Dan's voice that he intended a dig about my fibs and not about my fashion sense. So I didn't bother informing him that a dressy pants outfit like this was fine for a wedding. Instead I said, "*That* dress is too dressy for a wedding unless you're the mother of the bride. You won't see me wear it until Jenny's wedding."

"In that case, I won't see it at all. How many times do I have to tell you? I'm having nothing to do with that farce!"

Fortunately, Dan was no more eager than I to start the lunch bunch gossiping about our marriage. A wedding being an occasion for which Lois would need the services of a designated driver, we'd arranged to pick her up on our way. As she slid into the backseat, slender and chic in a slim-cut linen suit, Dan switched on his smile. It lasted until the usher seated us on the groom's side of the aisle, three-quarters of the way back from the altar. I looked around and spotted Natalie's husband, Norman, at the far end of our row, by the wall. Natalie's soon-to-be ex, that was. He'd spied me as well. I couldn't very well ignore him, so I gave him a little wave just as Lois gave me a poke in the ribs.

"Will you get an eyeful of that," she whispered. *That* was Natalie's lover, Roberto, and he was indeed an eyeful. As in, easy on the eyes. A broad face; smooth, tan skin; high cheekbones and full lips that looked like they knew how to kiss. Dark pools of eyes framed by thickets of lashes. And I hadn't even gotten to that body yet. I was about to whisper to Lois that I could see why Natalie had fallen for him, when my attention was diverted by a sharp, indrawn breath from Dan on my other side. For a moment I attributed his gasp to outrage for poor Norman, until I realized Dan was focused not on Natalie and Roberto, but on the couple coming down the aisle behind them: Jenny and Tamara.

"You knew they were going to be here together," Dan accused me two hours later. We had just arrived at the hotel ballroom where the reception was being held, and had a moment alone while Lois was in the ladies' room.

"Natalie and Roberto? Oh, I should say Natalya before she walks in and overhears me. Didn't I mention it to you? She made a big thing about his being invited when we had lunch last month."

Dan gave me a look. "Don't be deliberately obtuse. You know I'm talking about Jenny and that friend of hers."

"I guess Jenny did say something about being invited," I said, in as offhand a voice as I could manage. "She asked me if I thought towels were too impersonal a present, because she really doesn't know Dennis Jr. and Shawna that well. LaVerne invited all the kids, but the trouble is they haven't kept up with each other since they got too old for us to drag them to play group." Hopefully, my babbling would cover the fact that I, too, was shocked to see Jenny and Tamara walk in together, obviously a couple. As well as the fact that I was surprised at myself for being shocked.

"Fine. So let her come by herself. Or with us. Can you give me one good reason why she has to advertise her relationship?" Dan demanded.

I could think of several good reasons, which I'd learned at PFLAG and which, as a member of our chapter's speakers' bureau, ought to be on the tip of my tongue. But even if I thought Dan would be receptive to my enumerating them once again, this wasn't the time for a speech. Instead, I said, "Ninety-nine percent of the people here don't know us or the girls and could care less. Here comes Lois. Let's get in the receiving line before any more of the crowd shows up."

"*Mazel tov.* Congratulations," I told LaVerne as Dan and I reached her. She looked like a queen in her flowing gown, and beamed even more when I told her so. Dan moved on to congratulate her husband, Dennis, and agree that the four of us really had to get together soon. I took another moment to add, "Shawna is such a beautiful bride. And the children are adorable. The baby is precious, even cuter than the pictures you showed us." The baby was being held by Shawna's younger sister, who was simultaneously trying to distract little Denzel from grabbing hold of his mother's wedding gown.

Her smile widened. "I'm glad you got a chance to see her in the flesh. And I'm so glad to see your Jenny and," she paused, searching for the right word. "And her *friend*," she added, gesturing toward the girls, who were just entering the reception area.

"Is that what you call no one noticing who Jenny is with?" Dan growled once we'd gotten out of earshot.

"LaVerne isn't no one," I retorted. "She's one of my closest friends.

Of course we talk about our families when we get together." I'd found our place cards on the table where they were set out in alphabetical order, and was now trying to find the table number marked on them on the adjacent chart. Dan normally took over such tasks, but he was looking over his shoulder at Jenny and Tamara. They were still in the receiving line, talking now with Dennis Jr. and Shawna.

"So now your daughter is letting the bride and groom in on her relationship," he grumbled.

I gave him a poke with my elbow. "Everyone in the ballroom is going to hear *you*," I said, which at least shut him up. He took a miniature quiche from a tray being passed by a waiter and swallowed it with as much enjoyment as if it were cardboard, before heading toward the bar. We found Lois there, as I thought we would, exchanging a drained wineglass for one freshly poured. "I found our place cards," I told her. "We're all three at table eighteen with Natalie and Roberto."

Close up, Roberto was even more gorgeous than at first glance, oozing charm through his pores as he pulled out Natalie's chair. "My associate — and *very* good friend — Roberto Garcia," she said as we introduced ourselves around the table. In addition to the five of us, there were two business associates of Shawna's father, their wives, and Dennis Sr.'s old college roommate.

Dennis Sr.'s roommate turned out to be an orthopedist who, as soon as he learned that Natalie operated a gymnastics studio, launched an attack on the sport of girls' gymnastics. "I'm talking youngsters of ten and twelve who are pushed by their parents and coaches until they show up in my office with fractured limbs. Not from falls, mind you, but from the kind of day-to-day pounding that growing bones were never meant to withstand."

"Not at our gym," Roberto said. "You won't find any stress fractures at Natalya's School of Gymnastics." His voice was compelling, intelligent and assured, with a sexy trace of accent. *Our* gym, I thought, watching Natalie look at him adoringly as he explained the safeguards in their program. Natalie had never let Norman speak for her like that, but then she and Norm had never been of one mind, either.

It must be nice, I thought. To find someone on your wavelength, who not only cared about the same things you did, but was wrapped in such sexy packaging as well. Looking at him, I understood how Natalie could bring herself to walk out on her marriage. Lois was hanging on his every word. The businessmen and their wives were listening with what looked like more than polite interest, as well. Only Dan appeared turned off, probably still dwelling on Jenny and Tamara. Roberto's spiel would do nothing but remind him of the girls, with Tamara being the girls' gymnastics coach at the high school they taught at.

I glanced surreptitiously through the lushness of the floral centerpiece to see where the girls were seated, and spotted them at a table of younger people. Jenny was talking with the daughter of LaVerne's next-door neighbor. I barely recognized her. She'd grown from a scrawny preteen with a mouth that seemed too wide for her face, into a young woman with the looks of a model, her smile radiant and her hair done up in an elegant cascade of cornrows that must have taken hours to achieve.

Jenny turned from her conversation and noticed me looking at her. She gave a little wave. Then she and Tamara rose and made their way to our table. "Hi Mom, hi Daddy," she said, giving us each a peck on the cheek. She leaned over her father a moment more. "Daddy, thanks so much for the check you and Mom gave us for the band. It really meant a lot to me that you decided to send it."

It was obvious to me, if not to Jenny, that Dan was taken aback. But he could hardly tell her he'd done no such thing at the moment. "Well, you're welcome," he said finally. "But —"

Jenny was already launching on introductions. "Aunt Lois, Aunt Natalya, I want you to meet my partner, Tamara Goldberg. Tamara, these are my mother's other two best friends that I told you about."

"So we meet you at last," Lois said. "We've heard so much about you." Lois had drunk enough by now that who knows what embarrassing comment might fly out of her mouth. While I was holding my breath, "Aunt Natalya" and Tamara uttered delighted exclamations of surprise. Natalie jumped from her chair and the two of them hugged one another.

"I knew Jenny's friend was named Tamara, but I didn't realize it was *you*," Natalie said. "My prize gymnastics student. What are you doing these days?"

Once the formal bridal dance was over and general dancing started, I dragged Dan onto the crowded floor. We've always danced well together, and Dan automatically pulled me close to him as the band started a slow dance. We danced without speaking for a few minutes, the silence filled by the music and talk around us, the air sweet with floral arrangements and flowery perfume. Natalie and Roberto brushed by, dancing ostentatiously cheek to cheek, her Clairol-blond bob sunny against his shoulder-length hair, luxuriously thick and black. Over Dan's shoulder I noted her husband, Norman, who'd been placed at a table of singles, asking a good-looking redhead to dance, and then leading her to the floor. Natalie's eyes swung in Norm's direction; I was certain I saw her flinch before she turned back to Roberto with a comment I couldn't overhear and a trill of laughter.

I brought my mind back to Dan and me. "Thank you for letting Jenny think the check was from both of us," I said.

He stiffened, so that now I felt he was holding me at arm's length. "Did you think I was going to make a scene? That I was going to start a fight with her in the middle of this affair?"

"No, of course not," I murmured soothingly. "I just meant I was glad you didn't say anything to hurt Jenny's feelings."

"I do *not* go around trying to hurt our daughter's feelings!"

"I know you don't mean to. It's just that —" I broke off as I became aware Dan was no longer listening, that his attention had shifted to something behind me. He was staring over my shoulder just as I'd looked over his at Roberto and Natalie. "What is it?" I asked. But before he could respond, I had maneuvered us around so I could see with my own eyes: Tamara and Jenny dancing together.

If Dan had been rigid a moment ago, he had rigor mortis now. "What in God's name does she think she's doing making an exhibition of herself like that?"

It hadn't occurred to me either that Jenny and Tamara would get up and dance together in front of everyone there. Especially not slow dance, so that nobody could mistake that the two of them were a couple. But I pulled myself together and said, "There's no reason that they shouldn't be able to dance like anyone else. Relax, will you? Nobody but you is paying them any attention."

"*Everybody* is looking at them," he hissed.

As if to prove him right, a middle-aged couple near us turned to gawk. The woman turned back to the man. "Will you look at that? Mmnn, mmnn. Two such pretty girls and they're that way!"

"Now are you happy?" Dan demanded.

Only five minutes earlier I'd been enjoying myself, but happy was the last word I'd have used to describe my mood now. I didn't feel like dancing anymore. But the band kept playing as if this were some kind of dance marathon, and Dan kept shuffling us grimly around the floor, like a contestant determined to last till the bitter end.

"Honey," I said finally, "There's nothing wrong with the girls dancing together. If people make remarks, it just means we need to educate them."

"Will you listen to yourself! *We need to educate them,*" he mimicked. "Where do you think you are — a classroom? You're going to get up at a podium and tell everyone how wrong they are?"

It was a rhetorical question, but I answered it anyhow. "I meant through my work with the PFLAG speakers' bureau, not here at the wedding." I thought a moment. "No, I take it back about not here at the wedding. If you want to know, Jenny and Tamara are educating people just by being here and dancing together. By letting people know that two nice, pretty girls can be in love with each other."

"By making a spectacle of themselves, you mean!"

"You said that already," I snapped.

"As if *you* don't sound like a broken record, parroting all that stuff from your flag whatever group." Dan remembered we were in public and lowered his voice. "You and that damn speakers' bureau! Even if you were able to change one or two minds, what are you planning to do? Spend the rest of your life running interference for Jenny every time she decides that the whole world has to know about her sexuality?"

"If I have to, yes!" Though Jenny seemed to be doing fine without my "interference" at the moment. I tried to pull away from Dan, but he held onto me.

After what seemed an eternity of moving around the floor in silence, he burst out, "I don't understand what's wrong with you. I look at Dennis and LaVerne, bursting with happiness over their son married, two beautiful grandchildren...." He fell silent, and I wondered if he was remembering that the grandchildren had come before the wedding. Apparently not, for he went on, "I look at them, and at this wonderful affair the bride's parents put on, with their family and friends present to celebrate their happiness, and I could just cry. Can you tell me you don't want this kind of happiness for your daughter, you don't want to see her happily married with a family of her own?"

Put like that, I had to admit to myself the answer was yes. It might be a step backwards, but I, too, was still partly in mourning for the life I'd dreamed of for Jenny, the script that had been in my mind from the day of her birth, and that she would never follow. I was about to admit as much to Dan, when he added, "Well, obviously not, because from the day she came out to us, as you call it, you've done everything in your power to encourage her, to see to it that she'll never have a husband and children, she'll never get married, we'll never know the pleasure of giving her a wedding like this one, a wonderful affair where we can feel proud to invite everyone we know."

So it was all *my* fault Jenny was a lesbian! This time I did jerk out of Dan's arms, just as the band sounded the final notes. "You've forgotten. Jenny is going to have a wedding less than two months from now. And I intend to do everything in my power to help her make it just as wonderful an affair as this one!"

I felt so close to tears, I made a beeline for the rest room, just stopping at our table to grab my purse so I could repair the damage. Lois was still at the table. She gave me a look and said, "What's wrong?"

"Dan's mad because the girls were dancing. So it's my fault. I'll tell you when I get back from the ladies' room."

She got up from her chair. "Tell me now. I need to go myself." I filled her in while we were walking out of the ballroom and down the hall to the ladies' lounge.

"And if he's not having a good time, he's determined to make me miserable too," I said, as we walked into the carpeted outer area with its lighted makeup tables and mirrored walls.

"Look, nobody can *make* you miserable if you don't let them. So just make up your mind to have a good time," Lois said. She pushed open the door that led into the marble-floored space that held the toilet stalls and sinks. "After all, this is some unbelievable affair."

A toilet flushed with a discreet gurgle and the stall door opened. Natalie emerged. "If you're going to talk about me, you can do it to my face," she said.

Both of us stared at her. Lois found her voice first. "So who's talking about you?"

"The whole bunch of you. You think I don't have ears?"

"We didn't say one word about you," I protested. "Ask Lois."

"I don't *need* to ask Lois," Natalie said. "I heard her not ten seconds ago. She can't believe the affair I'm having. And you and Dan too. The whole time you were dancing, in fact from the moment Roberto and I walked into the church, Dan's been giving me looks that could kill. Don't you look so innocent, Sheila. I heard what you were talking about when the two of you were dancing. I may not have heard every word, but I heard enough. The whole afternoon, you've had nothing on your minds but my affair."

Chapter Seventeen

I phoned Lois at nine the next morning, but it was four before she returned my call. And then all she wanted to talk about was Natalie. "For someone who's been flaunting her affair the way she has, she was uptight enough about it. I thought we'd never convince her that you and Dan were carrying on about the girls, and not about her and that hunk of hers. If you ask me —"

"Speaking of the girls," I interrupted, "carrying on is exactly what Dan is doing. I don't know how I'm going to bring him around in time for their wedding."

There was a moment's pause, then Lois said, "We need to get together so you can tell me everything. I have to be at the office in fifteen minutes, but let's have lunch later in the week."

I needed to talk now, not later in the week. Besides, I'd sensed the discomfort in Lois's voice, her sudden hurry to get to the office. I was certain she'd have been willing to spend a few more minutes speculating on the future of Natalie's relationship with Roberto.

I ran through a mental list of friends who would understand the issues I faced and be available immediately. Only one person came to mind: Naomi. The pictures she'd done for *Plaza Suite* were still in my van. Returning them would be the perfect excuse to pop in on her.

It was five to five when I walked through the door of The Soaring Eagle. As I'd expected, Naomi was just closing the shop for the day. "You didn't need to make a special trip with those," she told me.

"I've got an ulterior motive. I was hoping you'd have time to talk a few minutes," I said.

Naomi laughed. "That's different, then. I always have time to talk to a friend." She locked the front door of the shop, placed the Closed sign in the window and took the two paintings from me. "You could have kept these if you wanted," she added, as I followed her upstairs. "I just dashed them off. They're not anything I needed back."

"They're good," I protested. "The composition and the colors — well, not as good as that Western sunset in your bedroom, but...."

Naomi gave her infectious laugh again. "I'm afraid I'm attached to that one."

"I wasn't hinting. It belongs right where it is."

"It reminds me of where *I* belong. But at least I have a trip out West in a few weeks," she added, as she carried the paintings into her bedroom. "I think I told you. I'm multitasking. Combining a buying trip with a couple of days as a vendor at the national PFLAG conference. Well," she said, returning to the kitchen, "sit down and let me pour you a glass of wine. Red or white?"

"White, please."

She poured two glasses of Chardonnay and sat opposite me at the kitchen table. "So, what's up?" she asked.

"More of the same with Jenny. Only things are coming to a head now." I took a sip of cold wine, then filled her in on everything that had happened since the closing party for *Plaza Suite*. "Seeing the girls dance together yesterday was the final straw for Dan," I concluded. I took another sip and admitted, "To be perfectly honest, I was a little shocked myself. But if I tell him that, it will just give him ammunition to try to keep me from supporting them. And my other friends think the whole thing is too bizarre for me to talk to them about it. You're the only one I can tell how I really feel."

"Your friends may surprise you. Your husband too. But I'm happy to talk, anytime you want. More wine?"

I'd drained my glass without even realizing. "I'd better not," I said. "I have to drive home."

"Don't worry. You won't be drinking on an empty stomach. I made a spinach lasagna this morning. It just needs heating up."

"Oh, I can't stay for dinner. I've got to get home," I said, surprised.

"In the middle of rush hour? It'll take you longer to drive through all that construction on 395 if you leave now, than to stay for supper and go in a couple of hours."

I'd forgotten about rush hour when I impetuously jumped into my car to see Naomi. "But I need —" I needed to cook dinner for Dan. He'd have a fit if there was nothing on the table when he got home. But I was getting good and tired of his fits. Let him fix his own dinner. "I need to call Dan and let him know I won't be home. Mind if I use your phone?"

I left a message on our machine while Naomi took a nine-by-thirteen pan of creamy lasagna from the refrigerator and put it in the oven. "That looks marvelous," I said. Marvelously fattening too, but I knew better than to say that to Naomi and invite another lecture on how my body image had been shaped by the patriarchy. Instead I wondered, "Are you expecting some more company?"

She gave me a look. "No. Why do you ask?"

"I can't believe you went to the trouble to make lasagna just for yourself."

"Why not? Why shouldn't I treat myself as well as I would treat a friend?"

I shrugged. "I guess if you like to cook. I don't cook if I don't have to. If I know Dan is going to be out, I buy myself a Lean Cuisine. Anyway, I'm drooling."

Naomi laughed. "You can nibble on the salad stuff while we cut it up. Or the bread," she added, producing a crusty bakery loaf. Her cutting board was hanging on the wall, an oiled piece of beautifully grained walnut that I would have thought too good to use. She set it between us on the small table, along with two well-sharpened paring knives and plastic Baggies of baby lettuces, carrots, radishes and celery. She selected a ripe tomato from a pottery bowl on the counter and sat down to slice it. "Getting back to the reason you came here, do you think your ambivalence about your daughter's wedding has anything to do with your conflict over your own sexuality?"

"No," I said, startled. "Not at all. I mean, I don't *have* any conflict over my sexuality."

Naomi smiled at me. Her lips looked warm, soft and desirable. Too late I remembered how much I'd admitted to her when we'd sloshed our way through lunch at Santa Fe East. "And if I wanted to talk to a therapist I would have paid one," I snapped.

"Sorry," she said, a little snappishly herself. "I thought you wanted to talk."

"I wanted to talk about what I'm going to do, when Dan is so against the girls' ceremony."

Naomi picked up the slices of ripe tomato she'd cut up and dropped them into the salad bowl. Juice trickled onto her fingers and she licked them with delicate relish, the way she might lick a lover's nipples. "It sounded like you've made up your mind."

"I have. I'm going to support Jenny no matter what. Even if I do have reservations. I just needed to talk to someone who could tell me, 'I know how you feel.'"

"I *do* know how you feel," she told me. "From experience. Only I was in your daughter's position when I had to come out to my family. My ex-husband took it pretty well. I think he'd had inklings of my feelings for Jody even before I did. But my children were another story — shock, hurt, embarrassment, acting out, you name it. But we worked through it, with the help of a very good family counselor. They're grown now, and they accept me completely."

I stared at her. What did she mean by saying that her husband had inklings of her lesbian feelings before she did? Was she saying that I simply hadn't realized *my* feelings yet?

"But I think it's wonderful that you're supporting your daughter and her partner, despite your reservations," she added.

I mumbled a halfhearted thank-you and reached for a large radish just as Naomi took a stalk of crisp, green celery. Our fingers brushed together, a momentary, unintentional caress, and she gave me another warm smile.

Suppose she was right, I asked myself. Suppose I was a lesbian and simply hadn't realized it yet? Suppose I were to "come out" to Dan and move into this tiny, colorful apartment with Naomi, the two of us sitting like this every night, smiling and talking as we prepared some wonderful, exotic dish, our fingers touching the way our lips would later. We'd help plan the girls' ceremony together, joining forces with Tamara's mother and her husband to assist them in putting on a marvelous affair, then dance at their wedding. We'd stay up late talking about art and theater, and work on every show at BAT together like Jack and Jim.

It would be a shock to my family, of course, and to my friends, but they'd get over it. After all, hadn't Natalie done as much, leaving poor stodgy Norman for her "soul mate?" And hadn't I realized weeks ago that I had more in common with Naomi than I'd ever had with Dan? So why not admit to myself that Naomi was right about me? Admit that I could almost feel her hand close the space between us, her fingers sending tingles through me as they moved with gentle persuasion on my body.

Her voice murmured, "Sheila —" and I jumped, brought back to myself, a married woman with no reason to doubt my heterosexuality.

Naomi's hand rested on my arm. "Earth to Sheila," she said. "The lasagna is ready to eat."

"Oh," I said, as she opened the oven door and placed the pan on a trivet between us. "I was just — that is, it looks...seductive."

I'd promised Jenny to shop for a wedding gown with her the next day. We'd agreed to go to David's Bridal, a shop in Springfield that advertised moderate prices and a selection of off-the-rack gowns that could be bought and taken home the same day. The shop had been Jenny's choice. "I want a nice dress, but I don't want to spend a fortune on something I'm going to wear once in my life," she'd told me. That was fine with me, especially since I suspected it would be me and not Jenny who would whip out her plastic at the register.

I'd also promised Marlene weeks earlier to take part in a lunch-hour panel discussion at AT&T, arranged by its gay and lesbian employees' association, so it was nearly two by the time I picked Jenny up.

"How was the panel?" she asked as I pulled onto I-395.

"Very well attended. I was surprised how many people showed up who weren't part of the gay employees' group."

"It's great all the work you're doing with PFLAG. I just wanted you to know I appreciate it, Mom."

I would have given her a hug and kiss but I knew better than to take my hands off the wheel at fifty-five miles an hour. "Thanks, sweetheart. It means a lot to have you tell me."

Jenny was silent a moment while I changed lanes. Then she said, "Dad seems to be mellowing a little, don't you think? You know how he doesn't like to come right out and admit he was wrong. So giving us the check for the band was probably his way of apologizing for what he said on the phone last week."

For an English teacher, Jenny seemed to be lacking in basic literacy. Otherwise she would have noticed that the signature on the check read *Sheila* Katz, not Dan. But perhaps she reasoned like Dan. Since he earned the money that went into our joint checking account, any expenditures on my part should be limited to ones that would meet his approval.

I hated to burst her balloon. And why should I put words in Dan's mouth? Let her ask her father if she wanted to know how he really felt. I compromised with, "Well, it's always possible," followed immediately by, "Can you believe this traffic when it's not even rush hour?"

A smiling saleswoman with henna-red hair welcomed us to David's Bridal and told us that her name was Barbara and she would be our bridal consultant. "When is the wedding?" she asked brightly. Told it was the end of August, she said, "Then you've come to the right place. With our selection you can find the perfect dress at the last minute."

The girls' ceremony was just over six weeks away, definitely last minute as far as finding a wedding gown went. But Jenny would have no problem finding a dress to fit her, I thought, as the saleswoman led us toward the racks of sixes and eights. Physically, Jenny is every inch Dan's daughter, slender and slim-hipped, with shoulders broadened by years of swimming laps. Clothes fit her as if she were a model.

"We pride ourselves on our range of styles," Barbara was saying. "Full skirts, sheaths, A-lines, informals, cathedral-length trains. What time of day is the wedding planned for?"

"Afternoon," Jenny said. She seemed a little overwhelmed by the rows of gowns, satins and laces, tulle and organza.

"Then you may want to make a selection a little more on the informal side. Though if it's a big church affair there's no reason not to choose a ballgown if you want. With your figure, honey, you can wear anything."

Jenny smiled. "Thanks, but I'm looking for something a little less ornate."

"Something simpler, of course. I really do think that would suit you better," Barbara agreed. "Now we have some nice sheaths here." She pulled two from the rack and held one up with each hand. "Simple but elegant. You could wear it afterwards to a dressy occasion."

Jenny studied the dresses, two simple columns of sleeveless white silk, as Barbara rotated them on their hangers. "That's more what I had in mind, but those are almost *too* plain. Maybe I should just look through the racks myself a minute."

"Of course. Take all the time you want. Just give me a shout when you need help. That's Barbara, remember." She flashed another smile as she replaced the two dresses and headed toward another set of customers.

"Let's divide up, Mom," Jenny said. "You look along the rack to the right and I'll look to the left."

A few minutes later, we each held several gowns. I was about to ask Jenny if she was ready to try them on when Barbara, the sales consultant, reappeared. "Would you like me to take those to a dressing room for you?" she inquired.

Jenny nodded. "I guess I've got plenty to start."

Barbara turned to me. "Why don't you make yourself comfortable," she said, gesturing toward an island of blue plush-velvet couches set on a deep piled rug. "I'll help your daughter and then she can come out and model for you."

I sat down on a couch at right angles to one occupied by two black women, apparently the mother and grandmother of a girl just emerging from the dressing room in a ballgown like the one the saleswoman had suggested to Jenny.

"Let me see the back," her grandma commanded. "Mmnn, I don't know. There's something about that train...."

"It's the front people look at," the mother said. "Can't you just see her walking down the aisle in it? Look how that neckline flatters her."

"Still you don't want to rush such a big decision. Let's see that last one on, sugar."

The girl nodded and turned back toward the dressing rooms. Her mother gave a muted sigh and snuck a look at her watch. Our eyes met as she looked up, and we smiled at each other.

"It did look good on her," I volunteered.

"This is the *seventh* she's tried on just in this store," the mother said. "My husband and I have four children, but the three oldest are boys. So being this is the one and only wedding we'll be putting on, we want everything to be picture perfect. Ron, my husband, says, 'Don't worry about the cost. Go on and max out the plastic, woman.'"

I smiled again, and she asked me, "You have more than the one girl?"

"Just Jenny," I said. "She has an older brother."

Jenny emerged right then in a fitted torso, dropped-waist gown that fell into soft, fluid gathers that only a girl with Jenny's slim hips could have carried off. The scooped neckline and cap sleeves were embellished with lace that gave the effect of an open-work necklace. She looked so stunning that it took my breath away.

She gave me a radiant smile. "Sorry to keep you waiting, Mom. I tried on three of the others in the dressing room but I didn't like them enough to bother coming out to show them to you. But this one, well, it's just what I dreamed of."

"You look like a dream in it," I told her, getting up from my seat and walking toward the mirror with her. "It's perfect for you. You've got good taste."

She smiled again. "Actually, you're the one with good taste, Mom. It's one you picked out. The only thing, it's also the most expensive of the bunch. It's nearly $800," she added, with a touch of hesitation.

"That's no problem," I said immediately. "I was planning to take care of it, and that's certainly not out of line these days."

"Oh, I didn't mean that you should —"

"Of course I should," I insisted. I'd told Dan I was going to do everything in my power to help Jenny, and I meant to do just that. "We've always expected to give you a wedding. So why should it be different just because you love another girl? Speaking of Tamara," I added, "do you want to have the dress held so she can come in and take a look at it before we buy it?"

Jenny shook her head. "No. And she's not going to try on her dress for me either. Stacy shipped it to her in case it needed alterations, so I've seen the dress — it's beautiful, more of a ballgown style. But we're not going to see each other in our wedding gowns before the ceremony. We just think it'll be more romantic that way."

I nodded, as Barbara, our saleswoman, appeared.

"I can tell by your faces that you've found the perfect gown," she said. She was smiling as broadly as if she'd just located a wedding gown for her own daughter. "You have a good eye, I can see that. That's a designer gown. Simple but subtle touches. All handwork in that neckline." I could see Barbara was right. You pay for subtle touches. She walked around Jenny, inspecting her from every side. "You couldn't have found a better fit if you'd had it custom made. And the length is right too. When you put on heels, it will bring it up a little, but it will still be fine without any alterations."

Jenny's bare feet showed beneath the gown. It hadn't occurred to me to tell her to bring shoes to try it with; it obviously hadn't occurred to her either. She smiled and said, "I never wear heels."

"For your wedding though," Barbara said, "a special day like that —"

"I can't see wearing shoes that hurt for the sake of fashion, even for my wedding. And I'm taller than my partner anyway, so there's no point in us looking like Mutt and Jeff. I'm sure I can find a nice pair of dressy flats."

"Oh, if you're taller...." Barbara said, seizing on the explanation that made sense to her. "But you don't need to run all over looking for shoes. We have a lovely selection here. If you'd like to have a seat again, Mother, I'll just take Jenny over to the shoe department." She led me back to my seat by the two women.

The younger woman gave me a tired smile. "I can't believe your luck, finding the right dress on your first try. It's simply gorgeous. And wait till your husband sees her in it! If he's anything like mine, he's just bursting with pride to see his little girl a bride."

"I guess you could say he's really beside himself," I told her.

By the time we got to the checkout counter we'd added a pair of white satin flats, headpiece and veil, and the total was well over a thousand.

"Mom, I can't thank you enough," Jenny told me, as I signed the charge slip. "We had no idea how much it really costs to put on a wedding, even trying to keep it simple. Even the invitations — at least you'll be glad to know we've taken care of those ourselves. We just got them out, in fact. You should be getting yours in the mail any day now."

The invitation arrived the following day. It was hand lettered, on stationery of a better quality than I'd have expected the girls to spring for, and simply and informally worded: *Tamara Goldberg and Jenny Katz invite you to share in our joy as we exchange vows of holy matrimony,* followed by the date, time, address and the words *Dinner Reception to follow immediately after.* I left it on the hall table for Dan.

He looked at it in silence a long moment. "At least Jenny had the sense to leave us out of it," he said at last.

Watching Dan toss the invitation into the wastebasket, I felt a rush of relief that I hadn't told him I'd just charged over a thousand dollars at David's Bridal. He knew I was committed to helping Jenny put on the wedding; there was no need to update him on every detail. I waited till he'd gone into the den. Then I retrieved the invitation and took it upstairs.

The rest of the week brought a welcome diversion. Anita and Jeffrey had agreed to let Stephanie come for a one-week visit. Jeffrey was driving her down, and then staying for the weekend. Dan and I were on pins and needles until his Toyota wagon finally pulled into our driveway Saturday afternoon.

Dan was prepared to give up his Sunday golf game to visit with his son, but Jeffrey had made plans to take Steffi to the zoo with Jenny and get in some "sibling bonding" as he put it. He brought a tired Steffi home a couple of hours after Dan returned from the golf course. "Be a good girl," he told her as he kissed her goodbye in front of the house, before climbing behind the wheel of his station wagon. "Mommy and I will talk to you on the phone every night, so you can tell us about all the fun you're having with your grandparents."

"I will. I'll be *so* good," Steffi promised. She wiggled out of his arms. "I'm a *big* girl."

"You know what, Grandpa, Grandma," she said, as she walked up the front walk with us once her father had driven away, Dan and I each holding one of her hands. "I saw bears and lions and elephants and you know what?"

"What?" Dan asked, on cue.

"A fox ran through the elephant cage and the elephants all got mad. They got *so* mad. And Aunt Jenny said he was a wild fox."

"A wild fox? Really?"

"Uh huh. And Aunt Tamara said foxes used to just live in the country, but now people built so many houses where there used to be country that wild animals have to come right into the city to live."

"*Aunt* Tamara?" Dan said, taken aback. "I didn't know Tamara was going to the zoo with you," he added after a moment.

"Uh huh, she did. And guess what?"

"What?" he asked warily.

"She and Aunt Jenny are gonna get married."

Dan gave me a look, over Steffi's head. "Steffi, your Aunt Jenny and her friend Tamara are both girls. So —"

"I know that," Steffi said, letting go of our hands to pull open the screen door. "I know they're girls, silly Grandpa. And they're both going to wear beautiful white dresses and have lots of flowers and, and guess what?"

"I can't," he said heavily.

"I get to be a flower girl."

The only downside to having Steffi visit was the toll on our privacy. "If she feels lonely at night, she'll just crawl between you," Jeffrey had assured us blithely. Having a five-year-old who may pop into bed with you at any time puts a damper on any couple's sex life. Normally, Dan would have found giving up our Sunday-morning romp the next weekend as frustrating as I did. Now, he seemed to welcome an excuse to skip it.

I still hadn't told him about the charge on our Visa bill. Nor did he check it online; with Steffi visiting, her doting grandfather turned on his computer only to introduce her to the educational CDs he'd stocked up on.

The week just flew by and before I knew it, Steffi's visit was over. I worried that Dan would start a fight with Jeffrey when he came to pick her up. But he kept his feelings about Steffi taking part in Jenny's "mockery of a wedding" to himself, rather than make a scene in front of his granddaughter.

So it wasn't until Monday evening, the day after she'd left, that the other shoe dropped.

Monday morning I'd intended to tackle the housework I'd neglected for a week while taking Steffi to the library, the mall, the "dinosaur room" at the Smithsonian and even to swim at our country club. But I was interrupted by constant calls from Debby Goldberg.

At nine that morning, she said, "You said you'd be too busy to talk while your granddaughter was visiting. I hope this is a good time, because we have a staggering amount to get done the next few weeks. Now I want you to join forces with me on this: If the girls are going to persist with that potluck idea of theirs, then we have to absolutely insist on hiring a caterer to coordinate everything. Just pray it's not too late. Otherwise, can you imagine the kind of disaster we might have? Our temple had a potluck once with nothing to eat but lasagna."

At noon, she called to say, "It's so easy to forget incidentals. Not that having a record of the big day is incidental. We need a list of what the photographer calls 'must have' shots. The girls coming down the aisle, and taking their vows, of course. Cutting the cake. By the way, I assume you want a copy of the photo album for you and your husband. Stan and I are getting a duplicate of the girls' album; I know I won't be able to bear leaving out any of the shots. Now," she said, pausing barely long enough to breathe. "Do you have any thoughts about the video?"

At three, she remembered that we hadn't discussed the rehearsal dinner. "Now that's normally the responsibility of the groom's family, but in this case...." In this case, I found myself agreeing to make all the arrangements, for which we would then split the cost.

At four the mail came. I sorted Dan's from mine and mine from Occupant's, and then stood holding the Visa bill between my forefinger and thumb. Jenny's dress wouldn't be on it so soon, but the bill would surely remind Dan to check our account online. If I were to drop it into the wastebasket along with the junk mail, I thought.... I sighed, set it on the table with the rest of Dan's stack, and went to the kitchen to decide on a recipe that might improve the bad mood I knew Dan would be in once he'd discovered the charge.

By the time Dan came home, I had one of his favorite dishes, seafood paella, simmering on the stove in my best porcelain-clad saucepan. A dozen stalks of fresh, green asparagus lay on the counter, ready for the steamer. "Something smells good," he said, sniffing appreciatively. Sure enough, he sounded in a better humor than he had in weeks.

"I hope so; I've been in the kitchen all afternoon. Dinner will be ready as soon as I steam the asparagus," I said, as I laid the spears in the steamer and turned the burner on high. "I've got a bottle of Riesling chilling in the refrigerator, if you want to open it."

"Let me go online a couple of minutes first."

It occurred to me that it might not be a bad idea to warn him of what he was going to find. "By the way, I forgot to tell you —" I said, but he'd already headed into his den. I could hear the annoyingly cheerful chord that Windows plays as it loads. Five minutes later, Dan stomped back into the kitchen.

"I see you've gone and done it again! I should have known when I found you doing your Julia Child act. The only time you cook a decent dinner is when you want to butter me up before you spring some new surprise on me!"

I turned from the stove where I'd been about to lower the burner under the asparagus. "I wasn't trying to spring anything on you. I don't know how many times I've told you that I intend to help Jenny out."

"And I don't know how many times I've told *you* that I absolutely forbid you to spend one penny more on this —"

"Since when do you have the right to forbid me! I'm going to spend whatever I feel is right. I'm sorry if you don't like it, but you're not going to stop me!" I was trying to reason with Dan, to speak as calmly as I could, but I could hear my voice come out of my mouth high-pitched and shrill.

He slammed his hand down on the counter. "I might as well be talking to the wall! What I say counts for nothing around here! I'm not going to stop you, am I? We'll just see about that!"

He spun on his heel and marched into the foyer.

"Dan, dinner is ready. We can talk about this while we eat," I called. There was no answer. I hurried into the foyer after him. I'd left my purse on the table there. Dan was digging through it. "What do you think you're doing?"

"What I should have done months ago! Where — aha, there it is!" He pulled my Visa card from my wallet.

"Give me that!" I grabbed for the card. Dan moved his hand out of my reach. "Dan, will you give me back that card!"

I made another grab for it, and Dan said, "You want your card back?" He sidestepped around me back into the kitchen. The kitchen shears were out on the counter where I'd been using them. He grabbed them up.

"Are you crazy! Give me those!" I screamed. "Give me back my Visa."

The shears sliced the card in two for Dan's answer. He let the two halves fall to the floor. "All yours."

I stared down at the two halves of the card. *Sheila* was neatly bisected from *Katz*. "Are you crazy?" I demanded again.

"I'm canceling the card in the morning and getting one in my name only."

"Have you gone insane?" I repeated.

He gave me a triumphant look. "You're burning dinner," he said.

I whirled toward the stove, suddenly taking in the scorching smell from the stove where my good copper-bottomed steamer had burned itself dry. I grabbed up potholders. Dan waited till I'd moved it from the stove, then calmly took a plate from the cabinet, helped himself to a large serving of paella, and stalked out of the kitchen. I could hear the den door slam behind him.

The phone shrilled as I shoved the ruined asparagus down the disposal. I snatched it up. "Yes. What is it?"

"Oh, I hope I'm not calling at a bad time," Debby Goldberg chirped. "I was just thinking. Wouldn't it be a wonderful idea to put an announcement of the girls' wedding in the newspaper?"

Chapter Eighteen

I ate my supper standing at the sink while I cleaned up the kitchen. Then I retreated to our bedroom, where I waited for Dan to apologize. By ten, I had to admit he wasn't about to. I turned off the TV I'd been pretending to watch, changed into my nightgown and went to bed. I lay as close to the edge as I could without actually falling on the floor, my back pointedly turned to Dan's half of the bed. He came up half an hour later. I lay in silence, waiting for him to make the first move, but the only sounds were the rhythmic swish of his toothbrush and the plop of his dirty clothes as he dropped them on the floor for me to pick up. He climbed into his side of the bed and I could feel the sway of the mattress as he turned away from me. His breath came with the slow, perfect ease of feigned sleep. It occurred to me that he was waiting for *me* to apologize to *him* for supporting our daughter the way I'd told him I would. Well, he would have a long wait. I lay awake fuming for another hour before I got out of bed to sleep in the guest room.

In the morning, I stayed in bed until I heard the rumble of the garage door as Dan headed to work. It was ten by the time I'd dressed and finished my coffee. I fished the two halves of my Visa card from the silverware drawer where I'd hidden them, and dialed the number for reporting lost and stolen cards. "I feel so stupid," I said, once I'd been connected to a customer service representative. "I never destroyed my old card when I got my new Visa this year, and last night I thought I should have, so I cut it up. Only," I added, with the self-deprecatory little laugh I'd rehearsed, "I went and cut up the wrong card." I held my breath until the woman

226

assured me it happened all the time and did I still have the two halves, in which case I just needed to mail them back and my card would be replaced. I thanked her profusely and hung up.

At least Dan hadn't closed the account the way he'd threatened. Or closed it yet, I amended. The day wasn't over. There was still the checkbook of course, but Dan had used it last. I jumped up and hurried into his office. As I'd guessed, the checkbook wasn't in its cubbyhole; he'd doubtless taken it with him to work. With no checkbook or credit card I'd be hard-pressed to buy groceries for dinner, let alone help Jenny. It suddenly dawned on me that, in my agitation, I'd forgotten the cards I'd hidden under my panties. Unlike Dan, I preferred not to carry all our credit cards wherever I went. I generally used the Visa that gave us frequent-flier miles and left the others home. I ran upstairs to the bedroom and yanked open my underwear drawer. I sighed with relief at the sight of my American Express and MasterCard.

But my relief was only temporary. As sole wage earner, Dan was the primary cardholder on each and every credit card I had. And it was obvious he intended to keep me from using "his money" for any of the girls' wedding expenses. In his present mood, I wouldn't put it past him to close out our other credit-card accounts if he discovered any more wedding-related expenses on them. Years earlier, when I'd opted to spend my time at an avocation while my friends were starting careers, Lois had told me that one day I would regret being financially dependent on my husband. That day had come.

Since I wasn't about to land a high-paying job in the next few days, I had to figure out some means of pressuring Dan into loosening his stranglehold on my purse. For one thing, I decided, I'd forget the trip to the supermarket I'd intended to make. I couldn't very well charge our groceries to the Visa card he'd destroyed, after all. I could, of course, use one of the others, but why should I? I served up leftover paella for dinner, rubbery from being left on the stove too long. Instead of complaining, he ate it in grim silence before vanishing into his den again.

I'd just put on my nightgown and stretched out on one of the guest-room beds, when I heard Dan use the toilet in the "family" bathroom and close the door behind him as he went to bed in Jenny's old room, apparently without noticing that our bed had been vacated by both of us. Since we weren't speaking, I didn't bother letting him know that both of us were sleeping in a guest room.

Wednesday was a repetition of Tuesday, except that dinner was a can of unadorned tuna fish served with celery sticks. If nothing else, it was low calorie.

Thursday morning, the phone woke me at nine. Debby, I was sure. I'd been putting her off about the rehearsal dinner for two days. Well, that's what machines were for. I let it pick up, and Marlene's voice sounded. "Sheila, this is urgent. Call me back the second you get in. My number is —"

I picked up before she could finish repeating it. "Hi, I'm here. Just a little slow getting to the phone. Is something wrong?"

"As a matter of fact, yes. I can't go to the PFLAG conference this weekend. I've come down with shingles."

"Shingles?" I tried to clear my brain; I hadn't had my morning coffee yet. "You don't mean there's something wrong with your roof; you're talking about the disease, right? But only old people get that."

There was a moment's silence, and then Marlene said, "Thanks, you've made my day."

"I didn't mean — how are you feeling?"

"I have never in sixty-three years felt worse. I ache in joints I didn't know I had. I've got hideous blisters all over the side of my face. I was up all night because it hurt too much to put my head on the pillow. I can't even put my eyeglasses on without pain and my doctor tells me if I'm lucky I may feel better in a month. When I hang up with you, I'm going to put in a call to Dr. Kevorkian and see if they'll spring him from jail long enough to do me in."

I laughed. "Well, if you can still make jokes, you're probably going to live," I assured her. "Is there anything I can do?"

"There most certainly is. Do you have plans for this weekend?"

Only camping out with Dan in the midst of an Arctic chill. "Nothing special, why?"

"I want you to fill in for me at the conference. Nobody else from our chapter is going this year, and I want us to be represented."

This called for sitting down. "You want me to go to a conference in Scottsdale, Arizona? On a moment's notice?"

"Why not? My plane ticket isn't transferable, unfortunately, so you'll have to buy one at full price. But I'll see to it you're reimbursed, even if the difference comes from my own pocket. My husband thinks that under the circumstances we'll be able to use ours at a later date. Anyway, the room won't be a problem; I'll call the hotel and change the name on the reservation. It's a nice room, by the way. Two queen-sized beds; we like to spread out. I know you'll have a wonderful time. In fact, why not take your husband and make a little second honeymoon of it?"

The last thing I felt like doing was having a "second honeymoon" with Dan. Right now, I regretted we'd ever had a first. Going away without him was becoming more appealing by the moment.

"He's tied up this weekend," I lied. "But I guess I can go."

"Sheila, you're a lifesaver! Now, I'd like you to attend the regional caucus, the chapter development workshop and the panel on bisexuality. I'm especially interested in getting a report on the bisexuality panel."

Only natural since her son had proved to be bi rather than gay. "Caucus, chapter development and bisexuality panel," I repeated obediently.

"Right. And don't forget to enjoy yourself. The national conference is a wonderful experience. It can change your life."

I had my suitcase open on the bed when Dan came upstairs to change from his suit after work. He stopped in the doorway and did a double take. "What do you think you're doing?"

"What does it look like?" I countered, and folded the top of my raw-silk pants suit. Marlene had told me to take something dressy for the banquet Saturday night.

Dan sat down heavily on the side of the bed. "You're leaving me over the damn Visa card? Don't you think that's overreacting?"

At least he was worried over the prospect. "I'm only leaving you for the weekend. I'm going to Scottsdale for the national PFLAG conference. Marlene got sick and asked me to fill in for her." I snatched up my silk pants before he could wrinkle them. "Don't worry," I added sharply, "my hotel bill is taken care of."

He'd sounded alarmed — I told myself — at the thought that I might actually be walking out on him. But now he said, just as sharply, "In that case, it's not a bad idea for us to get away from each other for a while."

I'd been expecting a featureless glass high-rise, but the hotel shuttle deposited me late the next morning in front of a sprawling, stuccoed pink edifice. The lobby was decorated in a desert theme, with mission-style couches in an oak finish and salmon pink cushions. Every couch and chair was taken. Those in the center of the lobby were occupied by guests sipping drinks from frosted glasses while talking to each other or on cell phones. The rest held harried-looking travelers surrounded by luggage, apparently waiting for spouses or partners to check in for the two of them. Long lines inched along in front of the half-dozen desk clerks, like supermarket checkouts the day before Thanksgiving. As I would at the market, I picked out the line that seemed to be moving fastest and took my place at the end, wheeling my case behind me. From signs I'd seen in the lobby, apparently two other groups were also having their national conventions there that weekend: an organization of orthopedic surgeons and a conservative women's group that called itself Mothers United in Concern for Kids. I wondered if they'd picked the name because or in spite of an acronym that spelled MUCK.

I looked around as I poked along — as too frequently happens at the supermarket, I'd picked the slowest line — but couldn't tell the concerned mothers from us presumably unconcerned PFLAG moms. I didn't see a soul I knew either, not surprising, since Marlene had told me no one else from our chapter was attending. It struck me that under normal conditions, this was the type of luxury hotel I'd be thrilled to check into with Dan for that "second honeymoon" Marlene had suggested. I suddenly didn't know what I was doing there alone. But once I hooked up with PFLAG, I'd be sure to find friendly company for the weekend, I lectured myself as I finally reached the head of the line.

"Reservation for Katz. Sheila Katz," I told the desk clerk.

He frowned at his computer screen. "Sorry, nothing here under that name."

"There must be. No, wait. I'm filling in at the PFLAG conference for someone else. She phoned in a reservation change. Marlene Wilkins. Or, it might be under her husband's name, Bob, I mean Robert, Wilkins."

"Let me check. Wilkins, Robert. Okay, we had a reservation under that name, but it was canceled yesterday."

"It wasn't canceled; it was transferred to my name. His wife couldn't make it because she's sick. She said they'd call the hotel to change the name."

"They must have forgotten. I just have the cancellation."

"I'm sure they wouldn't have forgotten. Would you check again, please?"

"Sorry, Ms. Katz, nothing under that name."

"But — look, never mind the reservation. I need a room for one person for tonight and tomorrow night." I pulled my wallet from my purse and extracted my MasterCard.

He waved it away. "No can do. We're full up. Sorry."

I stared at him, my credit card clutched uselessly in my hand. "What do you mean you're full? I've just flown halfway across the country to get here."

"Sorry," he said again. He didn't sound half as sorry as I was.

"Well, can you find me a room in another hotel around here?" Even as I said it, I realized there was nothing else anywhere "around here." I couldn't simply walk down the street to another hotel; we were in an area of gated enclaves, and miles from downtown Scottsdale, a location that I presumed did feature civilized sidewalks.

He shrugged. "I'll see what I can do. But it may take a few minutes. There's a lot of conventions in town, taking advantage of off-season rates. If nothing else, maybe I can find you something at one of the airport motels. If you don't mind waiting till I help these other folks...."

I did mind, but there seemed no choice. I moved to the back of the line, wishing *I* had someone to go deal with the desk clerk while I rested. The only person I even knew who'd be attending the conference was Naomi; she'd taken a vendor's table in the exhibition area. I'd have to look for her if I ever got settled.

The clerk was now checking in a couple with a crying baby and two small boys chasing each other around the nearest potted cactus. At least I had nothing in tow but a wheeled overnight case, I thought, as a tall, graying woman walked through the lobby entrance pushing three huge bags on one of the hotel's self-serve luggage carts. Then I smiled happily and called out to her. "Naomi!"

She wheeled her cart up to me. "Well, hello neighbor. You didn't tell me you were coming to the conference too."

"I didn't know it until yesterday. I'm filling in for our chapter president; she got sick at the last moment. I tried to call and let you know, but your partner said you'd already left."

"Three days ago. But I just got to the hotel; I've been visiting artisans I buy from in this area. In fact I really need to get checked in. Let me give you a call later. What room are you in?"

"I don't have one yet," I said gloomily, reminded of my dilemma. The line had moved up without me while we were saying hello. "In fact,

I'd better get back in line," I said, as I closed the gap between me and the man ahead of me. "Marlene told me she would switch her reservation to my name, but they claim to have no record of it. I'm sure she wouldn't have forgotten, so someone must have forgotten to write it down."

Naomi got in line behind me. "They didn't forget. You've been walked."

"What?" I said.

"Walked. Bumped. Hotels overbook these days, same as airlines, and changing the name gave them the excuse."

"The clerk said he'd try to find me something in an airport motel," I said, nodding at "my" clerk, who was now helping a tanned, silver-haired couple so energetic and fit looking that they could have posed for a vitamin ad in *Modern Maturity*. "Otherwise it looks like I'll be camping out in the lobby."

Naomi laughed. "It's a big season for conventions because rates are low in summer."

The silver-haired couple walked off, smiling at each other, and the clerk nodded to the man in front of me. "He told me," I said, inching ahead. "I shouldn't have come," I burst out. "I don't know what I'm doing here. I had this terrible fight with Dan, and then Marlene called and asked if I could leave the next day, and I thought why not, anything to get away. And now I don't even have a room and I don't know a single person here."

"You know me," Naomi reminded me.

"True," I said. "Look, you might as well get ahead of me. It's going to take him a while to find me something. You were in a hurry to check in, weren't you?"

"I am. Thanks," she said, as I moved behind her. "Naomi Pearlman," she said to the clerk, and then turned back to me. "I just had a thought. If you don't mind a roommate, you're welcome to share with me. I have one bed — a king-size — but if he can't switch it to a double room, I'll ask them to send up a rollaway. These conventions are a lot more fun if you stay in the conference hotel."

"That would be a godsend! If you're sure you won't be crowded," I added.

"Not at all. I hardly spend any time in the room anyway. And it'll be a help to have someone split the cost."

Five minutes later, we walked into room 328. The bed was a king-size, but the clerk had promised that a rollaway would be delivered within the hour. Naomi set up the luggage rack and lifted the largest of her cases onto it, unpacked several rolled flannel pouches that looked like those I kept my good silver in, and put them into a canvas carryall. "I'd love to sit down for a chat, but I have to get to the exhibition area and set up. I paid good money for sales space at the conference, and I need to get this stuff downstairs while people still have time to browse before the conference starts. No one is going to buy something pricey like Native American jewelry when they're hurrying between sessions. I've got to get them before or after the panels. But if you'd like, we can meet for dinner later. Is eight too late for you?"

"That would be fine," I told her.

"Good." She picked up her bag and gave me a smile. "Then I'll see you tonight."

I hurried to the opening luncheon — Friday featured a luncheon, Saturday the gala banquet — and then to the afternoon sessions. The afternoon was spent dutifully taking notes at the sessions Marlene had asked me to attend. When the sessions had ended and attendees stopped milling around the exhibits room, I helped Naomi pack away her wares before we went to dinner.

"Do you mind eating in the hotel?" she asked me. "I've been driving around for three days, and I hate to get behind the wheel of a car again. They've got a good Mexican place here; it's not your typical hotel restaurant."

It must have been good — the line of patrons waiting for tables spilled out of the entrance. After a five-minute wait, we lucked out. A table for two became available in the bar, and the couples ahead of us opted to wait for seats in the outdoor courtyard.

"How do you like Scottsdale so far?" Naomi asked, as the waiter set down the pitcher of margaritas she'd ordered.

"I haven't seen anything but the inside of meeting rooms yet. I've been too busy taking notes at panel discussions."

She smiled. "We should have waited for a table in the courtyard then. There's a little more atmosphere there."

"Hot atmosphere," I told her. "I figure if God had wanted us to sit outside in eighty-five-degree weather, He wouldn't have invented air conditioning."

Naomi laughed. "Or She wouldn't have. So what have you been attending?"

"Mid-Atlantic regional caucus, chapter development. Those two I could have done without, but Marlene specifically asked me to go to them. And bisexuality, that's another one she wants me to attend. That's tomorrow. For the rest, I get to pick the ones I'm interested in."

"Which are?"

"Well, I thought I ought to go to the panel on same-sex marriage. What with Jenny and Tamara planning one and all the *tsuris* that's been going on about it. Other than that I don't know." I reached for a tortilla chip and dipped it in the salsa, popped it in my mouth, and then reached frantically for my margarita and took a big swallow. "I didn't know this salsa was so hot!"

Naomi laughed. "It's an acquired taste. Try putting just a dab on your chip."

I did as she said, and took another sip of my drink. The cold liquid slid smoothly down my throat, a marvelous mixture of tangy and sweet, the salt forming delicious little crystals around the rim of the glass. "There's a workshop on improving as a public speaker," I said, picking up the thread of our conversation. "That might be a good one to go to if I'm going to stay on the speakers' bureau. Then there's, let me see, Countering the Arguments of the Religious Right. That's another training kind of workshop. A couple of the parents I ate lunch with were going to both. One on designing web pages, which isn't for me at all. One called Coming Out of Marriage —"

"I was on a panel on Coming Out of Marriage," Naomi exclaimed. "For your PFLAG chapter, actually, back about five or six years ago. I'm still a member of the chapter, you know. I don't have time to be active anymore, but I still pay my dues."

"It might be interesting," I said, taking another swallow of margarita. "Though right now, I'm not sure I want to listen to anything concerning marriage. For two cents, I'd trade Dan in for one of the kitties at BAT."

Naomi laughed again. "Cats are great companions, but they have their limitations. Now that I think of it, you did say something about having a fight with Dan before," she added in a more serious tone. "You two haven't worked out your issues over your daughter's wedding?"

"*He's* worked them out. What he says goes; that's his idea of working out issues. I bought Jenny a wedding gown and he cut up my Visa card." I took another big gulp of margarita, draining my glass. Naomi's was nearly empty as well; I refilled both our glasses from the pitcher.

Naomi was staring at me. "He cut up your credit card? That's an incredibly controlling thing to do. How did you react to that?"

I reached absentmindedly for a tortilla chip. "Oh, I've got plenty of other cards."

"But that's not the point. You're talking about a pivotal power struggle in your relationship."

"The way Dan was talking when I left, I'm not sure we're still going to have a relationship; he said it might be a good idea if we separate for a while."

"Really! I had no idea things had gotten that bad. How do you feel about it?"

I felt stupid for inadvertently giving her the impression that Dan and I were separating, when — no matter what the issues between us — we were just spending a weekend apart. What I really needed was advice on bringing Dan around before Jenny's wedding. But Naomi was slipping back into her one-time role of clinical social worker. I wasn't interested in being psychoanalyzed. Especially when I remembered that the last time I'd had a few margaritas with Naomi, I'd blurted out to her that she'd been starring in my X-rated dreams. Better to keep the conversation off myself. So I told Naomi, "I really don't want to talk about it now. I've got to —" I searched for the right word. "I've got to *process* it on my own first."

That seemed to do the trick. Naomi nodded and said, "I understand. But feel free, anytime you want to talk...."

I murmured okay back at her, ate another salsa-laden chip and swallowed a large gulp of my margarita. At the next table, a dark-haired woman lit a cigarette, holding it in a way that reminded me of Lois, before her doctor ordered her to quit. Her smoke drifted toward us, the scent reminiscent of Lois's kitchen, when we'd sat together with cups of coffee, watching our kids play in her yard, our conversation circling around the idiosyncracies of husbands and children. "You were saying you were on a Coming Out of Marriage panel," I said, just as the waiter came to ask if we were ready to order. "I was thinking of going to that panel," I told her once we'd ordered dinner and a second pitcher of margaritas. "I'm kind of curious about how someone decides she's a lesbian, after maybe years of marriage. I know you said you fell in love with your neighbor, but...."

"She was my best friend, as well. And I didn't *decide* I was a lesbian, I *realized* it. I couldn't be crazy in love with another woman without coming to realize I was attracted to my own sex."

235

"That's the part I find hard to picture," I admitted. "Not the sex, I mean." I paused, wondering if I had just implied that I *could* picture sex between two women. "I just can't imagine falling in love with one of my friends," I added quickly.

"I know. You told me," Naomi said. She took a couple of sips of her margarita, while I tried to think of a different topic. My mind was blank. I lifted my own glass, turning it to the side still rimmed with salt. When I put it down, our waiter was walking toward us. He set our dinners in front of us, taco salad for me and crab enchilada special for Naomi. The sight of the food made me realize how hungry I was. I dug into my salad, trying not to eye Naomi's enchilada with envy. It occurred to me that my salad, laden with beans, beef, guacamole and sour cream, was no less caloric than the sauce-rich enchiladas I had so virtuously passed up.

Naomi took a bite and gave a happy sigh. "Delicious."

"It looks it," I admitted. "I was just wishing I'd gone ahead and ordered it myself."

"Want a taste?" Naomi cut a bite-sized piece off one of the enchiladas. I waited for her to lay it on the side of my plate. Instead, she held her fork up to my lips, pausing expectantly until it occurred to me to open my mouth and let her feed me the tidbit.

"It's wonderful," I said, a bit disconcerted. "So, what were we talking about?"

Naomi smiled. "You were asking how I could fall in love with my friend. And the answer is that I've never felt that being friends has to be mutually exclusive with becoming lovers."

"Oh," I said. "Well, I guess....I guess that's true for you, then. But like I said, I still can't imagine falling for one of my friends."

This time she gave what looked like a wicked grin. "Maybe not. Or maybe you just haven't been imagining it with the right friend."

We lingered over our margaritas, and then gorged on fried ice cream, which Naomi talked me into trying. It was well after ten when we unlocked the door to our room. I didn't know about Naomi, but I was ready to drop. Unfortunately, the rollaway the desk clerk had promised to have sent up hadn't arrived. I went to the phone and called the front desk. I counted thirteen rings before a harassed-sounding clerk picked up and asked how he could help me. "Let me check with Housekeeping," he said, once I'd explained about the missing rollaway.

Two minutes later I hung up the phone and said to Naomi, "I can't believe it! They don't have the rollaway they promised us. That mothers' group has taken every folding bed in the hotel."

"Oh? Well, par for the course." She disappeared around the corner, where an alcove offered hanging space and the luggage rack where she'd set her suitcase earlier. I suddenly wondered uneasily if she would sleep in the nude, remembering how she'd been naked under her robe the first time I'd dropped in on her, when she'd dressed so nonchalantly in front of me. Instead, she reappeared wearing a T-shirt that reached halfway to her knees. I was still sitting on the side of the bed by the phone. "I'm dead on my feet. Mind getting up so I can take this bedspread off?" she asked.

"But what are we going to do?" I said, as I got off the bed.

Naomi yanked off the spread and tossed it in a crumpled heap on the chair. "*I'm* going to sleep," she said.

"But —"

"It's a king-size," she said. "We won't crowd each other. Unless you want to sleep on the floor." Put like that, there seemed no alternative to getting my own nightgown and toilet articles from my bag. When I emerged from the bathroom, Naomi was already asleep, lying near the edge of the bed on her side, face turned toward the wall.

I slid carefully under the covers, positioning myself on the opposite edge, a no-woman's land of two feet between us. At least the mattress didn't sag — the last thing I needed was to roll on top of Naomi during the night. After all that I'd let slip to her over the past few months, she'd be sure to get the wrong idea. It was bad enough that I'd packed my oldest nightgown, a garment so threadbare, it was virtually see-through. Imagining Naomi waking up and seeing through it, I pulled the covers up to my neck.

I'd been exhausted, but now I couldn't sleep. The room was full of sounds I hadn't noticed when the light was on: the drone of the air conditioner, the slam of a door closing down the hall, the quiet rise and fall of Naomi's breath. On the other side of the wall there was a sudden excited squeal, followed by a woman's voice entreating, "Oh, yes, OH!" I strained to hear the rest of the words, but couldn't make them out. Some lucky couple on their honeymoon, or maybe celebrating a second honeymoon, I thought enviously. It had been over a month now, since Dan and I had made love.

A second voice answered, murmuring indistinct, sexy nothings.

Startled, I realized it was a woman's. So it was a lesbian couple in the room next to ours. I supposed that wasn't surprising with the PFLAG conference in the hotel. I tried to picture what they were doing together or, more accurately, how they were "doing it." My mind was painting a scenario not too different from the way the dreams I'd had about Naomi would have turned out if I hadn't woken up first. The first woman cried out again. Naomi's slow, even breathing quickened. She stirred. I froze, as if I expected our next-door neighbor's lovemaking not only to wake her, but to inspire her to follow suit. After a moment, she turned onto her back and started to snore and I let out my own breath in a sigh of relief.

I turned onto my back and listened to Naomi's breathing, steady and slow, steady and slow. I was about to drift off when a high-pitched squeal sounded from the other side of the wall, almost like a cat this time. It was a cat, I realized as my fingers felt fur, Naomi's big orange tomcat, settling himself in the space between us. But this time, Naomi sprang up and said, "Oh no, you don't. Out you go." She turned on the lamp on her bedside table as she rose to put him out of the room. She must have taken off the T-shirt, I thought sleepily, for now she wore nothing but a rich suntan, her nipples dark and succulent against her breasts, ripe for a lover to tongue them. She smiled at me once she'd shut him outside the door. "We won't let him get in the way this time, will we?"

"No, we won't," I said. I started to sit up and hold my arms out to her, but my tummy looked so much flatter lying down that I lay back again and waited for her to come to me. Then we were lying face-to-face, breast to breast. My nightie had vanished and my naked body pressed against hers. My nipples stood up and I throbbed down there. Outside the room, the cat kept crying.

"Poor kitty. I should let him in," she teased me.

"Oh no, you don't," I said. "Not now, when I've got you where I want you." I rolled on top of her, pinning her down, my extra pounds coming in handy for once. "I've been dreaming about this," I told her. She smiled, her lips so inviting that I kissed her, then kissed her again. Our tongues met and danced till we both needed to draw back for a breath.

I bent toward her again and she licked her lips and whispered huskily, "Sheila! What in God's name are you doing?!"

I woke with a start. Incredibly, I'd rolled onto Naomi's half of the bed in my sleep. Not only that, I was lying on top of Naomi. My legs straddled her thigh, my hand cupped her breast and my nightgown was hiked up to my neck. "I — I was dreaming," I said. My brain told my body to scoot back to my side of the bed, in fact to dive right under the bed in embarrassment. But my body didn't respond. I lay right where I was, throbbing between my legs where I gripped Naomi's thigh, my palm tingling from touching her breast.

"Must have been quite a dream," she murmured. "Uh, Sheila, I can't move with you lying on top of me like this."

"I know." I knew, but I still couldn't bring myself to get off her. "The cat got between us again, but you put him out."

His demanding meow sounded again, and Naomi said, "There's your cat." Not a meow, but a squeal from next door, our neighbors still at it hot and heavy.

"They're two women too," I said.

Naomi pushed herself up on one elbow, forcing me to roll off her. "Sheila, wake up. You're saying you were dreaming about me?"

"I've been dreaming about you for months," I confessed, moving no more than an inch away. "I told you that a long time ago. When we had lunch and drank too many margaritas."

"Like we did tonight." She reached over to turn on the lamp by her bedside, and rubbed her eyes.

The light made me aware that my gown was still rolled up practically to my neck. My brain told me I should yank it down and cover myself, but my hand didn't move. If it had, I might have jerked off Naomi's T-shirt instead. "You told me dreams send you messages about what you should be doing in real life."

"I suppose I did, but —"

"But nothing." Before I could stop myself, I took her face in my hands and kissed her. Her lips were as warm and inviting as they'd been in my dream, but the faint aftertaste of lime and cilantro let me know this wasn't a dream. I sat back astonished at myself, filled with a confusion of emotions of which only one was clear: I wanted more.

Naomi was staring at me with a bemused expression, half smiling, half alarmed. "Sheila, I'm not sure just what's going on here, but you know I didn't ask you to share my room so I could seduce you."

"Who said you did? I'm the one seducing you." My hand went to my nightgown. Instead of pulling it down, I jerked it off and tossed it aside, then reached for Naomi's hand and placed it on my breast. She left it there a moment, long enough to send tingles all through me. Then she pulled it back.

"You told me you found me attractive," I said, sulky with disappointment.

"I do. But —"

I knew just what she was going to say. "But my weight really does turn you off."

"No, of course it doesn't. I *like* your weight." She let her eyes go up and down my naked body a moment. "Sheila, I really do think you're lovely."

"But not lovely enough to make love to."

"It's not that. I'd like to make love to you. I really would. But you're a straight woman."

"Well, so were you once."

She smiled, then reached out and took my hand in hers. "That's true. But you're at a very vulnerable point in your life, in the middle of a separation —"

"I am?" I supposed I had given her that impression. "All the more reason I could use a little tenderness."

"And besides, I'm not interested in a romantic relationship with you, Sheila. I really do think you're a beautiful, marvelous woman. And I hope we'll always be friends. But we aren't on the same wavelength. Not enough to sustain the kind of relationship I'm looking for."

"So who said *I'm* looking for a relationship? Anyway, I'm not actually in the middle of a separation; Dan just likes to blow off steam. And I don't know if I'm really a lesbian underneath. But for whatever reason, I haven't been able to get you off my mind. I've been dying to get you into bed practically since I met you," I admitted. "So here we are in bed together — it just seems like fate brought us together tonight. Why not make the most of it?" Naomi was still holding my hand; now I took her two hands in mine and moved them to my breasts, her left hand on my right breast, her right hand covering my wildly beating heart. "Pretty please," I whispered.

This time she let her hands remain. And then they were stroking me the way I'd been dreaming of. And I was caressing her, feeling the wonderful strangeness of a woman's body under my touch. Her T-shirt came off and I traced her curves with my fingers, ran them up and down her body, circling her nipples, twining my fingers through that wilderness of pubic hair and then delicately down below, toward that wonderful, pleasurable little button, knowing just where to stroke as if her body was my own. Her breath quickened and she whispered, "Oh God, that feels wonderful. You're a wonderful lover, Sheila. You must have been a lesbian in a previous life."

I couldn't answer her because I was gasping with excitement, as if I was making love for the first time. Her tongue caressed mine, and her exploring mouth made my nipples stand up. Then we were lying side by side, her hand curving over my mound, pressing and circling. I arched my body and her finger slipped inside me, going right to that Good-spot Dan has such trouble finding. I gave a little cry, my body moving in helpless rhythm against her, losing track of everything but her hand circling and pressing and circling, moving me to a fever pitch of excitement till I came and came and came.

Chapter Nineteen

*T*he clock radio woke me at six-thirty in the morning. The obnoxiously cheerful voice of a disc jockey found me nude, lying with one arm over Naomi, our nightclothes in a tumbled heap on the floor. Carefully I slid back to my side of the bed, closed my eyes and opened them again. Nothing in the scene had changed except that Naomi had opened her eyes and was now looking back at me with an expression of concern. I took a deep breath. "This wasn't one of my dreams, was it?" I asked her.

"Not unless we were having the same dream." She looked at me searchingly. "Are you all right, Sheila?"

I pondered the question. Which wasn't easy considering that I had a pounding headache and my brain felt fuzzy as a ripe peach. Not to mention the fact that it wasn't every day that I woke up in bed with someone I'd just had sex with. Someone other than Dan, that is. Someone still naked as a jay. Foggy as I was, I realized that whether or not Naomi could move without a qualm from being friends to lovers, I couldn't. Not that I knew whether Naomi had any intention of having the kind of long-term affair the word lovers implied.

"I'm fine," I fibbed, "except for a hangover."

"Sure?" she asked. She glanced at the clock and I could sense her impatience to open her sales table for business well before the morning sessions.

"I just said so," I said. "After all the dreams I've had about you, last night was like...was like a dream come true." She smiled. Looking into her eyes, I couldn't tell whether or not she believed me but she swung her legs to the floor. Her body was as exciting as I remembered.

"We both have to get going now," she said, "but we need to talk. We need to sit down together and have a long talk."

I nodded numbly. She walked to the bathroom as casually as if she were fully dressed, but this time I averted my eyes. It wasn't until Naomi had closed the bathroom door behind her that it occurred to me that she hadn't said a word about our lovemaking being a dream come true for *her*.

With all that was going around in my head, it was a wonder that I managed to get myself dressed and to the first conference session on time, with two cups of strong, black coffee and an order of French toast under my belt. Or where my belt would have been if I could still have found my waistline. But nine o'clock found me sitting in the third row of a discussion on coming out of marriage, notebook in my lap. The panel consisted of three women and a man, who had realized only after marriage that they were lesbian or gay, respectively. The man and one of the women explained that they'd had feelings for their own sex before their wedding day, but thought that getting married would "cure" them. The other two women told stories remarkably like Naomi's. As the younger of the two, a fortyish redhead with a figure to die for, put it, "I hadn't a clue to my real orientation until I met the most wonderful woman."

The other members of the audience nodded attentively, waiting until the moderator called for questions, then asked how the panelists' children had adjusted, whether or not they had come out to their aging parents. I was sure that not one of the other mothers present was questioning *herself* the way I was, wondering what it meant that *she* had met the most wonderful woman. Not a one, I was sure, had spent the night before having hot sex with her female roommate.

The redheaded woman began describing how she and her partner visited her children's teachers to explain that the youngsters now had "two moms." But she wasn't answering *my* questions: How did she feel the first time she made love with another woman? Did she know she was a lesbian first or did a light bulb go off in her brain the first time they kissed? Did she really have no sexual feelings for her husband all the time they were married? Did her husband suspect her affair before she told him?

For all his faults, I was sure that Dan had never cheated on me. And in the bright light of the overhead fluorescent panels, being angry at Dan seemed a weak excuse for going to bed with someone else.

I wondered whether Naomi had felt this guilty when she'd first started in with Jody. The session ended, my questions still unanswered. I went on to the next morning session, ate lunch in the hotel coffee shop with two mothers who'd been sitting next to me, and then attended the afternoon workshops. When I went to my room to change for the banquet, my emotions were still in a whirl.

Naomi returned to the room while I was putting the finishing touches on my makeup. "Hi," I mumbled, from behind "Blushing Scarlet" lipstick, thankful that I wasn't still in my bra and panties.

"Hi, yourself." She dropped her jewelry satchels on the table and sat on the edge of the bed. "You been doing okay, so far?"

I wasn't, but I couldn't think how to tell her that without making her feel bad for giving in to what I had started. "I guess. I went to that 'Coming out of Marriage' panel you suggested. It gave me a lot to think about." My sexual orientation mostly, but I wasn't ready to get into that. "And the one on same-sex marriage," I hurried on. "I was kind of disappointed in that one. I thought it would be more on how parents dealt with their kids' same-sex marriages, but it was mostly political. What's going on in Vermont, that kind of thing."

Naomi smiled. "It's a pretty political subject. But I meant, how are *you* doing? I was hoping we'd touch base sometime during the day, but I haven't seen you at all."

Because I'd been avoiding her all day was why. I'd purposely steered clear of the vendors' tables; it would have been too awkward to make casual conversation with her. "I've been rushing from one thing to another," I mumbled.

"I hope you haven't been stuck inside the hotel all the time. Once you get out of Scottsdale the scenery is magnificent. I've got this conference sandwiched in the middle of my buying trip, but I can spare a few hours to show you around tomorrow afternoon."

"I wish I could," I said, turning to face her. "But I have to leave for the airport right after the brunch tomorrow."

"That's a shame," she said. She looked me in the eye. "Not just on account of the scenery, but it would give us a chance to talk about what's happened between us."

"Oh," I said lamely. I knew she was right. What we'd done in bed had changed the character of our friendship and I couldn't keep ignoring it. There was no time like the present, I supposed, with a quick glance at my watch.

Naomi's eyes followed mine. "I know you're in a hurry to get downstairs. It'll have to wait till I get back home then. As a matter of fact, I bought a banquet ticket myself, so I need to change clothes and get downstairs too. It's kind of dressy, isn't it?" She didn't wait for my nod to head to the alcove where her clothes were hanging.

"I'll see you downstairs then," I said, and hurried out of the room before she could strip.

The cocktail hour before the banquet was already underway when I reached the ballroom. I asked the bartender for a glass of white wine; from now on I was steering clear of margaritas. I sipped slowly, keeping an eye out for Naomi, and finally spotted her not far from the entrance to the ballroom. I must have missed seeing her come in; she was already holding a drink. She was talking animatedly with another woman, a dark-haired younger woman with a long braid hanging down her back and dressed in a loose, crinkled cotton gown. Naomi herself looked stunning in slim black pants and a simple beige tunic set off by a turquoise bear-claw necklace.

I started threading my way toward them, then paused. The woman was probably another of the vendors; I didn't want to barge into their conversation if they were talking business, or keep her from catching up with an old friend. I waited till Naomi glanced my way, over the other woman's shoulder, and waved at her. She gave me a little wave in return. I wasn't sure whether or not it was an invitation to join them. While I was hesitating, I heard my name called. "This way, Sheila! We're saving a seat for you." I turned and joined the two mothers I'd had lunch with, who were saving me the last seat at their table, one close enough to the stage to have a good view of the after-dinner entertainment.

The dinner was surprisingly good. Like the restaurant Naomi and I had eaten in the previous night, it was a cut above most hotel food, Mexican with a Continental flair. I finished my glass of wine, then split a bottle of good merlot with my new friends. By the time the after-dinner speeches, vocalist and comedy routines had ended, I was feeling considerably more relaxed. The three of us chatted as the dancing started, a mix of male, female and heterosexual couples crowding the floor.

The band switched from rock to a slow dance. I spotted Naomi and her friend amid the couples dancing cheek to cheek, dancing what the chaperones at high-school dances would have termed a respectable distance apart, and still talking to each other a mile a minute. I wondered if Naomi would feel obliged to ask me to dance. I hoped not. Unlike Natalie, I wasn't ready to flaunt my affair in public. Assuming that Naomi and I were even having an affair, that was, and not just a one-night stand. I wasn't sure of my feelings, let alone hers. I was growing uncomfortable again and I quickly turned back to the other women, bringing up the panel on same-sex marriages in general and going from there to the issues between Dan and me over Jenny's wedding, as if we were holding a mini support group.

"So Dan has dug in his heels and, meanwhile, Tamara's mother keeps pressuring us to split the costs with them for the six-piece band, a rehearsal dinner with French service, the works. You have to give her credit; she wants to give Tamara a wedding that isn't inferior to what they gave her sister. But she calls me so many times a day about one detail after another that I'm thinking of asking her what long-distance carrier she uses, so I can buy stock in it." The other two mothers laughed at my little joke but I sat bolt upright. A way to resolve at least one problem had just occurred to me.

The three of us said good night shortly after that. The room was empty when I went upstairs; Naomi was presumably still on the dance floor. I brushed my teeth and got into my nightgown. Then I sat on the edge of the bed wondering if I should call the front desk and see if I could talk them into scrounging up that missing rollaway. But what was the point now, I thought, as I crawled into bed.

I lay awake asking myself what I wanted to happen tonight. My conscience told me not to be unfaithful a second time, while my memory was beginning to recollect the long lines of Naomi's thighs. But would Naomi be willing to make love again without processing our relationship first? I wasn't sure what I would say to her when she asked, but I knew I wouldn't be able to sleep a wink. Then my eyes opened to bright Arizona sunlight seeping around the edges of the room-darkening drapes. A glance at the bedside clock told me it was nine-thirty, well past the time I should have been up if I was going to pack and get to the ten o'clock brunch in time. Naomi was already gone from the room. She must have woken before me and turned off the alarm, letting me sleep.

I didn't know whether to be relieved or aggrieved that she hadn't woken me when she went to bed. But I couldn't worry about it now. I got up and dressed in record time and threw my things into my suitcase. I barely had time to check out before the brunch, leaving my bag in temporary storage behind the front desk so I could catch the bus to the airport right after. I left Naomi a scribbled note in the room, saying I'd see her when she got home from her buying trip.

It was just as well I didn't have to come up with words to tell her goodbye in person, I thought as the brunch came to an end. I exchanged addresses and promises to keep in touch with the two mothers I'd met. Then I fled for home.

Dan and I had very little to say to each other Sunday night. Just enough to make it clear that he hadn't budged a bit about the girls' wedding.

And though it had been a month of Sundays since the last time we'd made love, he turned his back to me and went immediately to sleep. I, on the other hand, lay awake, planning what I would say to him once I'd checked our financial records. When I finally fell asleep I dreamed I was in Naomi's bed, her cat hogging one half, so the two of us had to sleep curled up in each other's arms.

Once Dan had left for work the next morning, I went into his office and thumbed through his file drawers until I came to the hanging file marked Stock Holdings. There were two folders inside. The one in front was labeled Dan's Stock Holdings. Directly behind it was a folder that I'd all but forgotten about, until my jest about calling our broker to buy shares in Debby's long-distance service brought it to mind: Sheila's Stock Holdings.

Ever since we'd been married, Dan and I had had joint checking and saving accounts. During the time he was in law school and I was teaching, it was my earnings that had kept our checks from bouncing. But since that time, Dan had taken over as family provider. I'd been happy to leave our finances up to him. We had an equal partnership, I joked to my friends: He earned our money and I spent it. They'd all laughed but Lois. "Girls, you've got to take personal responsibility for your financial well-being," she'd warned, ever since she'd been deserted by the rat.

I hadn't taken her advice to heart until the issue of Jenny and Tamara's ceremony had come up, and Dan had started telling me what I could and couldn't spend "his" money on. I'd been kicking myself ever since for not having seen to it that I had some funds of my own, when all the while it had slipped my mind that a large chunk of our assets were, in fact, in my name, Dan having taken the advice of the lawyer who drew up our wills several years earlier to split our investments between us.

It was no wonder that I'd forgotten about the stocks I owned. The change had been in name only. Dan still took care of all our investments, telling me when to call our stockbroker, his friend Rick, to buy or sell one of "my" stocks. That was going to change, I decided. In the meantime, I sat down and looked carefully through my portfolio. When I'd made up my mind, I slipped the folder with the list of stocks back into the file cabinet, and went upstairs to dress.

I waited until just after dinner — plain skinned chicken breasts with rice and steamed veggies, heart-healthy but definitely not gourmet — to spring my announcement on Dan. "Oh, by the way," I said, as he started to push back his chair. "I'm calling Rick in the morning. I'm going to sell my IBM stock."

He froze so suddenly that I was afraid he'd topple backwards, chair and all. "You're going to do *what*?!"

"Sell the IBM stock," I repeated.

"Are you out of your mind? Do you know what the capital gains tax would be? Not to mention the growth potential it still has —" Dan took a deep breath, as if trying to get control of himself. "Sheila, leave the investment decisions to me. Please."

"This isn't an investment decision. I need the money. I'm calling Rick and asking him to sell my shares as soon as the market opens tomorrow."

"I said, no! In fact, I'm going to call Rick at home right now and tell him I don't want those shares sold."

I gave Dan a look. A long look. "Oh, really? I wonder what the Securities & Exchange Commission would have to say if a broker disregarded the instructions of the stock's legal owner?" This was a shot in the dark. I was only guessing the SEC would be the agency to enforce rules about buying and selling stocks, but I was virtually sure Dan couldn't do what he wanted with my shares without my say-so.

"Maybe, as a lawyer, you can tell me," I added sweetly, as I got up to clear the table. "But I need money to pay our share of the girls' wedding expenses, and since you so childishly destroyed my Visa card, you don't leave me much choice. I'm going to open a checking account in my name with the proceeds."

As far as I could see, this was a win-win situation. Either Dan would cave in on my using our credit cards for the girls' wedding or I would go ahead and sell the IBM, just as I'd threatened. I'd looked the IBM up online that afternoon. I would just as soon hold on to it, but I'd sell it if I had to.

"I never should have put any of that stock in your name!"

"Too late now," I pointed out. "Done with your plate?" He got up without answering, which I took to mean yes, so I carried it to the sink, rinsed it off and stuck it in the dishwasher. I could hear Dan in the den, opening file drawers and slamming them shut, presumably checking just how many shares of IBM I owned. It had split several times since he'd first bought it. I waited, measuring soap carefully into the dispenser, and in another moment he was back.

"I don't want you to sell that IBM. It would be crazy, totally short-sighted, to sell it at this point."

"I realize that. But I don't see what other choice I have."

He gave an explosion of a sigh. "No, you've fixed it so I have no choice. Call up and get yourself a new Visa card."

"I already have," I told him. "It came in today's mail."

"Fine. Wonderful. Then go ahead and put whatever goddamn thing you want on it. Just leave me out of this cockamamie affair."

So at least I could go ahead and help foot the wedding financially; the money was there now that I'd maneuvered Dan into letting me use it. But I'd promised Jenny he would attend the ceremony as well and I hadn't budged him as far as that went. I lay in bed trying to convince myself that what Chuck had told me at PFLAG months ago was true: I should stay out of whatever was going on between Jenny and her father. But I couldn't help thinking if I'd handled the whole thing differently, Dan would be singing a different tune. And no matter what Chuck said, I knew Jenny would be far happier having her father at her side as she walked down the aisle than if I'd bought her a Paris original wedding gown.

I could tell by his breathing that Dan was as unable to sleep as I was. Still, I had to ask him, "Dan, are you asleep?" He didn't answer, but I suspected it was because he simply wasn't speaking to me. I reached over and took his hand. "I know you're mad at me," I said.

His hand jerked out of mine and he rolled to the far side of the bed.

In a queen-sized bed, one side isn't that far from the other, but Dan and I might as well have been on separate ice floes in the Antarctic. It only followed that he was giving me the cold shoulder. "Don't pretend you're sleeping," I said. "I need to talk with you. I know you're upset but —"

"Upset does not *begin* to describe it. Upset is like saying that Hitler wasn't a nice man. I've always believed that the basis of a marriage has to be trust and you've been abusing mine from the day this whole thing started!"

If he only knew. I could just imagine how he'd react if he knew that two nights earlier I'd been making love with Naomi. But I couldn't afford to dwell on what had happened with Naomi right now. Or to give up on Dan. Jenny's happiness was at stake. "Honey, I told you before, you had a right to be angry over the way I fibbed to you. But please, don't take it out on Jenny."

"That is just like you! To assume I would take something out on my daughter because I'm angry over your behavior. Maybe that's the way you operate, but I don't!"

"You think you don't, but why else are you acting like this? You told Jenny you accepted her, but you're doing everything in your power to prove you don't. All her life she's been your pet, and now you don't care a thing about her happiness!"

Dan jerked up to a sitting position. "I am not going to have the same fight every night, goddamn it! I'd say I care about Jenny's happiness a good deal more than you do, with your trying to push her into this thing to show, I don't know, how fucking politically correct you are!"

"Will you stop shouting like a maniac!" I yelled, sitting up myself. "I'm not pushing her into anything! This is something she and Tamara decided they wanted on their own!" I heard my voice rising to match Dan's. I could feel my blood pressure spiraling upwards like the heat index on a Code Red day. "I can't see why you won't at least make an effort to understand her. I mean, if your own mother can come here for the wedding, the least —"

"My mother is *not* coming. I spoke to her this weekend; she had no idea the girls were actually intending a mock wedding ceremony. And I'm tired of telling you, I have a little more concern for Jenny's future than you do. She's a teacher — if this thing gets out, her job is on the line." He stood and grabbed his pillow. "Now, since you won't shut up, I'm going to the guest room where I can get a little peace and quiet!"

After a moment I thought to call after him, "Her principal is on the guest list!" But two doors had slammed between us and I knew he didn't hear me.

It wasn't until after Dan had left for work the next morning that I calmed down enough to remember what he had said about his mother. Jenny was disappointed enough that her father was refusing to attend her wedding, without having her favorite grandmother boycott it on top of that.

So it wasn't going to happen if I could prevent it. It was obvious that Dan had talked Rose into changing her mind. It was up to me to change it back. The way Rose and I got along, that was easier said than done. But I intended to make the effort. Which meant going to New York to talk with her face-to-face. If she knew I'd schlepped over three hours on the train to see her, she'd at least hear me out.

Not to mention that right now I welcomed any excuse to put some distance between me and Dan.

My mother lives in the same section of the Bronx as Rose. By late morning, I'd called Mama to tell her I'd be staying with her a few days, checked the Metroliner schedule and repacked the bag I'd just unpacked. Then I left a note on the hall table with the mail, where Dan couldn't miss it, to let him know I'd gone home to my mother.

All I'd told Mama was that I felt like a visit with her, but I hadn't been in her apartment a half hour before she had the whole story out of me — with the exception of what I'd done with Naomi.

"Dan has a point," she said, as the two of us sat in her kitchen sipping iced tea. "Teachers are in a vulnerable position."

"Jenny knows that," I said. "But having a wedding ceremony means everything to her. Anyhow, she teaches in Alexandria and the city has passed a law making it illegal to discriminate on account of sexual orientation. In fact —"

"They can repeal it as easily as they passed it. But she's made her bed. She'll have to lie in it."

Lying in bed wasn't what I needed to think about right now. And my mother's next words got my full attention. "I'm with Dan on this one. Jenny and her friend sent me an invitation, but I don't know about schlepping to Virginia in the heat to see whatever it is they're going to put on."

I'd assumed she was coming. I'd been counting on her. But what came out of my mouth was, "It's hot here too."

"But at least here I don't have to get all dressed up. Who wants to put on fancy clothes and nylons in the middle of summer?"

"Who wants to stay in the Bronx, where all you have is window units, when you can stay with us in a comfortable house with central air? And nobody said you have to get all dressed up. Wear what you want."

"Because it's not a real wedding, you mean. When you go to a wedding, you dress." Mama poured herself more tea from the Tupperware pitcher and stirred in a packet of NutraSweet.

I gave her a look. "Fine, then *get* dressed up. Wear that new suit you look so good in. They're having the wedding in an air-conditioned building."

"I'll have to think about it. There's still the traveling. With the way traffic is, even if you take the shuttle, by the time you get to the airport you might as well have gone on the train. And —"

"Now you're making up excuses. You've always loved to travel."

"But not to this affair of Jenny's. I'm not at all sure I approve of what she's doing."

I knew that already, but it hadn't occurred to me she'd actually refuse to attend. It was time to bring out my argument of last resort. "Mama, I hate to say it, but you're getting to be just like Rose."

"Like Rose! I'm nothing like Rose. Where do you get off telling me —"

"Because she's also too close-minded to attend the girls' wedding. She promised Jenny she was coming to her wedding, but one word from Dan and she's breaking her promise. Instead of thinking for herself, she's giving in to old-fashioned bigotry."

This time Mama gave me a look. "Did you ever think that maybe she's right to change her mind? That she's using her head for a change?"

This, I couldn't believe. Not only was my mother letting me down, but she was siding with Rose against me. I suddenly felt as if I were a twelve-year-old begging her to let me see the movie that all my friends were allowed to see. I felt near tears. But I wasn't a child anymore, I reminded myself. I was a grown woman, with a daughter to whom I'd made promises.

"Mama, I told Jenny I would help her, that I would be there for her. And with Dan so against me, I really need some support myself. I mean, I've been going to a support group ever since Jenny told us that she's a lesbian. But that doesn't take the place of family. And with Dan — I *need* you to come to the wedding, Mama. Even if you think it's a mistake for the girls to have it, can't you do it for me?"

I held my breath until Mama said what she'd always said in my childhood. "All right, I'll take what you said into consideration." She got up and went to check the contents of her refrigerator, saying half under her breath, "It's warm enough, I thought just cold cuts for supper." I knew it would have to do for the time being.

I waited until we'd finished eating to call my mother-in-law. I didn't want my mother to catch on to the fact that seeing Rose was the main reason I'd come to New York. So after Mama had twice refused my offer to do the dishes — "A couple of plates? It'll take me five minutes. Besides, there's only room for one in this kitchen, and I'm the one who knows where everything goes," — I casually said that I supposed I really ought to give Rose a call.

"You might as well bite the bullet," Mama replied.

"So you're visiting your mother," Rose said, once we'd exchanged greetings. "And do I get more than a phone call?"

"Of course you do. I was planning to come by and see you. Is tomorrow okay?"

"Don't come in the morning. I see the doctor then — he should tell me what I already know, that I'm an old woman. Afternoon's not too good either, that's when I do my shopping. I tell you what. Come for supper. I'll make you a kosher meal, like I'll bet you're not getting by your mother's." I glanced at my mother, hoping Rose's voice hadn't carried to her. I was using the wall phone hung over the dinette table we'd eaten at, and Mama stood rinsing plates a few feet away. As a matter of fact, we'd just eaten kosher cold cuts on seeded Jewish rye, with mustard and pickles. But then Mama had brought forth a dessert I knew Rose would deplore — slices of Sara Lee reduced-fat cheesecake.

While I was imagining what my mother-in-law would say if she knew we'd just mixed milk and meat, Rose added, "I know what you're thinking. You don't want to desert your mother for the evening, when you're only here for a few days. So you'll bring her along. Myrna and I don't see enough of each other anyway."

I suspected that my mother felt she saw entirely too much of Rose already. Not to mention that the last thing I needed was to have to deal

253

with my mother and mother-in-law at the same time. "I think my mother may have made plans for us to go out for dinner, but I can come for a couple of hours before —"

"She didn't even know you were coming, what kind of plans could she have made already? So she made reservations — big deal, she'll change them to another night. I'm not coming to her house, either, in case she's about to invite me. I wouldn't put it past her to mix milk and meat." She had Mama's number there, I had to admit to myself.

"Now, I'm not taking no for an answer," Rose said, when she finally wound down.

There seemed no choice but to tell her we'd both be looking forward to seeing her the following night. And to warn my mother not to say anything that would set my mother-in-law off.

Rose served us cheese blintzes with sour cream and strawberry preserves. "It's summer, so I decided to make dairy," she explained as we sat around the oak table in her dining room, which had once served as Dan's bedroom. I had to admit to myself — though never to Mama — that Rose far outdid her as a cook. Rose's blintzes melted in my mouth, the sweetened cheese rolled up in the thinnest of pancakes; I knew she'd prepared them from scratch. I could feel the cholesterol collecting in my arteries with each delicious bite. I could worry about my diet later, though. Here I was face-to-face with Rose, with the added complication of having my mother along, and no idea how best to bring up the topic of Jenny's wedding. Before I could hit on the right words, Rose said, "So I hear you and my son aren't on speaking terms. How long were you going to keep me in the dark?"

I should have known Dan would fill Rose in on every word that had passed between us. Or didn't pass, as the case might be. I reminded myself that if I wanted to talk Rose into coming to the wedding, I needed to stay on her good side. So I said, as calmly as I could, "We're just having a little bit of a rough patch. It happens in every marriage. There's really nothing to —"

Before I could finish, my mother, as if she hadn't grilled me about our quarrel from the moment I walked into her house, demanded to know, "Since when is a mother entitled to be privy to every moment of her child's marriage?"

Which Rose didn't hear, because she was saying, "He tells me that you're pushing Jenny into some kind of imitation wedding ceremony."

This was so patently unfair that I nearly choked on my last bite of blintz. While I was grabbing for my glass of seltzer water I had a few seconds to remind myself not to antagonize Rose, no matter what came out of her mouth. So when I set the glass down again, I made my voice as sweet as her cheese pancakes. "Dan may have gotten the impression I was pushing her into something," — no calling her precious son a liar —"but having a ceremony to show their commitment to each other is something the girls came up with on their own. I just gave Jenny a little help when she asked me."

"But it's true that what Jenny and this girl are talking about is some kind of, I don't know what you would call it, but–?"

"Counterfeit," my mother supplied, out of the blue, looking so smugly pleased with herself I could have throttled her. "Like a dollar bill that's made on a Xerox machine. A fake."

I threw Mama a look that could kill. It was bad enough she was taking Dan's side. She didn't need to put words in Rose's mouth. "It's not an imitation or a fake," I said, not using bigger words than I needed to with Rose. "Jenny and Tamara are simply planning a ceremony, a traditional Jewish service," I said, putting a little stress on *Jewish* for Rose's benefit, "to let everyone know how much they care for one another, and that they plan to establish a Jewish home together."

The two of them were quiet an instant, just long enough to give me hope, and then Rose said, "So they're not really having a wedding ceremony?"

I sighed. "I thought Jenny had told you on the phone...." I knew she'd talked with Rose. Unless Dan had simply changed his mother's mind, Rose had obviously misunderstood what Jenny was telling her. I could downplay the "wedding" part of the ceremony, of course. But if Rose were actually to attend — and I was determined to talk her into it — she would see it for herself. So I had no choice, but to say, "They are having a ceremony. They're having a traditional Jewish marriage ceremony, with their rabbi officiating. Under a *chuppah*."

Rose was staring at me. "And this is somehow according to the Jewish religion? You, I know you're an ignoramus when it comes to your own religion, but I thought Jenny had become so observant, how does she come to dream up something like this? A wedding with another girl?"

I sighed again and began racking my brain. If it was put to her the right way, Rose might be willing to see that Jewish tradition could be

255

broadened to make a place for Jenny and Tamara. She herself didn't always adhere to strict Orthodox laws, even traveling on a Friday night to see me in *Fiddler on the Roof.*

It was her favorite musical, I remembered. She'd said it had a Jewish heart. "Rose," I started, hoping a sudden inspiration would pan out. "They're like Tevye's daughters in *Fiddler on the Roof.*"

"Jenny and her friend are like Tevye's daughters? That's supposed to mean something?"

"It means they follow Jewish laws and traditions," I said quickly. "But they have to reinterpret them — make them fit — with their own time. The way Tevye's daughters fell in love with boys the matchmaker hadn't picked out for them."

"With boys," Rose pounced. "Even the one who fell in love with a goy — she should have been ashamed — didn't fall for another girl."

"But Jenny isn't going to fall in love with a boy," I said. "I know she explained to you that she's a lesbian. That's what it means, that she's only capable of loving another girl. It's the way God made her," I added, again inspired. Personally, I didn't believe that God's intentions extended to the individual makeup of each of the 6 billion people on earth, but Rose needn't know that. I continued quickly, before Mama, who liked to call herself an agnostic, stopped stuffing her face and launched another verbal salvo. "Of course we can't know all His reasons, but I know Jenny didn't tell us she's a lesbian to be fashionable," which was what Mama had claimed a few months back. "She doesn't have a choice. She has to spend her life with Tamara, or, if not her, then another girl she could love. Otherwise, she would be without anyone, like a hermit or...or a nun."

"A nun? She should turn Catholic yet like your son?"

Count to ten, I told myself. Even Rose couldn't misunderstand plain English this much. But I couldn't afford to respond to her dig at Jeffrey right now. "Rose, you know perfectly well that Jenny tries to be as good a Jew as she can. As good a person. She wouldn't be doing this if she thought it was wrong."

"Who said anything about my Jenny not being a good girl?" Rose demanded.

"I know that wasn't what you meant. But what would you have her do? Marry someone she doesn't love, to please other people? The way Tevye tried to make Tzeitel marry the old butcher before he understood how miserable that would make her?"

"God forbid!"

I allowed myself a small sigh of relief. It was premature.

"So did I say she had to get married?" Rose demanded. "But like my Dan says, why have this — what your own mother calls counterfeit?"

Mama nodded and I threw her a glare.

"Can't they just live together the way they've been doing?" Rose continued.

Did I have an answer? To be perfectly honest, it was a question I still asked myself from time to time. *Improvise,* I told myself. *Pretend the actor you're onstage with has just missed a cue.* "If it was a boy that Jenny was in love with, would you tell them just to live together?" was what I came up with. I didn't wait for them to respond to my rhetorical question. "Jenny and Tamara's feelings for each other are just as real to them as if they were a man and a woman. So it's natural that they don't want to just live together or pass themselves off as roommates. They want to pledge themselves to each other, to make a commitment to creating a Jewish home together — that's why they want a Jewish service. I mean, they want to live their Judaism as fully as they can, that's why they're standing up under a canopy, with a rabbi, and observing all the traditions they can. They're even going to a mikvah beforehand."

Mama threw down her fork. "A *mikvah*? In this day and age they're going to wash away their impurities in a ritual bath? Here I thought Jenny was at least a feminist and instead she's following an old, superstitious ritual that —"

"Where do you get the nerve!" Rose demanded. "Where do you get off making fun of your own granddaughter for taking it on herself to be an observant Jew? You know what I say? I say, good for Jenny! And shame on you!"

For a change, I was with Rose against my own mother — to whom I intended to give a piece of my mind once we left. "So Jenny can count on you coming after all, Rose? She's really hoping her family, all the people she loves most, will attend," I added.

"Well, I don't know. When I spoke to Dan...."

Another step backward. I groaned inwardly, and then gave a silent moan as Mama put in, "You make some good arguments, but you still can't say that a same-sex wedding is traditionally Jewish."

"The girls are *adding* to the Jewish tradition," I said, nearly hissing in my mother's face. "It's not a sin to change a tradition. Like the way they changed things in *Fiddler on the Roof* by having men and women dance together at Tzeitel's wedding," I pointed out, for Rose's benefit.

"That's true," Rose admitted.

I turned my back on Mama, speaking just to Rose now. "Jenny told me how much she'll miss you if you don't come. You know how close she feels to you."

"She's always been a darling. I just worry my son has his reasons."

All of a sudden, I'd had enough. "Fine, go along with whatever Dan says! I should have known better than to talk to you. I thought I could explain how much this means to Jenny, but I might as well have been talking to a wall! I should have known you're simply too old to take in a new idea, to understand a new tradition like this service the girls are going to have." I might have gone on to vent every grievance I'd held against Rose for the last thirty years if she hadn't started shouting back even louder than me.

"Too old! Too old my foot! Did you hear that, Myrna? I know you're not more than a year or two younger than me." There were close to five years between them, but who was counting? "Your daughter thinks the two of us are senile; we belong in some old-age home somewhere where they don't let you go out in public."

Mama shrugged, with considerably less concern than Rose. "I heard her. My hearing is in good shape, just like my thought processes. Sheila knows that I read the *New York Times* front to back every day. The front section, the financial pages, even the sports. I'll challenge anyone to a test of mental acuity any day."

"That — whatever test that is — you just tell your daughter to give it to me too. Are you listening to me, Sheila? Maybe I don't read the *Times* like your mother — I always liked a paper with some human interest — but I don't miss a day of the *Post*. So don't you get off with I'm too old to understand my granddaughter. Tell her I'm coming to her affair — no never mind, I'll call and tell her myself. And whatever I don't understand, I know she'll be willing to explain, without going out of her way to insult an old woman."

My mother and I took a taxi back to her apartment. I was too furious at her to speak a single word on the way back, except for, "I'll pay," when the cabdriver pulled up to the front of her apartment house.

"There's a reason you're not speaking to me?" she asked, once we were in the apartment.

I turned on her. "Yes, there's a reason. I didn't want to tell you what I thought of you in front of the driver, or your neighbors in the elevator, but I can't believe the way you've been treating me tonight. I told you how much it meant to me to support Jenny, how much I wanted you to come to the wedding service, and you not only refuse to attend but you do your best to see to it that Rose won't be there for her either! I know what you think of Rose, but you have no right to try to ruin her relationship with Jenny!"

"Ruin her relationship? If Jenny prefers Rose that's her business. But here I thought you'd thank me for convincing Rose to attend this affair. All I was doing this evening was helping you out a little with your mother-in-law."

I fell onto the couch. "It's been a long day. Maybe I'm not hearing right. How were you helping me by taking Dan's side against me?"

My mother smirked. "By playing devil's advocate, that's how. You know how Rose and I get along — like cats and dogs. Do you think if I told her she should be going to this ceremony of Jenny's that she would have agreed? You did the same thing yourself, after all. I thought that was a brilliant tactic on your part, to tell her she was too old."

I opened my mouth and closed it without saying anything, since for once I was speechless. After half a minute, I managed, "Mama, you're going to drive me crazy. You thought I blew up at her on *purpose*? And all that stuff you said — why would you be trying to maneuver Rose into going to the girls' wedding anyway? I thought you said you disapproved of it as much as Dan."

"I do disapprove. I know how much Jenny's teaching career means to her. I still don't see why she should risk it over this ceremony."

I closed my eyes and leaned my head against the cushions of the sofa bed, wanting nothing more than to unfold it and climb in. "You're not making sense. If you disapprove of it —"

"Maybe your mental processes are getting too old to follow me. I said I'd give it some thought, didn't I? So I did. I decided, if it meant that much to my daughter for me to come to this affair, then I'll come for your sake. And do my best to see to it that Rose gets there too. But I still think Jenny will live to regret it."

I opened my eyes again. "It turns out not to be such a threat to her career. The other teachers in the school all know about Jenny and Tamara's plans. As a matter of fact, the girls invited their principal and she sent back an acceptance."

"I'm amazed! Times must be changing faster than I realized. You could have mentioned it before."

"I told you."

"You did not."

I could have sworn I did, but why argue? "I thought I did. Maybe I belong in that old-age home of Rose's."

"There's nothing wrong with your memory but menopause. There was a big write-up in the *Times* science column. You ought to see your gynecologist about getting on hormone-replacement therapy."

"I'm *taking* hormones. Already. So you're definitely coming?"

"What did I just say? But I want you to tell me the truth, now." She got up and started out of the living room.

"What? Well, what do you want me to tell you the truth about?"

"I'll be back to ask you in a minute. I'm going to put on the suit you told me to wear, and I want your honest opinion on how it looks on me."

Chapter Twenty

*D*an talked with his mother at least once more while I was in New York. To my relief, Rose called to let me know that she was sticking to her decision to attend the wedding despite his arguments. "I talked to Jenny after you left and let her know I was definitely coming. And like I told Danny when he called, I don't go back on my word."

Not surprisingly, Dan hadn't called me. Or I him. I'd accomplished what I went to New York to do; I could have returned home the following day. Instead I saw my grandchildren and stretched out my visit with Mama till the end of the week, taking the subway into Manhattan with her to window-shop and buy tickets at Broadway's half-price outlet, then spending sleepless nights on the same convertible couch that I'd slept on through my college years. Newly slip-covered, but the same yielding cushions where I'd lost my virginity to Dan. My mother, still clinging to standards of morality that my generation laughed at, would have had a fit if she'd known, though I told myself at the time that even Mama had to see how right it was, when I'd found the man I meant to spend my life with — handsome, ambitious, kind and so tenderly loving. I felt as if I'd waited my whole life to leave my mother's house and join my life with his.

Now it was time to say goodbye to Mama once again. I didn't anticipate any tender, loving welcome on Dan's behalf. But there was a limit to how long I could stay with my mother, if for no other reason than that my back could no longer take sleeping on the sagging sofa-bed mattress. I caught the Metroliner back to D.C. Saturday afternoon.

By the time I reached home, it was evening. Dan was out, probably having dinner at the country club. I'd left him to worry about his own meals for a change, and I doubted he'd set foot in the kitchen other than to pour his morning coffee. Not that he had my sympathy. I was sure whatever he was eating tonight was better than what passed for food on Amtrak.

I checked the mail — nothing for me on the hall table but a stack of catalogs — and the answering machine. The red light was unblinking, indicating no messages, either new or saved. If anyone had called me, I'd have to depend on Dan to tell me about it.

It was nearly ten before he got home. I'd unpacked and changed into a nightgown, but I was too wrought up to go to sleep. Instead, I sat thumbing through a copy of the Victoria's Secret catalog, fantasizing about having a figure good enough to wear one of the sexy bikini and bra sets they featured, and wondering whom I would wear them for if I did. Not Dan, apparently, who, when he walked into the bedroom, just said, "I see you finally decided to come home."

"I only went for a visit. What did you think?" Dan sat down to take off his shoes, ignoring my rhetorical question. I asked, "Did I get any calls? There's nothing on the machine."

"What did you expect? That I would scroll through a dozen messages every day when I had no idea when you were even getting home?"

"You could have at least —"

"Written them down." After thirty years, mad or not mad, he could still finish my sentences. "What makes you so sure I didn't? As a matter of fact, they're on the planning desk in the kitchen, on a yellow pad. But I'll tell you who called. Your friend Lois, wanting to know how you could go out of town without informing her first. That Marlene woman, from your support group, who said she'd been expecting you to call up and fill her in on the conference. And last, but not least, that ditzy mother of Tamara's, who says she needs to talk to you about the rehearsal dinner."

So Naomi hadn't called yet. To drive that thought out of my head, I said, "She may be a bit much, but she and her husband are going all out to let Tamara know they're behind her, and I, at least, wouldn't feel right not to do as much for Jenny." As soon as the words were out of my mouth I knew they would start a fight I was in no mood for, so I quickly added,

"What about Jenny? Didn't she call at all?"

"She called me," he said smugly. "We had quite an interesting talk."

"Oh?" I said. Dan got up without saying anything further and headed for the bathroom to retrieve his pajamas, forcing me to add, "Well, what did she call about?"

"She called about that wedding gown you put on the Visa bill," he said finally, walking back and buttoning his pajama tops, "She said when you offered to pay for it, she was too excited to think it through. But now that she'd had the chance, she didn't feel right about our financing the dress and whatever else you bought, knowing I was still opposed to her going through with the ceremony."

I let the catalog fall to the floor. "You agreed I could go ahead and use the Visa to buy it for her."

"Don't you mean that you forced me into agreeing? But according to what Jenny said, you all but told her that I'd changed my mind, that *we* wanted to pay for her to have this wedding the same as we would if she were having a normal wedding."

"So I suppose you set her straight," I snapped.

"Unfortunately, that seems to be beyond my power."

"Very funny."

"I thought you would think so, since you've been doing everything in your power —"

"If you're about to say that I made her a lesbian, you're wasting your breath. No one can make anyone else become gay or lesbian; it's born in them. So what did you tell her? That we weren't going to help her out at all?"

Instead of answering, Dan walked over to his side of the bed and turned down the covers. At least he expected us to sleep in the same bed — unless he imagined I was going to start sleeping in the guest room.

"What did you tell Jenny?" I asked again. He slid into bed in infuriating silence. "Well?" I should become a dental surgeon, I thought. I suddenly seemed to be getting a good deal of experience pulling teeth. I got up from the lounge chair where I'd been sitting, went over to my side of the bed and got in. "Do I have to call Jenny up and ask her?"

"I told her we'd talked it over and agreed that we would help her out with the affair financially," he said finally, speaking to the ceiling. "I didn't let her know how underhanded you've been about the whole thing, if that's what you're worrying about."

I stared up at the ceiling myself, not sure whether to thank him or blow up at him. Before I could do either, he added, "I told her that I still can't go along with attending her affair, but since she's committed herself financially, based on what you gave her to understand, it doesn't seem fair to leave her in a financial hole. Though from what she let slip, it seems the what's-their-names, that mother of Tamara's and her husband, would be willing to cover her expenses as well as their daughter's. But she doesn't want to accept their help and I wouldn't want her to. I don't want that woman, Debby whatever —"

"Goldberg. Debby and Stanley Goldberg," I said automatically.

"Whatever. Anyhow, they don't need to think our daughter is some kind of charity case."

"Of course not," I murmured. "That's just what I was saying. That we should want to give Jenny the same support that they're giving Tamara." I reached for the remote-control clicker to turn off the ceiling light. Dan gave me a look that I caught as the globe winked out.

"No, that is *not* what I said. I've maintained all along that this ceremony the girls dreamed up isn't something we should be supporting. I'm just trying to deal with the situation you created here. Now do you mind letting me get a little sleep?"

"Fine," I said. "Good night." It was still early for a Saturday, but he doubtless had a golf game first thing in the morning. He certainly wasn't resting up for a Sunday morning in bed, even though it had been weeks since we'd had sex. Or since *he* had, at any rate. Naomi was the last thing I needed to think about right now. To get my mind off her, I asked, "Did Jenny have anything else to say?"

"Such as what?" he demanded. "I was almost asleep, if you care to know."

"You were not," I said. "You were breathing like a racehorse. What else did Jenny tell you?"

Dan sighed. "Nothing unusual. She had her tires rotated. She and Tamara rented the video of *Shakespeare in Love*, and she's toying with the idea of showing it to her English classes next fall."

"Speaking of school, you might be interested in knowing that Jenny's principal —"

"She told me," Dan cut in. "She and Tamara invited the principal of their school to this affair, and she's actually coming." It seemed to me he was telling me this bit of Jenny's news with reluctance, though he surely knew I'd find it of more interest than a saga of her trip to the auto-repair shop. If I hadn't brought up the topic, he wouldn't have mentioned it at all.

"That's what I was trying to —"

"That did come as a surprise. I hadn't realized attitudes toward homosexuality had changed so muci.. I would have thought a teacher.... Anyhow, it relieves my worries about her career future somewhat. As a matter of fact," he added, even more grudgingly, "Jenny says the principal asked if she and Tamara will serve as faculty advisors to a new extracurricular organization, a what-did-she-say gay/straight student alliance."

That last was news to me. But I'd been trying to tell Dan about the girls' principal for weeks and each time he'd cut me off. "I could have told you that their principal was on the guest list weeks ago. If you'd only —"

"Then I wish you would have!" he snapped, simultaneously turning his back to me in the clear attitude of a man not intending any further talk. "Instead of letting me drive myself crazy worrying that she'd be fired if anyone in the school system found out she's gay."

I returned Debby's call maliciously early in the morning. She answered with such a chirp in her voice that I knew she must normally be up at seven-thirty, which is what it was in Chicago. "I'm so glad you called," she told me. "I was going to call you this morning; I just thought you might not be up this early. I hope you have some news about the rehearsal dinner."

"I've been working on it," I lied. "But I haven't made the final arrangements yet. Something came up on short notice and I had to go out of town."

"Your husband told me. But time's short till the girls' wedding too. Incredibly short. If you want me to arrange something from this end just let me know." An exasperated sigh gusted through the phone lines from the Windy City. "At least Jenny says you've finally found her a dress. I must congratulate you on getting such a bargain. My older daughter, Stacy, and I shopped for months before her wedding, and we couldn't find anything decent for under $2,500. But then, it never occurred to us to look in a low-end shop like David's Bridal."

I counted to ten, unclenching my fingers one at a time as I did so, and then said pleasantly, "Jenny insisted on keeping the costs down. But luckily, with her figure, she looks stunning in anything she puts on."

"Oh, I'm sure both girls will make beautiful brides."

Both girls. I felt myself taking two steps backwards, like my PFLAG buddy Candy Sue. This wasn't the wedding day I'd dreamed of for Jenny.

I waited till a more reasonable hour for calling Lois. We hadn't talked since before I'd left for Scottsdale, so as soon as she was finished with hello, how are you, and what do you mean jetting around the country without a word to your best friend, I told her all about my blowup with Dan.

"Cutting up your Visa card! I can hardly believe it of him," she said. "But don't say I didn't tell you; it's a mistake to be totally dependent on a man. I can't blame you for not wanting to go back to teaching, but you need to find yourself some independent source of income. There's an opening for a couple of new agents in my office, matter of fact. With your brains and memory, getting a real-estate license would be a cinch."

"I can't do anything that's mostly evenings and weekends; that's when I'm busy with theater stuff," I reminded her. "Anyhow, right now I have enough to do planning a rehearsal dinner for the girls' ceremony."

After a week of trying, I still hadn't lined up a restaurant for the dinner. What's more, I realized as I got ready to leave for the PFLAG support group the following Sunday, I'd forgotten to call Marlene to fill her in on the conference. I punched in her number and got her machine. A good sign, I thought; she was feeling well enough to get out of her house. She'd probably left for the meeting already. Something I'd better do myself, if I didn't want to be late.

Marlene was setting out literature when I arrived. By the time I'd apologized for not having called her before leaving for New York, a half-dozen others had arrived. The support group never draws a big turnout in summer, and once Marlene had read the guidelines and made a few announcements she said, "I see there's no one new today." Besides the two of us, the circle consisted of Candy Sue, Alison, Chuck and three or four other old hands.

"Does anyone have a new issue they'd like to bring up?" Marlene continued. I had the issue of Jenny's wedding, but I'd been sharing that story with the group for months. I could tell them the latest developments with Dan and Rose, but what I really needed to get support on was my night with Naomi. That was an issue I didn't see myself bringing up in a million years. Just at the thought, my mouth felt drier than the desert Naomi loved so much.

I shook my head along with the others and Marlene said, "Since no one has anything new, rather than telling the same stories we've all heard before, I'd like to ask Sheila to give us a rundown on the national conference. For those of you who don't know, she was good enough to fill in for me on a moment's notice when I got sick the day before the conference."

Marlene still didn't look completely well, her forehead covered with the remains of crusted blisters. "I was meaning to write up the notes I took," I told her apologetically, "but I'm afraid I haven't gotten to them yet."

"Not a formal report," she said. "You can let me have that later. But if you could give us the highlights of one or two of the workshops you attended, off the top of your head. Did you happen to attend the one on bisexuality?"

That was now the subject closest to Marlene's heart. "Yes, I made a point of it," I said. "Let's see. It was a panel, with three speakers — a man and two women — but they all said more or less the same thing: Sexual orientation is more complex than most people realize. And both gay and straight people have stereotypes about bisexuals: either that they're really gay and afraid to come all the way out of the closet, or that they would go straight if they just met the right person of the opposite sex."

I paused to think, and Alison put in, "You hear it if you're gay, too. My mother's finally gotten used to the fact that I'm a lesbian, but for the longest time she was always mentioning these young guys she worked with, and wanting me to meet them." Dan, I recalled, had blurted out the same type of thing the time I'd gotten him to go to the support group. I wasn't sure if even now he accepted the fact that Jenny was a lesbian, and there were times even I —

"Getting back to the panel discussion," Marlene said, "did they cover more ground that you can remember without your notes?"

"I remember most of what they said," I told her. I don't take hor-mone-replacement therapy for nothing. "Another thing all three of them stressed is that being bisexual doesn't mean a person can't have a monog-amous relationship. I mean, if they're in a relationship with someone of the opposite sex, they don't have to have someone of their own sex on the side, the way a lot of people think they do."

Marlene nodded. "Absolutely. Any more than one of us married women would have someone on the side just because she'd met someone more attractive than her husband."

I winced. That was true of Marlene, I was sure, but not of me. Not anymore. Did one night count as having an affair? Or would it be only one night? Of course Marlene was thinking of an attractive man....

"Anyway," I said quickly, "they also said that people who are bisexual are less likely to come out to their parents than people who are gay or lesbian. I guess it's because not everyone is as understanding as Marlene. Parents tend to say something along the lines of, 'If it's possible for you to fall in love with someone of the opposite sex, then why would there ever be a reason for you to have a same-sex relationship?' And not to be supportive when they are in a same-sex relationship."

"I can see why," Candy Sue blurted. "It's one thing for someone like my son, who can't help himself. I mean, he's explained to me, he's just not capable of falling in love with a girl. But if someone —"

"Candy Sue," Marlene said, a little sharply for her, "why don't we let Sheila finish her report, and then we can discuss any issues it's raised."

Candy Sue gave a reluctant nod, and I said, "I suppose that's why they chose this panel for the conference, to get more support for bisexuals from PFLAG. Anyway, the panelists explained that they don't go around saying to themselves, well, I'm going to fall in love with a man now. Or with a woman. They meet someone they're attracted to, just like anyone else. I mean, it's like, well, like my son. He's not bi," I said hastily. "But we're Jewish, and I suppose he always expected to fall in love with a Jewish girl. But when the time came, he met Anita, who happens to be Catholic. He wasn't looking to marry out of his religion, but she was the one for him. He just fell in love with her as a person."

"Yes, but —"

I ignored Candy Sue's interruption so as not to lose my train of thought. "I remember one of the women on the panel made the point that she, how did she put it, self-identified as bisexual long before she had a relationship with a woman, because she had strong feelings of attraction toward other women. But she was with a boyfriend then, and didn't act on her feelings until after they'd broken up."

"But that's different than marrying someone of a different religion," Candy Sue said stubbornly. "You're saying your son fell in love with this Catholic girl for her personality, but...but you don't *sleep* with a personality."

Everybody, even Marlene, broke out laughing. "Well you don't," Candy Sue persisted. She looked from one to another of us, and said, "I wouldn't say this if there was anyone new here. But as long as it's just the few of us who all know each other, I still can't understand how, if she was able to have feelings for her boyfriend, she could up and decide to be with a woman instead. I know you all don't think that's a politically correct way to feel, but I just can't help it."

"There's no politically correct way you *have* to feel, Candy Sue," Marlene said. "PFLAG welcomes people at whatever stage of the acceptance process they're in. But the point Sheila was making is that this woman on the panel didn't *decide* she would choose women from then on. She simply realized she was attracted to women as well as to men and could be open to a relationship with another woman. Just as my son realized that he could be in love with a woman and not just with another man."

"But he realized he could fall in love in a normal way while —" Candy Sue broke off as she realized what she'd said, perhaps alerted by the fact that Alison had jerked her head towards her so quickly her dangling earrings were jingling.

This was a giant step backwards for Candy Sue, especially considering that she'd been coming to the support group months longer than I had. I opened my mouth to go on with my report before she could embarrass herself further, but before I could get a word out, Alison said, "It was *normal* for her to be with a woman; being with a guy was what was wrong for her. I bet she was in denial the way I used to be. I had a couple of boyfriends, before I admitted to myself I was a lesbian. So this woman broke up with her boyfriend after she realized she was a lesbian."

"Actually, that's not quite what she said," I said. "This was the bisexuality panel, remember. All three of the panelists said if they were to break up with their current partners, they could envision themselves in a relationship with someone of either sex. But the other woman panelist did say that she felt that she really had been heterosexual to start with."

Marlene gave me a startled look now. "You mean, she was in denial about her bisexual orientation the way Alison just told us she was about her lesbianism?"

"No, what she said is that a person's sexuality can change at different stages in their life," I persisted. "That it's fluid, not fixed. Well, she said she *knew* it wasn't the politically correct position, but the other two seemed to agree with her."

"But I thought we learned that people were born gay or lesbian," Candy Sue objected, "and now you say —"

"I'm not the one saying it, Candy Sue. Marlene asked me to report on the panel and I'm just —"

"Denial," Chuck cut in authoritatively. "When your panelists thought they were straight or gay, they were in denial. They simply hadn't come to terms with the full range of their sexuality yet."

I supposed Chuck was right. But then, what about Naomi? Hadn't she admitted enjoying sex with her husband before she realized she had stronger feelings for her best friend, Jody? Had she had feelings for other women, which she'd suppressed, before falling for Jody? I'd have to ask her next time I saw her. If there was a next time, that is. But surely she'd want to see me again, at least to talk, and maybe.....

More to the point, what about me? I was totally turned on by Naomi, but try as I might I couldn't remember having the slightest romantic feeling for another woman before, not even a high-school crush. I'd managed to report on the bisexuality panel as if I were giving a lesson to a class, as if I were telling the lunch bunch some interesting item I'd read in the paper. As if it had nothing to do with me.

But it did. And suddenly I couldn't keep it bottled up any longer.

The rest of the group was directing its attention to Chuck now, Candy Sue pleading, "So I'm right, my son was born gay?" while Alison and Billy chimed in with their own experiences and Marlene tried to regain control of the meeting.

"I believe the panelists," I said, speaking as fast as I could before I lost my nerve. "Because I really have always been straight, and now I'm attracted to another woman."

Every person in the room, Marlene included, broke off talking in midsentence to turn to me. "You're saying *you're* a lesbian, Sheila?" Alison asked for everyone. She was staring at me with an expression of surprise and something that might have been delight. Candy Sue looked just as startled, but the look on her face was closer to horror. Whatever their expressions, though, they were all waiting for me to respond.

"I'm not anything," I stammered. "I'm me, Sheila." What was it we advised people to tell friends or family they were coming out to? And was I coming out? "I'm the same person I've been all along, except, well, I've realized that every once in a while I do feel a kind of attraction to another woman. In fact, there was a woman I saw at the conference —" I managed to shut my mouth before I blurted out any more. What had taken place between Naomi and me in bed was my own business.

Candy Sue still looked stunned. "But you're saying...."

"I'm saying I had a few daydreams about this person, that's all," I improvised, a lot more lightly than I felt. "Okay, more than a few. Enough to bother me. I couldn't bring myself to say it when Marlene asked if there were any new issues, but, well, I guess that's my new issue."

"That you're just beginning to realize you're a lesbian," Alison repeated.

"I'm not beginning to realize I'm a lesbian. I mean, well, yes, I am attracted to this woman. But there are plenty of men I find attractive as well. So if I'm anything, I'm bisexual. Like Marlene's son. I'm in good company," I managed to add, smiling weakly.

Marlene beamed back at me. "I think a lot more people than we realize would call themselves bi, if they were as honest with themselves as you are."

I felt a sudden lightening of the load I'd been carrying. "I don't think I'd have brought myself to be so honest if I hadn't been attending this support group so many months."

Everyone present at the support group nodded supportively.

"We're very glad you felt able to share that with us, Sheila," Chuck said.

As if programmed, everyone nodded again, all but Candy Sue looking genuinely happy for me.

"It's a relief to have come out with it," I admitted. Everyone was looking at me so earnestly that no one picked up on my unintended play on words. "Not to hide what I've been feeling. But really, it's a moot point. I'm a married woman. So it doesn't matter who I find attractive," I continued, my mouth on autopilot now. "I love my husband, and I'm not going to do anything to change my life."

Everybody — including Candy Sue this time — nodded approvingly. So apparently I was the only one wondering whether I actually meant it.

The other thing I didn't know was how Naomi felt about me. The last time I'd talked with her was in Scottsdale, before the banquet. I wished now I had arranged to stay another day and taken her up on her

271

offer to show me the desert scenery. Not just so I could see it, but to give us the opportunity, as she'd put it, "to talk about what's happened between us."

What's happened between us. Happened in the past tense. Did that mean it was over, as far as Naomi was concerned, nothing more than a one-night stand? Or happened as in we now happened to be in a new kind of relationship? One that was still happening.

I'd told the support group I had no interest in straying from my marital vows. Then why was I carrying on like a teenager, afraid to leave the house for fear of missing Naomi's call, even though we had an answering machine? When I'd been in high school, dying to know if the cute boy in my solid geometry class liked me back, I called my best friend to go over every word he'd ever said to me and ask her what she thought. Lois was my best friend now, but there was no way I could tell her I was having an affair, the same as Natalie, only mine was with a woman. A woman who made my heart race every time I thought of her.

Instead, I picked up the phone and dialed Naomi's apartment. After two rings, she greeted me in that low, sexy voice of hers, saying, "Hi, this is Naomi." Just the sound of her voice sent tingles of excitement through me. Quickly, I said, "Hi yourself, I know you're probably still unpacking from your trip but I just wanted to touch base because you're right we do need to talk —" all in a rush, before I realized that I was talking to her answering machine, which was going on to say that she couldn't come to the phone right then. I hung up without leaving a message and called The Soaring Eagle. Her business partner answered the phone and told me that Naomi had extended her buying trip and was still out of town.

"Is there a message?" she asked, her voice distracted and impatient.

What kind of message could I leave? *I've been thinking about you night and day?* "Just tell her Sheila called," I mumbled and hung up.

It was Monday now. Twenty-four hours since I'd blurted out my issue to the support group. As I'd told them, it had relieved the burden of secrecy I'd been carrying around. What it hadn't relieved was my growing obsession with Naomi. How much longer would she stay out of town? And why? Was it a simple business decision — she'd heard of some new craftspeople whose work she had to check out? Or was it because of the night we'd spent together? Did she want to put off seeing me out of embarrassment over what we would say to each other? Or did she need the time to decide how she felt about pursuing our relationship?

There was no way to find out till she returned, a realization that sent me into such a frenzy of impatience that I went straight to the freezer for a bowl of Ben & Jerry's Chubby Hubby. Only in this case it was the wife getting chubbier from scarfing down the ice cream. This had to stop, I told myself. I was going back on my diet. And I was going to stop mooning over Naomi night and day.

I reminded myself that I had plenty else to occupy my mind. Starting with finding someplace for the rehearsal dinner before Debby took it into her head to book the Ritz-Carlton and send us a bill for half. All I had to do was find a restaurant with a private room that would seat all of our out-of-town family and all of the Goldbergs. That would be elegant enough for Debby's pretensions and family-friendly enough for Jeffrey and Anita to bring Steffi and the baby. Oh yes, the girls and Rose would be happier if it was kosher. And Dan would be happier if it didn't cost an arm and a leg.

I hadn't found anything nearby. Now I sat down to try restaurants in Silver Spring. It was an hour's drive around the Beltway, but it did have a large Jewish community. I started making calls, concentrating so hard that I jumped when Dan came home from work.

He glanced around the kitchen, taking in the unset table and the stove with nothing bubbling on it. "I hope that's a recipe for supper you're studying so intently," he said.

"Oh my God, supper! I forgot all about it."

This was so unlike me that Dan collapsed onto the nearest chair. "You *forgot* about it?" He gave a martyred sigh. "It's not enough you run off for a week without even a thought to whether you've left anything in the house for me to eat, but now that you're finally back home it just happens to slip your mind that I'd appreciate something besides tuna fish and crackers once in a while."

If Dan had been existing on tuna fish while I was gone, it was freshly grilled tuna at the country club. And in the week I'd been back, I'd fixed his dinner every night. Ignoring his griping, I said, "I got involved trying to plan dinner for when your mother and everyone is here."

"I can't believe you sweet-talked my mother into attending this affair, against her better judgment. But all right, the family is coming from New York, so we have to feed them. Is there some reason you have to plan the menu *now*? Instead of cooking supper tonight?"

"It's a dinner party," I pointed out, carefully not mentioning the

273

phrase *rehearsal dinner*. "You can't leave something like that to the last minute — by rights I should have planned it weeks ago. But you have no idea how hard it is to find a place to have it. I've been on the phone for hours." A glance at my desktop would have shown him that. The pad I kept there for shopping lists was covered with scrawled notes and scratch-outs through the names of restaurants I'd eliminated.

"So why do we have to take people out? What's wrong with right here? We had everyone at our house for Passover with no problem."

"That's because you didn't have to do the cooking."

"Why would I, when I'm married to someone who cooks like you do?" Dan said, getting up to find himself some cheese and crackers. This was probably the nicest thing he'd said to me in weeks, and I hoped it wasn't inspired solely by his hope that I would start using those culinary skills in the very near future.

"I appreciate the compliment," I told him, "but it's still a big job. It's not just our family who'll be here, you know. The Goldbergs — Tamara's parents and her sister and brother-in-law — will be in town. Besides," I added, talking fast before he could get upset all over again about the reason why they would be in town, "I wanted to find someplace kosher for your mother. You know how she complains whenever she eats here."

"Once, she complained," he said, around a mouthful of crackers and cheese, "and you make a federal case of it."

Once a meal maybe. "How about cutting me a slice of that Gouda?" I said. Diet be damned. "She'll be happier eating kosher, but the only kosher restaurants I found are in Silver Spring and I hate to drag everyone that far. Anyway we really need a private room and —"

"What are you talking about, there's no kosher restaurants? There's a kosher deli less than a mile from here."

"Moe's? It's a hole in the wall! I need to find seating space for twenty people. Besides —"

"So do carry-out."

I could just imagine the look on Debby's face. "Dan," I said, as clearly as if I were talking to one of the high school freshmen I used to teach, "you don't serve cold cuts for a rehears — for a company dinner."

"They have hot things. Corned beef. Hot pastrami on rye. My mother was crazy about it." Dan looked as if he was about to drool. "Now do you mind at least throwing together a salad for *our* dinner? Now?"

"Wait a minute. Let me think."

"You can't think and make dinner?"

Not with this many factors to consider. There was the time factor, first of all. Debby was right. It wasn't easy to line up a place at the last minute. Moe's Deli was kosher. Rose would be pleased and so would the girls. They'd said they wanted to keep things simple, hadn't they?

But it was Dan I was considering most of all. When he realized it was the rehearsal dinner, would he dig in his heels and refuse to attend? I still had hopes of getting him to both the dinner and the wedding itself. And he could hardly stay away from his own house with his mother and the rest of our family there.

Still, I could just see Debby's face. Though when I thought about it, I wouldn't mind seeing her expression when she was served corned beef on seeded rye at the rehearsal dinner.

"We'll eat in five minutes," I said. "Just let me get my purse."

Dan gave me a look. "You're going to pull something to eat out of your purse?"

"I always take it when I go out. We're eating at Moe's. Hot corned beef and pastrami." After which I would ask Moe if he would consider catering a dinner.

Moe's Deli was in the same shopping center as Dan's favorite sporting-goods store, so while I was talking with Moe I sent him off to look for the new golf shoes he needed. We both went to bed with a pleasant feeling of getting an errand out of the way, me over getting Moe to agree to cater — details and menu to be worked out later — and Dan over his new shoes. My feeling of accomplishment lasted until we were lying in bed together, and it occurred to me that a rehearsal dinner typically follows a wedding *rehearsal*. All I'd gotten Dan to do was agree to eat dinner with his family. As far as I knew, he was still planning to boycott the actual ceremony.

I couldn't help heaving a sigh at the thought. Dan must have been lying awake too, for he immediately asked, "What is it?"

The last thing I wanted right now was to start another fight about the wedding, especially when Dan was in a good mood for a change. On the other hand, did it make sense to wait to bring it up till he was in a bad mood again? So I said, "I just don't understand why I can sweet-talk your mother, as you call it, into coming to the girls' ceremony, but I can't get through to you no matter how much I try."

"Maybe because you haven't been talking to me in a way I'd call exactly sweet," he said drily.

He had me there. Though he'd deserved most of what I'd said. But I needed to put Jenny's feelings ahead of mine, so I said, "You're right. I'm sorry, I didn't mean to be picking a fight all the time."

But if what Dan had just said was true, then I was right that he was going to disappoint Jenny just to get back at me. I opened my mouth to say so, but before I could, he said, "Not to mention running around making arrangements behind my back and telling me one lie after another about them."

"I already told you I was sorry for fibbing to you."

"That's what really gets me," Dan went on, as if he hadn't heard me. "The one thing I've always believed is that no matter what disagreements come up in a marriage, it has to be built on trust. And until this year, I always assumed you felt the same way."

He didn't know the half of it. Hiding my preparations for the girls' wedding was nothing compared to what I'd done with Naomi. I couldn't begin to imagine what he would say if he knew about the night we'd spent in Scottsdale, or my continuing obsession with her. All of a sudden I felt so anguished I almost blurted out a confession. Instead, my throat choked up and I began to sob. "I didn't mean to do things behind your back, it's just that one thing led to another," I managed.

My outbreak startled Dan even more than it did me. "All right, all right, calm down," he said, sounding worried as well as surprised. He slid over and patted my shoulder. "There's no need to get hysterical. I just wanted to get what was bothering me off my chest."

"I know," I said, calming down to a sniffle. "I'm sorry." I reached for Dan's hand as I said it, and he let me take it; then he closed his over mine.

We lay in uneasy silence a few moments. Then Dan said, "Still, I have to tell you that it does get to me that you were so busy planning this affair for Jenny, and yet you couldn't take the time to mention that the school administrators already knew about her relationship with Tamara and that luckily they weren't going to make an issue out of it. You knew how worried I was about her losing her job, and yet you couldn't set my mind at ease with that one simple bit of information."

That hadn't been for lack of trying. If Dan hadn't stormed out of the room every time I'd tried to discuss the girls' ceremony, I would have told him long ago. But saying so would be sure to set him off again. Then I remembered Chuck and his advice at PFLAG. "I was going to tell you that Jenny and Tamara were out at school already," I said. "But then I decided it was up to Jenny to tell you. I got some advice from a therapist, and he said that what I was doing was typical of a lot of mothers — getting in the middle between you and Jenny."

"You saw a therapist? I hope you didn't forget to give your insurance information. I haven't seen any paperwork on it from Blue Cross."

It was just like Dan to worry about insurance instead of listening to what I was trying to tell him. And apparently it had become just like me to shade the truth. Instead of admitting that the advice I had gotten was an off-the-cuff comment in the middle of the support group, I said, quickly improvising, "It was an introductory visit. He doesn't charge for the first visit, and I decided I didn't need to keep seeing him. But anyhow, what he said was that it sounded as if I kept getting in between you and Jenny — with the best intentions, of course. That I was interpreting what you said to her and vice versa, putting the best face on what you said to each other, so as to smooth things over between the two of you. But that in the long run your relationship with your daughter wouldn't improve until you and she communicated directly with each other."

"And this is why you kept me in the dark?" Dan retorted. "Because you think that Jenny and I have such a poor relationship that we're going to be on the outs from now on because I don't approve of this so-called wedding?"

"That is not what I said. I just said I didn't want to hurt your relationship by running interference for you. After all, there was no reason Jenny couldn't let you know that she was out at school herself."

"Well, I'm sure she would have mentioned it earlier, only she assumed you wouldn't have kept it a secret from me. You don't need to worry about my relationship with my daughter." Dan's words were full of confidence, but he couldn't fool me. He knew how much he'd let Jenny down. No matter what he said, I could hear the worry in his voice.

"Honey, I know she's always been crazy about you," I said. Dan gave a mollified grunt. "But don't you see how that makes her all the more disappointed when you refuse to take part in her ceremony?"

Dan was silent just long enough for me to start congratulating myself on finally getting through to him. Then he said, "Sheila, do you ever listen to yourself when you talk?"

This was not the question of a man who had been brought around. "I don't know what you're talking about," I said.

"I'm talking about the fact that not five minutes ago, you informed me that you couldn't so much as mention that Jenny had already let her principal know about her relationship with Tamara because you didn't want to interfere with her relationship with me. So do me a favor and keep on doing what you claimed to be doing — just stay out of my relationship with my daughter." He rolled onto his side, his back to me. In an infuriatingly short time, he was snoring blissfully.

Five minutes earlier, I'd been sobbing with guilt over betraying Dan. But listening to Dan snore, I felt as lonely as I had on the sofa bed at Mama's. Despite my remorse, I couldn't help wishing it was not Dan, but Naomi, in my bed.

Chapter Twenty-One

W ith a wish like that, it was inevitable that I would dream about Naomi again. Only this time, I was lying naked on a bed of sand between Naomi and Dan, each of whom was vying to win me away from the other. The sun-warmed grains tickled my bottom while Naomi played with my pubic hair, whispering, "Let me show you my cave, you sexy Mama Bear." I turned to her, breathing hard, when Dan caught me from behind. His hands cupped my breasts. "You belong in my bed, not hers. You promised yourself to me," he growled.

I sat bolt upright, my heart pounding until I had woken up enough to realize I was alone in my bedroom. The alarm clock read 9:00 a.m. Dan would be at his office by now. It didn't take Freud to interpret this one, I told myself. I felt guilty, as well I should. My guilt trip was interrupted by the ringing of the phone. I grabbed for it so quickly that I knocked the telephone base off the nightstand.

"I didn't wake you, did I?" Lois asked.

A flood of disappointment washed over me on hearing the voice of my best friend. "No, I was up. Just going down to have coffee." I swung my legs to the floor, still shaken up by being torn between Dan and Naomi in my dream. Why couldn't I have dreamed I was in Naomi's bed? Then, I'd walk out of the bedroom into her cozy kitchen, come up behind her and give her a kiss on the back of her long, lovely neck. She'd turn, smiling, and we'd put our arms around each other and kiss, soul to soul, then sit at the table with pottery mugs of coffee, talking about the day to come. I'd look across the table into Naomi's warm eyes instead of the back of Dan's business section.

"Sheila? Are you still there? Don't go back to sleep on me."

"Oh, Lois! Sorry, I was....I was just wondering. Back when you were with the rat, did you ever have an affair?" I was so astonished by the question I had just blurted, I nearly dropped the receiver.

"I should have. He deserved it. But I left the running around to him. What brings it up?" Lois paused, then gasped. "Sheila, don't tell me you're having an affair? Is that it? Am I right?"

I was tempted to tell her everything. I needed to talk. Badly. But telling Lois a secret was like setting up a Web page and registering with every search engine in existence. So I said, as quickly as I could devise a plausible comeback, "Don't you know me better than that? I was just thinking about Natalie and Roberto this morning, for some reason."

"Oh. Well, that's a coincidence. Because I was going to tell you the latest."

"What latest? Don't tell me there's trouble in Paradise."

"Don't ask." Which meant I needn't bother, because she was about to tell all in any case.

I dropped Lois off after a long, liquid lunch — chardonnay for her, two Diet Cokes for me. Back home, I headed for the kitchen to think about dinner. Instead I found myself dwelling on Lois's latest. Not that her news was so surprising. The bloom was off the rose as far as Roberto went. Too bad that Natalie had already left Norman for him.

I didn't have to drive anywhere that evening, so I poured myself a glass of wine — heart-healthy red — and sat down at the breakfast table. Wasn't it just weeks ago that Natalie had gushed about Roberto all through lunch, painting him as a paragon of perfection, from the part in his hair to the perkiness in his penis? Now, he'd virtually moved into her studio apartment, despite her stated intention of living alone. And it seemed that living with him day in and day out had toppled him off his pedestal. Was it only the excitement of starting a new relationship that had made Roberto so attractive to Natalie?

And could that be all that had attracted me to Naomi — the excitement of something new and different? I'd be tempting fate if I kept up my affair with her. Dan would find out sooner or later, just as Norm had. What then? Could I be like Natalie and give up my marriage, my home, without a backward glance?

I picked up my glass and wandered from room to room. Each one held some memento of the life Dan and I had built together. The hall to our bedroom was lined with family portraits: the two of us, Jeffrey and Jenny, a new one every couple of years till the kids were grown. The dresser held our wedding picture, Dan and I smiling joyfully into each other's eyes as I left my mother's house for wedded bliss. Which reminded me, in turn, of how I'd lain awake at Mama's recalling the thrill of making love with Dan on that very couch.

The excitement of something new, I reiterated to myself. That's all this whole thing with Naomi amounted to. I'd be crazy to risk my home and marriage for the thrill of carrying on an affair. Dan didn't deserve that, no matter what differences we had. I should put the energy I'd spent fantasizing about Naomi into working on our marriage. No matter how Naomi tempted me, I'd tell her I'd made up my mind not to repeat our lovemaking.

I repeated my vow to myself all the rest of the evening, while I cooked one of Dan's favorite meals without springing a thing on him, and all the next morning, while I ran to the theater to let in the commercial cleaning company I'd hired, and while I reassured Debby at least five times that yes, everything was arranged for a catered rehearsal dinner.

I was still repeating it to myself when Naomi finally called four days later, Sunday morning, just after Dan had left for the golf course.

"I thought you'd never get back," I blurted, before she'd even finished saying hello. Fine way to back off from a relationship, I scolded myself. "I've been wanting to talk to you," I added, in what I hoped was a less eager tone of voice.

"Absolutely. We definitely need to talk," she said, her voice even warmer and throatier than I'd remembered. "But we really can't have this conversation on the phone."

"No, I guess not."

"So why don't you come by tomorrow. Can you make it for lunch? My partner can hold down the fort in the shop for an hour. I'll make us an omelet." Naomi was purring at me now, sounding so sweetly sexy that I knew just what she really had in mind for lunch. Should I tell her I'd rather meet at a restaurant? I opened my mouth to do just that, but then thought, what if someone I knew happened to overhear us?

"I'll be there around one, if that's good for you," I said instead.

No matter how Naomi tried to entice me, I would hold firm to my resolve to call a halt to our affair before it went any further. I repeated that resolution to myself as I drove to Old Town and maneuvered into a parking space six inches longer than my car. Her business partner waved me to the staircase and I repeated my resolution once again as I climbed upstairs to Naomi's apartment.

The door was ajar and Naomi looked up from the table where she was chopping onions and peppers for the promised omelet. Her smile was as warm as an embrace, and then she rose and hugged me tight. The feel of her arms around me reminded me of how I'd felt in bed that night, so I quickly stepped back out of her embrace and sat down on a kitchen chair.

"I thought you'd be back long before this," I said.

"So did I. But I needed to change my plans. I was sorry to put off seeing you again for so long. I've been thinking about you a lot. Are you sure you're all right?"

So it *was* on account of her feelings for me that she'd extended her trip. She was probably just waiting for a signal from me.... I reminded myself once more that I was a happily married woman. A married woman, at any rate. "I'm fine," I lied. "Been busy with a lot of family stuff. The girls' ceremony coming up and all."

Naomi nodded and began cracking eggs into a bowl. She added pepper, salt, nutmeg and what looked like heavy cream, and began beating the mixture together so vigorously that I could see her breasts jiggle under her ribbed T-shirt. I looked around the apartment to take my eyes off them. It didn't take long, only three rooms, the tiny kitchen, an archway leading to a living room with a deep reddish-brown leather couch and several stunning Native American pottery bowls, and the bedroom where I'd gazed on Naomi naked for the first time.

To distract myself from *that*, I pondered, as I had months before, what it would be like to live in this apartment. Not much to take care of. Twenty minutes with the vacuum and you'd be done. Not that I actually minded vacuuming and dusting. Unfashionable as it was, I rather enjoyed taking care of my house, plumping up the pillows I'd chosen to accent each room, dusting the picture frames that held our family snapshots, pausing to remember the occasion when each had been taken.

Natalie had left all her family portraits — she'd told Lois, LaVerne and me — moving into a studio apartment even smaller than this. I wondered again if I could live like that. Like this. But of course, I'd be living with Naomi. It wasn't the number of rooms you had, after all, but who you lived in them with.

"Lunch will be ready in a minute," Naomi said, startling me from my reverie. She was pouring the eggs into a skillet of sizzling butter.

"Let me wash my hands," I said, getting up. "Mind if I just use the kitchen sink?" She stepped back to give me room. Not far enough, though; I had to squeeze past her, close enough for my arms to brush her breasts, close enough to feel her breath hot against my neck, to breathe in her scent. I couldn't help myself. I turned and took Naomi in *my* arms, and pressed my lips to hers, pressed my tongue between them. I felt her hesitate an instant, and then she was kissing me back, her tongue as warm and eager as mine. When we stepped back from each other at last, I reached for the pan of eggs and moved them from the burner. "You know, I'm not really hungry for an omelet right now," I said. The implication of what I was hungry for hung none-too-subtly in the air.

"Oh, Sheila. I can't," Naomi said, pulling abruptly away from me. Her voice was so dismayed that I gave her a look of disbelief.

"But — I don't understand. I thought just now that you.... Don't tell me you weren't just as...you weren't at least a little attracted," I stammered.

"More than a little. You're a very attractive woman, Sheila. I keep telling you that. But I shouldn't have done that just now. I can't let myself get carried away with you. I'm starting a new relationship and —"

"A relationship?" I interrupted. "You told me you were single."

"I was. Well, I still am, technically. We're both too mature to just rush into something. Like that old joke, what does a lesbian bring on a second date? A U-Haul."

I was dying inside and she was telling jokes. I plopped onto a chair again. Unfortunately I picked the wrong chair. Naomi's cat sprang off it, yowling his dismay, and startling me so that I ended up sitting on the floor, the chair tipped over behind me.

"Are you okay?" Naomi extended a hand to help me up.

I gave her a look. "Fine. I have a well padded tushie." As she well knew. I checked the other chair for the cat and sat down.

Naomi smiled. "I didn't mean to upset you."

"I'm not upset; I just feel so stupid," I said. I sniffled, and then faked a sneeze so she wouldn't know I was fighting back tears. From her reaction, it wasn't working. She sat down, pulling her chair up so that our knees were nearly touching, pressed linen to practical polyester, and took my hand. Not the way a lover would, but like a nurse about to check my pulse.

"I've been afraid you'd feel like this. Neither of us made any promises, Sheila. We spent a wonderful night together. And I might have been very willing to explore the possibility of a longer-term sexual relationship with you, if that's what you wanted. Though I wasn't at all sure you would, in the clear light of day, so to speak. You are a married woman, after all."

So I was. Funny that it was Naomi who'd remembered that fact right now, not me. But now that she'd reminded me, I said, "As a matter of fact, that's what I came here to tell you. That I'd just slipped up the one time, and I wasn't going to risk my marriage by having an affair." I pulled my hand from hers and blew my nose. "I just forgot myself for a moment when I saw you," I said, trying to assume an air of dignity to cover my embarrassment, the way I would slip into a long suit jacket to cover my hips.

"Me too," she said, venturing a strained smile. "But what I wanted to tell you was that I've started seeing a woman who —"

"When did you start seeing someone? I thought you've been on a buying trip the past two weeks."

Naomi got up and turned to the stove. "I think these eggs are salvageable," she said. "A little more scrambled than an omelet should be, maybe. I hope you're still willing to eat lunch."

"When haven't I been willing to eat? But you didn't answer my question."

"I met her on my trip, actually. At that dinner dance PFLAG had. I think you saw her. Didn't you wave to me when we were dancing together?"

I had. I'd been expecting to sit with Naomi that night and trying to imagine what in the world we'd make dinner conversation about. "I thought that was just some friend of yours. Someone else who was selling stuff at the expo."

"I did have an old friend there, matter of fact, someone who owns a bookstore — Women's Words — you might have noticed her table. She introduced us. Ruth was just attending the conference." Naomi caressed the name with her tongue as she repeated it, smiling to herself as she sprinkled grated cheese into the pan of eggs.

I stared at her, startled from my misery. "Ruth and Naomi? And that's why you fell for her? On account of her *name*?"

Naomi laughed. "It is funny, isn't it? But we're hardly mother and daughter-in-law the way Ruth and Naomi are in the Bible."

I decided not to dwell on what they *were* to each other. Instead, I picked up my fork to attack the eggs Naomi was dishing onto my plate.

"I should have tracked you down and explained before you left, though. You must have wondered when I was out all night."

"Out all night?" The eggs were delicious. I'd have to ask Naomi what kind of cheese she'd used — if I decided ever to speak to her again.

"After the dinner dance. The one we were just talking about."

"Oh." I thought back. "I didn't realize you were. I mean, I thought you came in after I'd fallen asleep and then got up and out before I did in the morning." Hadn't the sheets on her side been rumpled? Or had I messed them up myself, tossing and turning? "So where *were* you? You spent the night with this Ruth person?"

Naomi nodded. "But not the way you're thinking. We went out for a drive to the desert, and just sat and talked the whole night. About everything. Our past lives, our dreams, my shop, the house she's building herself in Santa Fe, her writing, my painting, the colors of the sunrise. At which point I realized that I needed to be back in the vendor's area at the hotel in less than two hours. By the time I felt I could leave my table to shower and change, you were gone from the room." She took a bite of eggs and gave another blissful smile — presumably inspired by the memory of that night, though it could also have been the cholesterol-filled richness of the omelet.

"I know it was only one night, but by morning I knew I'd met the woman of my dreams. The one I've been searching for my whole life," Naomi added, confirming my first guess as to the reason for that Mona Lisa smile. "My soul mate. I suppose that makes me sound like I'm seventeen."

"Fifteen, but who's counting?" I finished the last bite of my omelet. "But what kind of relationship can you have when she's a thousand miles away?"

"Not for long. I was getting to that. Like I told you months ago, I always knew I'd move West one day, when the time was right. And it is. I'm leaving this area and moving to Santa Fe. Roz is going to buy out my share of the shop."

"You spent one night with this woman and you're moving in with her?"

"Close to two weeks. And I didn't say I was moving in with her," Naomi said, finally letting a hint of exasperation into her voice. "I'm looking for a place of my own for right now. I might sound like a teenager, but we're mature women, Ruth and I. We want to give ourselves time to develop a relationship, not rush into it. But it's hard enough to maintain an existing relationship by long distance, let alone explore a new one."

That made sense, I had to admit. I stared down at my empty plate. There seemed nothing more to say, so I stood up. "I'd better be going. Thank you for lunch. It was delicious. Too delicious. I guess now that we won't be seeing each other any more, I'll get back to my diet."

Naomi caught my arm as I turned toward the door. "I was hoping we could have this talk without hurting your feelings. It's not as if we'd been in a long-term relationship." Nor one that she had initiated, she didn't have to remind me.

"Next thing you're going to tell me you hope we can still be friends," I told her, trying to smile as I said it.

"I do, very much so. But I'll understand if it isn't possible for you. By the way, I already returned my RSVP card saying I would love to come to your daughter's wedding. But I suppose under the circumstances, you'd prefer it if I stayed away?"

"I —" I opened my mouth to say I thought that would be for the best, when I remembered how I'd turned to Naomi time and time again for help with all the grief Dan was giving me over the girls' ceremony, and with my own secret misgivings about it. "No, of course I want you to come," I reassured her. "I don't know why I'm carrying on like this." Which was nothing but the truth. Hadn't I come with the avowed intention of telling Naomi I couldn't have an affair with her? It didn't make sense for me to feel anything but relief. But rationality didn't seem to be my strong suit this afternoon. "So what are you going to do in Santa Fe? Workwise, I mean. Will you open another Indian jewelry store?"

Naomi shook her head, relief showing on her face at my friendlier tone. "The market for Native American art is crowded already in that part of the country. But Ruth knows a gallery specializing in Western art that needs an assistant manager. Or will, starting in September. I had a long talk with the owner on the phone and basically the job is mine, though I do have an appointment for a formal interview once I've relocated."

"Isn't that going to be a comedown, after running your own shop?"

"Not at all. It's long hours, a lot of responsibility and paperwork running a place like this, even with a partner. And this will be a good opportunity to learn more about the art world. Plus give me a little more time to spend on my own painting."

"And if you're working in a gallery, maybe you can display a few of your own works there."

She laughed. "My work is nowhere near that quality. This is a gallery that handles R. C. Gorman, among others."

"Oh," I said, making a mental note to look up the name if I could remember it. "Well, I love your painting at any rate." I glanced at my watch. "I'd better get going."

"Wait a second." Naomi darted into her bedroom and returned holding out her painting of the sunset that I'd so admired. "I want you to have this."

"Oh!" I said again. "I didn't mean — I wasn't hinting —"

"Of course you weren't. I want you to have it." She handed it to me, and I cradled it in my arms.

"It's beautiful. But I shouldn't take it from you," I protested. "I mean, you love it."

"Because it reminded me of country I love. But I won't need a reminder now. I'll see the real thing every day."

I smiled. "I'll miss you," I said.

"And vice versa. I really do treasure your friendship, Sheila, even if there isn't the possibility of a romantic relationship between us." She stepped forward and gave me a hug, and I transferred the painting to one hand so I could hug her back. A friendly hug, no romance involved. "Though who knows?" she shrugged, as I turned toward the door. "If we'd met one another years ago, before you met your husband and I met my ex, it's possible we'd be keeping house together today."

"Who knows?" I echoed her and walked out her door.

Naomi was getting ready to move to Santa Fe and live happily ever after, but I had to get home to make supper for Dan. Once I'd walked into the family room from our garage, I set Naomi's painting on the couch. I began looking up the recipe for low-fat chicken divan, but I couldn't keep my eyes off the painting. Did I need a daily reminder of how I'd humiliated myself? Still, it was so beautiful, so evocative of Naomi.... The picture hanging over the couch was just an art-museum poster. I took it down and hung Naomi's in its place.

I thought Dan would be bowled over as soon as he walked into the house, but he headed straight for the front hall to go through the mail, and then into his den to check his e-mail. So we ate dinner without him noticing the painting — our conversation consisting mainly of his grumbling about a $439 Visa charge to have BAT's theater and kitchen scoured by Dirt Diggers, the heavy-duty cleaning company I'd picked to get the place ready for the girls' ceremony.

"The least you could have done was write a check for that amount to the theater and let them pay the bill from their treasury, so we could have taken a charitable deduction on our taxes. You remembered BAT's nonprofit status when you wanted to pull the wool over my eyes, but now that you've gotten your way, you just pull out your plastic without a second thought." Dan gave a snort of disgust as he pushed back his chair and headed toward his recliner in the family room. He stopped, as the glowing colors of Naomi's sunset caught his eye. He gave it a good look. Then he turned and gave *me* a look. "You bought a new painting on top of all the expenses for this so-called wedding?"

"It was a gift," I said hastily. "My friend Naomi, you remember her? She owns that Indian jewelry shop in Old Town where I bought my silver necklace? Anyway, she painted this while she was on one of her buying trips."

"She's the one who used to be a social worker? Very intelligent person." Dan turned to take in the painting again, mollified by the realization that I hadn't spent several hundred more on a work of art. "Not bad. A woman of many talents."

You don't know the half, I thought.

"So what was the occasion for her to give you a present like this?"

I shrugged, as if the whole subject was beneath mention. "She's moving out West and trying to get rid of stuff. I guess you could say it's kind of a going-away present."

"Well, it's not bad looking," he said, glancing at it appreciatively once more. "But shouldn't you be the one giving her a going-away present?"

Other than a night to remember? "I suppose I should," I said. "Only I just found out today that she's leaving the area. It came up suddenly. She met someone while she was on her buying trip and made a really impulsive decision. She seems very happy about it," I added, and my voice was so obviously unhappy that Dan gave me another look.

"You sound like you've lost your best friend. I didn't realize you were on such good terms with her. You've hardly mentioned her, except for inviting her to a couple of cast parties."

For good reason. I felt overwhelmed by a rush of guilt, with a sudden urge to confess all. I took a deep breath and got hold of myself. I couldn't imagine what Dan would do if he knew, and I wasn't about to find out. Never in a million years would I tell him.

There wasn't a soul I could tell, in fact. I'd shared enough with the PFLAG group. Nor would I tell the lunch bunch, not even my best friend Lois. The only person to whom I might ever divulge my secret was Jenny. Not now, of course, but some day thirty or forty years off, when she and Tamara came to visit me in the nursing home and the three of us sat rocking on the front porch, at a loss for conversation.

Dan was still standing, apparently waiting for some response from me, so I said, "Actually, I met her for lunch a number of times. I needed someone that I could talk to about Jenny and how upset I've been about the way we've been fighting over the girls' wedding."

"Oh." Was it my imagination, or did he sound a little abashed?

"I mean, I've got the support group, but that's not the same as talking to a friend. And most of my friends wouldn't understand. Jack and Jim might, but when I see them it's just for theater stuff. But Lois and the rest.... So I've been having these heart-to-heart talks with Naomi, I guess because she can understand the issues, being a lesbian herself."

Apparently this was news to Dan, but to my surprise he just murmured, "Oh, really," as if my having a lesbian friend was completely unremarkable.

"So I am going to miss her, because what you said was right, Naomi was becoming one of my best friends." Which, when I thought about it, was plain truth. Not the whole truth, but the truth. "And when you think about it," I added, "I don't have that many close friends." I heard the beginning of sobs in my voice, and I shut up before Dan could grow suspicious, blinking back tears as I pretended to blot my lipstick on my napkin.

Dan was silent a moment too. A long moment. But instead of turning on me with an accusation of adultery, he said, "Honey, I hope you're counting me as one of your best friends. Because that's the way I think of you, no matter what disagreements we have."

One of my best friends. Even before all the difficulties we'd had this year, it had never occurred to me to think of my husband in those terms. As a companion, lover, provider, father, yes. But as a friend — that category was reserved in my mind for my girlfriends, people like Lois and LaVerne and Natalie. Friends were the women with whom I shared confidences *about* our husbands.

There was no way to say *that*, so I said, "Of course I do." I got up and walked past Dan, sinking down on the family-room couch. He'd been headed toward his recliner, but now he came over to sit next to me. I opened my mouth to reassure him further, but what came out was, "But you haven't been very friendly to me lately."

He drew back a bit. "And you have?"

He had me there; there was no getting around it. I'd been fantasizing about Naomi for months, been obsessed with her. Then I'd topped it off by actually having sex with her. And I couldn't tell myself it was a once-in-a-lifetime slip, because if she'd been willing I'd have been in her bed that very afternoon, the rays of her painted sunset illuminating our naked bodies as we rolled on her sand-colored sheets. I bit my lip, glad that I couldn't see that vivid reminder of her from where I sat on the sofa.

And Dan said, "You've acted as if my views about this affair had no validity whatsoever. You've manipulated me, outright lied to me —" I nearly jumped out of my skin. Dan *knew* about my affair?

"I never meant it to happen," I said. "I just —" Without warning, my voice caught in my throat, tears started down my cheeks.

Dan put an arm around my shoulder and gave me a little squeeze. "I didn't mean to make you cry about it. It's just that it's seemed to me lately that the only people whose opinions you take into account are in your support group. Them, or Tamara's mother."

I jumped again. I'd been wallowing so in my guilt that I'd entirely misunderstood him. It would never dawn on him that I'd been unfaithful. But I owed Dan a little honesty for a change. Not total honesty, but a little. I took a deep breath and turned to face him.

"To tell the truth....to tell the truth, I started off feeling the same way you do about the girls having this wedding. But I kept it to myself. Partly because I thought that I shouldn't feel that way if I really accepted her —"

"That's certainly what you've been preaching to me."

He had me there again. "I know I have. Because I think the right thing for us to do is to accept Jenny. I mean accept her sexual orientation and support her relationship with Tamara. But to be honest, I did have a lot of reservations about this whole wedding business. It's just that I didn't want

Jenny to know about them. I didn't want to make her unhappy. And I suppose I didn't want her to be unhappy with me."

"So instead, you made me the bad guy."

"I didn't make you anything! You were the one who dug in your heels. In fact, I've done everything I could to smooth things over between the two of you. I don't think you have any idea how much you've hurt Jenny by your attitude."

"And what happened to letting us work out our own relationship, the way you say that therapist told you?"

"Therapist? Oh, Chuck, right."

"Did you even care about my relationship with Jenny, or were you just trying to prove how much you loved her by giving in to her on this wedding business? Or maybe even trying to show that you loved her more than I did?"

I drew in a breath that was more like a gasp. "How can you say that? First you say you want to be my best friend and then...." I burst into tears in earnest and Dan had no choice but to give me a hug.

"I didn't mean to make you cry," he said again. "Sheila, Sheila come on, stop now. I didn't mean that the way it sounded. It just came out wrong."

He sounded so apologetic that once I had sniffled back my sobs, I found myself blurting, "I don't know. Maybe I was a little jealous of how you and Jenny usually get along together. With mothers and daughters, it's not that easy. But I would never dream of trying to make it seem like you didn't love her." I wouldn't, would I? Not consciously anyway, I assured myself. And if I ever wanted to explore my unconscious motivations I'd do it with a therapist, not my husband. Which reminded me of what Dan had thrown up to me a minute ago.

"I know I told you that according to this therapist I shouldn't get in the middle between you and Jenny. But I couldn't help wanting to keep you from having a big rift with her. I mean, maybe his advice isn't always right. I think sometimes if you care for someone, you've got to tell them when you think they're doing the wrong thing." I had a sudden sensation of deja vu. Had I told Dan all this already? No — "Oh my God, I sound just like Rose!"

"Like my mother?" Dan pulled back enough to give me the kind of quizzical stare you give someone who seems to be going off the deep end.

I nodded. "I was saying just the kind of thing she's always saying:

'When you love someone you tell them their faults.' You know how she always says that."

He did know; he relaxed enough to grin. "Well, that's one for the books — you turning out to be just like my mother. I'll have to tell her." He took my hands in his, and then said, much more seriously, "But you've been hounding me about this ceremony of the girls' because you do love me. I'm very glad to know that."

"Of course I do! Maybe it hasn't seemed that way to you. I'm sorry if I ever made you doubt me. But I've always loved you, always." Which was nothing but truth. No matter what fights we had. What couple didn't have fights? But what I had with Dan was stronger than any fights, a whole life we'd built together. I squeezed Dan's hands back and said, "Why do you think I've spent half my lifetime with you?"

He grinned happily again. "Now you sound just like Golde."

"Who?"

"In *Fiddler on the Roof*. When Tevye asks her, 'Do You Love Me?' And she answers, 'After twenty-five years, if that's not love, what is?'"

"Oh, *Fiddler on the Roof*. I didn't know you remembered it so well."

"I remember everything you've been in. And do you remember what Tevye says back after Golde admits she loves him?"

Of course I did. But I waited for Dan to say it.

"'And I suppose I love you too.'"

I sighed happily.

Dan hesitated a moment, and then said, "I don't want to start quarreling again, but I would like to ask you about something you said a few minutes ago."

"Is it about what I've put on Visa? I think the only other big item —"

"No, no, nothing about money. I told you, spend whatever you feel you need to on this," Dan said. "Within reason, of course," he added, sounding more like his usual self. "No, what I wanted to ask — you said you started off with the same reservations about the girls actually going through with this ceremony. So I'm wondering now whether you still have them underneath, or whether you've worked through them? Maybe I should ask how you've worked through them? If you have."

"Oh." What I felt about Jenny and Tamara. Did I even know what I felt? I thought back a few months, when I'd winced inwardly at seeing the two of them give each other a little kiss on the lips. Never dreaming that not too long after, I'd find myself in bed with another woman, eager for her kisses on my lips, not to mention on several more X-rated spots.

I had to admit, my desire for Naomi was infatuation, not the kind of lasting love I had with Dan. Maybe I wasn't quite over it yet, but I would be in time. But for the space of that one enchanted evening — to dredge up a musical-comedy song from my mother's era — our passion for each other had felt as right as rain.

But suppose I hadn't met Dan first? Suppose it had been Naomi I met when I was scarcely out of my teens, as she'd momentarily imagined as we said goodbye? Assuming that I'd been able to realize back then that I could fall for a woman as easily as a man, wasn't it perfectly possible our infatuation could have matured into the kind of lasting love Dan and I shared now? Of course it was. In which case, wouldn't I have wanted the two of us to be able to take vows of wedded love, just as Dan and I had?

"Of course," I said, not realizing I'd spoken aloud, until Dan said, "You mean, of course you've worked through your reservations?" and I remembered he was still waiting for my answer.

I nodded. "I think I am all right with it now. Jenny and Tamara feel the same way about each other as...as you and I did when we were married. So it really is right for them to have a wedding just like we did."

"That's just what you've been saying all along to convince me to change my mind," Dan said. "But I'm still wrestling with this whole thing. The last thing I want to do is to hurt Jenny, yet the idea of the two of them standing under a canopy....How did you get *all right* with it, as you put it? Was it your PFLAG group? Or what?"

"Partly. Going to a support group was a big help. So was knowing people like Jack and Jim. You remember we went to their ceremony?"

"That was before Jenny ever came out. I can't relate it to her somehow. But that did it for you? That and your support meetings? You just came to think about it in a different light?"

"Not entirely. I mean it's a process. Emotional stages you have to go through. That I had to go through." The most important part of which was the one thing I had to keep to myself. "But maybe it was easier for me because I'm a mother. Or a woman," I added, coming as close to being totally honest as I could. "So it might have been easier for me to put myself in Jenny's place."

Chapter Twenty-Two

The few days left before the wedding flew by. I devoted myself to helping Jenny and her intended plan their big day, just as I'd always imagined doing in my daydreams about Jenny's future. Nothing was changed but the gender of the imagined groom.

The theater building was ready. True to their name, the Dirt Diggers had dug grime out of the crevices between the old floorboards and waxed them to a mellow glow, sucked up dust and dried paint chips with an industrial-strength vacuum cleaner, washed the windows and rest rooms, scoured the oven that the potluck committee would use to hold the covered dishes committee members brought, and even removed the cobwebs festooning the beams below the twenty-foot ceiling. Sam dropped by to make sure nothing had been disturbed in BAT's storeroom, and remarked with grudging approval that we'd have to hang artificial spiderwebs before the Halloween play.

Sprucing up the theater was just the tip of the iceberg. The girls had final meetings with the photographer, musicians and the chairperson of the potluck committee. The cake — the one item the food committee wasn't providing — had to be picked up at a kosher bakery in Silver Spring; I'd volunteered to do that. I'd also told the girls I would check on the rental cushions and the rented dinnerware and glasses. The poles of the *chuppah* needed to be decorated with greenery, but not till the last minute, to keep it fresh, and I'd promised to double-check with the florist, as well.

Not to mention that I had to get ready for six houseguests — Jeffrey,

Anita, the children, Mama and Rose — plus the rehearsal dinner. Since our talk, I hadn't pressed Dan. Nor had he said whether he might bring himself to take part in the ceremony, or at least attend it. Although I'd been spending several hours a day with Jenny and Tamara, it was three days before the wedding when I finally admitted to Jenny that her father would probably not be taking part.

"I shouldn't have told you I could guarantee Daddy would be there. I shouldn't have gotten your hopes up like that. But I want you to know that it's not —"

"Mom, don't you think I knew that? I'm not a child."

The two of us were in the girls' living room, sitting at a quilting frame on which was stretched the nearly finished canopy under which the wedding party would stand. Tamara had run out for groceries, and I'd taken advantage of this rare time alone with my daughter to bring up her father. Jenny wasn't interested in conversation, though. She was more intent on stitching together the remaining squares that a quilting party of their friends hadn't finished. Her head was bent over the frame, so I couldn't make out her expression. But she sounded pissed, whether at me or Dan I wasn't sure. "I didn't mean to imply you were, just that I made you a promise I shouldn't have," I started again, when Jenny again interrupted.

"I didn't expect you to wave a magic wand. I know how stubborn Daddy is," she said, sounding for the moment like one of her students. "Anyway, this is between him and me."

That was the way Chuck had advised me to leave it, the way I'd told Dan I was going to. Still, I couldn't help adding, "I hope you know that even if he can't bring himself to take part in the ceremony, he still loves you very much."

"Yes, of course I know," she said impatiently.

Her impatience was catching. "Well, don't bite my head off," I snapped.

She looked up at that. "Sorry, Mom. I didn't mean to yell at you. You've been really great anyway, the way you've supported us from the very beginning."

At least to all appearances, I thought. I owed Jenny honesty about my unspoken reservations just as I had Dan. It might even help her understand her father's conflict better, if I confessed them. *To tell the truth honey, I haven't always felt...*No, that was too negative. *I really am behind you now, but....*That was a better start, but what? *But I had to make a journey to get* *to that point.*....Marlene would approve of that wording. Though could I assure Jenny I'd reached the end of my journey toward full acceptance? Or was I still on that journey, despite Naomi, despite — I took a breath.

"Actually," I began.

Just then, Tamara's key turned in the lock. She pushed open the door with her hip, balancing two grocery bags and singing out, "I bought us ice cream. Chocolate. I thought we deserved a treat."

I couldn't help breathing a sigh of relief. So much for admitting my ambivalence. The moment had passed. Jenny sprang up to help Tamara, took one of the grocery bags from her, and then turned back to me. "I just wanted you to know how much I appreciate it. I'm sure it was a struggle for you at first, just the way it was for me, when I first came out to myself."

Though I'd finally accepted that I couldn't force Dan into attending the ceremony, I couldn't help going at it indirectly. So that evening, once we'd sat down to eat, I said, "After supper, would you mind bringing the crib down from the attic?"

"You want the crib down?" he echoed, in a voice as quizzical as if I'd told him that instead of being in the full flush of menopause, I was about to present him with a change-of-life baby.

"We haven't had it down since Steffi outgrew it. I want to give it a good going-over with the vacuum."

Dan was still looking at me with what appeared to be shock.

"You do remember that everyone will be here the day after tomorrow?" I reminded him. "My mother. *Your* mother. Jeffrey, Anita, Steffi. And little Jeffrey. So we need to get out the crib."

He finally nodded. "Of course. I hadn't realized it was so close. That is, I knew it was, but I still need time to...." It was obvious he wasn't talking about getting the crib, a five-minute job once the pull-down stairs had been wrestled into place.

"But you have just two days," I pointed out, as gently as I could. "Your mother is coming all the way from New York," I repeated.

"And I still can't get over it."

Neither could I, as a matter of fact. If anyone had told me six months before that Rose would be taking my side in an argument with Dan, I would have *plotzed*. I decided it was best to keep this thought to myself.

"She used to be so insistent on following every Jewish law," Dan added.

"There's nothing in Judaism against two women having a wedding ceremony," I said. "I mean, I admit it's not...not traditional, but there's nothing in the Torah against it. I went to a panel on religion at the national conference."

"Still, my mother used to get so upset if anyone even mixed the milk and meat dishes."

I remembered too, after thirty years, how she'd screamed at me for drying the roasting pan with her *milchig* dish towel. "But Jenny is her granddaughter. She's more important to Rose than keeping the dishes separate."

"They are amazingly close," Dan had to agree. "Of course she hasn't felt the same about Jeffrey since he went and converted, and with Judy's children on the other side of the world.... I can only imagine what *she* would have to say if she knew about this wedding business."

"Your sister? Oh, that reminds me, the mail is in my car; the mailman handed it to me just as I was pulling out," I said, jumping up from the table and hurrying through the door to the garage. "There's a letter from her," I added, as I returned. "The rest is all junk."

I handed it to Dan. "Why don't you read it out loud?" I said, as he opened the envelope.

"All right. '*Dear Daniel and Sheila, I sent a gift, a bronze menorah by an Israeli artist, to your daughter's home, to commemorate the ceremony she is having with her friend, but I–*' How does she know about the girls' plans?"

"I sent her an invitation. I didn't think she'd actually come, all the way from Israel, but —"

"You might have asked my opinion first."

"To write my own sister-in-law?" Even if we were practically strangers, living as far apart and such different lives as we did. "I didn't want her to feel left out. So go on. Read."

"'*But I wanted to write directly to the two of you. A few years ago, I would have found such a ceremony joining two women bizarre, perhaps even offensive. I would not have understood how two parents could condone such a thing.*' I knew it. I'm surprised she actually sent them a —" Dan started to say, before his eyes fell on the next line.

"'*But two years ago, our own Rachel told Chaim and myself of her love for another girl, a comrade whom she met during her service in our country's armed forces.*'" It occurred to me, irrelevantly, that Judy's written English had grown increasingly formal, even stilted, as if, after all these years, it was English that was her second language and Hebrew her native tongue.

"*And so my eyes have been opened,*" Dan read on, with dogged surprise. "*though not without much struggle and weeping. As a result of which I can imagine the sadness that you, my brother, and my sister by marriage, must have likewise experienced. I want to tell the two of you how much I admire your strength, and the love you are showing to your child, by celebrating with her her commitment to her chosen mate. She is fortunate in you, and you in her.*

"*It is impossible for us to make the journey to be with you for this occasion, but I — and Chaim too — will be with you in spirit. Your loving sister, Yehudit.*"

Jenny didn't find it remarkable when I told her about Judy's letter the next day. "Didn't you know, Mom? Being gay runs in families."

"Well, I only hope —" I broke off before I could say anything to upset Jenny. Such as, if your aunt can attend your wedding in spirit, I hope your father can bring himself to show up in the flesh. "I hope Judy does come over for a visit one of these days. It's been years since we've seen her," I said instead. "Speaking of relatives, Jeffrey called. He said they're going to get an early start tomorrow — pick up Mama and Rose, then head straight for the George Washington Bridge. So they'll get here in plenty of time, with the rehearsal so late." The wedding was Sunday; the rehearsal Saturday evening had to wait until after Sabbath ended at sundown, and the rehearsal dinner following couldn't start till ten or so. It was lucky I'd come up with a caterer who understood.

"I'd better get off the phone and get the house ready for company," I told Jenny. "I want everything to be perfect before Debby sees it."

Tamara's parents had no sooner checked into their hotel the next day than Debby was on the phone with me to double-check the time of the rehearsal dinner. "Just wondering if there'll be time to change, or if I should dress for dinner before the rehearsal?" An hour later she had to know the color of the corsage I'd be wearing to the ceremony. Half an hour later, she realized she'd forgotten to get directions to BAT for the rehearsal and she hated to bother the girls when they were so busy.

Normally, I would have put Dan on to give directions, but this time I came up with them myself. "See you tonight," I told her, not mentioning that it might be only me she'd be seeing. Why explain Dan's absence when it might not be necessary?

With admirable restraint, I didn't demand to know if Dan had come to a decision. Instead, I kept busy with last-minute arrangements with Moe, my caterer, and with setting up TV trays around the living and family rooms. With so many people, any dinner had to be buffet. The afternoon flew by. Suddenly I realized not only that I didn't know whether Dan would be at the rehearsal, just hours away — and by implication take part in the wedding — but that Jeffrey and the rest of the family from New York were late. Traffic, I thought. I walked into Dan's den and said, "You know, we'll have to leave for the rehearsal almost as soon as Jeffrey and Anita get here. Is there some chance you've decided to come with us? It's kind of hard not knowing."

Dan's computer was turned on, but instead of checking our investments or his e-mail, he was rereading Judy's letter, which was lying on top of his keyboard, the page sharply creased as if he had read it and then folded it back into its envelope over and over. He sighed. "I know I've made things difficult for you. I'm sorry," he began, when the phone shrilled next to him. He picked it up.

"What? Where are you? What happened? No, never mind, you can tell me later. No, don't spend the money on a rental — I'll pick you up. Give me an hour and a half, but if I run into traffic it could be as long as two. Okay, I'll look for you by the yogurt place."

He hung up, and I demanded, "Well??"

"That was Jeffrey. His clutch went out and they're stuck on I-95. Luckily they're at a rest stop — Maryland House — but they can't get it repaired till Monday. He should have replaced it years ago — he'd have been able to afford a new car if he'd listened to me about going to law school instead of deciding he was God's gift to the stage.... Anyhow, I told him I'd schlep out there and pick them up," he said, in as annoyed a tone of voice as he could summon up. It sounded to me like relief at getting off the hook, at least as far as the rehearsal was concerned.

"I'll have to take your van," he added in an afterthought as he headed for the garage. "Hopefully, we'll be back in time for your dinner."

I drove Dan's car on automatic pilot to BAT, trying to guess what Dan had been about to say when he'd been interrupted by Jeffrey's call. The girls and Tamara's parents had already arrived, and I was barely out of my car when Debby fell on me with a flurry of air kisses, followed by breathless introductions to her husband, Stanley; Tamara's sister, Stacy;

and *her* husband. After which, Jenny and Tamara introduced the rest of us to their rabbi, a stocky, graying woman named Laura Bernstein; Adam; and Adam's fiancee, Jennifer. I'd forgotten that Jenny had asked her former boyfriend, Adam, to be her "best person," as Tamara had Stacy. I hoped my surprise didn't show as I greeted him and murmured "so glad to meet you" to his intended.

I had seen Jenny's face fall when I got out of the car without her father, so as soon as the last introduction had been made, I explained the rescue mission he'd been forced to run. Instead of being relieved, as I'd expected, she said, "Oh, but Jeffrey is an usher; he's supposed to be here for the rehearsal. And don't you remember, we told Steffi she could be a flower girl?" Those facts had totally skipped my mind — either due to my preoccupation with Dan, or to a simple senior moment.

"We'll have to wait till they get here," Debby snapped, at which Rabbi Bernstein informed us that we would have to rehearse without her, in that case. So our rehearsal proceeded as scheduled, with me walking Jenny down the aisle alone — just as I would doubtless have to do the following day — and Tamara escorted by her father and her very miffed mother.

Chapter Twenty-Three

*T*he van pulled into our garage just before ten, approximately five minutes before the rehearsal dinner was scheduled to start. Dan and the others filed inside and milled around the kitchen and family room, looking hot, tired, disheveled and cross.

"Well, you made it just in time," I said. "People will be here any minute, so why don't you all go on up and get dressed. I gave you the same rooms —"

"What do you mean, dressed? It's just family, isn't it?" Jeffrey said.

Anita lit into Jeffrey before I could say a word. "Just family? So it's all right to look like a slob when you can see how your mother's knocked herself out for this?" She waved her hand toward the kitchen, where Moe at least was knocking himself out, setting out wine, liquor, mixers and platters of hors d'oeuvres on the counter. "And since it was just your family who was concerned, it was all right to forget taking the car to the garage? Your son," she added, turning to me as if I were still bringing him up, "was supposed to have the clutch checked before we started on a five-hour trip. Only he decided it was more important for him to go to an audition. It doesn't matter if six people get stuck on I-95, as long as he makes his audition." Anita doesn't often lose it, but when she does, she can outdo Rose herself.

"It wasn't an audition, it was a callback," Jeffrey said mildly.

"You got a part!" I exclaimed.

"Well, I haven't gotten it yet, but —"

"I'm *hungry,*" Steffi broke in, tugging at my arm.

301

"We're going to eat soon." I grabbed a few carrot sticks from a veggie platter and handed them to her. "Eat these in the meantime."

"I don't want carrots, I want peanut butter."

"Stephanie," Anita said, "you can eat those carrot sticks or you can wait until dinner. Now march upstairs so I can get you and your brother ready for the party." She picked up little Jeffrey, still asleep in his car seat in the midst of all the commotion, and handed him to her husband. "If it isn't too much trouble for you to carry up your son." Mama and Rose followed without joining the argument for once, and Dan straggled after them, carrying both their bags. I took a deep breath, about to run upstairs myself to see if anybody needed anything, when the doorbell chimed. I opened it to Stanley and Debby Goldberg, with their daughter, Stacy, and son-in-law, Michael, behind them.

The Goldbergs had gone back to their hotel to change, and now Debby was arrayed in a mint green, beaded silk sheath, as if she thought I was hosting the rehearsal dinner at the Ritz Carlton and not in the family room of my house. Her husband was in a suit and tie, though he had the grace to look uncomfortable. "Come in, come in," I urged, smoothing my loose, crinkled cotton dress, which had seemed totally appropriate until this moment. From upstairs I could hear both showers being turned on nearly in unison, then a faint "damn!" as the water pressure left the first bather in the cold.

"Are we too early?"

"No, of course not, Dan just ran into a lot of traffic. Please, have a drink. Make yourself at home. Oh, hi, Tamara, Jenny," I called out as the two of them got out of Tamara's car and hurried down the walk. Jenny was lugging an overnight bag and carrying a long, opaque plastic garment bag.

"What in the world do you have there?" I asked her as they walked into the foyer.

She sighed. "Would you believe my wedding gown? Debby thinks I should stay with you guys tonight. That it's more romantic or something."

"You're staying *here?* Jenny, do you realize we have six people staying with us already?"

"I know, Mom." Jenny shrugged helplessly. She added in a whisper, "I tried to tell her, but —"

"My mom likes all these little traditions, so we thought it wouldn't hurt. It really does make it more romantic," Tamara put in.

"Everyone knows it's bad luck to see each other before the ceremony," Debby called over her shoulder, with the nonchalance of a woman who didn't have to figure out where to put a seventh houseguest. She was closing in on the bar Moe had set up.

I would have thought that changing the tradition of having one of the marrying couple be a groom would have allowed for changing other traditions, but I had no time to argue. Jenny was still standing like a statue, her arms full of clothes that belonged home in her closet. "All right, give me those; we'll figure out something later. Be down in a minute."

"What have you got there?" Dan said, as I laid Jenny's things on our bed.

"Debby thinks Jenny should spend the night here. They're downstairs already. And Stanley's in a suit," I added meaningfully, as Dan reached into our closet for an old Hawaiian shirt.

"Well, good for him," he said, starting to button his shirt. "But aren't the hosts supposed to set the dress code?" he asked, as I tore off my cool cotton dress and reached in the closet for my dressier raw-silk pantsuit. I pulled it on without stopping to answer, pausing just long enough to lower the air conditioning on my way down, garbed in a long-sleeve outfit as I now was.

"You didn't need to change, Mom," Jenny burst out after I'd reached the first floor and hurried down the center hall to the rear of the house.

Debby, who was perched on one of the chairs at the breakfast table — separated from the kitchen by one side of the counter — gave me the once-over at that.

I said, "I was just wearing the other to get ready. Everything's been so hectic."

"Too hectic," Debby muttered. "I don't know what kind of ceremony we're going to have with half the people missing at the rehearsal. Oh, and Sheila, I don't know if you know it, but there's a truck from some delicatessen right in front of your house. I can't imagine that one of your neighbors.... I don't suppose you know who it belongs to, to ask them to move it, that you're having a party, but...."

It occurred to me that I could have parked my car out front, and told Moe to pull into the garage. It would have been easier for him and less of a shock to Debby's delicate sensibilities. Too late now. "It's my caterer." I waved a hand grandly in Moe's direction.

"From a deli??" She sounded as horrified as if I'd said the main course would be fried grasshoppers.

Moe, who was busy setting additional hors d'oeuvres on the counter, gave her a look. "Not just any deli, lady. One of the premier delis of Brooklyn, New York, now transplanted to the Commonwealth of Virginia. Everything guaranteed kosher. All your traditional delicacies, but we're not afraid of haute cuisine either." Which he pronounced howt. "Care to be the first to sample our baked brie?" He stooped to pull a dish out of the oven and set it proudly on the counter.

"Baked brie? Just a bite," Debby said, and then sat there expectantly. I should have told her that Moe's speciality was food, not service. But before another second went by, her husband, Stanley, had jumped up from his seat to fix her a plate of appetizers.

"Freshen your drink, while I'm up?" he asked her, and then offered to mix one for me as well. I took the frosty gin and tonic thankfully. The doorbell rang. It was Adam and his fiancee, Jennifer, the last to arrive. Everyone was on hand now, though half the guests were still upstairs, putting on outfits that I hoped would meet with Debby's approval. Jenny, Tamara, Stacy, Michael, Adam and Jennifer were hanging out at the end of the kitchen counter closest to the dining room, drinking Perrier and dipping veggies into the sour cream dill dip, leaving me to talk to Debby. Stanley, apparently, was the strong, silent type, his conversation consisting mainly of, "Get you another?" as he leaped to his feet to wait on his wife. She was on her second martini when Dan finally arrived downstairs, still in a Hawaiian-print shirt, though he'd made the concession of putting on a new one in subdued blues and beige. Anita, Jeffrey and Steffi followed on his heels, looking cleaner and cooler than before. Rose and Mama descended fifteen minutes later, during which Anita gave in to Steffi's pleading for peanut butter and we all refreshed our drinks.

As soon as Moe brought forth the first course, I knew I was in for *tsuris*. Since it was summer, and since I didn't want to offend Debby by having a main course of pastrami on rye, I'd decided with Moe on a dairy menu, with cold borscht topped with creamy sour cream for starters. Not until this moment did it occur to me that beety red borscht was possibly not the best choice for a buffet dinner in a house where the dining and living rooms boasted real Oriental rugs, and the family-room carpet, though heavy duty Berber, was white.

But it was Debby's pale green silk that got splattered, as she and my granddaughter collided when Steffi decided to help herself to another peanut-butter-and-jelly sandwich just as Debby was ladling out a bowlful of borscht. I whisked Debby off to the laundry room, where I had a new bottle of cleaning fluid Lois had recommended. To my relief, the fluid actually worked; the stains were gone so fast that we returned to the gathering in time to hear Dan ask Stanley, "Just between us, while our better halves are out of the room, do you really feel good about this ceremony our daughters are having?"

Neither of them noticed Debby freezing quietly beside me; they were filling their plates at the counter, backs to us. Anita and Jeffrey were talking earnestly to Steffi. Jenny and Tamara, along with Stacy, Michael, Adam and Jennifer, had commandeered the living room, out of earshot at the front of the house. Only Mama and Rose, sitting at opposite ends of the family-room couch — a room separated only by pillars from the breakfast room and kitchen area — appeared to have their ears cocked.

"Between us?" Stanley repeated. "Well, don't repeat this, but it's not what I would have chosen for Tamara." He lowered his voice as he said her name, as if afraid it would carry over the clatter of crockery into our front parlor two rooms away. "And I take it from your question that it's not what you would have chosen for your girl, but —"

"But of course we support her absolutely," Debby said, an ice statue coming abruptly to life.

Stanley jumped. "Of course, of course. I just meant if we'd had our druthers —"

"And we couldn't be prouder of her. We couldn't be happier to be walking her down the aisle tomorrow. Just like the two of you must be," Debby overrode him.

The two of you being Dan and me, an awkward silence ensued. Anita broke it. "Mrs. Goldberg, I just wanted to say, I'm so sorry about your dress, and Stephanie is too, aren't you, Steffi?" She waited for Steffi to give an embarrassed nod. "My husband and I will be happy to pay for any damage."

Debby waved her apology aside. "It's good as new. Sheila has a product that works miracles on stains. I'm going to have to get some."

I could see Anita give a quiet sigh of relief at having her offer of paying for what looked like a designer original so politely refused. She must have been on a roll with apologies though, because now she turned to me, and said, "Before I forget, my mom wanted me to tell you how sorry she and my father are to miss Jenny's ceremony. But they signed up for this cruise months ago; it's the first real vacation from the restaurant they've had in years."

"I don't think Sheila or I were really expecting them," Dan said. "After all, with their being Catholics, and this being a — a lesbian ceremony...."

"No, really, they would have come. After all, Jeffrey's grandmothers are religious and they're here."

"Not me. I'm an agnostic," said Mama. "I only advised against a same-sex ceremony because of Jenny's career. But my daughter assures me it's no problem where she teaches. By the way, this borscht is delicious, Sheila."

"It's the sour cream," I said. "He mixes it in, it's not just a dollop on top. The kind of stuff that goes right to your hips. But for a party...."

"Right to your arteries," Mama said, about to go off on one of her health-food kicks. Well, better the conversation should veer to calories and cholesterol than to a fight over the wedding tomorrow.

But Rose had the tenacity of a bulldog. "What, you don't believe in God? You think the whole universe came from nothing?" she demanded of Mama. "Well, you think what you want, but I'm proud to tell you that I'm an observant Jew. Just like Anita here says."

"I said agnostic, not atheist. There's a difference, in case you don't know. But I don't follow every religious superstition, no."

"Superstition! Because I believe in keeping the traditions!"

"That's why I was surprised you were willing to come," Dan told his mother.

"Why should you be surprised? When my Jennela explained to me how much this ceremony means to her, I made up my mind to come for her sake."

"That's a wonderful attitude, Mrs. Katz," Debby said. "Especially for a woman your age."

"My *age*?" Rose repeated. "What's my age got to do with it? You think I'm too old to understand when my granddaughter talks to me?"

"No, no of course not. I just meant...."

"Ma, she was trying to compliment you," Dan said.

Debby nodded yes. I told myself I shouldn't be enjoying her embarrassment so much.

"Compliments about my age I don't need. Besides, I didn't do anything to deserve praise for. I'm sure your own — your parents are still living?"

"My father passed away ten years ago, but my mother is still alive,

306

thank God."

"And she doesn't feel the same way about your own daughter? Even if she couldn't make such a long trip in the heat?"

"Uh...." Debby seemed at a loss for words. Very uncharacteristically for her.

"Well, actually," Stanley said, coming to her rescue. "My wife's mother isn't that.... That is, she's a little older than.... Well, we just decided it would be for the best not to mention anything about all this."

"Well," Rose said, turning to Mama. "It's lucky you and I keep our minds active so our children don't think they have to treat us like little children."

"You can say that again," Mama said. I was so struck by the sight of Mama and Rose beaming at each other in perfect harmony that I barely noticed the three couples trooping in from the living room — where they'd missed the entire exchange — to fill their plates with the next course.

"Who's treating you like a little kid, Grandma?" Jenny asked. By her tone she obviously thought she'd walked in on the tail end of a joke.

"Me? No one. But your friend here, her grandmother is missing out on your affair because her parents think she's too old to understand about you and her caring for each other."

There was a moment of silence while everyone took that in. Debby was in the closet about Tamara to her own mother, Debby who'd been calling me day and night, telling me we should put a wedding announcement in the newspaper.

"You kept my wedding a secret from my *grandmother*? What about the letter I wrote her? You promised to see she got it. Didn't you give it to her?" Tamara demanded.

"Tammy — Tamara, you know my mother can't even live on her own, so we just thought that trying to explain to her —"

"Grandma's in assisted living because she broke her *hip*. There's nothing wrong with her *mind*."

Tamara's words were punctuated by a yell so loud that everybody jumped. But it was just the baby monitor, which Anita had apparently plugged in at one end of the counter. She rushed upstairs to take care of little Jeffrey, looking relieved to get out of the fray. Steffi trailed along behind her.

Tamara and Debby were still glaring at each other from opposing sides of the kitchen counter, gearing up for a knock-down drag-out mother-daughter fight, when Moe said, "Watch out folks! Next course coming out." Everyone backed off while he set down a platter heaped high with grilled shiitake mushrooms with balsamic vinegar and another of slender, cold asparagus with Hollandaise sauce. A good caterer is worth his weight in gold.

Once they'd filled their plates, Tamara followed her mother into the living room and plopped down next to her on the couch. "You promised to hand deliver Grandma's invitation," she hissed, in the kind of whisper that with only a little effort can be heard by everyone in a room.

"Tammy, I —" Debby stammered.

"I told you not to call me that! Here I thought she didn't even care enough to answer. I tried to call her half a dozen times and every time the damn receptionist told me she was taking a nap or in therapy or I called too late, she goes to bed at six p.m., or some damn thing and it turns out she doesn't even know about my wedding, maybe she couldn't have traveled here, but even so...." Tamara stopped berating her mother only because she had broken down in sobs.

"Honey, I'm sorry, I never meant...." Debby began.

"Your mother thought it was for the best," Stanley said simultaneously while Jenny hurried to Tamara's side and put an arm around her shoulder, stroking her hair and murmuring into her ear.

Tamara sniffled. "Jenny's grandmas are here. *Her* parents weren't too cowardly to let them know about our wedding."

Jenny stroked her hair again. "I know just how you feel, sweetie. But I really don't think your parents were ashamed about the wedding; they just didn't realize that older people aren't necessarily out of it. And at least *they're* both planning to walk you down the aisle tomorrow. My father won't even be there. He probably wouldn't be at this dinner if it wasn't at our house." She'd spoken softly, into Tamara's ear, but I couldn't help hearing from where I was standing with a bottle of wine I'd been about to offer around.

It was evident that Debby, sitting on Tamara's other side, had heard as well. Debby stopped fumbling for apologies and turned on Dan, who had claimed his recliner across from the sofa. "You're not going to be there tomorrow? Sheila said months ago that you were unhappy about the girls' wedding, but I thought by now you surely — My mother could never have made it here in any case, but you — Don't you realize how much this means to Jenny? A girl looks forward her whole life to her father walking her down the aisle."

She'd caught Dan with a mouth full of mushrooms. While he was simultaneously trying to gulp them down and come up with a response, I snapped at Debby, "A Jewish girl looks forward to her father *and* mother walking her down the aisle. And Jenny can count on me escorting her tomorrow."

"Me too," her brother said. He left off refilling his plate and came over to squat on the rug in front of Jenny. "Jen, don't worry. If Dad won't do it, I'll walk you down the aisle with Mom, and Anita can take my place as usher."

I wasn't sure if Dan had heard Jeffrey or not. But he finally managed to start, "As a matter of fact, as far as tomorrow goes —" But Debby didn't appear to be listening. Neither did Jenny. She was smiling at her brother with tears in her eyes, and a loving look I never thought I'd see when they were kids squabbling in the backseat of the car.

"Listen. I know it's the last minute, but I wouldn't give up on Dad," Jeffrey continued in the kind of stage whisper some drama coach must have taught him would project to the back of the auditorium. "Remember what a fuss he put up when Anita and I got married. He didn't agree to attend our wedding until two days before we were married."

"I didn't necessarily say I wouldn't attend —" Dan was continuing; he broke off when he heard Jeffrey. "Your wedding and this were two entirely different things."

"I should hope they're different," Rose said loudly, from where she and Mama were now sitting at the breakfast-room table. "Jenny and her friend here are promising to make a Jewish home together, kosher kitchen, candles on Friday night, while your son married a shiksa. Not only that —"

"Grandma!" Jenny protested.

"Rose, be quiet, she'll hear you," I hissed at the same time, thankful that with strangers in the house Anita had chosen to stay upstairs to nurse.

"It's your son who should hear me. Anita, I have nothing against. She's a nice girl for a shiksa. A very thoughtful person. But your son had no business marrying her."

Jeffrey rolled his eyes. "Grandma, it's a little late. We've been married five years. We've got two children." That he could say it so calmly astounded me.

"It's on account of the children that I keep after you. It's not too late to give them a Jewish upbringing."

"Enough already, Ma," Dan said.

"Rose, that's enough!" Mama seconded.

The sound of my husband and my mother voicing the same sentiment stunned me for a moment. Only a moment.

"No," I said, glaring at my mother-in-law, "it was enough long before you opened your mouth tonight! I'm sick and tired of you attacking my son every time you lay eyes on him!" I knew I shouldn't antagonize Rose on the eve of Jenny's ceremony. But I was through weighing every word that came out of my mouth. "If you're going to be a guest in my house, then you can keep a civil tongue in your head!"

"Sheila, shh, you've got other company. Don't embarrass people," Mama whispered.

I ignored Mama's admonition. "Or if you have to pick a quarrel, then pick it with me. Just because you've always had it in for me, you don't have to take it out on my son."

"What are you talking about, I have it in for you?" Rose sounded thunderstruck, too astonished to be insulted. She was staring at me, as was everyone else in the room, Moe included.

"You took a dislike to me from the minute you met me," I said.

"Dislike? I don't know what you're talking about," Rose repeated.

"I still remember the look you gave me when Dan brought me home to meet you and Morris."

"The look — What was I supposed to do, turn my back on you?"

"Like something the cat dragged in. I still remember your exact words: 'So this is who my Danny picked to marry.'" Rose was giving me a look now — a look of total bewilderment. Even to my ears it suddenly sounded a feeble excuse for holding a grudge all these years.

After what seemed like an hour of dead silence, Rose shook her head. "You've got too good an imagination. I always thought you were a good match for Dan. But even if I hadn't, I accept my children's choices. Look how I accepted Judy's decision to go live in Israel and bring up her children so far away I'd have trouble recognizing any of them if I met them on the street. She told me it was right for her, and I accepted that. I don't interfere in my children's lives."

"So why can't you accept your grandson's choices? Did it ever occur to you that Jeffrey chose a wife and a religious faith that are right for him?" I came back at her, but quietly, reasonably.

"What's right for a Jewish boy —"

"Grandma, please!" Jenny pleaded.

"Both of you, stop already. Sheila. Ma."

Rose sighed and spread her hands. "All right, what's done is done. I won't say another word. At least he picked a lovely girl in Anita," she admitted. Just in time. My daughter-in-law appeared from the direction of the stairs, carrying the baby, in a new romper, wide awake and ready to play. Behind them, Steffi paraded. She had changed as well — into the ruffled, powder-blue dress she was supposed to wear the next day for her role as flower girl.

"Did I hear my name?" Anita asked brightly. Tactfully, she didn't wait for an answer. "My sleepyhead is up at last, all fed and ready to be shown off. This is Steffi's little brother," she added, to Tamara, Adam and the rest of the group who hadn't yet seen the baby. "Jeffrey Paul."

"Will you look at that smile," said Debby, jumping up to admire him as everyone oohed and aahed. "And you've named him after his father. I always liked the idea of a boy carrying on his father's name." Rose gave her a look, which fortunately she didn't catch. Debby turned to Steffi. "How lucky he is to have a big sister like you. Did you help your mommy give brother his dinner?"

"Uh uh," Steffi says. "Cause he drinks milk out of my mommy's breasts. But I got out the diaper wipe when Mommy changed him. And his clean sleeper. And *I* put on my new dress that I'm going to wear to be a flower girl."

"Careful not to get it dirty now, Steffi," Anita warned.

"Why did you let her put it on tonight?" Jeffrey asked her, standing up and coming over. "Here, let me hold the baby so you can get yourself some food."

"Try the mushrooms; they're delicious," Debby told her. "Who would have thought? When I saw that truck from the deli I was expecting pastrami on rye."

"We serve pastrami at the deli," Moe put in from the kitchen, where he was now arranging miniature blintzes on trays for dessert. Jewish cannoli, he'd called them when we'd gone over the menu together. "But for a party like this, we do the haute cuisine."

Anita handed little Jeffrey over to his father. "Steffi insisted on putting it on. She wants to show it to your father because he won't be at the wedding tomorrow," she explained in a whisper.

I wondered why so many people with no dramatic training don't understand that the expression "stage whisper" reflects the fact that whispers carry. Sure enough, Debby picked up on it immediately.

"You mean, he refuses to attend," she said.

"Mom," Tamara told her, "it's between Jenny and her father."

"Not to mention that the child has ears," Mama pointed out.

By "the child" I assume she meant Steffi, who fortunately was twirling her way to her grandfather instead of listening. "Look, Grandpa, it goes way out when I turn around."

"I see," Dan said. "That's a very pretty dress."

"It's a *beautiful* dress, Grandpa."

"Then it suits a beautiful little girl like my Steffi." Dan lifted her onto his lap. He looked relieved to be able to focus on his granddaughter, ignoring the rest of the party. Everyone else seemed focused on Dan though, except for Stacy, her husband, Michael, Adam and his fiancee, who had all retreated to the dining-room table.

"You know what, Grandpa?"

"What?" Dan asked her.

"I'm going to be a flower girl. At Aunt Jenny's wedding tomorrow. I'm going to walk down the aisle ahead of her and Aunt Tamara, and I'm going to have this basket of flowers and throw some to everybody."

"Well," Dan said, after a moment.

"And everybody is going to see me in my new dress. Except you. Because you can't come," Steffi said. "Why can't you come, Grandpa? I *want* you to come." Her voice had changed to that demanding whine five-year-olds are so richly capable of.

"Well, actually, Steffi," Dan said. "I think maybe I can come, after all. I'm not so sure I can walk down the aisle with your Aunt Jenny, but I'll come and sit in the audience — I mean the congregation — and watch you be a flower girl. Okay?"

"Thank you for agreeing to come to the ceremony tomorrow," I told Dan when we were finally in bed, hours later. The house was full. All four upstairs bedrooms were in use, including the sewing room off our bedroom. Poor Jenny was bedded down in the one bed left, the sofa bed in the family room, probably the least comfortable mattress in the house. She'd protested once more, as everyone left, that her staying over was ridiculous, but gave in to Tamara's insistence that her mother was right — it would be so much more romantic if the two of them didn't see each other again until the wedding.

"It means a lot to Jenny that you're coming," I added now to Dan. "Even if —" I stopped myself before I could upset Dan with my nagging. He'd obviously come as far as he could. I'd have to be satisfied with that.

"Even if," Dan repeated, sounding not upset but rueful. "I suppose Steffi will be happy with that, at any rate. You know, I'd been trying to say half the evening that I'd come to realize I couldn't just...just boycott the ceremony entirely. Not without really hurting Jenny. But every time I opened my mouth, Tamara's mother jumped down my throat."

"She is a piece of work," I said, with feeling.

"I hope we're not going to be thrown into their company too much after this...this *wedding*." Dan gave a sigh. "It still amazes me that everyone but me seems to accept it as a bona fide wedding. A marriage like you and I have."

"That's how Jenny sees it, honey. And Tamara. I know it's difficult for you to accept. Remember, I told you it was hard for me to accept Jenny's sexual orientation too, at first." Not to mention that my own was a bit more elastic than I'd realized.

"I know, you told me. But it's not actually the thought of them having sex that bothers me...."

I was opening my mouth to tell Dan that sexual orientation was about so much more than sex — loving someone, wanting to make a home together, seeking recognition from society — when he knocked me off my soapbox by adding, "I don't know. Maybe it really is the thing that bothers me most. You know, it's always struck me so funny. Sex is so good with the opposite sex; why would anybody bother trying it out with their own sex?"

This was a question I was not about to answer. Instead, I blurted, "I don't know. It's been so long since we've had any, I almost forget what it's like."

Dan turned to stare at me a moment. The lights were out, but my eyes had adjusted enough to the dark that I could see his lips curving into a grin as he reached out for me. "Well, no time like the present."

I held back a second. "They'll hear us," I murmured, glancing over to check that the pocket doors to the sewing room were completely closed.

"Not if we're quiet. Remember how we used to make love on that sofa bed of your mother's and she never knew a thing?"

If I hadn't remembered, Dan's hand sliding under my nightgown would have reminded me. His touch was as familiar as my own breathing, yet so new, so exciting, after these weeks of hiatus, that my body was steaming as if I had the mother of all hot flashes. I gasped with pleasure as Dan's hands found my nipples, encircled my breasts and after a suitable time of exploration moved down toward my nether regions. They stopped halfway there to give a squeeze to my tushie and circle the mound of my tummy.

I stopped gasping with pleasure and said, "Oh, now you're feeling all the fat I've put on. I've gained five pounds tonight alone."

"So?" Dan murmured, keeping his hands right where they were. "More of you to love."

I woke the next morning to Dan's snores; the house was remarkably quiet otherwise, considering there were nine people under our roof. The others, even baby Jeffrey, were apparently sleeping in. That wouldn't last for long, so I hurried downstairs to make coffee and enjoy my first cup in peace, trying to make as little clatter as possible so as not to wake Jenny, who was sprawled on the sofa bed on the other side of the breakfast room. I'd just switched the pot to "on," though, when she crawled out of bed and stumbled past me to the powder room in the front hall. Over the sound of the coffeepot chugging, I heard the toilet flush, water run and then a heartfelt, "Shit! Oh shit!" from my daughter.

"Jenny?" I knocked on the door. "Is something wrong, sweetheart? Are you okay?"

"Oh, Mom, everything's all wrong. I don't even have a toothbrush. I had to drag so much stuff with me I forgot all about it."

"Is that all? I always buy spares. I'll get you one."

Jenny opened the door and I saw that that was not all. Her eyes were filling with tears and when she started to speak again she had to choke back sobs. "And where am I supposed to take a shower? It was stupid for me to stay here. I never would have done it if Tamara hadn't insisted that it would be so romantic."

"You don't have to use the powder room. We have three full baths, remember; use the one downstairs," I said.

Jenny ignored me. Her concern was not logistics, I saw, as she went on. "It doesn't make any sense, but Tamara's mother thought we shouldn't spend the night together, so Tamara just had to go along with her. She says she just wants a simple, meaningful ceremony, but then she turns around and has to add every frill that Debby suggests. It's like I don't even know her anymore. Like I'm marrying her mother instead of her."

By now, Jenny was crying full force. I gave her a hug. "Just between you and me, I find Debby a little hard to take at times. But she and Stanley will be going back to Chicago tomorrow and you'll be here. Come on, sweetheart, it's not worth crying over where you spend one night."

"But that's just it, Mom. I'm not thinking about one night; I'm thinking about every night for the rest of my life. It's like I don't even know what I'm doing. I'm supposed to get married in a few hours and maybe it's all wrong. I mean, I've always believed marriage should be for life. How can I get married if I'm not sure?"

"Jenny, sweetheart, it's not like —" I bit back my words so fast I nearly bit my tongue. Surely I hadn't been about to tell Jenny that it wasn't as if it was a real wedding! I couldn't believe that I had nearly taken such a giant step backwards. Jenny didn't pick up on what I'd started to say, though; she was turning toward her father, who'd come down the stairs and into the front hall while I was racking my brain for some better words of wisdom.

"You're not sure?" Dan asked, in an astonished tone of voice. "I couldn't help overhearing. You're saying you're not sure you're a lesbian?"

Jenny stopped crying and gave him a look of equal amazement. "Of course not, Daddy. I can't imagine myself with anyone but another woman. It's just...well all of a sudden it dawned on me, like I just told Mom, that I'm about to promise myself to Tamara for the rest of my life and I don't know if I'm ready. Or if she is. If I'm going to be more important to her than her mother, or...or if I can even stand her mother."

"Oh," Dan said. He was silent for a long moment, and then asked, "But you were sure about your...your feelings up to now? All the months you and she have been living together?"

Jenny nodded. "It's not that I don't love Tamara. I do love her. It's just...just...." She spread her hands helplessly. "I don't know, it's just that this is making everything so final."

"Oh," Dan said again. Another moment passed. "Well, in that case, it sounds to me as if you have a classic case of wedding jitters."

These were the last words I expected out of Dan's mouth, especially in such a calmly reassuring tone of voice, and both of us stared at him.

"Wedding jitters?" Jenny echoed.

"You've never heard of them? They're almost a tradition. I remember, I was ready to run out of the *shul* before your mother and I got married."

"Really? You were scared before you got married, Daddy?"

"Ask your mother. She'll tell you how my hand was shaking like a leaf when I put the ring on her finger."

I shook my head. "I was too nervous to notice."

"And talk about mother-in-law problems," Dan said. "Don't get me started."

Me either, I thought, but kept my mouth shut. Dan went on as if he were reading my mind. "And as she demonstrated last night, your mother has some problems along those lines too. Yet I would say things have worked out very well between us. I'm certainly very glad we went through with the marriage."

"That goes double for me," I said, which Dan may or may not have heard, as he was going right on with his spiel.

"Anyway, what I was getting at is that if everyone waited until they were 100 percent sure, there would be very few brides and grooms." Or brides and brides either, apparently.

"In fact," Dan added, slipping into his jovial argument-for-the-sake-of-argument mode, "the custom of having the bride's father walk her down the aisle probably originated as a way to keep her from bolting at the last minute. And Jewish tradition goes that a step better. Both halves of the couple walk down the aisle — between two parents if at all possible."

Jenny stared at him for the inhalation of a breath, her eyes suddenly shining so that I imagined I could see rainbows reflected off her teardrops. Then she threw her arms around her father. "Daddy, thank you! I knew you'd come through for me!"

Chapter Twenty-Four

When our family climbed out of our vehicles in the BAT parking lot, Dan still wore the dazed look of a man who hadn't realized what he was saying until it was too late. And it certainly was too late, with Jenny now radiant with happiness as she carefully held up the hem of her gown to keep it from brushing the pavement. I felt my heart catch in my throat, the way it had when she'd put it on at our house. Tamara and the rest of the wedding party hadn't yet arrived; at Anita's suggestion we'd managed to get there early so that Jenny could go over the order of the procession with the members of the wedding party who had missed the rehearsal. That meant Jeffrey, Steffi — and now, Dan.

"Jenny, honey, we'd better get inside the theater and have our mini-rehearsal before guests start arriving," said my practical daughter-in-law. Jenny nodded and turned to lead the way. Jeffrey took his daughter's hand and followed, with Anita, holding baby Jeffrey, going along to help coach Steffi. Only Dan lagged behind.

"I can't believe I've agreed to go through with this," he admitted once the others were out of hearing range, and just as Adam and his fiancee pulled in and parked alongside us.

"Mr. Katz, I hope it's not out of place for me to tell you how happy I am to see you here. It means a lot to Jenny," Adam said, getting out of his car.

Dan nodded. "I've come to realize that. It looks like I've promised to walk her down the aisle, and I won't go back on my word. But as long as Jenny is out of earshot, I don't mind telling you I wish it was you she was marrying here today."

Adam laughed. "I don't. And I doubt Jennifer does either," he added, reaching for his fiancee's hand. "Seriously, Jenny and I are the best of friends, but that's all we are. There's never been anything more between us."

Watching Dan's face as he took that in, it crossed my mind that if this were a musical comedy, Adam would break off his engagement on the spot and walk down the aisle with Jenny, his childhood sweetheart. But whatever illusions I might have harbored in the past, this was real life, and I knew there was not a spark of romance between Adam and Jenny. And so did Dan, because he merely nodded again and said, "I'd better catch up with them and see what I'm supposed to do."

An hour later, Debby's insistence that it was bad luck for the bride and bride to see each other before the ceremony had to fall by the way-side as the girls signed the *ketubah* — the traditional Jewish marriage con-tract — in the presence of their rabbi, their parents, and Adam and Stacy, the two "best people." The first guests began parking their cars and head-ing toward the theater, where Jeffrey and Michael were waiting to escort them to their seats. The photographer took Jenny and Tamara off to get a few shots of the two of them together while the rest of the wedding party waited in the adjacent house owned by BAT. Left to our own devices in the lounge, Debby drew Stanley and Stacy into a corner, where she appeared to be doling out some last-minute instructions, while Steffi chattered to her mother, as well as to Dan, Rose, Adam and Jennifer.

Mama ignored the others to give me a running commentary as the wedding guests streamed past our window. As always, she identified everyone by a usually unflattering, salient characteristic. "There goes your best friend with the loose lips."

"Lois," I told her. "Please, Mama."

"And that one whose ribs stick out. Don't tell me that's her husband with her."

I took a look. It was Natalie, all right, but definitely not Norman. Not Roberto either. This one was blond and even younger. I could hardly wait to see who Norman would be with.

"And your friend the accountant." From a distance, being black is probably LaVerne's most salient characteristic, but Mama prides herself on being color blind.

"Those two men, arm in arm?"

"They're a couple, Mama. The dark-haired one directed *Fiddler on the Roof* last spring. You met them at the cast party."

"You expect me to remember every face I met a year ago? Wait till you're my age. That one I don't know either, the one with the knockout jewelry. Though I always thought Indian jewelry was maybe a little informal for a fancy occasion."

That one was Naomi. I followed her with my eyes as she was swallowed up in what looked like dozens of Jenny and Tamara's friends from their congregation. Then I walked over to Dan, straightened his tie and reminded him to put on his yarmulke.

The girls, Debby and I had been planning the wedding for months, down to the smallest detail. The music had been chosen, the order of the procession fixed. Only one detail had been overlooked: which bride would march down the aisle first. At the rehearsal, Debby had taken the lead, she and Stanley walking Tamara down the aisle ahead of Jenny and me. Now, she was adamantly insisting that Jenny go first, leaving Tamara second. And Tamara was adamantly insisting that we follow the same order as at rehearsal.

So there we were, ten minutes to curtain time, with mother and daughter squaring off. I couldn't see what difference it made which of the girls went first, unless Debby felt that she and Stanley bringing up the rear might keep Dan from bolting.

Tamara seemed to have a different theory. "Mom, we're doing it the way we rehearsed it. All you're trying to do is show off, because my gown is fancier than Jenny's." Which I wouldn't put past Debby. After all, in the traditional wedding the bride came last so that all eyes would be on her. And I had to admit that the gown Tamara had borrowed from her sister was far frillier, nothing like the simple, flattering lines of Jenny's dress. (More flattering, I congratulated myself secretly, than Stacy's dress was to Tamara.)

"That's not what our wedding is about," Tamara added, "Anyway, if either of us should get featured billing, it should be Jenny. She has half her family here while —"

"How about flipping a coin?" Dan cut in. Stanley laughed and Debby glared at him.

"Sweetie, it really doesn't matter," Jenny said. "If it will make your mom happier for you to go down the aisle after me, that's fine."

"It will make *me* happier if you go last," Tamara said stubbornly. "After all, your mother did a lot more of the work getting this off the ground. Your family is, like, hosting the wedding. Besides, it's my wedding, not my mother's."

"It's *our* wedding," Jenny corrected her. The two of them smiled at each other, and Debby threw up her hands in defeat.

The time had come that I had been dreaming about for years: the two of us, Dan and me, escorting our daughter down the aisle. Only I hadn't imagined being overcome by stage fright as we awaited our entrance at the rear of the theater. Jeffrey and Michael ushered Mama and Rose to the front row, and then returned to take their places in the procession. At a whisper from her father, Steffi marched slowly down the aisle, sprinkling petals to each side with the air of a queen dispensing favors to the commoners. I could sense Anita holding her breath until Steffi reached the front and took her seat with a reluctant air. Michael and Jeffrey followed, and then the two "best persons," Stacy and Adam, walking side by side.

With a toss of her head, Debby moved in stately fashion to her daughter's left, Stanley moved to Tamara's right, and the two of them slowly escorted their daughter down the aisle. I couldn't help wondering: If Jenny had gone first as Debby had wanted, would Debby have been struck by the sudden unreality of seeing her daughter's soon-to-be spouse, adorned in white lace, move down the aisle ahead of her?

A quick glance at Dan revealed that he felt as disconcerted as I, but from the corner of my eye I caught sight of Jenny's smile, now radiant as a spotlight, under her veil. Tamara and her parents reached the end of the aisle; the music sounded our cue; and Jenny, with Dan and I on either side, started the slow, solemn march toward the *chuppah*. Rows of faces turned toward us. The lunch bunch and the cluster of the Goldbergs' friends seemed to be doing their best to hide quizzical looks. But the girls' friends watched with glowing faces, women as well as men wearing yarmulkes, I noticed with a flicker of surprise.

Then we had reached the front where Tamara awaited Jenny, her hand outstretched. We parents took our seats while the two brides climbed the steps to the stage together and moved as one under the *chuppah* that had been set up there. Hands clasped, they faced the rabbi, with only Stacy and Adam by their side. The quilted roof stretched above them, and the poles wrapped with greenery and blossoms framed them like the door to a honeymoon cottage. As the rabbi started chanting the traditional Hebrew blessing, I reached for Dan's hand and held it as our daughter held her love's hand under the wedding canopy.

Though their synagogue, Bet Chaverim, generally followed a Conservative tradition in its services, the girls and Rabbi Bernstein had decided to blend Reform elements into their wedding — particularly the use of enough translation to ensure that everyone present could follow the ceremony. So the rabbi repeated the Hebrew greeting in English. Then she added, "As we welcome the marrying couple, their friends and family gathered here this afternoon, it's appropriate to remember that the guests at a Jewish wedding are no mere audience. Just as the Jewish tradition commands you to rejoice, to follow the marriage ceremony with song and dance, so too it obliges you to become a loving and supportive community in which their love for each other, and for living a Jewish life together, will grow and flourish."

They'd need that support more than an ordinary couple, I thought, wondering if that had occurred to any of my friends besides Marlene, the PFLAG chapter president, who I could see from a glance over my shoulder was nodding her head several rows back. The rabbi chanted the opening blessing and the blessing over the Kiddush cup that the girls would drink from later in the ceremony. They murmured amen, and then it was time for the exchange of rings.

Adam produced the gold band for Jenny to place on Tamara's finger and Stacy did the same for her sister. Then Jenny recited, in a clear, sweet voice, "With this ring, I pledge myself to love and care for you for the rest of my days, in times of joy and in times of struggle, to make with you a Jewish home and to seek with you to live a life in accordance with the faith of our foremothers and fathers and the traditions of Moses and Israel."

Tamara began her vows in turn, but the quiet of the congregation was broken by what I devoutly hoped was the cry of a baby. I turned toward Anita — the only person holding an infant — but little Jeffrey was sleeping peacefully in her arms. Which meant that I'd heard the plaintive meow of BAT's perennial nuisance, Nudnik. Tamara hesitated an instant, and then started reciting again as a second meow sounded from directly under my feet. Having found me, Nudnik sprang into my lap. At least she hadn't leapt onto the stage and disrupted the ceremony. But here I was, in my $450 mother-of-the-bride dress, with a nervous cat about to sink her claws through the silk and into my leg.

There was only one thing to do and that was to stroke Nudnik gently behind the ears until I felt her relax and curl up for a nap as Tamara ended her vows. Steffi immediately began to beg her mother, "Can I hold the cat?" Anita and her two great grandmas simultaneously shushed her. I kept my eyes carefully averted from the Goldbergs as the rabbi began the second part of the ceremony with the reading of the *ketubah*, or marriage contract, modified for two brides.

When she finished reading, Rabbi Bernstein said, "The renowned rabbi, the Baal Shem Tov, is quoted as saying, 'From every human being there rises a light that reaches straight to heaven. And when two souls that are destined for each other find one another, their streams of light flow together and a single brighter light goes forth from their united being.'"

As if on cue, a ray of sunlight slanted in the window and lit up the two brides. "Is that the light going to heaven?" Steffi squealed, causing laughter to ripple gently through the room while Anita, Rose and Mama shushed her again.

Rabbi Bernstein smiled and I thought to myself that not every five-year-old could have followed that quotation.

"Maybe it is the beam of light given off by Jenny and Tamara's love for one another," the rabbi said. "There's no knowing for sure. But what's certain is that these two young women are bright lights in our congregation, and to their friends and families who have gathered here to witness and rejoice in their love for one another. But Tamara and Jenny, as you may know — and if not, as you surely will learn — love alone is not enough to sustain a lifetime together through the unforeseen difficulties that lie in wait. Or through the daily annoyances that can eat away at relationships even more than life's catastrophes — the burned dinner, the cap off the toothpaste tube, the overdraft on the charge card." There was another quiet ripple of laughter. I glanced at Dan and caught him giving me a rueful smile. I gave his hand a squeeze and he squeezed back.

"So love must be joined by commitment, by vows made under a *chuppah*, as commanded by God for the sanctification of marriage," Rabbi Bernstein went on. "Each of you, Jenny and Tamara, has a mother and a father who have kept the marriage vows they made through good times and bad, and who have now come together to rejoice with you in your love. As they have honored their marriage vows, so you honor your parents by following their loving example, cleaving to one another as partners in love and in life. And you in turn will set an example for your children in the creation and continuance of a loving Jewish home."

Dan started next to me at the rabbi's suggestion that Jenny and

Tamara might become parents. Apparently he hadn't heard of the lesbian baby boom. I'd have to fill him in. For the moment, though, my attention was taken by Nudnik, still in my lap and startled into wakefulness by Dan's sudden movement. I stroked her behind the ears again until her body relaxed into another catnap. Then I gave Steffi a look as her stifled giggle reached me. Fortunately, the rest of the congregation had their attention on the rabbi, who was now reciting the first of the Seven Blessings, and on the marrying couple. I breathed a quiet sigh of relief.

"Blessed art Thou, O Lord our God, Creator of the universe, who created the fruit of the vine," the rabbi repeated in English, and continued with blessings for love, joy and a world of peace and harmony. The girls faced each other as their attendants lifted their veils for them to drink from the cup of wine — a ceremonial silver goblet that Debby had provided and that the rabbi now produced from the small table behind the *chuppah*.

Strictly speaking, no further vows were called for once the wine had been drunk, but now the two brides said, in unison, "I am my beloved's and my beloved is mine."

"May the Lord bless and keep you in love and in joy," Rabbi Bernstein said. "You may now exchange your first kiss as a married couple."

Months earlier, I'd been secretly shocked when the girls gave each other a quick kiss, but now as they moved together they seemed, as the rabbi had said, right for each other, a union made in heaven. The rabbi brought forth a wineglass, wrapped in a napkin, and Jenny and Tamara smashed it underfoot together, the clatter of breaking glass sounding through the hushed assemblage. Nudnik squirmed again, but now it was because of the tears that were streaming down my face and plopping on her fur. It didn't matter though, because the whole crowd began cheering and yelling, "*Mazel tov!*" The cat streaked out of the theater.

A moment before I'd been blinded by tears. Now I was blinded by the girls' smiles as the band struck up the music for the recessional — at Debby's insistence, "Sunrise, Sunset," from *Fiddler on the Roof*. We stood to file out after the wedding party, and Rose suddenly grabbed Dan's sleeve and commanded, "Look at your daughter's eyes."

"Do what?" he said.

"The song, it reminded me. When Tevye wanted to marry his daughter to that rich butcher, like you thought Jenny should marry her friend who has a girlfriend of his own anyway."

"Ma, I only said —"

"But then he sees how much she loves the tailor, and he says to himself, 'look at my daughter's eyes.' So that's what I'm telling you to do."

"Well," Dan said. He cleared his throat. "Well."

The girls ducked into the adjacent house to spend the traditional fifteen minutes or so in seclusion, while volunteers from Bet Chaverim scurried about setting up the buffet table inside the theater and rearranging the rows of folding chairs around rented tables decorated with white cloths and centerpieces of floral arrangements. The rest of the guests streamed into the lobby, milling around talking, or heading for the rest rooms to freshen up. The girls had opted to forego a formal receiving line, so Dan and I, along with the Goldbergs, Mama, Rose and the rest of the wedding party, waited in the lobby with the others as the theater was transformed for the reception. Steffi spotted Nudnik as the outside door swung open and made a beeline outside to pet her. Debby followed Steffi with her eyes. Then she turned on me, demanding, "How did that animal get in and nearly ruin my daughter's wedding?"

Not to mention *my* daughter's wedding. I looked Debby up and down, in her designer sheath that made me suddenly feel like a fat frump in my own flowing designer dress. How could anyone look so perfect and be such a pain?

"I have no idea. It's never happened before," I told her coolly.

So much for giving up fibbing. I turned to Dan, who gave me a secret wink and put an arm around my shoulder. "Thank goodness that pest didn't ruin your dress," he murmured in my ear. "After you sneaked it into the house just for this occasion. By the way, we were in such a rush this morning, I didn't have time to tell you, but you look stunning in it. Worth every penny."

I had just enough time to beam at him before friends began to crowd around us. By the time we'd accepted some dozen congratulations and introduced people to the Goldbergs, the theater was transformed into a reception hall, and we made our way to the head table. When everyone was seated, Jenny and Tamara entered, pausing in the doorway, hand in hand. Everyone rose and cheered as the brides threaded their way through the room to join us. A loaf of challah had been placed on the table between their seats, and the two of them said the blessing over it.

"Now can we eat?" Steffi piped up, so loudly that laughter spread across the room.

"Absolutely," Jenny told her. She took Steffi by the hand and led the way, along with Tamara, to the buffet table.

When we got to the table, Debby did a double take. "What is this, a brunch?" she hissed at me. "Bagels and lox?"

"Smoked salmon," I informed her. "What could be more elegant?"

"And *this*?"

This, even I had to admit, didn't look elegant. Latkes — potato pancakes — that should have been a golden brown, but instead were a strange, dingy black. "Those are okay to eat,"one of the potluck committee, who couldn't help overhearing Debby, assured her. "We thought we'd save time by grating the potatoes the night before; no one realized they'd turn dark. But they're absolutely delicious, really."

Debby all but rolled her eyes. "If you'd gotten a caterer, like I suggested, this never would have happened," she hissed at me.

Tamara turned. "Mom, stop making a scene. If you don't like them, then just don't take any," she said, in a voice that could have frozen ice cream.

Debby looked so abashed that she not only took one of the latkes but even popped it in her mouth. "They are okay," she admitted.

I popped one in my mouth too. "Absolutely delicious."

When everyone was nearly done eating, Adam tapped his spoon against his glass. "I'd like to propose a toast," he said. "To one of my closest friends and her life partner, Jenny and Tamara, friends, lovers, and now, newlyweds in the sight of God. *Mazel tov* to you both, and may you live a long and happy life together. *L'chaim*."

After everyone drank, Jeffrey and Stacy, who'd been sitting with their spouses at the far end of our table, stood simultaneously. "As siblings of the happy couple," they said, in a toast they'd obviously rehearsed together, "and on behalf of our spouses as well, we joyously welcome our new sisters-in-law into our families."

I had a feeling that I'd taken an inadvertent step backwards. Shouldn't Jenny and Tamara's parents have made a toast before a brother and sister? Wouldn't it have occurred to me if this had been a traditional wedding? I glanced at the other three and Debby met my eyes, apparently thinking the same, as she immediately stood.

"On behalf of my husband, Stanley, and myself, I want to drink to our daughter and our new daughter-in-love."

For a second I was floored, not having realized Debby was capable of such felicitous wording. But then I gathered my wits and seconded her toast with a loud, "Hear, hear!" in which Stanley joined in, and Dan, as well, after a discreet nudge in his ribs.

I should propose a toast of my own, I told myself, but before I could improvise one, I was surprised again when Dan rose. "Sheila and I are fortunate enough to have most of our family here today. And it looks like we've acquired a whole new branch. So we'd like to toast...." For an instant he faltered; then he raised his wineglass higher. "To family. Old and new."

As Dan sat down, the Capitol Klezmers struck up the first dance. Tamara and Jenny rose and moved to the dance floor together. They danced slowly around the floor, arms around each other, smiling and gazing into each other's eyes. I nodded to myself. Yes, I was right. They did look natural together.

The two danced their way back to us and held out their hands — not to their fathers, as I had expected, but to their mothers. Debby and I got up and danced with our daughters. At an apparent eye signal, the girls switched partners. I put my hands on my new daughter-in-law's shoulders. Or daughter-in-love, as Debby had put it. Not at all a bad turn of phrase. Debby caught my eye and smiled as the girls danced us past one another, and I felt myself warming toward her. I might as well. For better or worse, we were family now.

After the girls had danced with their fathers and fathers-in-love in turn, the bandleader stood up. "I know a lot of you are waiting for us to play our brand of klezmer, so you can dance the hora and hoist the brides up on chairs." Applause laced with laughter met her words. "But the brides have asked us to play one more social dance first, an old-fashioned mixer, something that's been popular at other weddings we've done. So here's how it works. Take your partner in your arms and dance. When we pause in our playing, switch partners. That's it. And one more thing: Really mix it up. You lesbians out there, don't be afraid to twirl around with a guy, and you gay men with a girl. Same goes for you heterosexual couples. You don't have to be stuck with the opposite sex this afternoon. So everyone, loosen up and dance!"

Dan took me in his arms and we danced without needing words, our rhythms matching, my head on his shoulder, his arms holding me close. The music stopped. I found myself dancing with Mama, then my mother-in-law, then Jack of Jack-and-Jim, each switch taking everyone farther from the cluster of people they'd sat with. Dan was dancing with Candy Sue. I could hear her congratulating him. Remembering the steps backwards she'd confessed at PFLAG, I wondered if she secretly felt she should be expressing condolences instead. Then I overheard her add, "I just wanted to tell you what an inspiration you've been to me. From what Sheila — No, what we say in the group is private. But that time you came with her, last year, I could just tell you weren't sold on the thought that you had a lesbian daughter. And now here you are, making toasts at her lesbian wedding. I can't tell you how much you've encouraged me to go on and finish the journey to accepting my son's sexuality."

I couldn't see Dan's expression as the music paused again. I stopped trying, as I found myself face-to-face with Naomi. Her arms were gentle and familiar, a pleasant memory now slipping into the past. "I'm so glad you came," I told her, meaning it.

"Me too. You put on a wonderful wedding; your daughter will treasure it in her memories. And I'll treasure my memory of you," she said, smiling as the band stopped for another moment, and we went our separate ways.

I switched partners again and again as the band played on. There was Jack swirling Mama now, and Jim with the rabbi, Natalie with LaVerne, looking like two high-school girls waiting for a boy to cut in, and Stanley with the potluck coordinator. Natalie's new boyfriend held a young blond woman so close I hoped she couldn't see, and her soon-to-be-ex Norman swept by, looking befuddled to have Jeffrey in his arms.

Sam claimed me next and confessed, "Liveliest affair I've been to in a while. Turned out better than I expected."

Before I could think of a reply, I was swept away by my son, then by a young woman with flaming red hair and then by Tamara's father. Jeffrey was dancing with Anita now, the two of them making a circle of their arms to include Steffi, and LaVerne had reclaimed her husband, clinging to his neck. "Girl, this is something else," she mouthed as they danced on by.

The music was slowing for what surely must be the last set. I glanced around for Dan and found him moving smoothly with Naomi. I picked another partner: my best friend, Lois.

"So you got Dan here after all," she said, slurring her words as she usually did at the end of any occasion where liquor was served. "Don't take this wrong, but do you mind if I ask you a question?"

In the tenth of a second that Lois normally allows between that preliminary and her follow-up question, I prepared myself to say *Yes, I really*

am happy for Jenny, or No, Dan didn't give me any more tsuris over the bills
— when Lois went on, "Let me ask you. Look over there." She maneuvered us into viewing range of Dan and Naomi, tossing her head in their direction. "Don't you think they're dancing awfully close? And the way they're talking a — I don't mean to suggest there's anything going on between them, but...."

I was so startled I stopped dancing and Lois whispered, "Keep moving or he'll know you're watching him."

"Lois, if you mean to imply they're having an affair, you're wrong," I said, moving my feet obediently. For the briefest of moments I thought of telling Lois who *had* had an affair with Naomi, but of course I didn't. I love my friend, but not her loose lips. Instead, I took the lead and danced us in the other direction.

"I know you trust him absolutely, but look how Norm trusted Natalie — Natalya. Not to mention how I trusted the rat. He looks awfully interested in her."

"Lois, trust *me*. Dan is not having an affair. That's just not him. And even if it was, Naomi is the last person he would choose. She's not his type."

"How can you be so sure?"

"Well, for one thing, I know her. She just started a relationship with someone she's crazy about. And for another, she's only interested in other women."

"Oh. You could have said," Lois added after a moment.

"I just did. Besides, even if she wasn't a lesbian, Dan wouldn't go for her. I told you, she's not his type. Look how skinny she is. Hardly any boobs." I swung my plump hips happily. "He likes them built like me. *Zaftig.*"

I stepped back from Lois as the music began to die down. Dan appeared, arms outstretched, at my side. The dance was ending, but even so, I glided into his arms, where I belonged.

Suggested Reading Group Discussion Topics

1. At PFLAG support groups, like the one Sheila attends, parents of gays and lesbians often say that when their children come out of the closet, they go in. Why?

2. Do you have gay or lesbian family members or friends? How would you describe your family's reaction? How might you react if one of your children, or a close friend or family member, "came out" to you as lesbian or gay?

3. What are your feelings about Jenny and Tamara's ceremony? Should lesbians and gays be allowed to marry legally? Why or why not? If you were in a committed relationship with someone of your own sex, would you wish to be married?

4. When Dan tells Sheila that she is his best friend, her unspoken response is that friends are the women she talks to about her husband. Can a husband and wife be friends? What is a friend?

5. Are Sheila and Dan equal partners in their marriage? Why or why not?

6. Sheila manipulates Dan and hides her support for their daughter's ceremony from him. Under what circumstances, if any, are such deceptions justified in a relationship?

7. Both Jenny and Jeffrey deviated from the "script" that their parents had in mind for them: marriage to a Jewish partner of the opposite sex. Which disturbed Dan and Sheila more? Why?

8. Sheila experiences guilt after her brief "affair" with Naomi. Would she have felt more or less guilty if she had had an affair with someone of the opposite sex? How might Dan have felt if he had known about it? Do you see a difference in an affair with a person of the same sex compared to one of the opposite sex?

Author Biography

Rochelle Schwab lives with her husband near Washington, DC, and is active in Parents, Families and Friends of Lesbians and Gays (PFLAG). Her work in PFLAG, and her relationship with her two daughters, spurred her to a fictional exploration of family issues. She's author of three previous novels; the last, *In a Family Way*, was included in *Reading Group Choices: Selections for Lively Book Discussions 1997*. *A Departure from the Script* has been selected as one of the titles featured in the 2002 edition of *Reading Group Choices*.